No Ordinary Love

Anita Notaro

TRANSWORLD IRELAND

TRANSWORLD IRELAND
an imprint of The Random House Group Limited
20 Vauxhall Bridge Road, London SW1V 2SA
www.rbooks.co.uk

NO ORDINARY LOVE
A TRANSWORLD IRELAND BOOK: 9781848270329

First published in Great Britain
in 2010 by Transworld Ireland,
an imprint of Transworld Publishers
Transworld Ireland paperback edition published 2011

Addresses for Random House Group Ltd companies outside the UK
can be found at: www.randomhouse.co.uk
The Random House Group Ltd Reg. No. 954009

The Random House Group Limited supports the Forest Stewardship Council (FSC),
the leading international forest-certification organization. All our titles that
are printed on Greenpeace-approved FSC-certified paper carry the FSC logo.
Our paper procurement policy can be found at www.rbooks.co.uk/environment

Typeset in 12/15pt Ehrhardt by
Kestrel Data, Exeter, Devon.
Printed in the UK by
CPI Cox & Wyman, Reading, RG1 8EX.

2 4 6 8 10 9 7 5 3 1

Anita Notaro is a freelance journalist and producer/ director. She worked for RTE, Ireland's national broadcaster, for eighteen years and continues to work as a drama director on *Fair City*. She has directed the Eurovision Song Contest and the Irish General Election, as well as programmes for the BBC and Channel 4. Her last book, *Take a Look at Me Now*, won the Popular Fiction Book of the Year award in 2008 at the Irish Book Awards. She is a regular contributor to RTE and TV3.

www.transworldireland.ie

For my best friend, Dearbhla Walsh. We've shared so much down through the years that I couldn't do life without you, so don't let that Emmy award take you too far away from me!

1

WE ALL HAVE BAD DAYS AND I'M NO EXCEPTION. I'VE EVEN HAD a few seriously crappy ones, but my today could easily have featured in a commercial for headache tablets. You know the kind – where the woman can't get a seat on the full-to-overflowing train, then the strap of her €500 handbag catches on the turnstile and snaps, and after that the heavens open just as she prepares to walk the last fifty metres home. Well, multiply that by a thousand and you have a snapshot of my day. The only difference is that in TV-commercial life the woman puts her key in the door and gets handed a glass of wine by a Dr McDreamy type who has already run her a bath, lit the fire and popped a steaming pot of something bursting with freshness on the stove to finish cooking while she unwinds. In my case, the lights weren't even on when I eventually let myself into an apartment so cold the two-week-old rancid flowers were back standing to attention and what remained of my morning coffee had either seriously congealed or was frozen solid. I took off my sopping-wet trenchcoat before the cold got right into my bones, kicked off my shoes and burst into tears. I'd had it with life – at least the kind of life I was leading at the moment.

On paper, you see, I had it all. I was a psychologist with my own practice, but I'd been lucky enough to get a job which meant I was attached to a large private hospital and was based there two days a week. That meant I had a guaranteed income – and they paid very well – and still was my own boss. And yes, I met lots of eligible men there, but somehow I never got a chance to get past the nodding stage with any of them. Even the ones who referred patients to me did it by phone or email because they never seemed to be free at the same time I was. Also, my work was very intense, with long hours, because a lot of clients worked and wanted early or late or weekend appointments. That meant no down time, no long lunches or nipping off to shop when my mood dipped and, because I was still building my practice, virtually no life outside work. Even thinking about it now made me want to see a shrink myself.

An assault of whingeing texts on the world brought only two offers of help and saw my closest friends join forces, hit the Chinese takeaway and grab a couple of bottles of whatever they could find in the fridge at the local twenty-four-hour Spar.

After they'd uncorked and plated, both tried unsuccessfully to tease out the crisis that was simmering away in between my alternating long sighs and expletives. Everything was annoying me, so they hardly got a word in for the first ten minutes. In the end, though, Maddy got four in before I exploded.

'So, Lou, what's up?'

'What's up is that I've had it with life. I'm sick of getting up in the middle of the night just to get parking in Dublin city centre. If I have to listen to another moaning south-county Dublin yummy mummy whose husband annoys her just because he forgets to buy organic avocados and occasionally buys orange juice from concentrate, I'll puke. I'm sick of eating plastic, overpriced sandwiches on the run. What's more, I never seem to get a day off. Even when I don't go in I'm at home writing case notes and catching up. Most working days, all I get are rich-bitch problems one after the other and then I come home, late, to a freezing-cold, empty apartment, eat from a silver tray and fall into bed, only to do it all over again the next day.'

'Well, you could always put the heating on a timer,' Clodagh, ever practical, said, smiling. 'In fact . . .'

'Don't even go there, darlin',' Maddy warned. 'She's on a timer herself at the moment and the dial is turned to "explode", I reckon.'

That little interchange summed us up in a way and explained why we worked so well as a trio. Clodagh was the practical one; always there, permanently calm and a rock of sense. Maddy was the artistic one, not of this planet most of the time, but always up for anything and she never failed to make me laugh.

I was somewhere in the middle, not as sensible or organized as Clodagh but lacking the courage that Maddy had to grab life by the balls.

Without Maddy, I reckoned that Clodagh and I would be two old grannies in rocking chairs by now, and in my case it would not be by choice, but because I was too stressed and tired to make any effort. Put simply, Maddy provided the only bit of fun and madness in my life

9

and Clodagh picked me up and put me together when I splintered.

'Go on,' Maddy grinned at me now. 'Let it all out, what else do you hate?'

'I hate it that all my money goes on trying to look younger than I am, that everyone in the world seems to have a significant other and that somehow I've ended up doing a job where the only skill involved seems to be asking, "So, how does that make you feel?" Frankly, I've reached the point where I don't give a toss most of the time.'

'Now hang on – you're well paid and respected by your peers. And most of your clients are in fact men, or had you forgotten?' Maddy asked cheerfully. 'Also, you had that massive write-up last month in the *Indo* and you were photographed the other week at that big party with what's-his-name, the singer? And you've always gotten satisfaction from your work. All I get is hate mail.'

'That's true.' Clodagh grinned. 'You even gave me a lecture on the subject only the other week, remember? You were urging me to . . . "break free of the cycle of doom and gloom" was how you put it, I think . . .' She'd cleared the takeaway containers and opened a box of Maltesers.

'So, how come you suddenly "can't get no sat-is-fac-tion",' Maddy sang tunelessly as she played her air guitar in an effort to make me laugh.

'I dunno. My life just doesn't seem to be working for me any more but I think I've only started to notice it recently. I'm stressed all the time and everyone out there is so aggressive, have you noticed?'

'Well, em . . .'

'Even today a blue-rinser jammed her trolley into my back as I picked up a panini, then had the audacity to tut at me as if I was the one causing the problem.'

'Oh yeah, the pensioners are the worst,' Clodagh agreed. 'I never go near the DIY stores on Thursday, when the over-65s get a discount. They're always annoyed about something. They act as if they resent you just because you still have your teeth.'

'And don't get me started on roadworks . . .' I ignored Clodagh because I didn't want anybody muscling in on my moan. In fact, by this stage they'd made an unspoken pact to just nod, I suspect, because they let me rant on again for ages.

'OK, Lou, we get the picture,' Maddy said eventually, nudging Clodagh, who was trying her best to stay awake. 'And yes, you do seem to spend an awful lot of time and energy trying to help people who are so self-obsessed they make Victoria Beckham look carefree. But listen, we've been here before, no? And it's always the same: when push comes to shove you don't want to give up your well-paid career and your gorgeous apartment and your life, basically, and who could blame you? Not me, anyway, an actress who's permanently topping up her Credit Union loan.'

'Hang on a sec, just spool back a bit.' Clodagh sat up straight and Maddy shot me a 'she's on to you' look. 'Answer me one question, Lulu – and it's one that you usually avoid during these sessions – what would you do if you could choose any job in the world?'

'I've no idea, that's part of the problem.' I was depressed just thinking about it.

'Hang on a sec, I think I know.' Maddy shot out of her chair. 'And it's so obvious I can't believe one of us hasn't made you think seriously about it before.' She grabbed a photo off the mantelpiece, a black-and-white, creased portrait of my first ever dog, and thrust it at me. 'You'd work with four-legged creatures instead of two-legged monsters.' She knelt down beside me. 'Look me in the eye and tell me that ever since you lost that ugly-lookin' mutt you haven't secretly wanted a job that involved helping animals.'

'Probably,' I muttered.

'But didn't you consider that at one point? You even did that year-long course in animal behaviour after college.' Clodagh shook her head at Maddy. 'Nope, that's not it.'

'It is, I promise. She's just always been too sensible, too worried about what people think, I'm telling you, Clodagh. Am I not right?' She made a face at me.

'Probably,' I muttered again, knowing she'd hit the nail on the head.

'Of course I am. I can't think why I never pushed you on it before. It was seeing that photo, so out of place in your posh apartment, that did it. How come I'm only noticing it now?'

'I usually keep it in my bedroom,' I admitted.

'Well, I suppose working with animals might actually be better than some of the clients you've had over the past few years.' Clodagh grinned.

'You said it.' Maddy was on a roll. 'Well-heeled lunatics, most of them. Now, who's for a top-up while we analyse the potential of dogs dumping on you rather than humans?'

As usual, we didn't get very far and, eventually, they left, but not before making me promise to at least consider my life. I was so pissed off because I knew Maddy was right that I even forgot to contribute towards dinner. By eleven I was in bed with the electric blanket turned to 'burn' on the dial and, of course, just to end that perfect day I fell asleep and forgot to turn it off. When I woke at three thirty I was swimming in my own sweat.

Next morning I resolved to dust myself down, start over and all that shite. But it was becoming harder. Even I – the queen of bouncing back – noticed it was taking longer to regain my energy. Still, I consoled myself that days like yesterday didn't come along very often, so I put on my high patent shoes for a bit of zing and headed off. Twelve hours later I was comatose on the sofa, coughing and sneezing and ringing anyone I could think of for a moan.

Maddy was in London that day doing a voiceover for a commercial, Clodagh was probably at the gym working off the excesses of the night before, and I drew the line at calling my sister, mainly because she looked like a model and would listen for precisely ten seconds before telling me all the good things that were happening in her life. Becky was a bit of an issue for me, if I'm honest. She was everything I wanted to be and it rankled sometimes. Anyway, even I'd had enough of me by that stage, so I went to bed early – again – with enough paracetamol to kill a cow, and dreamed of having a life.

The week didn't really improve much. I had two sessions with a new client, a man called Marcus who was addicted to porn on the internet. I had specialized in sexual–addiction counselling at college and so a fair amount of my work was in this area. On paper, Marcus had it all – a Page-Three stunner for a wife, five-year-old twin girls who looked like angels, a main residence as well as a holiday home in Ireland and a villa in Portugal. And tons of money, a good portion of which he spent downloading images from various sites and masturbating while his wife and kids slept upstairs. After he'd almost been caught twice – once by one of his daughters – he came to me for help. Oh – and did I say? Marcus was six foot tall, great-looking and one of the most self-absorbed men I'd ever met.

'So why are you here if you don't feel you're doing any-thing wrong?' I asked for the third time.

'I suppose it's how other people might see it . . .' He looked sulky.

'Like who?'

'I dunno, a work colleague, my mother. It's getting harder to hide the stuff.'

'And what about your wife, you say she's no idea?'

He shrugged. 'She's happy, why wouldn't she be? She has everything she wants. Anyway, she spends the summer holidays, mid-term breaks and any other long weekends in the sun with her girlfriends and all their kids while the husbands earn the dough, so she's not around a lot of the time.'

'I don't think that's the issue though, is it? She could and will be around. And the incident with your daughter nearly coming upon you . . .'

'That was unfortunate.' He was silent for a while. 'I'm not harming anyone really,' he said quietly, but he didn't look at me as he spoke.

14

'Could you stop if you wanted to?' I finally asked him directly.

'Yes, yes of course I could.'

'Do you want to?'

'I'm not sure.'

'What are the reasons you might consider stopping?'

'I suppose, I dunno, I guess because I feel it's not normal to want to lock yourself in a room at night and jerk off to live action on a screen.'

'So how do you feel when you're doing it?'

'Excited, the anticipation's the thing. And the risk. But then, afterwards there's a brilliant buzz for a while but then it's not so great . . .' He tailed off, not wanting to think about the shame I knew came crushing in.

We talked a bit more. It wasn't going to be easy for him. These cases were rarely straightforward, and I wasn't entirely convinced he was ready to tackle his. In fact, my guess was that he was looking for someone to tell him it was OK.

I had a full day and by the time I arrived home, shivering, the dreaded bug had finally taken hold. I was doubly annoyed because I'd decided earlier I couldn't stand another night in on my own so I'd arranged to meet Clodagh and go to the movies. But then I felt so exhausted I ended up cancelling, which depressed me further. To her credit, she sent a text offering to babysit you with chips, ice-cream and Lemsip, but I eventually decided I couldn't face even her.

By that stage I couldn't even pluck up the energy to shop, so I had another night in with a zillion TV channels, most of which I watched for about ten seconds before I surfed again. I acted on the 'feed a cold, starve a fever' theory that my granny swore by and ate two giant packets of crisps and munched on a packet of chocolate crinkle crunch, drank a very large hot whiskey with cloves and lemon – the Irish cold cure – and fell on to the bed, fully dressed, to watch a late movie. I woke at 6 a.m. in the same position, icy cold, still with the remote in my hand. My breath tasted of cheese and onion, my eye make-up was down around my jaw and my new trouser suit, which had just come back from the cleaners, was only fit to use as a duster.

I had one of those truly awful moments as I realized I desperately wanted to crawl under the duvet and howl, then sleep on and off in between watching mindless TV all day, with my BlackBerry – and everything else that meant contact with the outside world – on silent. It was then I finally knew for certain that something had to give. All the months of trying to pull myself together had come to nothing. I was sick of pretending I was happy, convincing myself I was lucky while struggling just to remain upright. Something had to give, and the change had to be significant enough to get me out of this enormous black hole. I just wondered if I was up to it.

result. So, after all the smaller things had been done, it just left the biggest, scariest change of all. But I was determined and, besides, that famous conversation with the girls had finally hit home – maybe because I'd been feeling so low at the time – so while I was, for the first time, actually taking steps to change my life, I set about updating my skills.

I really did have a qualification in animal behaviour, as Clodagh had reminded me, and I'd managed to do a couple of refresher courses over the years, mainly as a means of getting away from the intensity of my life and to stop myself going completely bonkers with the kind of stuff I was listening to all day. So while I was ploughing through my list of major changes, I took a bit of a break and headed off to London for a course with a visiting American expert whom I'd always admired. He held a once-yearly clinic for problem pets in the British capital and combined it with a really intensive workshop where you got to see him in action and even help out. He only took people with a recognized qualification and yet the course was full by the time I had managed to extricate myself from my commitments, but it helped that I knew this guy's work and had read all his books. I begged the organizer by email and was put in touch with Professor Harrison's assistant. After I told him how desperate I was to change my life, he relented and put me to the top of the cancellation list, and when he emailed me to say someone had pulled out I rang Maddy and screamed with glee, then tore off to pack my bags without even asking how she was. Being plunged into that world full-time for several weeks was so uplifting that when I spoke to her on the phone from London she said she hardly recognized my voice any more and threatened to close down my practice in my absence if I didn't finally do something. And I knew her, she was capable of breaking into my office, telling all my clients I'd no longer be seeing them, giving my books to the accountant to wind up the company and hiding all my contacts and files.

'I'm serious,' she stressed as she picked me up from the airport on my return. 'I haven't heard you so energized in a very long time and I'm not about to let you off the hook this time.'

'I know, I feel great,' I admitted. 'The course was amazing. We were thrown into so many real situations with our tutor at his clinic that it rekindled my love of animals – and dogs especially. He was amazing to watch. I learned so much.'

'Well?' Maddy asked.

'Well what?'

'Are you going to do something finally and give us all a bit of peace?'

'I think I am,' I laughed, and she nearly crashed the car trying to give me a hug and drive at the same time.

So, after a final bout of agonizing about whether I had the courage to go through with it, I eventually realized that it was now or never. With Maddy and Clodagh's help – which took the form of a million 'yes you can' texts followed by hundreds of threatening phone calls – I decided to go the whole hog and opt for a total change of lifestyle. To kickstart the plan I simply put an ad on the back page of the *Irish Times*.

DOGGY DATES

Is your Labrador lonely?
Your Schnauzer sulking?
Or maybe your Westie whines all day?
Go on, bring him on a doggy date next Thursday
and
Let US can your canine concerns!
Call 088 – 222 333 444
Who knows? YOU might get lucky too!!

Yes, I know it was a mass of clichés and that everyone, me included, was sick to death of all those 'Prefer bread to broccoli?' 'Crave toffee rather than tofu?-type ads, but I wasn't at all creative, so it came down to Maddy and her actor friends, who were all bonkers. Between them they decided it was a winner.

'You'll be inundated with calls, I promise.' Clodagh laughed hysterically when she saw it and, believe it or not (and no one was more surprised than me), I was. OK, it was mostly hesitant females and overenthusiastic gay men, but hey, beggars and all that. Admittedly, a lot of the women sounded desperate. It took me a while to cop on, but when my third female caller in a row asked where they could buy a dog in time for next Thursday I began to get the picture, but I gave them all the number of our local dog sanctuary. The tag line at the end – which Maddy had only put in at the last minute as a gag – had clearly hit home. Eventually the little-known dog-rescue centre 'Doggies 'n' Moggies in Distress' rang and asked me to stop giving out their number. I suspected I was distressing the volunteers bigtime.

It was funny, but even dealing with dog *owners* lightened my mood. The mere possibility that I might be able to make a living by putting my talents for solving people's problems to use with animals made me smile. And at least I'd never have to deal with another addiction case again. It had all gotten way too heavy, I realized as soon as I stopped. Time to have fun again after years of 'proper' behaviour and countless days spent watching my words.

The only slight cloud on my otherwise Cif-bright horizon was that I didn't actually own a pet myself. And wouldn't, not after the last time. I still couldn't think about my much-loved pet Gnasher in that old photo without feeling sad. However, as soon as I arrived at the local church car park – half an hour early, in order to get my act together – I decided this was, in fact a blessing in disguise. It was bedlam.

I hadn't the faintest idea what to do so I blew my whistle, the one I kept in my handbag beside the canister of pepper spray in case I was attacked on the way home some night. Chance would be a fine thing, my sister Becky always said. Mind you, it was easy for her to say that. Men were always hitting on her, mainly because she was blonde and 'out there' in every sense of the word. In looks and manner she was the image of my mother, or Martha, as she insisted we call her.

To my amazement, the whistling worked. All of a sudden it seemed as if forty pairs of eyes were on me and, if you counted the dogs, they were.

'Hi.' I cleared my throat and slipped the whistle into the pocket of my pink velour tracksuit, which I'd bought in an effort to finally rid myself of the dour counsellor image.

'Eh, welcome,' I beamed, as I bent down and put on what I hoped was my pet-friendly voice.

'My name is Louisa (only my mother called me that) and I'm your, er . . .' my voice petered out. 'Eh, let's just say I'm your Growler Guru.' I gave a nervous grin, but no one responded. 'By the way, everyone calls me Lulu,' I stammered, trying to get past the gaffe. Maddy and I had decided it was the most pet-friendly version of my name, and I needed all the help I could get, quite frankly.

Actually, what Maddy had said was that Lulu reminded her of a Chihuahua. Not a compliment had been my immediate reaction.

My face was scorch-your-hands hot by now so I went into cease and desist mode immediately. One thing I definitely did know was when I wasn't working. It rarely happened, because I generally never lost control, but when it did it was usually trying too hard that was my undoing.

'Right, well, why don't we all introduce ourselves then?' I was acutely aware that my face now matched my tracksuit, not a good look for anyone. I mentally shook myself and smiled at the nice thirtysomething with the white Labrador. He was cute, I decided. Shame he was wearing a pinstripe suit and a tie covered in frolicking dogs – the ones with the barrels round their necks. It was so yellow it looked like a badly done Van Gogh.

'I'm Ronan and I'm here for my gran. Her dog, Deputy, is becoming a bit too attached to me.' He tried to shift the overweight mutt who was stretched out, snoring, right across his feet. 'Last night he growled at my mother and wouldn't let her into my house, which is rather unfortunate, because she was delivering my ironing at the time.' The women all looked as if they'd like to mother him themselves but, personally, I couldn't get past his stiffness. He looked so uptight he made Prince Charles seem loose.

'My gran – Myrtle – is getting on a bit, so I take him for walks, that kind of thing,' he explained. 'But he keeps running away from home – my gran's – and ends up scratching at my front door at all hours.'

I gave him one of my 'that's enough' smiles. This guy was way too intense and more than a tad anal for my liking.

'Right, well we can certainly work on that . . . fatal attraction thing.' I smiled encouragingly, even though I didn't have a clue how I was going to persuade Deputy to stick to four-legged males.

'Now, who's next to come to confession?' I said in what I hoped was a teasing voice. I'd been practising for days, ever since my sister told me yet again that I needed to loosen up.

Next up was an elderly couple called Doreen and Arthur, sweet and neat with a front garden filled with narrow borders of white alyssum and blue lobelia in clumps – I'd bet my life on it. God, I'd have loved them for parents. They were nice and sensible. She wore flat, laced-up shoes with thick tights and a pleated skirt and had a shiny, homely complexion. He was roundy and sported a flat cap and a hand-knitted cable cardigan with leather toggle buttons. They had two lazy-looking Westies. They really should have been signing up for Unislim classes they were so fat – the dogs that is, not Doreen and Arthur. Apparently, they were called Syd and Vicious and no, their owners had never heard of the

Sex Pistols. Syd had Australian ancestry, and the other one wasn't the most sociable of creatures, according to Doreen, who explained that they had no friends left at this point.

As they smiled at each other and held hands and told the class everything about themselves, my mind drifted to my own family and especially my mother. Martha was not what you'd call conventional. Even Maddy, who accepts everyone as she finds them, found her weird.

'She likes to think of herself as bohemian, a free spirit,' I'd told Maddy and Clodagh when they first met her years back.

'Sorry, Lou' – Clodagh made a face – 'but to refer to your mother as bohemian is an insult to hippies everywhere.'

'Now if I said that you'd take it with a pinch of salt,' Maddy grinned. 'But coming from Clodagh' – she whistled – 'well, that sums it up really. Martha is bonkers.'

'Bonkers she may be, but she was bloody tough on me as a child. I spent my whole life trying to conform, to live up to her standards. Is it any wonder I'm so uptight?'

'What was your father like?' Clodagh asked. 'Any clues there?'

'I've no idea really.' I didn't easily discuss my father. He and my mother had split shortly after I was born and my mother always implied that he was a waster. Any time I misbehaved, Martha punished me and told me that if I wasn't careful I'd end up just like him, so as a result I worked much harder than any other kid my age and always tried to make it up to her.

'Well, your stepfather was OK and he probably had more of an influence on you growing up?' Maddy smiled.

'Yes, but he never got involved really. He left us girls to Martha most of the time.' The truth was that Ron adored my mum and couldn't believe his luck when she married him so, while he was a strong businessman, he was putty in her hands. I think he loved it that Martha just seemed to float through life expecting everyone to take her into consideration, and of course they did. I suppose the fact that they had Becky shortly after they married meant that I always felt like an intruder, even though Ron was a dote and never made me feel anything other than his daughter. But I wasn't his and Becky was, and in my mind that was huge, especially as Mum seemed determined to keep the reins on me much more than Becky, who got away with murder, because she was the baby, I guess.

Suddenly I realized that Doreen and Arthur had finished their introduction and I hadn't heard a word, so I smiled at the young woman standing beside them. A bright-eyed, pretty girl of around thirty, she introduced herself as Emily, and I decided I liked her immediately. She was carrying a cat in a basket, which explained why the Westies were sitting on her boots, looking like they'd just spotted dinner.

'Eh, do you have a dog with you, as well?' I asked hopefully. That cat was not going to last long around here.

'No, I hate dogs,' she responded cheerfully. 'Actually, Rover here belongs to my mum.' She grinned.

Rover? Everyone stared but no one asked. They all looked at me expectantly. Go on, you're in charge, their eyes seemed to challenge.

'My mum thinks he's a dog, you see,' Emily apologized. 'Reincarnated, of course.'

'Naturally.' I tried to look like I was used to this type of story.

Emily continued, 'My father was killed by an Organic Farm Produce truck while out walking the original Rover – who was definitely a dog, trust me, I spent my life keeping out of his way – but he legged it and hasn't been seen since. This Rover appeared in our back garden that night crying to be let in. My mother is convinced that he's Rover – the original dog now a cat – sent by my father to keep her company.' Emily looked constipated with angst by that stage and one of the Westies started snoring, which was where I was headed myself.

To their credit, not one of the class laughed.

'But why wouldn't your father have just sent another dog, if he did send, eh, Rover?' a very camp voice asked. Gay Godfrey (the nickname I gave him, Maddy had said it would help me relax if I could give them all a pet name) wanted to know. What is it about gay men and the need for detail?

'Because my mother was actually afraid of dogs, but she loves cats, you see.' I could feel a migraine coming on. 'And now she's certain that this is Rover brought back, so she's happy. The only thing is she's been trying to teach him to fetch the ball and he won't budge, which is why I'm here. Sorry.' She seemed to know just by looking that we all thought she had a screw loose.

'No, no, don't apologize, it's . . . fascinating, I think,' I said in what I hoped was an encouraging manner. 'Let me get back to you.' I looked around quickly for a bit of normality.

'Hello.' A very uncomfortable-looking man half thrust his hand in my general direction then changed his mind.

26

'Sorry we were a bit late.' He grinned. 'The truth is, Louis had to drag me out.' He pointed to an absolutely stunning guy – outdoor type, I immediately thought, until I noticed his nails were clean and his loafers way too expensive.

'Hi.' Louis smiled, revealing teeth that really should have worn shades. 'I hope we haven't missed any juicy stuff.' He poked his mate and grinned in a coy way. 'As Mike said he was . . . somewhat reluctant.'

Why, oh why do all the gorgeous ones have to be bent as Turkey Twizzlers? I thought, trying not to look as if I'd just lost interest.

'We're flatmates,' Mike continued, without being asked. Everyone had assumed they were a couple as soon as they realized Louis was gay. Now they were working up to asking what 'flatmate' meant exactly, I reckoned.

'My partner, Emerson, died recently,' luscious Louis chipped in. 'He was in the hospice for months. Pedro' – he pointed to the Collie, who had the saddest eyes I'd ever seen – 'was the hospital dog, and when Em died he pined like mad.' Louis bit his lip. 'I had no choice but to take him home with me. He was whining continuously and unsettling the patients, who have enough problems of their own, quite frankly. So I advertised for a flatmate, because I don't do walkies. Makes me hot and sweaty,' he explained. 'And bores me silly. I'd much rather be in the gym chatting up scantily dressed instructors by the water cooler.' And not the females ones, unfortunately for us girls. This guy really was gorgeous.

'Anyway, Mike had just returned from London and he needed to find a place quickly, and so far it's working out.'

He grinned at everyone. 'And Pedro's happy; he gets his constitutional every day.'

'And by the way, these classes were *not* my idea.' Mike looked like he'd rather be at the dentist. 'I'm here under extreme duress.'

'Well, we'll try and make the experience as painless as possible then, and if all else fails I can prescribe painkillers.' I grinned at him. He had possibilities, I decided, cheering up.

'Is that everyone?' I asked hopefully.

'Hi, we're Matt and Sally,' said a thirtysomething, well-to-do guy whose hand was being tightly gripped by a pretty young woman.

'Hi, Matt,' everyone chorused as if we were all in rehab, which we sort of were.

'We don't actually own a dog, yet. We're in the process of adopting a baby, and I thought we should get in some practice by taking responsibility for a dog. So we came here hoping to pick up some tips before we hit the dog shelters.'

'Great, well you could always borrow one in the mean-time. We seem to have more animals than humans here tonight.' I looked around.

'And last but not least, I hope, we're Bronwyn and Susie,' a voice – that I imagined would have the same effect as honey and lemon on a raw throat – purred softly. All eyes turned to look at the most divine pair of females I'd seen in a long time.

'I'm Susie, actually, and this is my friend Bronwyn,' the Vicks voice giggled. 'Hi, everyone.'

At that moment all hell broke loose so we were forced to

abandon the introductions. A couple of strays had infiltrated the class, and Syd was having none of it and was trying to see them off. When I'd dealt with that, it was time to start the class. I quickly went through a few key points in relation to animal behaviour and then we made a few attempts at 'sit', 'stay' and 'come', as I tried to get the owners to see things the way a dog would. We walked round and round the car park and practised like mad and, all in all, it was fun and people seemed to make friends easily, which was a relief.

'So, that's just about it for this evening, then,' I told them when the hour was up. 'This was always going to be a free introduction, an initial get-to-know you.' I smiled. 'I have leaflets here if anyone would like more details of the type of services available.' I reached into my satchel. 'I do have a website, and you're welcome to stay in touch by email. There is a suggestion that we might get various classes going if there's enough interest, so I'd really welcome your comments.'

I did a quick recap in my head. So far we had a handful of gays, a few pensioners, an anorak and a woman trying to turn her Siamese into a Shiatsu. And Mike, whom I hadn't yet got a handle on. Just as well I was trained as a counsellor.

3

MY FIRST ONE–TO–ONE CLIENTS TURNED OUT TO BE BRONWYN and Susie, or the delectable dykes, as Maddy insisted on calling them, even though we'd no idea whether they were gay or not.

Apparently, Bronwyn and Susie had Googled me after the class and decided I was exactly what they needed. I was a qualified psychologist and also an expert in animal behaviour – according to some little-known journalist whom Maddy had persuaded to interview me. Of course, I knew none of this as I made my way excitedly to my brand-new office in the Sandyford Industrial Estate the following Monday afternoon, for my first ever canine-counselling session.

Part of changing my life meant never working on Monday mornings again. EVER. In fact, ideally never working at all on that day. My plan was to start my week on Tuesday, thus avoiding that Monday-morning feeling for the rest of my days, I told my friends.

'Doesn't that just mean you get that Tuesday-morning feeling instead?' Clodagh was nothing if not logical.

'No, it's not the same because the week has started so it's

not Monday.' I think I knew what I was talking about here.

'But it's now your Monday, is it not?'

'I give up.' I dragged her out for coffee to try and give myself some energy.

As it turned out, Bronwyn and Susie were only free on Mondays so I was forced to compromise my principles fairly early on, but I told them firmly I could only see them after two o'clock. Consequently, I had a lie-in, followed by a swim and sauna and then a leisurely lunch with Maddy.

'Wow, Lou, what have you done to yourself?' she smiled.

'Lulu,' I warned.

'Sorry?'

'Lulu, I'm now called Lulu, remember, not Lou?'

'Sorry again.'

'No worries. Anyway, do you like it?' I wasn't sure what there was to like really, except that I was wearing casual trousers and a T-shirt, hardly trend-setting in the style stakes, I would have thought.

'Your hair is a different colour.' She sounded amazed. 'You never colour your hair.'

'Well, I'm just practising, to tell you the truth.' I was thrilled she'd noticed. 'I put in one of those wash-in rinses. Black Cherry, it's called. Does it look any different? I feel like Penelope Cruz in that hair ad,' I told her, flicking my glossy mane while running my fingers through it and pouting. Normally, my hair gave 'mousey' a bad name and, since my mum had had orangey hair most of her life, I'd never been brave enough to experiment, even with a wash-out–after–six-shampoos–type colour.

31

'Yeah, it's got a purple tinge.' Maddy was impressed, I could tell. 'Very cool. And you look rested or something. Have you had Botox?'

'No, dumbo.' I wasn't quite sure whether to be annoyed that she thought I needed injections, or pleased that I wasn't frowning any more, obviously. 'It's just that I'm not stressed. It's my new life. And I'm wearing less make-up,' I added for good measure. It was part of my simplified life, plus it was saving me a fortune – crucial if you looked at my appointments diary. I loved talking to Maddy like this. We'd known each other since childhood and so we had an unspoken agreement that we could say anything we liked to each other without consequences.

'Christ, I wish I had the guts to quit my job.'

'Maddy, you're an actress, you don't have a job.' Actually that wasn't fair. She did have a small part in *Southside Girls*, a sitcom about a group of country nurses who work in Whitecliff Clinic, an exclusive, south Dublin private hospital where everyone who's anyone goes – if they can't buy their way out of getting sick, that is. It was a huge success when it hit the television screens two years ago. Unfortunately, Maddy wasn't one of the 'girls' as such, she was a member of the kitchen staff, which meant she got to wear a rather unappealing, vomit-green nylon coat and hairnet and her only line for the past year and a half seemed to have been 'Chips or mash with that, love?' Still, I adored having a friend who was in television, because there weren't many laughs to be had in my profession, that's for sure. Hopefully, though, all that was about to change. Besides, she did get the odd freebie, which she was happy to share in return for free psychoanalysis.

Anyway, Maddy was only contracted to the series for ten weeks each year, which is why I'd been teasing her. Other than that she drew the dole, did the occasional voiceover and 'rested' a lot. But, hearing her talk about quitting anything was unusual, so I listened intently.

'We've just been told that there's a new producer starting on the show, and rumour has it that it's Pauline Charleston,' she sighed. 'If it's true I'll slit my wrists. Honestly, the woman hates me, Lou, she—'

'Lulu—'

'Lulu, sorry, hon, I forgot. Anyway, I have to find a new job and you're a great ad for it – you look, well, I dunno, you look . . .' She searched for the right word.

'"Stunning" would do,' I laughed, using one that nobody would ever use in relation to me.

'You do look great, honestly,' she said kindly.

'I look great for me, is what you mean,' I told her. I was used to it. You see, part of my problem was that having grown up with a sister who was a stunner always made me feel, well, just ordinary, I suppose.

'No, I mean it. You look younger, less, em – structured, that's it.' She sounded pleased with herself.

'Well, that's it. I've heard it all now. Most actresses would say, "Darling, you look fabulous," or "Honey, you're amazing," but "Lulu, you look less structured" is all I get. Charming,' I sighed, and ordered broccoli soup and a salad with toasted pine nuts.

'You know what I mean.'

'I do. It's just that I wish I was a bit more . . . exotic,' I

33

told Maddy for the hundredth time. 'No matter what I do, I still look average.'

'You do not, you—'

'Yes I do and you know it, so don't you dare go all coy on me now. Look at me – I've lost a bit of weight—'

'Now come on, you never had any real weight to lose—'

'OK, not much, I'll give you that,' I conceded. 'But I've started doga classes, and my bum looks a bit tighter, I think.'

'What the hell's dog-a?'

'I said do-ga not dog-a.' I was enjoying my moment. It's rare to get one up on Maddy, who's a mine of useless information. 'Yoga with your dog,' I explained. 'It's the latest craze in the States, apparently, and it's just hit Ireland.'

'From Brooklyn to Bray. That's interesting. Does it matter at all that you don't have a dog?' Her brow wrinkled.

'Well, yes, obviously. It's hard to do the dog pose without one, I imagine, but I've only been to one class and it's been all stretches. Besides, I will have a mongrel shortly.'

'I suppose what I'm trying to say is that you've never shown any interest whatsoever in animals since Gnasher,' Maddy said softly.

'I have, it's just taken me some time to think about owning one again,' I said defensively, remembering the heartbreak I'd suffered when my first dog had died. I still couldn't talk about him, even after all these years. 'Anyway, I need one for my new career.' I banished all thoughts of my adored dog, it was the only way. 'Meanwhile, I've arranged to borrow my neighbour's two Yorkies for the next class. Unfortunately, they're called Pussy and Willie—'

'There, you see, you simply can't get away from body

34

parts,' Maddy said, in an I-told-you-so way. 'Look, can I just say one thing? Are you not going a bit overboard on this change-of-career thing by giving up all your old clients?'

'What? You encouraged me,' I spluttered.

'I know, and I do. Honestly. It's just that you trained for years to become a psychologist. You specialize in sexual addiction and, last time I looked, the only thing the dogs in our neighbourhood were addicted to was licking their balls or chasing that poor postman who has a heart condition . . . no, let me finish,' she pleaded. 'Besides, any dog addicted to sex simply humps the nearest female he can hop up on, so no problems there, I reckon. Please . . .' she patted my arm. 'Just be sure you want to sever the ties completely. You're great at what you do. AND you earned a fortune.' She sounded miffed at me for not appreciating that.

'Look, I know you're only looking out for me, but it's too late for all that. I've stopped practising and referred all my clients to other professionals. Besides, I've had it with counselling guys who don't know their arse from their elbow. I'm all burnt out, Maddy; it's very common among counsellors. And when I found myself one day wondering if I'd remembered to defrost the lamb chops for dinner in the middle of a client telling me how her lover had taken a call from his wife just as she was about to have an orgasm, I realized that I was becoming desensitized, to say the least.' I really wanted her to understand. 'Besides, I never got to meet any single men – well, not the type you could be seen in public with,' I moaned. 'At least dog owners tend to be sociable . . . and, in general, they don't take themselves too seriously' – although I wasn't quite certain about that yet.

'And I'm tired and talked out and, quite frankly, if I never have to see another man whose dick, I reckon, is a lot thicker than his brain, I'll be happy.'

'OK, OK, I get it, sort of,' she conceded. 'Don't mind me anyway, I'm just jealous. And feeling a bit insecure myself. Tell me everything – are you nervous?'

'Well, it hasn't been as hard as I imagined, actually. Of course, I have the cushion of having a bit of money in the bank to tide me over for a year – at a push. Ask me again when that runs out.' I slurped my soup, simply because I could. No more white shirts to keep clean just so I'd look the part for clients who couldn't care less. I had a flashback to one particular day when my feet were killing me from too-tight stilettos and my stomach never stopped rumbling because I was on the apple diet in order to fit into a dull black dress for an equally dull conference on cognitive behaviour therapy, and said a prayer of thanks that I was out of it all.

'Anyway, it's too late to turn back now. I have my first appointment in less than an hour's time.' I filled Maddy in on what little I hadn't already told her. Her final verdict was that Bronwyn and Susie sounded so luscious she'd be tempted to give them one herself.

As it turned out, they were a nice normal doggy problem: Susie wanted a dog and Bronwyn wasn't sure she could cope and was secretly hoping, I suspected, my skills as a psychologist would help persuade Susie this wasn't a good idea. However, I concentrated on the idea of a pet and what it would mean in their lives. The decision to get one was for them as a couple to decide, I told them. Their problem was right up my alley, and they were great fun to boot.

4

NEXT DAY I GOT A CALL FROM RONAN O'MEARA ASKING IF I could see him that evening at seven, and out the window went my plan for no overtime. So far so not good on the work/life balance then.

'Hi.' He shook hands formally as soon as we met at the top of the stairs.

'How are you?' I asked, and I really wanted to know. There was something about him that suggested he'd known too much tragedy for someone his age. I don't know how I knew that, it was one of the few things I was good at – reading people, being able to tell things about them before they let me know. He looked like someone who'd been dealt a major blow in life and been softened around the edges as a result.

'Fine, thanks for seeing me at such short notice.' He seemed a bit uneasy, I decided, watching him shove his hands in his pockets and shuffle about. I liked him in casual clothes much better, even if the dark-grey sweater looked like it had been in the tumble dryer once too often, his jeans hung around his bottom and his trainers needed a scrub.

'Pleasure. You didn't bring, eh, Deputy, wasn't it?'

'Christ, no, I'm trying not to encourage him.' He eased himself down on to the couch. 'Anyway, where would he sit?' He grinned. 'Not a blanket in sight. And I hardly think you'd want him scratching this,' he patted my million-dollar leather sofa.

Oh dear. How could I have forgotten a bed of some sort for the real clients? Canine couch, I scribbled on a yellow stickie, right next to pig's ears – foie gras for four-legged friends, according to one website.

'So, the problem is your gran's dog, from what you told me the other evening?' I decided to get straight down to business.

'Myrtle, that's right. It's doing my head in, to be honest.' He sighed. 'Don't get me wrong, I love dogs – I was even going to be a vet at one point.'

'Really? You'd make a good vet, I suspect.' I smiled at him.

'That's what everyone says.' He grinned. 'I'm mad about all animals, as it happens.'

'So how come you changed your mind?'

'Life.' He shrugged, and something about the way he said it told me not to push.

'What did you end up doing?' I enquired casually.

'Accountancy, like my father.' His voice sounded so flat I felt myself squirming and had to stop my mouth forming a silent 'Ouch!'

'Right,' I muttered instead, trying to keep my voice even. I could picture him as a classical musician, an IT specialist, a farmer even, but he just wasn't accountant material.

'I'd started training to be a vet actually. I was at college

38

studying, and then my father died and I sort of drifted into his practice. Eventually I went back to study part-time and, I dunno, accountancy seemed the sensible option. The only one, in fact,' he corrected himself. 'My father's business was a bit of a mess, you see, so I knew I'd end up there for quite a while. I felt I owed it to his staff, most of whom had been with him since school . . .' His voice tailed off and the sense of helplessness was almost tangible.

'That must have been hard on you?' I was sorry as soon as I said it. Stop counselling them, I chided myself.

'I suppose.' He shrugged. 'Shit happens, I guess.'

'So, you must have some understanding of dogs, then, if you were training to be a vet?' Hell, he was probably more qualified than I was.

'I do, at least I like to think I know a bit. That's what's wrecking my head, to be honest.' He yawned and stretched. 'My gran's dog adores her, I can tell. He doesn't even seem particularly pleased to see me half the time. Yet he keeps turning up at my door. If it's not him, it's my mother.' He grinned. 'Neither of them will leave me alone.'

'How come?'

'I dunno,' he said, but he did, I knew, because he looked so uncomfortable. 'But there's always one of them on the doorstep. Last night I tickled my mother's ears and gave the mutt a kiss.' He smiled faintly. 'It's getting hard to tell them apart.'

'You could always move,' I suggested, trying to give him a way out of a conversation he didn't want to have, I suspected.

'I live within walking distance of the office, right by the

sea, so it's not really an option. Wouldn't stop my mother anyway, I'm afraid. Do you ever have that problem?'

I didn't tell him that there was more chance of me tongue-kissing a python than finding my mother calling round unexpectedly to see how I was – even when she had lived in Ireland – but decided against it. 'Eh, no, she lives abroad.' I smiled. 'Anyway, I'm sure we can sort out the canine in your life, even if the humans might be more difficult.' I was at a loss actually, so I asked him a few more questions to buy me some time. Nothing obvious hit me even after more than half an hour's probing. I tried to stay focussed on the dog, rather than giving his problem human associations, which is what I seemed to be doing a lot.

'Tell me what happens when you bring the dog back to your gran?'

'Nothing. He seems delighted. He wags his tail at her as if to say, "Aren't I a good boy?" and instead of scolding him she gives him treats. I can't figure it out.'

Neither could I, but I wasn't about to tell him that. 'Tell you what, why don't we make another appointment and you can bring him with you? I won't charge you for this one,' I said, feeling a bit useless.

'I'm happy to pay you,' he smiled. 'Besides, didn't you say at the class this was a new venture for you?' He paused.

'Did I?' Christ, I must have let it slip. 'Well, yes, it is, but I have trained, I assure you, my qualifications are up on the wall in recep—'

'I wasn't implying anything, other than that you shouldn't turn down money at this early stage.' He held his hand up. 'I'd really appreciate any help you can give me. I feel I'm just too close, wood from the trees and all that. It's starting to take over my life, to be honest.' He ran his hands through his hair. 'I love my gran, don't get me wrong. We're great friends, but I seem to be spending all my time with her. It's ruining my social life.' He laughed shortly. 'Actually, that's not true. It's non-existent anyway. I meet more people through visits to Myrtle than I would if I went speed-dating.'

'Maybe she's lonely?' I was only half listening to him, wondering if I'd hit the nail on the head. Perhaps she was sending the dog around to his house so that he'd have to visit her.

'No, as I said, most times there's someone visiting when I return the mutt.' He sighed again. 'She's got a social network to rival most women half her age.'

That ruled that out so.

'In fact, I know loads of younger people who stay in night after night because they're exhausted and stressed,' he said, unknowingly describing my past existence, 'but not Myrtle, she's always on the go. It's the internet, actually. It's the new ballroom of romance apparently, especially outside Dublin.' He sounded like an old codger. 'Most of the women I know meet men in chatrooms.' He shrugged. 'Is that sad, or is it just me?'

'Are there still any lights left on in the Irish countryside?' I was only half joking. 'I thought the drink-driving laws combined with the smoking ban finished that off for young people, along with no outlet for pensioners, with all the sub-post offices closing.' I was trying to humour him, he seemed a bit intense. I suspected he needed to let it out.

'Oh listen, don't mind me, I'm ranting,' he confirmed.

'I'm just a bit pissed off today. The internet's been great for my gran; she was in a poker room the other night when I rang. She texted me to call her later,' he said wryly. 'I'm just annoyed because I can barely turn on the computer.'

The alarm on my phone buzzed. It sounded like a message coming in but in fact it was my way of reminding myself of the time.

'Well, let's see the two of you together then and see if we can't figure this out between us,' I suggested.

'Great, as soon as you can would suit me.' He stood up. 'I won't mention anything to my gran for the time being, though. I'll just offer to take him for a run in the park.'

'Fine.' He arranged to call me to make the next appointment, because his gran was going on holiday and he'd have the dog for a couple of days. Then he left, shoulders hunched. I wondered what the full story was there.

I spent the rest of the evening trying to figure it out in my head. There was a major piece of the jigsaw missing and I really wanted to help him. I looked up all my reference books, but nothing fitted. Maybe it would fall into place once I saw them together. I sighed and decided to go to bed early.

I'd have loved a long soak. Problem was, I didn't have a bath any more. You see, as soon as I committed to changing my job, I decided to go the whole hog. So I sold my soft-top yuppie car and bought a gorgeous Kawasaki motorbike, shiny black with a pink streak. It made me smile each time I saw it waiting for me. It was a huge change for me, and I have to confess I missed my coffees en route to work, but

I got everywhere so much quicker that I actually had lots of time to get ready in the morning and have breakfast and make any urgent calls.

The only problem with moving house was that I couldn't find anything that wasn't similar to my swanky apartment until Maddy heard of someone who was renting a mobile home in Bray, which was on the Dublin border, officially in County Wicklow but really like a suburb of the capital city. I loved it the minute I laid eyes on it, and so far no bath was the only downside to living in a caravan. I could still see the oversized, roll-top one I used to own but was always too tired to go to the trouble of filling.

Now, I wriggled my feet in my new pink (have to be careful not to overdo the girly colour) suede kitten heels and laughed. Moving here was the best thing I'd done. It made me feel that I'd left it all behind – the traffic, the stress, the aggression, the people who had no time for anyone and didn't even bother to greet their neighbours in the lift of the apartment block they shared.

Not for the new me, so now I lived in a trailer, worked in the latest 'hot' profession, and was learning to rollerskate. How cool is that?

Once I'd changed into jeans and a hoodie and scrunched my hair into a ponytail, I turned on all the lamps, as well as the lights on the deck, marvelling again at how easy my home was. It had a large kitchen/living/dining room, a main bedroom, a guest room and a tiny study (third bedroom), and a bathroom that had everything I needed except space. There was a lot of elbow-crunching as I moved around trying to dry myself in the morning. The other big downside was that there was virtually no storage but I had just acquired a garden shed, which was fab. No more stubbing my toe on the suitcase under the bed or keeping the Hoover and ironing board in the shower. That was my job for the weekend actually, sorting out my new shed. Anal, but fun, and Maddy had promised to help in return for a good feed.

Now I tidied up as I pottered about, getting everything ready for the morning. All I had to do was plump the cushions and arrange the tea towels on the handle of the oven door and, bingo, the place was tidy.

In bed, I could see the stars, thanks to a skylight and the fact that Bray was virtually in the country, so much less pollution.

Next day I had only one client, but I wasn't panicking. This was going to be a building exercise. It was Emily – the nice one with the cat called Rover whom her mother thought was her dog reincarnated. She told me the story again and we tried to thrash it out, but no matter what we came up with, there was one big obstacle. Rover was, in fact, a cat and we'd all be pushing up the daisies before he chased a ball, I reckoned, even if he had nine lives. And there was no way of knowing if he had ever been a dog, I told Emily, but for some reason, she felt she had to sort it out for her mother.

'It's just, they were the most devoted couple, and since Dad died Mum's been heartbroken and I can't bear it.' She had tears in her eyes. 'I simply have to figure it out.'

'So what exactly is your mother hoping for? She sees clearly that he's a cat, right?'

'Yes. I guess she's looking for a sign, anything, that he might have been a dog in a previous life.'

I wondered why Emily felt compelled to solve this problem when it was clearly her mother's delusion, but I suspected she was a solver generally, just like I used to be. It was a way of looking for love, I'd learned.

But I said nothing and so, for now, we went round and round in circles. At one point I even found myself down on all fours on the floor, playing with what was definitely a cat called Rover, wondering if I could, with a lot of hard work, teach him to show any doggy signs. The fact that he constantly meowed was a bit of a problem, but I wasn't giving up yet. I put down a number of toys. First, a nice, smelly, edible intestine – dogs adore them, according to Tim in *The Gourmet Dog* – next, a squeaky ball with a range of brilliant noises built in, then a plastic hamburger filled with mince which even had a use-by date (where do they think up these things?) and, finally, a small, grey, nondescript rubber mouse. Rover nearly knocked me over when he saw it. Within seconds he was circling the bit of plastic with the curly tail, and in no time it was being lashed around the place as he tried to annihilate it. No crisis of identity there then.

After almost an hour I gave up, but decided against telling Emily outright. I knew she'd be traumatized.

'OK, perhaps we'll leave it for today then. I need to rethink this one,' I told her, wondering if there was a website I could go on.

'Thank you so much for not giving up on us.' Emily was pathetically grateful. It hurt me to see it.

'Emily, I'll do my best, but if I can't help, then I won't be charging you, OK? It wouldn't be ethical, because I'm really not sure I can do anything at all. Rover is a cat, you see,' I said, which was totally unnecessary given that, by now, he had climbed up the curtains and was teetering along the wooden pole quite happily, something I'd never seen even the most agile puppy attempt.

'Oh no, please, I won't be able to come again in that case.' Emily looked close to breaking down. 'Honestly, I know it's a difficult case, but I have to be sure I've done everything I can, just in case he is Rover – the dog, that is – come back to us. You're my last hope, you see.'

'Well, I'll do my best, obviously. I do have a contact in the States who specializes in' – I was going to say 'nutcases' but changed my mind – 'eh, more unusual canine problems. I'll give him a call over the weekend and see what he makes of your case.'

'Thank you, I really appreciate it. I can't tell you how much. My mother means everything in the world to me, you see, she—'

My phone beeped and Emily stopped abruptly, and I was half glad, to be honest. There was only so much I could take in one session.

I spent the rest of the day Googling for cats who might be dogs but, for some sane reason, there weren't many sites. There was one guy in Oregon who'd managed to teach his pet snake to bark, but that was about it.

At six o'clock I rang Clodagh and suggested a drink.

'Love to, darling, but I'm off to do some circuit training. I'm running in the next New York marathon.'

46

'Of course you are.' She hadn't told me, it was just that Clodagh was always doing something.

'Fancy calling around to see the new pad later?'

'OK, sure, but I'm on the water – still, not sparkling. And today I'm only eating green food, so if you have anything in the fridge . . . don't go to any trouble . . .'

'I've a few nice, crunchy nettles in the garden. Soup, maybe?' I asked cheerfully, but it was lost on her.

'No worries, I've a bag of spinach in the cooler bag in the boot.'

'Fabulous. Maybe we could share it?' My sarcasm too was wasted. Clodagh was one of the most focussed people I knew. I'd bet she was making a mental list – and using word association to memorize it – while on the treadmill watching Sky News and chatting to me on her hands-free phone.

'Sure. See you around eight. Ciao.' She was gone. I wondered whether I should tell her about Rover, but decided against it. It might all be too much for her organized brain to take in. Clodagh was my dose of sanity. I adored her energy and get up and go. Nothing was ever a problem for her and I loved her for it. I'd pick her brains another time; meanwhile, in an effort to get through the rest of the afternoon, I headed out to buy a hot chocolate and macaroon bar to stave off the hunger pangs. It was all the talk of spinach that did it.

5

EVEN SHARING A SLIMY VEGETABLE WITH CLODAGH WAS invigorating. Mind you, that feeling was helped considerably by a very brisk walk in biting wind along Bray seafront. We ended up practically in Greystones, a village I hadn't been to in years. I hardly recognized it; I'd never seen so many new houses.

'My God, I feel claustrophobic,' I told my friend. 'How do people live like this?' I eyed up the rows of brown boxes that all looked identical (except for the different colours on the front doors), without a patch of green space between the crazy paving of the driveways. It was fairly typical of the entire commuter belt in Ireland, from what I'd seen.

Clodagh, of course, knew all about the houses and their occupants. Within two minutes, so did I. Within five, I wanted to own one – she had a way of telling a story.

'Super-cool arty types, media moguls, television producers. Lots of wife-swapping and dope-smoking, allegedly. Great parties, according to Una, a girl in the gym. She shares one of the terraced ones over there with a drummer and a Riverdancer.'

Back at the van, I could see she was having difficulty

coming to terms with my trendy new life, despite her lib-
eralism.

'But how? Where? – What I mean is, what do you do if
you need to, you know . . .?' she half hissed, half whispered
and pointed to her bum.

'You don't have to whisper, there's no one around,' I told
her. 'And if you want to pee just use the toilet,' I said with
a smile.

'But do those portable toilet bowls really get rid of the
poo or does it just float around for ages and then you have
to fish it out and bury it?'

'What planet are you living on? Chemical toilets went the
same way as Chemical Ali. Mine has a dual-control flush. I
have central heating, for God's sake. And a power shower.'

'Oh,' was all she managed, but I still think she was glad
her spinach was bagged and pre-washed.

Once inside, her jaw dropped. I couldn't resist giving her
the grand tour.

She said 'oh' about thirty times.

'Oh, you have a proper bed.' (Clodagh)

'What did you expect, a pull-out campbed that doubles as
a kitchen table?' (Me, delighted)

'Oh, it's a real fridge.' (Her)

'As opposed to a cooler box, yes.' (Me, sarcastically)

'Oh my God, is that a waste extractor in the sink?' (Her
again)

'No, it's where you mash up the poo if it doesn't go down
the loo.' (Me, giving up) 'Let's have a drink.'

An hour later we were giggling about it all. One thing I'll
say for Clodagh, she could definitely take a slagging.

'You're such a middle-class, spoilt brat,' I prodded her. 'Didn't you ever go caravanning as a child?'

'Yes, of course.' She was all hands and drama. 'Where do you think I saw those chemical whatsits? I went to Courtown with my friend Angie. But most of the loos were basically a hole in the ground with the lid of a pot on top and a box of scratchy, greaseproof squares of loo paper tied to the hedge. When I told my mother, she was so appalled she refused to let me go even to Angie's family home again for a play date, and she lived in Foxrock, they were loaded.'

'Your lot are so . . .'

'Snobby, I know.' Clodagh was never afraid to tell it like it was.

'I was going to say proper.'

'Thank God you and I met at college and by that time my folks had lost their power. I have to say, your mother gave me more of an education than TV ever could.'

'Yeah, that'd be Martha all right. Pity she screwed me up by being so strict when I was growing up.'

'I think she worried you'd go off the rails.' Clodagh smiled. 'She said something one time about not wanting you to turn out like your father.'

'Yeah, so while I spent years trying to be the perfect child Becky was running wild. And she still got more love and attention.' I sounded bitter, even to myself.

'So is that what all this is about then?' My friend waved her arms about.

'Maybe. I've wanted to break free for years, but I guess my mother started it. It was OK for her to be bonkers, but I had to be perfect.' I indicated the bottle. 'Top-up?'

'No ta, I shouldn't have even had one. Have to be up at six. Go on, I'm listening.' I corked the wine and put on the kettle instead.

'God, Clodagh, I'd become so dull, I never realized. Why didn't one of you tell me?'

'Not dull. Just . . . I dunno . . . sensible, I guess.'

That word again. If anyone applied it to me one more time, I'd clock them. 'Yeah, well, I'm through with dull, boring, predictable, whatever. I no longer have to worry about what my mother says—'

'So what's all this about really?' All my friends were now adopting my counsellor clichés, it seemed.

I thought for a moment. 'I suppose it's about wanting to have a more exciting time of it. A bit more Amy Winehouse than Mary Whitehouse.'

'I blame Bridget Jones,' Clodagh decided. 'Although, you're more like Keira Knightley, I think. Serene,' she sounded pleased. 'That's you.'

'All the hot girls in the movies these days are quirky and kooky, not serene,' I told Clodagh. For some strange reason I felt like crying for all I hadn't done with my life.

'They aren't real, remember? The movies isn't real life.'

'You know what I mean.' I wasn't about to be patronized.

'Lou, listen to me,' Clodagh said gently. 'We love you as you are. You're strong and loyal and dependable . . .'

That did it. I jumped up and practically knocked over her glass. 'But that's it. Can't you see? I don't want "dependable" written on my tombstone. Loyal people don't get laid. I've been sensible since I was five. I had to be; otherwise my mother might not have loved me. All my life

I've done the right thing. I got top marks at school, went to college, got a proper job, bought quality, durable (I hated that word) clothes, kept myself neat and tidy and never had a pair of Spanx rolled off me even by a doctor. And there's my baby sister, she's been having a ball, getting away with murder all her life. And my mother's never off the phone to her, whereas she doesn't even know I've moved house.'

'I think you've turned out fine,' Clodagh said softly. 'And Becky is nice, but she's, I dunno, vacuous, I suppose. And completely self-absorbed.'

'I don't want *their* lives necessarily,' I said. 'But Christ, Clodagh, at least they've lived, unlike me. If I was told tomorrow that I'd a terminal illness, I'd be gutted.'

'You'd be fucked actually,' Clodagh said, deadpan.

'You know what I mean.' I felt flat again.

'We love you, you don't need to change.'

'Yeah well, you'd better get used to it, babe' – I mentally picked myself up – ''Cause this is the new me.' I did a twirl, seeing as she hadn't yet commented on my Juicy Couture tracksuit. 'And quit wrecking my buzz.'

To her credit, she didn't laugh. 'OK, hon, let's see where this takes us. I'll come along for the ride.' She gave me a hug. 'But only if I can make a list.' She winked.

'Screw lists, I'm having an adventure.'

'You're on, so. How about we start by doing something this weekend?'

'Great. Maddy's coming round on Saturday to help me organize the shed. We could go out after?'

'A shed, eh? Very unconventional.' She gave me a look,

then ducked to avoid the cushion I threw at her. 'I'll meet you in Ron Black's at nine.'

Next day I had a new client. He was called Denis Cassidy and I was thrilled, because he'd been referred by our local vet in Stillorgan. I wondered if he was cute, single – young even? Rich would be a bonus. He was, in fact, sixtysomething and hadn't a bean, if looks were anything to go by. But his dog was a hoot, a tiny Jack Russell cross with a tail that would take your eye out.

'Mr Cassidy, sit down. I'm Louisa.' I decided to play it straight with the name with my older clients, in case they thought 'Lulu' was too flaky. 'And who is this cutie?' I tickled the dog's neck then straightened up and coughed, realizing I was talking to all dogs as if they were babies.

'This is Bartholomew,' he said with pride.

'That's an unusual name, why did you choose that?'

'I wanted something grand, you see. I hate my own name. All my life I've been called Dinny or Denny or Dinjo. At school I was Denis the Menace.' His eyes twinkled.

'I once had a dog called Gnasher.' I'd no idea why I told him. 'He was a bit of a rough diamond.'

'I'm a bit of a gouger too, you see.' He winked.

'I doubt that.' I laughed. Bartholomew had taken up residence on the brand-new Louis Vuitton-imitation canine couch, all brown and caramel check and fake leather. After he'd sniffed it for a moment or two he decided to christen it. I tried not to look too horrified or move too fast as he cocked his leg on my €100 fake-designer bed – and Denis was a bit slow out of the chair – so by the time we got to him he'd peed for Ireland and was wagging his tail in delight.

'I'm so sorry.' Denis looked really upset.

'No worries, he's just being a dog.' But I'd gone off him bigtime, I decided, as I scooped up a load of tissues I'd bought in case any clients burst into tears – a hangover from my old life when all I did was mop up after people. Not so different now then, I decided, although the smell was a bit gassier and I used not to have to wipe the seats. I took the bed to the bathroom and ran it under the tap then left it to dry on the radiator.

'I'll pay to have it cleaned,' Denis said feebly when I returned. 'Bad dog,' he said sternly, but he was stroking the mutt's head as he scolded, not the recommended way to deal with bad behaviour.

'So, what can I do for you, Mr Cassidy?' I said with a smile, ignoring the dog's wagging tail, having decided the little bollix could sit on the cold floor.

'Denis, please. I've never been called Mr Cassidy in my life, except when I was stopped by the cops and breathalysed last year.'

'Oh my God, what happened?' It was every oulfella's nightmare in rural Ireland these days. Denis had told me he lived near Ashford in County Wicklow so I imagined he was a farmer or something, judging by the dirt under his nails.

'Told him he'd have to catch me first and sped off,' he cackled.

'What?'

'He was on a pushbike, you see, and it was dark. And my back number plate was missing.' His face was that of a bold child who'd gotten away with robbing an orchard.

'Good for you.' It was a totally unprofessional thing to say, but it was out before I could stop myself.

'That's what everyone says. These new drink–driving laws have ruined rural life.' He thumped the table. 'I'm a responsible driver. I have two pints and go home the back roads and, anyway, my old jalopy wouldn't go over 30 miles an hour if you filled it with whiskey, even. Most of my neighbours won't go out any more, they're terrified of losing their licence. Have the police nothin' better to do than harass old folks like me? I asked a young fella in uniform the other day. He was about twelve years of age and givin' a ticket to Mrs O'Reilly, just because she was blocking a line of traffic for a second while she nipped in to get her pension. It's a scandal, that's what it is. Anyway, tell me about what you do, Miss?'

'Well, em, I'm, em, originally a psychologist, but I have studied with a world-renowned expert on dog behaviour. My certificates are internationally recognized and I did a BA in . . .'

'So you used to practise on humans, then?'

'Yes, I suppose, although prac—'

'I prefer dogs myself, most of the time.'

'Me too.' We smiled at each other, and I like to think both of us knew then that ours was a relationship that would endure, although Denis gave no indication of what he was thinking. In a way, he was the father figure I'd never had. I shook myself quickly, realizing that I wasn't about to go there.

'So, eh, maybe you'd like to tell me about Bartholomew?' I asked him after a second or two.

'There's something botherin' him,' Denis told me after a while. 'He's just not himself.'

'How do you mean?'

'He's moody.'

'Moody?'

'Yeah, a bit like a woman. Never know where you stand with him. One minute he's licking your face, next he's ignoring you, that class of thing.'

'I see.' I didn't.

'So, do you think you can help?'

'I'll certainly try. Perhaps next time I could come and visit you at home?' It was something I'd been avoiding, feeling I had enough to cope with, but I was beginning to understand that part of my job was going to mean travelling, to see my 'clients' in their normal environment. So here was my first opportunity, and I suspected I was going to have to do the same for Ronan O'Meara and his gran.

'That'd be great,' Denis said, and immediately got up to leave, as if he was afraid I'd change my mind. 'When?' was all he said.

'Eh, soon. How about next week?'

'Could you come tomorrow?'

'Not tomorrow, no.' I scanned my diary. 'But perhaps Friday? Does that suit?'

He nodded. 'As long as it's after twelve. I collect the oul pension on Fridays, and Maureen Kearns, the neighbour who brings me, always insists we have coffee afterwards. She's fierce posh like that.' He scratched his head as if he couldn't figure that one out either. 'Do you drink this new coffee, Miss? That frothy stuff with cocoa powder all over the place and very little in the cup that you can actually swallow?'

'I prefer tea actually.' I laughed at the face he made.

'Grand so. I have plenty of that. And a packet of ginger-nut biscuits to dunk in it.'

'I look forward to it.' I scribbled down his address and telephone number and we agreed a time.

He left happy, and left me even more intrigued. Like most of my new clients, there was more to Denis the Menace than I'd discovered so far – that I knew for sure.

6

I WAS LOOKING FORWARD TO MY NEXT APPOINTMENT. LUSCIOUS Louis was back, along with Mike and Pedro. Louis was wearing an exquisite charcoal suit; Mike looked like he'd slept in his shirt.

'Hello there.' I made straight for Louis. My God he really was a ride, and quite macho-looking too. I wondered if I was the only woman who secretly thought that cute gay men could swing either way, if they met the right woman. I'd wasted quite a bit of time on this notion over the years, and it hadn't happened yet.

'Cool room, I love the colour.' Louis was off exploring, so my plan wasn't about to come to fruition this time either, I reckoned.

'Aubergine melt,' I told his back. 'I had a bit of help from an interior designer. Apparently, dogs feel more at ease with certain tones, at least according to Giorgio's website. It's something to do with their acute sense of smell, apparently. Did you know that colours smell different?' I asked them.

Louis looked interested, while Mike looked like he was waiting for the punchline.

'Me neither,' was all I could think of to add.

'Fascinating,' and 'What a load of shite,' Louis and Mike said in unison.

'I can't believe you fell for that, he must be American,' Mike continued. 'Pedro here only gets excited by the smell of pee and wouldn't recognize aubergine melt if it appeared in his Pedigree Chum.'

'I suppose that's from his days in the hospice – the urine association?' I sympathized.

'No, it's because Mike's aim is always off and he never quite manages to reach the bowl.' Louis's lip curled. 'And Pedro follows him everywhere, so he invariably licks it up. Gross but true.'

'Don't they say piss is rich in something?' Mike wanted to know.

'The only thing yours is rich in is alcohol.' Louis sighed. 'No wonder poor Pedro is so stupid, he's probably half cut most of the time.'

Oh God please, I prayed silently. Not another couple who need counselling. I decided to move on pronto. 'Sit down, please.' I indicated the couch.

'The dog bed's a bit past it,' Louis commented, as Pedro sniffed excitedly then rolled around on it. 'Doesn't quite match the rest of the room.'

'Yes, well, it's brand-new but one of my other clients – Bartholomew – peed on it, and I put the fabric on a rad to dry and unfortunately it sort of melted and went all hard . . .' I'd been furious when I discovered it.

'Some bastard peed on the dog bed? Now that's gross.' Mike laughed.

'No, no.' I shook my head. 'Bartholomew is a dog – a Jack Russell cross. Denis, his owner, was mortified, actually.' I decided this pee thing had gone far enough. 'Anyway, Pedro seems more than happy.'

It was true. The Collie was trying to flatten the bed by thrashing it to bits, and doing quite well, actually.

'Ignore him, it means he loves it.' Louis gave the dog an adoring look. 'He'll settle in a minute, won't you, honey bun?' He got down on all fours and proceeded to roll about with the dog. I went off him straightaway, thankfully, as soon as he started asking, 'Who's your Daddy?' in a black rapper voice.

'And therein lies our problem.' Mike stretched and yawned. 'Louis thinks the mutt is human. It's killing me.'

'Right, well . . .'

'I don't, honestly, Louisa . . .' Louis made to get up.

'Last night he came home with a high chair for him – specially made – so that he could eat with us.' Mike mouthed, 'I swear,' at my incredulous face and raised his eyebrows. 'He has his own clothes rail, tracksuit and sun visor. The only difference between him and Louis is that Louis has a walk-in wardrobe.' They were behaving like an old married couple; I decided they were definitely partners. 'Last week I got into trouble for not making him sit in the baby seat in Louis's car and strapping him in.' Mike scratched his head. 'He weighs a ton because we feed him avocado and bleedin' chickpea purée or something and when Louis's away he claims I'm giving the dog diarrhoea simply because I open a can . . .'

'I refuse to feed Pedro anything I wouldn't eat myself.'

Louis looked sullen. 'How would you feel if you had to eat pig's intestines and blood and stuff?'

'Like I do every Saturday morning when I have black pudding for breakfast?' Mike grinned.

'OK, guys, let's take it from the top.' I pulled out my notebook and went into school-mistress mode. 'What's the basic problem?'

'I told you, Louis thinks he's human – the dog, I mean.'

'I do not. You just ignore him. Last week I came home and he was drinking the remains of your beer from a bottle you'd left on the kitchen floor, because there was no water in his bowl . . .'

'That's because we'd run out of Evian and you won't let me give him tap water.' Mike caught my snort. 'You think I'm exaggerating? Come and stay with us for a weekend some time.'

'You never wash him and, once, you forgot to feed him for two days.'

'That is not true.' Mike threw his hands in the air. 'I just didn't roast a pheasant for him and serve it with parsnip crisps.'

'You fed him one of those own-brand cheap-as-chips tins. He had the runs for two days.' Louis folded his arms and angled his body away from Mike, always a bad sign in a relationship.

'Look, I'm not doing this any more.' Mike stood up. 'He's a dog, for Christ sake. He does not need lavender oil on his pillow and his own armchair.'

'He's just afraid of what people think when they see him out with Pedro . . .'

'Too right I am, when he's a Collie wearing a pink tutu and a swastika or whatever you call those diamond collars . . .'

'Swarovski, asshole.' Louis was furious. 'You're just showing your ignorance.'

'Ah fuck it, I'm outta here.' Mike headed for the door while I was pretending to take notes.

'No, no.' I leapt up. 'Please, don't go. This is a . . . eh, more common problem than you might think,' I lied. 'And I'm confident we can . . . avoid a domestic crisis.' I tried to be diplomatic.

'Yes, but can you avoid having them both committed?' Mike started to laugh suddenly. I was biting my lip at that stage anyway. 'Next on his list' – he indicated Louis, who had his back to us – 'is finding a dog hotel where he can call every night to say hello via video link when he's away.' Mike winked and explained that there was even one hotel where the dogs could bring their favourite DVD with them, to help them sleep.

'You're a cruel bastard.' Louis hauled Pedro – who was snoring, genitals exposed – to his feet, and was out the door before I could stop him.

'Oops, better go, he's hell to live with when he's upset.' Mike looked like he enjoyed tormenting people.

'Excuse me . . .' Mary, the offices' receptionist, put her head round the door. 'Eh, Mr Cassidy just rang to confirm your appointment for later this morning.' She looked pointedly at her watch, in an effort to rescue me, I suspected.

'Eh, fine. Thanks,' I gave her a reassuring smile. 'I hadn't forgotten.'

62

Mike was halfway out the door. 'I really have to go,' he grimaced. 'Louis is driving and, if I don't get there fast, Pedro will be sitting in the front seat wearing my shades and I'll be crouching in the boot wearing a muzzle. It's a tough life.' He winked and was gone.

'Oh, and we owe you money. Fix you up at the next one,' he shouted over his shoulder. I headed for a giant chocolate intake.

7

TWO HOURS LATER I PULLED UP OUTSIDE A TYPICAL FARM-house in Wicklow – a plethora of sheds, muck everywhere and a mound of tyres. Bartholomew came to greet me, hurling himself in my direction from about ten metres away and somersaulting in the process, then landing smack on his back at my feet with a resounding thump.

'Ouch, I felt that. Are you OK?' I forgave him the bed incident immediately. He wriggled around, got to his feet, shook off the mud and acted as though nothing had happened.

'Typical man.' I grinned at him and rubbed his belly.

'Hello there, you found us then.' Denis Cassidy was in his working clothes, threadbare cardigan and check shirt with several buttons missing around the stomach revealing a vest the colour of used bathwater.

'Mr Cassidy, how are you?'

'Would ye give over with the Mr, Miss, my name is Dinny.' He ignored my outstretched hand.

'In that case, my friends call me Lulu.' I wasn't sure why I told him that. He had one of those faces; it made me want to dump my emotional baggage on him instead of the other way round.

He howled with laughter. 'What class of a name is Lulu?' He slapped me on the back so hard I nearly hit him in the eye with the apple I'd eaten on the journey down. 'If I call you that, the neighbours will think I have a fancy woman or somethin'. Mind you, Lulu's a dog's name, so that's good.' He cackled and turned on his heels and led the way inside.

The kitchen was much as it had been for years, I reckoned. A Formica table was covered with an orangey plastic cloth, the kind with bananas and apples printed inside squares. It matched the shiny red kitchen cabinet, from what I could see. The fireplace was a brown and cream concoction of cracked tiles with a coal scuttle and a packet of firelighters beside it, side by side with a brass companion set in the shape of a horseshoe, the rungs bare except for a half-burned, baldy brush and a blackened, stubby poker.

'I made you some dinner.' He'd half cleared and set the table – something that didn't happen every lunchtime, I imagined.

'You shouldn't have . . .'

'It's only soup.' He ladled out a glutinous mass that I knew had come from a packet. Country Vegetable, or something similar, I decided, as identical yellow and orange squares floated to the surface of a thick beige broth flecked with grass-coloured sprinklings. To go with it, he put heels of white batch loaf on a bread board, then left a plate of square pink slices of tinned corned beef in the middle of the table.

Saxa salt and Goodall's white pepper completed the meal. He used both liberally.

I tucked in, only so as not to offend him, and noticed he broke his slice of bread into lumps then dunked it in the soup to add to its wallpaper-paste consistency. We ate in silence, while the TV with rabbit's ears sat in the corner and spat out recipes for spiced pumpkin and chorizo broth and warm rocket and pesto salad with goat's cheese.

For afters we had brown mugs of strong tea and a packet of jam tarts in colours that didn't even vaguely resemble homemade preserve but tasted delicious nonetheless. I was touched that he'd gone to so much trouble for me. Eventually, we got round to discussing Bartholomew, who by now was curled up on his master's chair snoring.

'Sit over here by the fire and warm yourself,' Dinny insisted as he whooshed the dog down. I had another reason to be glad I no longer wore black suits – the mustard velour chair housed more hair than my shower plughole.

'Well, the dog seems content.' I envied him, carelessly stretched out on the hearth, as close to the mound of burning turf as he could get without scorching.

'Aye, he's OK today, but last night he growled at me when I wanted to sit in me own chair. And this morning he ignored me for ages, wouldn't come out of his bed.'

'Could he be ill?' I wondered out loud. It seemed too obvious. 'You had him checked by your vet before you came to me, though?' I remembered.

Denis nodded confirmation. 'Not a thing wrong with him – sure, look at the way he tore out to meet you.' He had a point there.

'How old is he?'

'No idea. I found him in the field one day about six years ago, no collar and skinny as a rake. I asked around and the postmistress put up a notice, but no one claimed him and, to be honest, I was glad in the end. He sort of grew on me, he's a bit of a chancer.' He winked. 'Like meself.'

'Well, he's a chancer who got lucky then.' Bartholomew had rolled over and was now lying on his back, paws in the air, gazing up at his master. I found myself thinking of Gnasher, something I was doing often these days.

'Tell me this,' Denis asked after a slight pause. 'Is there such a thing as the male menopause for dogs?'

'Pardon?' The television was now showing us how to wax our legs, complete with models in swimsuits. The girls were sprawled provocatively across the pink velvet couch, and I was terrified the demonstrator was about to move on to the bikini line. Daytime TV had changed a lot since I'd last seen it – Derek and Thelma and a group of old folks with Sonny Knowles and Anne O'Dwyer on piano, all singing along to 'I'll Take Care of Your Cares'. I mentally shook myself. 'Sorry, Dinny, you were saying?'

'You know, the same sort of thing that women get, mood swings and all the rest. I asked Mary Grimes in the grocer's and she said it happened to everyone, humans and animals.'

'Eh, I don't think so, but you never know. Hormones and all that, most of us have them. Tell you what, why don't I talk to your vet, Jim Harding, about his general health?'

'Ah no, don't go near him.' Denis went red in the face. 'He laughed at me when I asked him about it. Women are more sympathetic to that kind of stuff – must be the babies.' He'd lost me there, but I was desperately trying not to make him feel stupid. 'Is there anything I could give him? Mary Grimes mentioned some sort of oil – daffodil or primroses or something – but I hadn't a clue what that was and I didn't like to ask.' He looked like the world was changing too fast for him. 'Us men are supposed to know these things nowadays. Sure there's a Herb shop now in Wicklow. Imagine, a huge space that sells only dried weeds and twigs, things like parsley and thyme, I suppose, stuff we only ever used to stick up the turkey's arse at Christmas.' He coughed. 'Pardon me Miss, I'm not used to female company much.'

'Denis, the world's gone mad, and it's no different for me, either.' He was so sweet, a bachelor who'd been left behind in spanking-new Ireland. 'Tell you what, why don't we keep our eye on his, eh, mood swings, the two of us, and see if we can't figure it out between us? And meanwhile, I'll do some research on the internet and see if I can find out something about . . . dogs and their hormones.'

He brightened up immediately. 'Would they have that sort of thing on a computer?' He sounded amazed. 'Is that what this internet yoke is, even – a computer?'

I nodded, wondering how many more bemused elderly people like him existed in our cash-rich, time-poor nation. 'That's all it is, Denis. A box. Think of it as a giant encyclopaedia.'

'Well, holy God, what's the world coming to? Sure, soon you won't need to go outside your front door. I have a niece in Wexford, she never rings unless she wants something. Last week she told me she was doing all her Christmas shopping "online". I hadn't a clue. When I asked her about it she didn't have time to explain.'

'Well, next time you're in my office, I'll show you how it works if you like?' I stood up, mainly because daytime TV was now doing an item on celebrities eating worms in the jungle. The latest tasty morsel was a crocodile's penis, or 'croc shaft', as they kept referring to it. I wasn't sure how much more I could take, never mind Denis.

8

I DECIDED IT WAS TIME TO GET LAID AS SOON AS I AWOKE next morning.

I'd never had a one-night stand – not that anyone knew. Frankly, it wasn't something to be proud of, not among my generation, that's for sure. You see, deep down, I was an all-or-nothing girl. I wanted the fairytale – not that I had any right to expect it. Princes didn't suss out girls like me: there were too many of us, for a start. They wanted bubbly or sexy or funny or blonde hair and big tits. Take Maddy, for instance. She wasn't a stunner, but men actively sought her out in pubs and clubs. Maddy was vivacious, had great one-liners and legs up to her ears. But it was her here-I-am, if-you-like-me-great, if-you-don't-tough attitude that kept them coming. Me, I always tried too hard. Maddy had been shagged more times than I'd been shopping, and always on her terms. After thinking about it over three mugs of tea, I decided there was no option but to enlist her help. It was my only hope.

Stretching out, I revelled in my surroundings. Quiet was something I'd never really gotten used to. And here in my mobile home at the end of a seldom-used lane, even the barely happening bustle of Bray town seemed far away. I jumped up and had the kettle on, bed made and curtains open in seconds. Compact suited me, I decided.

Maddy arrived at twelve. She wore old jeans, several cheap, strappy T-shirts – one on top of the other – no make-up and her hair was in a scrunchie, yet you'd still ride her. We got started on the shed, and I waited until we were fully engrossed before casually mentioning that I needed a change.

'What sort of change?'

'I dunno. I love my new life but I'm still a bit bored with myself.'

'So what do you want then?'

'Excitement.'

'Lulu, baby,' she scolded, but it was playful. 'You've been saying that for ever.' She stopped assembling the shelf unit for the shed and sat on a tea chest. 'We've been through all this.' To her credit, she didn't look like she was bored to death with the topic. 'Your sister got all the mad genes and you got the nice, normal ones. And years of growing up trying to please your mother have taken their toll. You are what you are, which is pretty damn good from where I'm standing.' She redid her scrunchie. 'Trying to be something you're not never works. Men are attracted to women who are confident in their own skin – pretending to like snooker and beer and laughing at their weak one-liners was for when we were fifteen. Be yourself,' she chided gently. 'A big fat cliché, but true nonetheless.'

'I'm tired being me. It's dull. I know I can't fundamentally change who I am, but I want to be less uptight, less safe.' I sighed. 'I feel I am, deep down. If only I didn't worry all the time.' Even thinking about it made me scared it was never going to happen. 'And let's face it, if I think I'm boring, what chance has anyone else?'

'Well, you've moved from a house to a caravan, gone from a car to a motorbike, changed job and abandoned your power suits. I'd say you've loosened up considerably.'

'Really?' I was pleased. 'Well, could I make myself a bit more, em, jazzy, maybe?' I decided to cut to the chase. 'A bit more out there looks-wise. I fancy a fling.' I grinned.

'OK, tell you what. Once we finish here, let's wash your hair, for a start. I've always wanted to see it left to dry naturally.' She was warming to it, I could tell. 'And you could lose the drab brown eye colour you always wear, along with that nondescript lipstick you keep stocking up on.' She hesitated, wondering if she'd gone too far, I suspected.

'You're absolutely right.' Far from being insulted, I was thrilled. 'That's me – neutral. Well, not any more.' I threw my fist in the air, Che Guevara-style. 'My hair is not like Becky's though,' I warned, feeling nervous straightaway. 'It's more wiry than wavy.'

Clodagh arrived just as we started lunch. A few texts had persuaded her to join us early after all. She'd brought some sort of couscous muck, which she tucked into quite happily. Maddy and I had a deli roast stuffed chicken on warm baguette with lashings of butter and, for dessert, a coffee slice each. Clodagh nibbled on goji berries. We saved the wine for later and got back to work in earnest, filling Clodagh in on our plans as we worked. She was equally enthusiastic, and I was delighted, feeling I was really doing something positive with my image at last. Ditching the black suits was fine, but replacing them with anything other than Next or Zara plain casuals or an M&S white T-shirt was beyond me.

By five thirty we were all cream-crackered, so we had a pot of coffee (Clodagh had mint tea) and chilled for half an hour, then the girls got stuck into 'Operation Transformation'.

Two hours later, I looked like a dark-haired version of one of those brazen blonde barmaids in *Corrie* – a mass of curls and psychedelic and sparkle. The girls ruined their make-up laughing when I said as much, but they insisted I looked younger and, more importantly, hot. My lovely hair, my only comfort in life, was indeed 'natural'. It also totally redefined 'big hair'. My slinky top was a riot of colour, my padded bra was orange lace with a chocolate trim, and my earrings would fit around your neck. The jeans – the only thing I owned – were fine, but the shoes were red patent with polka-dot bows and the cute peep-toes revealed blood-red nails. Most of the stuff belonged to Clodagh's flatmate, our only option when we phoned her and begged her to come over and help. Oddly enough, I sort of liked it in a horrified but thrilled way.

Still, it was an indication of how desperate I was for a new image that I let them bring me to the pub looking like that. It was their insistence that the look was 'so now' that convinced me. Given that it had only been invented in the past hour, it was definitely what you'd call happening.

Each time I dithered about actually facing the public, they sold it to me on the basis that I looked cool – and cool was what I craved. Two equally cool beers in quick succession helped convince me to stay.

What happened next will haunt me for ever. Three guys approached us, and we chatted away for a while. We knew they were coming, they'd been watching us for ages, feigning nonchalance, as guys do. They ranged from not bad to middling to OK after a few vodkas – and guess which one I got? Still, I wasn't downbeat. He was an artist called Jason who played in a band, so he was definitely trendy, and Paul – the cute(ish) one who fancied Maddy – invited us to their next gig the following week in the only decent pub in Shankhill. So far, so definitely happening then.

We eventually made our way to the disco next door. At this stage I was nervous. I hadn't had enough to drink, so that sense of abandonment I craved hadn't kicked in – or been let out, in my case. In fact, that was another of my hang-ups I needed to deal with. I was always careful about alcohol – terrified in case I'd lose control, the ultimate shame.

Still, we took to the dance floor like we were fuel-injected. I noticed Jason hung back by the bar while his two mates joined us. After a while, I was exhausted, and my earrings were so heavy they were ripping my neck to shreds, so I wandered over to where he was standing.

'Hi.' I decided to go for it.

'How's it going?'

'Great. You?'

'Yeah, cool.' That word again. It was a sign.

'Actually, I should explain.' I knew this was a mistake as soon as I started. Guys didn't want to hear this kind of stuff. 'You see the girls sort of "did me up" for the evening. I'm not usually quite so . . . bright . . .'

'No, you're fine.' He swallowed rather a lot of his pint,

which I should have taken as a warning. Instead I took it as a come-on. It was his smile, I decided later. He had a nice smile. His mate left a pint down beside him and winked at me, another sign as far as my deranged mind was concerned. I took a deep breath and decided I'd quite like to kiss him.

'Eh, fancy . . . going outside?' No, I don't know what came over me. I think I must have had a brain seizure, actually. I hadn't 'gone outside' since I'd been asked to bring in a crate of minerals at the school disco when I was fifteen. In fact, I don't think the term exists any more. Worse still, I hadn't been on my own with him for thirty seconds and, besides, outside in this case was the main street and I had two choices – snog him in front of the taxi rank or buy him chips.

'Eh . . . no, thanks all the same.' He tried to smile, but his eyes had *panic* written across them as clearly as if he'd used my purple kohl pencil to do it. 'Sorry, I probably should have . . . it was just my mates . . . and yours . . . eh, I'll see you.' And he left a full pint as evidence of his desperation.

To my credit – Maddy insisted later – I didn't crumble. She swore I'd looked totally chilled the whole time. It felt like forever as I glanced around trying to pretend I hadn't just been dumped before I'd even been picked up. I waved vaguely at people I didn't know simply to keep my hands busy. The girls gestured at me to join them, but I avoided eye contact because of my halogen-hot face and bitten lip, so eventually they cut short their floor show and strolled back to the bar.

'Where's Justin?' Maddy wanted to know.

'Jason,' Clodagh insisted.

75

'Him too.' She looked at me.

'No idea,' I said in a bored voice.

'Have we had enough, girls?' Clodagh yawned. 'I'm up at six.'

'On a Sunday?'

'Yep, meeting a gang in Enniskerry at eight. We're walking a new route up the Wicklow Way.'

'Sure what else would you do before breakfast?' I tried to joke. 'Well, I'm happy to head for the hills myself.' I had to stop myself breaking into a gallop, in fact.

'OK so.' Maddy gave in rather quickly for her. 'Although I did quite fancy another dance with Paul . . .' She glanced around trying to spot him. 'I have a feeling he was waiting for someone, though. Intuition.' She shrugged.

'Come on, I've had enough.' I could have kissed Clodagh for saying that. 'Sure we know where they'll be next Saturday night if we want them.'

Yep and I knew where I wouldn't be. You'd have to tether me to a trailer to get me anywhere near that pub in Shankhill they'd mentioned, but I wouldn't be telling the girls why any day soon.

'Let's not appear too keen, eh?' Clodagh continued as she picked up her bag.

'She means you.' Maddy poked me in the ribs. 'I saw you . . .'

'Get a life.' I tried to flick my hair nonchalantly, forgetting I had a mop on my head – a hairsprayed one at that. 'I can't even remember what they were saying half the time. Bit too culchie for me.' Stop now, you're going too far the other way, I warned myself.

76

'Well, Jason said he's playing in that pub in—' Clodagh offered, but I cut her dead.

'Oh that?' I shook my head as if I knew something they didn't. 'I really don't think it's for us. So, anyone for chips on the way home?'

'Yes, please.' I knew Maddy would do anything for a fag and a large bag of greasy fries. She'd been moaning about being hungry since we'd arrived.

'Let's go, girls,' she said enthusiastically, confirming my thoughts. I only realized I'd been holding my breath when we were safely outside.

Clodagh got straight into a taxi, wrinkling her nose at the smell from the chipper, so Maddy and I strolled home to my place, eating spiceburgers and swapping stories. Eventually, of course, it came out. Maddy suspected something and was not easily put off the scent.

'You said what?' She pulled her arm out of mine and spun around. God, I hated that grin.

'I know, I know.' I was mortified. 'Please, I beg you, if you have any regard for our friendship, never bring it up again, or I'll die, I swear.'

'But . . . did you . . . actually . . . say . . . ?' Even Maddy struggled to deal with the magnitude of my gaffe. It was written all over her face. 'I mean, even if you'd asked him back to your place – but "outside", I mean, how old are you?' She was really enjoying this. 'And besides, there is no . . .'

'Shut up.' I hit her over the head with my chip bag, and the saturated bottom collapsed and vinegar dripped into her hair.

'Ow, get off.' She pushed me away. 'Yuck, what's that?' She put her hand up to her head.

'Grease, hopefully. And smelly vinegar.' I dodged the blows and ran on ahead, and we eventually fell on to my deck laughing. She was still singing 'Falling Slowly' through the wall an hour later as we lay in our rooms having drunk two pots of tea and made chip butties with what was left unsquashed of our supper. Not one of your best encounters was my final thought before I fell asleep, deciding that even if I lived to be a hundred I would never make a fool of myself like that again.

9

THE GIRLS WERE BACK IN TOWN. BRONWYN AND SUSIE WERE sitting hand in hand in the waiting room when I arrived at lunchtime on Monday, and Mary was trying hard not to stare. I loved our receptionist to death, but she was as holy as her name suggested and very straight-laced. Mind you, she did look after the entire building effortlessly and made endless cups of coffee and photocopied for Ireland, as far as I could see, so I wasn't about to complain any day soon.

Still, I suspect I was the most exotic thing she'd seen in a long time – my job, that is, rather than me personally – although I'd overheard her telling Miriam, our cleaner, that she thought I was 'wild' because I'd sold my house and now lived in a trailer. I was secretly thrilled.

I'd dressed in red today, as per Clodagh's instructions. Colour is vital – she'd sent me a text earlier that morning. Remember, how you appear is how the world sees you. So I imagined the entire universe now saw me as a tomato – I think maybe I'd overdone it slightly. All this was as a result of several conversations about my disaster with Jason, which Maddy filled Clodagh in on as soon

79

as she opened her eyes the next morning. Clodagh said I needed to build up my confidence, but perhaps a red suit *and* shirt *and* shoes *and* bag were a tad too much. Thanks to my 'black suits for life' code of dressing, I'd no idea about colour.

'Goodness, Lulu, you look cheerful today.' Susie jumped up and hugged me as soon as she saw me. I had to force myself not to flinch, another hangover from my childhood. My family didn't do affection.

'I think I've overdone it a bit on the colour.' I smiled. 'My friend said I was to wear red . . .' I felt like a bit of an eejit. 'I'm, eh, usually quite good at dressing myself actually, but then you can't go wrong with black and black, I suppose.' I grimaced.

'No, red is good,' Susie stressed. 'It really goes with your dark hair.'

'Scrap the suit,' Bronwyn said in a bored tone. 'It sucks. Actually, you need a new wardrobe. In fact, I'll donate a pile of stuff to you, we've just had new presses made and I need to de-clutter. I've got lots of tops you could wear with black or grey or even white linen trousers. More fluid.' She saw my confused look. 'Fluid is good,' she assured me. 'And never, ever wear those Mary Jane-type shoes. Your ankles are too thick.'

'That's brilliant to know.' I was delighted. 'No, it's OK, honestly,' I assured poor Susie, who looked as if she was going to throttle her partner. 'And thank you,' I smiled at Bronwyn.

'Pleasure. And I will drop loads of stuff in to you here in the next day or so.'

'I'll pay you for anything that fits and flatters.' I smiled, although I had my doubts. Bronwyn and I were poles apart.

'Not acceptable.' Bronwyn shook her head. 'Pay me back by sorting us out. The dog thing is really doing my head in now,' she groaned.

'We've found one.' Susie looked delighted.

'No, you've found one. But I am not having a rat roaming around our house.'

'Oh Lulu, he's adorable. He's a Chihuahua type and he's mainly white, with a black ear and what looks like a patch over his eye.'

'She wants to call him David, after her father.' Bronwyn checked her manicure.

'Bronwyn and my father don't really get along.' Susie looked uncomfortable.

'He refuses to accept that we're a couple,' Bronwyn said flatly. 'Anyway, he's an aggressive little fucker – the dog, that is; although her father's not the nicest either. Anyway, he already acts like he owns the place and he's peeing everywhere.'

'Well, puppies do take a lot of training,' I cautioned.

'He's not a pup. He's two,' Bronwyn told me. I could sense trouble as clearly as if a policeman with a grave look on his face had just walked into the room.

After that, the rest of the week seemed easy. I had another new client, which was exciting. Jonathan was an interesting guy, over six feet tall, with a Yorkie called Gilbert who barked day and night. I was in my element – this one was right up my street. Dogs about to have ASBOs slapped on them I could cope with in my sleep.

Next morning, Clodagh rang bright and early – too bright and way too early for me. She was vague – unusual for her – but the gist of it was that she'd be round late morning. The call was closely followed by one from Maddy, who also wanted to swing by. No one 'swung by' Bray – it was miles from anywhere. Still, after my week I needed some human company, so I wasn't about to argue.

'That's great, Maddy. Clodagh just rang, she's coming round as well,' I sat up in bed. 'What's with you all this morning, you especially? It's only ten thirty.'

'Fab. We'll go shopping.' She avoided the question. 'Oh and let's get our hairs done, darling, shall we?' It was all a bit showbizzy for me.

'Are we going somewhere? A TV thing?' I was out of bed now. Maddy's parties were always worth tagging along to. Last time, I'd met Ronan Keating, or was it Keith Duffy? Definitely *one* of the boy-band heads, anyway.

'No no. Just thought it would be fun,' she said airily. 'Anyway, gotta run. See you later.'

They arrived in one car, with Clodagh driving. 'We hooked up after I spoke to you,' Maddy told me, hauling a bag of goodies out of the car.

'Breakfast.' Clodagh smiled.

'What's that green stuff?' I pointed to a tray of grass peeping out of her bag.

'Wheatgrass, it's for juicing.' She moved past me and was fustering round my kitchen in seconds.

'I'm having an onion bagel with cream cheese and so are you.' Maddy had seen my face. 'And a Danish if we can fit them in after.'

We had a lazy breakfast on the deck; the days were still just about warm enough to eat outside so we decided to make hay and all that.

'OK, town anyone? I've made us hair appointments with Paul whats-his-name, by the way.' Maddy jumped up all of a sudden.

'The guy off the telly?' Clodagh sounded impressed.

'Hession, yep, he was on set the other day and I persuaded him to fit us in.'

'The three of us? Isn't that pushing things?'

'Ah well, you go first, new image and all that.' Maddy was being too nice to me.

'Then we'll head down Grafton Street, maybe pop into BT and get our make-up done in Mac. Triona's on, I think.' She tried to look vague.

'Have you two something planned?' This was all a bit too organized.

'No, no,' they said in unison.

'Swear.'

'Scout's honour.' Clodagh held up two fingers and Maddy made the sign of the cross on her neck.

'OK, lead me to it.' I grabbed my bag. 'Oh, by the way, remember I told you that one of my clients was going to give me a bag of her cast-offs?' I said to Maddy. 'Wait till you see the stuff. It's gorgeous.'

They looked at one another, arousing my suspicions again immediately.

'Better and better.' Maddy laughed. 'We'll try it all on later over a bottle of vino.'

'Look.' I threw down my handbag. 'You two must think I'm thick. I can smell a rat a mile away. So, tell me now, or I'm not going anywhere.'

'Tell you on the way.' Clodagh bustled me into her car as only she can.

We had a great afternoon. Paul Hession started on my mop and squeezed in Maddy. Clodagh had washed her hair that morning anyway, so she spent the time drinking free lattes – breaking her no-caffeine rule – and reading *Red* and *Cosmo*. My hair looked amazing by the time he'd finished. It was so shiny you could have skated on it, and the black-cherry colour made it look so thick I could've gotten a part in a L'Oréal ad myself.

Next stop Brown Thomas, the poshest department store in Dublin, its assistants so well groomed and intimidating they managed to penetrate all my training and make me feel like a twelve-year-old again.

Triona in Mac, however, broke that rule. She was a doll. Again, she opted for me first, and when she finished I looked so cool and sassy I was gobsmacked.

'But I don't look like me.' I kept preening in the hand mirror as all the assistants smiled and said things like 'Love that damson-curd gloss,' and 'That mocha really brings out the colour of your eyes.' I hadn't a clue, but I knew I liked it. The other two got their faces done as well, and we headed for a cocktail in the Shelbourne, laden down with free samples from several counters, because Maddy knew everyone.

'So, when are you going to tell me what's going on then?' I asked as I sipped my Bellini ten minutes later. 'And don't bother covering up any longer. I know when you two are up to something.'

10

'NO,' I SHOUTED TWO MINUTES LATER AFTER THEY'D eventually 'fessed up.

'Yes.'

'No. I mean it.'

'You're going whether you like it or not.' Maddy was getting into her stride and, backed by the other one, she was hard to stop.

'You can't make me.'

'Aw, come on, you look amazing, and when we get home we'll try on all those new clothes.'

'Absolutely no way,' I said, but it was weaker and they both knew it.

'Yes!' Maddy did a little dance around the Horseshoe bar until Clodagh – who knew almost everyone here – yanked her back down and ordered her to behave. 'You're embarrassing us,' she hissed. 'I have to deal with these people—'

'Would you go way out of that, sure there's your man from TV3, here since eleven this morning, I betcha,' Maddy interrupted, not to be beaten. 'He's hardly likely to object, seeing he can barely string two words together.' She poked me in the ribs. 'Just because you know a few of the radio and TV heads who frequent this gaff, don't go all snobby on us.' She made a face. 'Remember, I'm the media babe,' she taunted.

Clodagh was an account executive in one of the big ad agencies, so she always knew someone, no matter where we went.

In terms of their backgrounds, they were poles apart. Clodagh's family were very proper, whereas Maddy's mum, Connie, originally came from a part of Dublin where they've been known to eat their young. It always amazed me that they 'got' each other, but they did – apart from the odd little bitching session, like now.

'Listen up, you two. Quit arguing. I cannot – repeat, *cannot* – go to that gig tonight. I can never face that guy again, do you understand?'

'"Course you can. We'll be with you.' Maddy pooh-poohed my objection. 'He won't even remember, for God's sake. We were all pissed.'

'I wasn't, that's the trouble. His face haunts me last thing every night.'

'Well, let's go there glammed up to the nines and show the fucker.' She took a slurp of her Margarita through the straw and clinked her glass to my Bellini. 'Another one?' She had already gestured for replacements.

'Not me, I'm driving.' Clodagh shook her head at the barman, while I nodded yes furiously. I knew when I was beaten. It was going to be a nightmare, nothing surer.

The only thing I can say in my favour is that I looked as good as was humanly possible for a girl like me. I hadn't paid so much attention to myself since I made my communion, and that was only because I knew my mother would probably barely remember the date, so I spent months preparing. Bronwyn's clothes were deemed 'to die for', so much so that we spent an hour fighting over who'd wear the Dolce and Gabbana black dress, until I pulled rank and insisted that I did, in fact, own the clothes.

'But—'

'All of them,' I added for good measure.

'But . . . but, you've abandoned black for ever,' Maddy shouted when she'd run out of buts.

'Maybe.' She had a point there. 'However, this is black like I've never even had the courage to try on before.' I grabbed it triumphantly. 'Besides, it's more slate grey, I think.' I held it up to my face.

'It does really suit her,' Clodagh conceded reluctantly. She hesitated, then grabbed an olive-green top out of Maddy's hands. 'And this really suits me.' She ran into the bathroom and locked the door.

By nine o'clock, I'd forgotten my feelings of dread, thanks mainly to a glass of wine on top of the cocktails earlier. Still, I snuck into the pub behind the girls, just in case. To my horror, we'd come in a side door and instantly came face to face with the band, who were in full swing. They were a cross between Oasis and Def Leppard and they were certainly giving it loads, with the result that the place was heaving. Of course, the first person I made eye contact with was Jason. In fairness, he looked worse than I felt. He sort of hunched up his shoulders and tried to make himself invisible behind the drums – at least that's how I saw it.

'Tell me the make-up is hiding my mortification,' I mumbled to Maddy as Clodagh headed for the bar.

'What?' She glanced over my shoulder. 'Ah fuck him, he's only a drummer on the dole, and I'll bet his disgusting jumper is M&S rather than D&G.' She winked. 'Just keep picturing him in his jocks and be very glad you didn't go there.'

'Is he on the dole?'

'No idea, but he looks like you'd fling him a euro or two if you met him on O'Connell Bridge,' Maddy joked. 'Quit worrying, you're a babe.'

'You're absolutely right.' It was the drink talking, but who cares. Whatever gets you through was my philosophy to-night.

'Anyway, I'm much more interested in the lead guitarist.' Maddy nudged me. 'Oh, and there's Paul. He's coming over. Hi Paul.' She went all coy, just as Clodagh returned with the gargle.

They both blocked my view then, so I forgot to check out the guy in the band. Paul was OK though, she'd been right last week. And judging by his smile, he was giving her the star treatment.

'Ladies,' he said, just a smidgen too smoothly. 'You sneaked off last week without a proper goodbye. Glad you could make it.' He glanced at me as if he'd never seen me before, but he had eyes only for Maddy really.

Clodagh and I left them to it and moved off into the crowd, just as another half-familiar face gestured in our direction.

'Now there's a ride, who is he?' Clodagh wanted to know.

'It's Louis,' I shouted, as if I'd known him all my life.

'Louis who?'

'Luscious Louis, from the class.' I waved frantically as he made his way over.

'Lulu, I wouldn't have put you down as a rock chick.' He kissed me on both cheeks. 'But my, you've changed.' He twirled me around. 'You look amazing.' He took in every inch of me. 'Prada or Armani?' he wanted to know, and Clodagh's face fell.

'He's gay,' she whispered, totally unnecessarily.

'He is,' I said through my teeth. 'Louis, I'd like you to meet my good friend Clodagh.'

He kissed her three times. 'Have you come to see Mike?' he asked.

'Mike who?' we both said in unison.

'Mike, you know, my flatmate. He's in the band. There he is, on guitar.'

'If he's not gay, he's mine,' Clodagh said quietly as I struggled to see that far without my glasses.

'Oh, that Mike,' I said, a bit disappointed. But then Louis dragged us a bit closer, and I had to admit he looked all right. He was taller than I'd remembered, and he'd cleaned up a bit since the day with Pedro, when he looked like he'd just fallen out of the scratcher. He was obviously enjoying himself too, and it showed on his face. He was laughing at something, and his eyes – definitely his best feature – were crinkled and sparkly. They were all having great fun, I noticed, except for Jason, who was still peeping out uncomfortably from behind the snare.

'Fuck the lot of them, just for tonight I don't care,' I told

Maddy, as she and Paul joined us and Louis led us to a table on a raised platform area where we could see everything.

'The VIP booth.' He unhooked a rope, bowed and swept us in, and we all laughed and pretended we weren't in a pub in the suburbs.

An hour later I was really into the craic, helped along by a few more drinks. Louis turned out to be brilliant company, and he and I danced like lunatics for most of the time. The band eventually called time, and Mike wandered over to our table, pint in hand.

'Lulu.' He grinned at me. 'You've changed.'

'Have I? How?' I tried to sound nonchalant.

'I dunno, let's see.' He scratched his nose. 'Your hair's all done, you're wearing make-up, no glasses and . . . the dress is . . .' He whistled. '. . . Out there.' He grinned at me. 'That's it for starters.'

I was happy about the dress bit. My boobs looked big in it, that was the main thing as far as I was concerned. The balcony bra Maddy had made me wear certainly helped, as did the cotton wool I'd stuffed inside when no one was looking.

'Have you chicken fillets in?' Clodagh whispered, right at that moment.

'Nope,' I answered truthfully. 'I'd never buy them, it's not fair on the chickens, according to Jamie.' I headed for the loo, leaving her speechless for once.

I decided I liked Mike. In fact, I decided I fancied him, so I flirted outrageously, especially when Paul dragged a very reluctant Jason over to the table.

'Hi, Jas.' I slapped him on the back and he nearly choked on his pint.

'Remember me?'

He apparently did. 'Yeah, sure,' he mumbled, then disappeared pronto.

'I tried to get off with him last week,' I told a slightly bemused Mike, who hadn't even noticed us chatting, I suspect.

'And did you succeed?' He laughed.

'No, he ran off.' I tossed back my hair. 'Big mistake.' I was suddenly delighted with myself. I wasn't worrying, or being nervous or sensible. In fact, I felt a bit Maddyish actually.

'Yeah, from where I'm standing, it definitely was.' I liked the way he was looking at me, but I needed to sort a few things out in my head first.

'Are you flirting with me?' I said what I was thinking.

'I dunno, am I?' He sipped his drink.

'Are you gay?' I changed tack without thinking, afraid I'd forget to ask.

'What?' He spluttered his drink this time.

'You and Louis, are you a couple?'

'Hell no. What gave you that idea?'

'I'm not sure, I just thought—'

'Well, that's done a lot for my masculinity. I quite fancied myself as a bit of a hard rocker tonight.' He grinned. 'It was a good gig, though.' He wasn't really asking. 'I haven't played with the guys in ages.'

'It was,' I agreed. 'Are you bisexual or anything?'

'What's your problem?' He looked mystified.

I'd no idea. 'Want to dance?' I asked suddenly, without a trace of anxiety.

'Sure, I have to shut you up somehow.' He left down his drink and grabbed my hand. A DJ had set up after the guys had finished, and the lights were low and the music changed tempo just as we got there.

'OK, Lulu, what's going on?' He pulled me into his arms but held me far enough away from him so that he could see my face.

'Nothing, I'm having a great time, actually.' I meant it. I hadn't felt so relaxed in years.

'Good, so am I.'

'I feel sexy,' I admitted.

'You look hot.' He winked at me.

'Really?' He might as well have told me I'd won the lotto.

'Really.' He pulled me close. 'You're a different girl to the one I met last week. Far less uptight.'

I was delighted and sensibly decided to leave it at that. Unfortunately, it was one of the last sensible things I did for the night. All too quickly, the music changed, and the others joined us and Louis grabbed me, and between us we turned a few heads in the next half-hour with our antics.

'I guess it's time to go, girls,' Clodagh said eventually, just as I realized my glass was empty again.

'No way, it's early.'

'It's two o'clock, darling.' Maddy laughed at my bemused face.

'Anyone want a lift?' I'd forgotten Clodagh was driving.

'I could drop you off in my taxi if you like,' Paul offered

Maddy, and she said 'Yes please,' a bit too quickly, I thought.

'Are we going back to my place?' I asked Mike then, making her comment sound like the most subtle come-on ever uttered.

Clodagh looked like she was about to say something, then closed her mouth quickly as Maddy shot her a look.

'I think someone should deposit you safely home.' He tipped my nose with his finger. 'Want to share a cab?'

'Yep,' I said instantly.

'Are you sure? I could drop—' Clodagh interrupted, but I held up my hand. 'I'm a big girl, you know,' I told her. 'I can look after myself.'

We all left together, and Paul and Maddy and Mike and I headed for taxis. Clodagh waved and shuffled off with Louis, having discovered that his house was quite close to hers.

'You take the first one,' Maddy offered. 'Sure you're OK?' she asked me.

'Absolutely.' In fact I had been fine, a bit drunk, as in I'd lost my inhibitions, but now, out in the fresh sea air, I felt much worse for wear. Still, I knew I could hold it together. Hell, I'd had years of practice.

'Text me as soon as you get in, won't you?' Maddy waved us off.

'I only live a mile or two away.' I gave the driver directions and, within minutes, he was at our lane.

'I don't see any houses here.' Mike was looking at me and smiling. 'Have you forgotten where you live, Lulu?'

'No I have not. That's my house there.' I hopped out and

94

he followed. I thought I vaguely heard him tell the driver to wait, which was a massive disappointment.

'That's a mobile home, or whatever you call it.'

'Yes, thank you, I can see that. It's a van actually, to people in the know.' I wagged my finger at him. 'And it's mine.'

'You live in a trailer?' He asked, with a look I couldn't quite decipher on his face.

'Yep.' I fished out my keys. 'And that's my motorbike over there.' I was enjoying myself immensely. I sounded so much more interesting, even to me.

'Cool,' he said. 'How long have you lived here?'

'Ages.' I sort of lunged at the deck in an effort to appear nonchalant and nearly missed the step. 'Come in and have a look round.' I chucked my handbag away for good measure, having fished out the keys first, thankfully.

'I should be getting home, the taxi's waiting.' He grinned, ducking to avoid being strangled with a shoulder strap. I heard a thud as my bag hit the tree.

I'd managed to get the key in the lock, so I pulled Mike in after me, just as he tried to rescue it. 'Get rid of the cab.' I flicked the switch for the wall lights and turned on my iPod. 'I feel like getting laid.' It was at that moment that I decided I just might be more drunk than I realized, so I sort of pushed him down on the sofa in an effort to sit down myself.

'Relax,' I said, and lunged at him, sticking my boobs in his face. 'Let's fuck like tigers.' I grinned, flinging my leg across his lap. It was then I noticed the cotton wool peeping up from where my boobs should have been. I stood up – a bit too sharpish – to fix them before he noticed, but the effort took its toll. I belched, then swayed as everything went funny and the room started to spin. With absolutely no warning for either of us, I leaned over him once more and vomited all over his chest, with a spurt or two in his eye for good measure.

11

MY EYES WOULDN'T OPEN. I RUBBED FURIOUSLY, AND WHEN I finally prised my lids apart I wished I hadn't. Everything hurt. The taste in my mouth reminded me of a stale rice cake I'd once bitten into. It felt like maggots were rummaging in my stomach and someone was drilling my brain and hadn't bothered to anaesthetize me. I lay there, feeling worse than I imagined most living people felt no matter how near death they were, and tried to get my head around what had happened. I hadn't a clue, and the more I tried to piece it together the more panicky I became, until my heart was thumping so hard I knew I had to stand up to try and alleviate the pressure. That was a mistake. Even though I eased myself out of bed so slowly a pensioner would have beaten me to it, as soon as I was upright I knew I was definitely going to throw up, and I bolted for the loo, ruining my bathroom carpet in the process. When I couldn't take the smell of me any longer, I crawled into the shower, turned on the water and eased myself up the wall like an elderly drunk.

Ten minutes later, wrapped in a towel and dressing gown but still shivering, I drank three soluble tablets in a pint of water. Eventually I stumbled on to the banquette seating and stayed there for half an hour until the tablets had at least dulled the hammering in my head.

The phone rang. I'd no idea where the bloody thing was but, after three calls, my fuddled brain realized it was next to my bed. At least once there I could lie down again.

'He— hello.'

'Jesus, you sound rough, are you OK?' Maddy asked.

'What happened?'

'That's just what I was about to ask you. How did you get on with Mike?'

'Mike?'

'Yeah. He left you home, remember . . . ?'

And so it was for the entire day. In between trips to the loo I had a few conversations with the girls, rescued half the contents of my bag from the surrounding woodland and opened all the windows in the van in a futile effort to get rid of the stench.

Thankfully, my memory came back in stages; otherwise I'd have topped myself in sheer disbelief at what I could remember of my performance. Even at that I had no idea how I'd gotten to bed and whether I'd managed to undress myself – a scary thought. I had serious doubts as soon as I saw my clothes folded neatly over the back of a chair.

'Tell me the very last thing you remember.' Clodagh was on her third call of the day, and she was getting irritated.

'I've told you both, I can't really recall anything much after leaving the pub, although I do know I threw my handbag up a tree, for some reason—'

'Right, that tells me a lot,' she said with a loud guffaw.

'So, what time did Mike leave?' There was a hint of a 'did you or didn't you?' in her question but, unlike Maddy, she was being a bit sensitive given my fragile state.

'Listen, I don't even know if he came in, never mind what time he left. All I know is I woke up in bed, naked, with my clothes folded over a chair and my knickers draped over the bedside lamp beside my bra, which was dangling from a glass of water. The only thing saving my sanity is that if anyone had undressed me fully they're unlikely to have been so adventurous with my underwear, don't you think? Oh God—' I wanted to vomit again. 'I think I may have tried to have sex with him.' I suddenly had a flash of me throwing my leg over him. 'I definitely made a lunge at him and stuck my boobs in his face.'

'Crikey, will I come around with a bottle of wine and we can try and figure—' She was obviously desperate for the goss.

'No. No, please.' I knew I sounded insane. 'Even the smell of alcohol could send me over the edge.' I tried not to gag.

'Peppermint tea then? It's good for the—'

'No, I can't even stand the taste of the ordinary stuff at the moment. All I want to do is crawl into a hole and die.'

'Well, you can't. You just have to face the music.' She'd run out of sympathy, obviously.

'Oh my God, I've just remembered something else.' I buried my face in my hands. 'No, God, please no.'

'What is it? Tell me,' she screamed.

'I think I . . . oh fuck, I think I threw up on top of him, it was when I tried to pull the cotton wool out of my bra without him noticing.' I was so mortified by this time, I knew there was nowhere lower I could possibly sink.

She laughed so hard I hung up, disgusted. Maddy rang five minutes later, singing 'Stuck On You,' or something equally grotty. 'I'm sorry, but it's just that it's so unlike you it's fabulous. Please, I beg you; give me a blow by blow.'

'No. Go away. I hate you both.' I hung up. Again.

'Hear me out. It's what you wanted – a complete change of personality. I love the new you.' She was back within seconds.

Eventually I switched off my mobile, crawled under the duvet and watched TV until it got nearly dark and I could legitimately try to sleep. An hour later I was nowhere near oblivion, so I gave in, rang Maddy and begged her for one of her 'relaxer' tablets. She always had an endless supply, claimed it was the only way to get through an interminable day on set. She called around forty minutes later, bottle in one hand and Clodagh in the other. I got some sympathy when they saw how bad I looked.

'Have a cure, it'll help. One glass with a tablet will knock you out,' she suggested, not a recommendation I'd be reading on the packet, I reckoned.

'No, honestly, desperate as I am for sleep I would be violently ill if I even got a whiff of the stuff. Please,' I begged. 'I know you mean well but just give me a tablet and leave me to die in peace.'

'OK, OK.' Maddy gave in. 'My liver is shot anyway, I bet.' She grinned at me. 'Although you were downing them a lot faster than anyone else.'

'Out. Now.' I opened the door and practically threw them

both into the night. 'And if either of you *ever* let me get into that state again, there'll be hell to pay.'

'Actually' – Maddy ducked under my arm and grabbed the corkscrew and two glasses before I knew it – 'we'll have a drink out here on the deck. That way, you can stay inside near the loo and tell us what happened. You won't even have to look at us.' She sounded delighted.

'No,' I begged, but they refused to go anywhere until I'd gone over it once more.

Half an hour later, they linked arms and laughed their way to the car. I swallowed the tablet, which I just about managed to keep down, threw myself into bed and mercifully conked out.

Next day, the full horror of my actions hit me. It was my worst Monday morning in years. I could no longer hide behind a veil of sickness and cold sweats and wanting to die. Instead I had to face up to what I'd done – tried to seduce a client while he laughed at me, pulled the stuffing out of my boobs while wriggling them in his face and then, just to ensure he'd never forget me, I'd thrown up all over him. As Maddy had said, I'd been moaning for years about being dull, but really, I'd never been so out of control in my life. It was scary, and worse, I knew I could never face Mike – or Louis – again and I was determined not to have to. I spent the morning tracking down the only other qualified animal behaviourist I knew of, then asking her if she'd do me a huge favour and see a client because I'd sort of become 'personally involved' and felt it was no longer appropriate to treat their dog. God, I felt a complete eejit.

'Well, actually, the animal is your client, so as long as you're not "personally involved" with Pedro – was that his name? – then I'd say you're OK.' I could hear the laughter in her voice.

'Well, perhaps I'll just give them the option.' I wanted out of this conversation. Fast.

'Of course. I'd be happy to help. Give them my number,' she said kindly, sensing my distress – I imagined – from hearing my very high-pitched voice.

'Thanks so much, I'll do the same for—' I decided not to go there. 'Cheers, thank you.' I hung up, sweating.

By the time I reached my office at two o'clock, I was like a wet rag and still a bit hungover, this time from the tablet, I suspected, although Maddy said that was rubbish. 'I've often taken three – on a bad day, mind you – and felt no ill effects,' she scoffed. 'You're still suffering from liver poisoning, I suspect.' She laughed childishly. 'Any word from Mike?' she asked quietly, tongue glued to her cheek, I imagined.

'No, and don't go there,' I warned as I swept past reception, afraid to talk to anyone, so fragile was I feeling.

'Eh, just a few appoint—' Mary tried to stop me, but I brushed past her. 'Great, I'll pick them up later, thanks,' I muttered.

'It's just that I—' She tried again but I was having none of it.

'Sorry, just on an important call,' I hissed at her. 'Speak to you later.' I spent the next hour closeted away, on the phone, willing the time to pass so that I could go home.

I was chatting to Maddy when Mary put her head around the door.

'Sorry to interrupt, I tried to tell you earlier, but I took an appointment for you, because you'd nothing on.' She looked scared she'd made a mistake.

I was about to ask who it was when Louis walked in. I stood up so quickly I almost tripped over Pedro, and came face to face with Mike. I had such an instant surge of panic that I honestly thought I was having a heart attack.

'Eh, hello.' My eyes were wider than saucers, I knew. 'Hello, Pedro.' I practically threw myself on the animal in an attempt to avoid either of his owners.

'I was trying to tell you earlier,' Mary said cheerfully. 'Mr—'

'Louis, please darling. I keep telling you I ain't no mister.' Louis chuckled. 'Hello there,' he beamed at me. 'I hope you don't mind the short notice, but Mike was free and Mary said you had no clients scheduled, so I sort of muscled in, as it were. Great night on Saturday, wasn't it?' he said as Mary left. 'You sure can dance, can't she, Mike?'

'She has a lot of hidden talents, I'd have to agree,' Mike said quietly.

'Come in, please,' I gestured, wondering how long I could avoid (a) looking at Mike and (b) throwing up all over him. Again.

I've no idea what I said to them for an entire hour, but somehow I managed not to glance above Mike's Adam's apple while I lavished attention on the dog, gushed over Louis and generally behaved like a mentaller. Eventually, I shoved all three of them out the door claiming I needed to discuss their problem with a colleague in the States and that I'd be in touch in a day or two.

'But I thought we knew where we were going with this,' a bemused Louis stuttered.

'We do,' I said confidently. 'But just to be on the safe side . . .' I chirped. 'I'll be in touch. Bye.' I slammed the door after them and would have locked it if I could. Shivering and sweating, I sat down, nerves in shreds, finally understanding why some people kept a bottle in their bottom drawer for emergencies. I put my head in my hands and was just about to howl when I heard the knock.

'Mary, I'm really sorry, I was just about to explain.' I rooted in my drawer, afraid she'd notice how unhinged I was.

'It's me, I just wondered where I should leave my dry-cleaning bill?' said the voice of my tormentor.

I practically dived for cover. 'Em, just leave it at reception,' I mumbled.

'Actually, you're lucky. I managed to mop up most of the stuff with all that cotton wool you were . . .' He coughed '. . . getting rid of.'

'Yes, well, I'm—'

'You can't avoid looking at me forever you know. Louis already thinks you're bonkers.'

'Sorry to interrupt—' Mary cut in. 'Just I have a phone call from New York for you and I wondered if you might want to take it?'

'Call me,' Mike said.

'Fine. Yes. Great. Thanks,' I mumbled, along with every other word I could think of for 'goodbye'. I could definitely hear him laughing as he finally, mercifully backed away.

12

THERE WAS ONLY ONE THING FOR IT, I DECIDED. CONCENTRATE
on my career and forget the rest. This was, of course, easier
said than done, but I was pretty determined. I took every
bit of work I could get, kept my head down and avoided the
demon drink and the demonesses Maddy and Clodagh.

Ronan O'Meara was back, and this time he'd brought
Deputy.

The Labrador ignored him throughout the session, so
no clues there. In fact, we ended up going into our tiny
kitchen halfway through because he was snoring so loudly
we couldn't talk properly.

'There's something I'm missing here,' I had to admit as I
spooned coffee into two mugs. 'The dog is clearly not fatally
attracted to you, so why does he keep appearing at your
door?' I wondered aloud. 'Are you sure you don't live next
door to a meat factory?'

'Nope.' He shook his head as if taking the question
seriously.

'And there aren't any fabulous female dogs in the vicinity,
wearing pink tutus and diamonds?' I thought of Pedro.

'Uh uh.' He shook his head.

'I'm stumped.' I didn't mind admitting it.

'Me too.' He tucked into a plate of chocolate-chip cookies and didn't look worried.

'It's fine you being stumped, but you're paying me to solve the problem,' I told him. 'Those cookies are costing you dearly.'

'I had hoped for a fresh perspective and all that,' he said with his mouth full. 'But to be honest, I'd gone down every reasonable avenue myself before I came here.'

'OK, I need to see your house. And your gran's. And meet her,' I decided. 'So, what are you going to tell her about me?'

'The truth, I suppose, it's all I can do.'

'And are you happy to do that?'

'Yes, I'll do anything to sort this out, to be honest. As I told you before, I love animals and I enjoy minding him while she's away but really this is wrecking my head. I spend my entire life with my gran, and every time I go around she has visitors so clearly doesn't need me. Then I have to stay and make polite conversation, and if I'm forced to eat one more slice of her tea brack I'll throw up.'

'You're clearly too polite,' I told him, my mind made up. 'So, when can I call?'

We arranged a time the following evening and I spent an hour writing up everything I could think of in my notes, feeling even more inadequate when I'd finished.

Next evening I headed for Dalkey, a seaside village as far removed from Bray as Barcelona is from Benidorm. One of the jewels in south-county Dublin's well-encrusted crown, it was full to overflowing with people for whom life seemed effortless. Many of the homes I whizzed by were magazine-cover material and I saw more clipped box hedging and manicured lawns than I'd ever encountered before. The main street, however, was more quaint than ostentatious, although the understated clothes shops alongside cafés selling antiques and housing art galleries at the rear gave some clue as to the clientele. It was a charming place to get lost in, I decided, so I left the bike in the car park of the Queen's, a well-known local pub, and went walkabout, as I had time to spare. Most of the shops were closed or just about to, so I indulged in a bit of window-gazing and resolved to come back in daylight and explore some more.

I had arranged to meet Ronan outside his office and walk to meet his gran, so I texted him as soon as I arrived at the converted stone cottage and then sat on the wall to wait. It looked like a charming place to work, if the outside was any-thing to go by. The glass in the wood-framed windows was gleaming, and the sills were overflowing still with cascading autumn flowers in every imaginable colour, while the fire-engine-red front door was flanked by tumbling hanging baskets. In fact, apart from the giveaway brass plaque, you'd have sworn the house was occupied by a passionate retired gardener, which is what I told Ronan as he came rushing out, looking preoccupied.

'What? Oh, yes that's Maura, our cleaner, tea lady, collector of newspapers and laundry and general minder,' he said breathlessly. 'She loves the place and is regularly to be seen here on Saturdays. You should see what she's done with the back garden, it's full of strawberries and tomatoes in summer. And she never asks me for money – she swaps seeds, apparently.' He looked bemused then a bit guilty. 'In fact, you've just reminded me that I really need to buy her something nice as a present, it's her birthday this week and I totally forgot.'

'She must like working for you,' I remarked as we crossed the road and headed towards the sea.

'Yes, she does.' He sighed. 'It's what made me come back here in the first place. All Dad's employees are still here, and they're really decent people, they've sort of adopted me.' He shrugged. 'It's just that sometimes . . .' He tailed off, 'I dunno, I just wish it had all been different, I suppose. Between work and my gran, it's a very dull routine.' He shook his head as if to clear his thoughts. 'Anyway, Myrtle lives just over the road here,' he said, changing the subject. 'I told her you were helping me to try and figure out why Deputy seems so attached to me, although she said – and I'm using her words – that it was my fatal charm that had him fatally attracted.'

'Sounds like she's a fan of yours.' I smiled, and wondered for the tenth time what the story was with him, but I didn't ask. So many times recently it felt like I had a tiny role in lots of tangled lives, and today was yet another one of them. Funny that I thought I'd left all that behind in the last job. But somehow this was different, maybe because the human woes were actually not my concern at all, really. For once I wasn't trying to solve anything. This made everything appear simpler, or perhaps it was just that I had simplified my own life and de-cluttered my own head quite a bit in the process.

'Myrtle's great, by the way,' Ronan said with real warmth. 'I hope I haven't given you the wrong impression.' He looked worried. 'In fact, I'm lucky in so many ways.' He had a faraway look in his eyes that belied what he was saying. 'I'm surrounded by people who genuinely care for me. My mum is a friend more than anything else and all of Dad's employees would go to the ends of the earth for me.'

'So why do I suspect you don't feel lucky?' It was out before I knew it.

'Because I'm a selfish little shit who needs a kick up the arse,' he said without looking at me. When I glanced at him, his stony face put an end to any further conversation.

I mentally gave myself a kick as a reminder not to stick my nose in uninvited again.

'Here we are,' he said, pointing to a stone cottage not unlike his office, except that this one had pretty net curtains instead of blinds, and the door was that particular shade of blue that many older people seem attached to.

Myrtle, however, looked anything but set in her ways. For a start, she was wearing a multicoloured flowing skirt, T-shirt and jangly earrings. Her hair was streaked with grey but was cut in a very attractive long bob, and it swung about just above her shoulders. She was the trendiest granny I'd seen in a while.

'Come in.' She hugged her grandson and shook my hand firmly. 'I have a friend round for a chat.' She smiled warmly at me.

'She has more friends than I have socks,' Ronan whispered, as we followed her down the long, narrow hall to the sitting room. 'And they're all my age. I don't understand why they'd want to visit an old lady, unless they're after her money – and she has plenty.' He grinned.

'How many are there?'

'Lots. I've lost count of the number of seemingly busy career women who appear to enjoy spending time with her.'

Before I had a chance to reply, we'd reached our destination and Myrtle was introducing me as 'the dog shrink' in a giggly, girly tone. I shook hands with Rachel, a very attractive thirtysomething blonde.

'We met on the internet,' Myrtle explained.

I must have looked confused, because she added, 'At a bridge class. I play bridge regularly, but I like to invite my opponents for tea, so that I can see the whites of their eyes.'

And to think I'd imagined that all bridge players were in their dotage.

'You should get Skype.' I smiled, and then realized she'd probably never heard of it.

'Oh, I have it,' she replied easily. 'In fact, if my grandson had it I could keep an eye on him much more easily and check he's eating properly.' She winked at me. 'But somehow with bridge it's not the same as sitting opposite a person face to face. Now, Ronan, would you mind making Rachel a cup of coffee while I chat to Louisa about our shared scourge?' She giggled.

By the 'see what I mean?' look on his face, he'd entertained more than one of Myrtle's bridge buddies, although not many men I knew would shy away from getting to know Rachel.

'Sure,' he answered easily, as Rachel got up and let him lead her into the kitchen.

'You don't mind, do you?' Myrtle asked Rachel. 'This shouldn't take too long.'

'Not at all.' The young woman seemed perfectly happy. 'I'm dying for a coffee actually. No lunch.' She smiled at me. 'Again.'

'I've been there, too many times,' I told her, as Myrtle called 'Give her a slice of my rhubarb crumble too,' to Ronan's sagging shoulders.

'Sit down, please.' She indicated a button-backed chair. 'And tell me how you think I can help, Louisa?'

'Call me Lulu, everyone does.' I decided I liked this woman. 'It seems that your dog has become rather fond of Ronan, and keeps turning up at his door at all hours, and he's asked me if I can find out why.' I wasn't sure if she'd take to the idea of an animal behaviourist, so I was treading carefully. 'I hope you don't mind me calling to see you?' I asked. 'I'm just keen to find out as much as I can about the dog and his environment.'

'Not at all.' She looked perfectly at ease. 'So, have you any ideas?'

'Not yet, no,' I told her truthfully. 'Have you noticed any changes in his behaviour lately?'

'Can't say I have. He's always been very fond of Ronan, and no wonder. He's a lovely man, even if I say so myself.'

I nodded agreement. 'Can you tell me when it first started – what I mean is, when Deputy first wanted to be with him all the time, started going to his house on his own, that sort of thing?'

'Oh, it's not all the time, he just likes to visit him some-times, in the evenings, mostly,' Myrtle told me.

'I see. And have you any idea why?'

'I think he just likes to wander off on his own, or perhaps he gets a treat,' she suggested.

'No. That was the first thing I asked. Ronan simply brings him back here.' I was puzzled.

'Well, it does get him out of the house and gives him some exercise.'

'Ronan or Deputy?' I grinned.

'Ronan, but both, now that you mention it.' She had a tinkly laugh. 'Although Deputy gets plenty. I bring him for a good walk twice a day.'

'There must be some reason,' I said, more to myself than to her.

'It's a mystery,' she announced, and yet again I sensed that one of my clients knew more than they were letting on, although in this case Myrtle wasn't my client and was simply being co-operative. I wondered if she was lonely, a thought I'd had previously.

'Does it bother you at all?' I asked. 'Not knowing where he is half the time?' Most old people adored their pets and worried about them as they would babies.

'No.' She ditched that solution for me. 'I'm always so busy, you see. I swim, I play bridge, I'm in the ladies club and the local St Vincent de Paul. Half the time I feel guilty for not paying enough attention to Deputy. But he's great company late at night. Sits at my feet while I'm on the internet, which is a lot of the time. Chatting to people, making new friends.'

'In your bridge club?'

'No, no. Bridge players are mostly quite old and serious.' She giggled again.

'Not Rachel, though?'

'Definitely not Rachel,' she agreed. 'Actually, I spend time in chatrooms mostly.'

'Chatrooms?'

'Yes, and I meet lots of gorgeous young women there, all looking for love.'

My seriously muddled brain suddenly found me imagining I had a gay granny to add to my troubles.

13

'EXCUSE ME?' I SAID EVENTUALLY, SURE I MUST HAVE MIS-heard.

'I'll tell you what, why don't we take Deputy for a stroll and have a nice little chat?' Myrtle jumped up and picked up her scarf and a lead.

'But what about Ronan?'

'Oh, he'll be fine, don't worry.'

'Well, perhaps I'd better tell him, just in case—' I heard a noise and realized he was coming to investigate anyway.

'How's it going?' He looked at me appealingly.

'Fine, darling. We're just off for a little stroll with Deputy.' Myrtle brushed past him.

'But what about Rachel?' he whispered, and he glanced over his shoulder, as if afraid she'd suddenly appear.

'Take her for a drink or something; she'd love to see a bit of Dalkey. And the Queen's have a lovely evening menu, by the way,' Myrtle told him.

'Gran, I do know the Queen's very well, I eat there a lot, but I don't know this woman.' He sounded exasperated. 'And I've already plied her with more sugar than she's had this year, I imagine, and we've dissected the economy, agonized about the weather and predicted the budget.' He seemed about to say more but bit his lip.

'Perhaps she could come with us?' I suggested, wanting to help, as usual.

'Oh no dear, she's not the outdoor type,' Myrtle told me.

'But you just suggested I take her for a walk.' Ronan scratched his head.

'Just an idea.' Myrtle shrugged.

'Gran, I actually have to get back to work, I've got a job to finish tonight . . .' He stopped, not wanting to upset her, I figured.

'Well, don't worry about me,' I said, wanting to get him off the hook. 'My bike's parked up the road and, anyway, it was really your gran and Deputy I came to see. I'll call you.' I mentally shooed him away, sensing his awkwardness.

'Are you sure?' He was practically at his office as he spoke.

'Certain.' I grinned at his back.

'Well, in that case, I'll see if Rachel would like to stay and check in online.' Myrtle seemed resigned as she headed for the kitchen.

I put on my coat, and Deputy came bounding in, having heard the lead jangling, I suspected.

'Rachel's decided to head on back into town.' Myrtle seemed disappointed when she put her head around the door, and I wondered again if she wanted company. 'I'll just see her out and then we'll be off.' She disappeared.

Five minutes later, we were heading towards the harbour. Thankfully, I'd worn flat shoes and a warm jacket. No black suits and definitely no high heels on a bike, so I was well set up for a walk.

'Did you say you'd come all this way on a pushbike?' Myrtle asked.

'Motorbike,' I told her and she looked so thrilled at the idea I ended up promising to take her for a spin some time.

'Well, Myrtle, I don't mind admitting I've no leads on this case,' I said eventually. We'd laughed and talked and I'd told her about my life change by this stage, and I felt like we were old friends. 'Not great for my new career, eh?' I joked. 'I won't be getting many recommendations at this rate.'

She looked worried. 'I'll mention you to all my friends,' she said earnestly.

'Thanks.' I was touched.

'Lulu, can you keep a secret?' Myrtle blurted out. 'I really need to know I can trust you.'

'Of course,' I told her. She looked older and a little bit frail, and for a split second I was worried for her.

'It's just that . . .' She stopped. 'I haven't been entirely honest with you.'

'About what?' I was confused.

'I'm the one sending Deputy around to Ronan.'

'But why?'

'To get him to call around to my house,' she said, as if it was the most natural thing in the world.

So she was lonely after all. 'Myrtle, have you time for a coffee?' I'd spotted a cosy little café up a sidestreet we'd just passed and I sensed she might need a moment.

'I'd like that,' she said quietly. 'And Mrs Nolan back there

116

stays open late and she makes fresh jam doughnuts every day.'

'Perfect.' I smiled and we headed back the way we'd come. I wondered how I'd handle this one.

'How much do you know about my grandson?' she asked, when we were installed in a corner of the tea rooms beside a wood-burning stove with a huge pot of tea and a basket of warm, sugary doughnuts that might as well have had 'comfort' tattooed in jam on the top of them. They smelled divine.

'Not a lot.' I smiled as I bit into a little piece of heaven, and wiped the sugar from my nose. 'Just what he said about his dad and wanting to be a vet but ending up looking after the family business.'

'Yes, that was unfortunate. He takes on so much responsibility; he's always been an old head on young shoulders really. And these past few years he's gone into himself more and more. Sometimes it worries me.'

I waited, as I usually did when I sensed someone struggling with uncomfortable thoughts. 'Did he mention his wife?'

'No.'

'He doesn't, generally. I'm just hoping that someday he'll talk about it to someone, and I thought with you being a stranger . . .' She sighed. 'He's had such a lot to deal with. I just wanted to help him.' She looked at me sadly. 'Audrey was killed in a car accident. And when I tell you that she was his whole life, his universe, it doesn't even come close to letting you know what they had together. It was the happiest day of my life when they got married. I just knew it was a match made in heaven.' I could tell Myrtle was still deeply troubled by it. 'Unfortunately, that's where she is now.'

'When did she die?'

'Nearly two years ago. He's never gotten over it, and he never will, I fear.' There were tears in her eyes now. 'Please, you have to promise me you won't let on. He'd never forgive me.'

'I promise.' I tried to reassure her. 'My whole working life's been spent keeping other people's secrets.'

'Thank you,' she said simply and sipped her tea. 'It's been a terrible time for us as a family. He's been only half alive ever since, and I see the constant pain in his eyes. But in the past three months, I've seen a slight change, a tiny reason to hope he might get through it.' She looked sad. 'He puts up a front, you see. He's good, too. And he works like a black, which helps him forget.' It was so un-PC that I'd have laughed any other time.

'Sorry, I'm not allowed to say that, am I? Although I heard on the net the other night that the new expression is "works like a Barack".' She looked like a bold child. 'Anyway, I've been sending the dog to his house so that he'd have to bring him back. And I've been searching for a new girlfriend for him on the internet, which is why there's always someone there when he calls. It's how I've been setting up the meetings.'

'So Rachel just now . . . she was a potential partner?'

'Yes, but so far he hasn't shown any interest in any of them. And there've been quite a few. And now he's brought you in to solve the problem so I suppose I'll have to stop.'

'How on earth did you get Deputy to keep going to his

house?' I asked her, my practical side kicking in straight-away, but also because I felt she needed a bit of light relief.

'It took persistence.' She grimaced. 'I walked him there several times a day for weeks. But first I went myself and left a trail of his favourite treats from my door to Ronan's. I even taught him to cross the road.' She seemed amazed. 'I'm good, aren't I?'

'You certainly are. But how did you get him to scratch at the door until he got Ronan's attention?' I wanted to know.

'Ah, that involved the ultimate treat. I have a key, because I let in the cleaner once a week and put out his bins when he forgets. So I left a very tasty piece of chicken or lamb in a corner of the hall. Just a tiny morsel, tucked under the rug, so it couldn't be detected.' She looked pleased. 'Now, I only have to leave a trail once a week, and mostly I don't bother with the meat in the hall – just in case it goes off and Ronan cops on.' She sounded like your woman from *Murder She Wrote*. 'As soon as I let the dog out – having given him a sniff of Ronan's gym shorts first – he heads straight there and sits patiently until he gets in, even if Ronan's not there. I do have binoculars though, just to make sure he's in, because I usually have someone nice for him to meet and I don't want to waste their time,' she explained.

'Of course.' I smiled, hoping I looked as if I'd heard it all before.

'You'd be amazed at the response I've had to my post-ing.' She seemed intrigued. 'There are a lot of single young women out there looking for men.'

Tell me about it, I wanted to say. 'Your posting?' I en-quired instead.

'Yes, I have a little page on Facebook and on a few other sites as well. All heavily disguised, of course, in case he ever goes online,' she told me. 'Not that I have to worry on that score, he's computer-illiterate, really. Strange for anyone in business these days, don't you think?'

'Yes, now you mention it.'

'He's no interest, you see, and he has a couple of young boys and girls working with him who do use it, but a lot of the accountants I know are stuck in the past, still using ledgers and pencils and rubbers. Although everyone now files returns online, I hear. Even Mrs Nolan, who owns this place, does her VAT on the computer. Now if Ronan were a vet – doing a job he loved – he'd have a website, with photos – the lot. You mark my words. As it is, he barely knows how to email,' she said in disgust. It was definitely one of the oddest conversations I'd had with a pensioner, that's for sure.

'Anyway, I'm going to have to try a new approach, I guess.' She tutted. 'Even my daughter – his mother – doesn't know, by the way, so please be very careful.'

'I will, I promise.' I liked her immensely. 'But meanwhile, how are we going to solve this problem because, as you say, this way of meeting women isn't working at present, and the Deputy thing is driving him bonkers?' I decided to give it to her straight.

'Yes, I gathered that as soon as he brought you on board.' She looked at me, and it was as if a lightbulb had gone 'ping' in her head. 'Are you married?' she asked innocently.

'No.' I almost choked. 'And not looking, either.' I grinned

at her cheek but thought I'd better not encourage her. 'He's not my type, I'm afraid.' I made a face.

'Why not?'

'He's em—'

'You can be honest, I've a thick skin.'

Like a rhino, I didn't say. 'He's a bit too . . . nerdy, I guess.'

'Nerdy?'

'Anoraky?' I tried.

'Ah yes, he's always been like that. So, have you any suggestions?'

'Not right away,' I told her honestly. 'But I do have a number of friends who might be interested.' She cheered up at that. 'And if you call off the mutt I'll come up with an explanation and give you half the credit?' I tried.

'I suppose so.' She sighed for the tenth time. 'Seriously, though, have you any ideas for getting him interested in women again? Because no matter what either of us come up with, unless he meets them halfway, then I'm beginning to realize there's no point.'

'I think he just needs time,' I said gently. 'I don't believe you can hurry along grief. It's a natural process. He'll come through it when he's ready. That's been my experience in dealing with it anyway.'

'You're probably right. I just worry about him so much. He's wasted so much of his youth already. His father's death was a huge loss for him, and taking over the business meant putting his own life on hold. Then this happened and he's become a bit odd, I fear. I've been trying to persuade him to rescue a dog even, in an effort to get him socializing.

That's why I was so happy when he mentioned you. It's been so long since he's taken an interest in anything outside of work. I hoped it was a first step back.' She looked worn out.

'He'll be fine, honestly. Just give him time and space and be there for him, as you clearly are.' I patted her arm. I admired her enormously and envied Ronan a bit. She'd make a great friend and mentor for anyone, or maybe it was just that I'd been a bit short on role models all my life, so I was a bit needy that way.

'There's more,' she said.

'More?'

'To Ronan's story.'

'Yes?'

'Yes.' She looked as if she was really struggling now. 'When Audrey died she was nine months pregnant.'

'Oh my God, how awful.' I felt truly sorry for him. 'So he lost a wife and his unborn child?'

'No, no, the child survived. A boy. Lucas.' She rooted in her bag and took out a photo of a curly red-haired scoundrel with freckles.

'He looks nothing like Ronan.' I tried to make sense of it. This story was getting so far-fetched I was beginning to think maybe she was playing a trick on me.

'No, that's the problem.' Her eyes told me that this was no joke. 'He's the image of Audrey.'

'How old is he?' Had she said this all happened two years ago?

'He'll be two shortly,' she confirmed.

'And where is he now?'

'He lives with Ronan's sister Ellen, in Donegal.' Myrtle bit her lip.

'And how does Ronan keep in touch?'

'He doesn't. Ronan hasn't seen him in over a year and a half. Oh, he tried, initially, but more for my sake, I think. And his mother's. He simply can't cope with the child. It reminds him too much of what he lost that day.'

14

I GOT VERY LITTLE SLEEP THAT NIGHT, THINKING ABOUT Ronan. To most people, the idea of giving your child to someone else to care for might seem abhorrent, but I knew how complicated these things were and how sometimes it's easier to run away from emotions rather than face them, or – horror of horrors as far as most men were concerned – talk about them.

Next morning, my mobile rang at 8 a.m., just as I was having a leisurely bowl of muesli. It was Emily, and she was in a state.

'What's wrong, is it Rover?' I wondered where all this was headed for.

'No, no, it's something else. I'm so sorry to bother you; I just didn't know who to turn to . . .'

'What is it?' I was concerned, but she was so distraught she couldn't speak properly, and I ended up arranging to see her in the office at nine thirty, which meant the remains of my cereal went in the bin and my hair didn't get washed, which always made me feel grotty.

Even on the bike I spent ages in traffic and just being caught up in honking horns and BMW users who seemed intent on lane-hopping and cutting up other drivers, especially motorbikes, left me totally stressed, a feeling I'd forgotten. Arriving at the office at twenty past nine, more than a bit frazzled, made me feel very grateful I was out of the rat race.

'Rover's disappeared,' Emily told me as soon as she came through the door. Her eyes were wild, and she looked like she'd had a worse night than me. 'And my mother was so angry that she told me she never thought she'd regret the day she adopted me but she did now.' With that she collapsed in a heap, and I called for a cup of strong tea as I handed her the tissues.

'Please, Emily, don't upset yourself.' She always seemed a bit like an anxious child, which in turn made me revert to being an overprotective carer, as I had been so many times growing up. 'I'm sure your mother didn't mean what she said,' I tried to comfort her. 'I didn't know you were adopted, by the way,' I said without thinking, more to distract her than anything else. Boy, was that a mistake.

'Neither did I.' She choked and dissolved into a heap again. We got through a box of tissues in the next ten minutes.

'Is that what this is about?' I asked her gently.

'Yes.' She gulped back a sob. 'I always knew there was something. I always felt different. And I don't look like any of my cousins.'

'But you adore your mother, you've told me several times. Does it really matter that much?' But I knew enough about her to guess that it did.

'Yes,' she whispered. 'I've spent my whole life trying to be the apple of her eye but never quite managing it. I've never

125

been able to put my finger on it before. I always felt I just needed to try harder, which is why I was working so hard on the cat thing.' She shook her head. 'Now it all makes sense.' She blew her nose. 'I'm not really her child. That's why I don't feel the connection the way I should.'

This was becoming a bit too close for comfort, I decided, knowing exactly how she'd felt as a child. It was odd that hearing someone else talk about feeling left out made me see that I'd felt exactly the same way most of my life. I knew that I too was facing challenges that could really only be sorted out by talking to my own mum.

But the adoption thing had taken this to a whole new level for Emily. I let her cry, hoping the outpouring would help her deal with the situation.

'I need to find out . . . all the details.' This was another problem I'd dealt with before.

'Well, once you've had a chance to come to grips with things, why don't you sit down with your mum and talk it through? I'm sure she'll have lots to tell you.'

'Do you think so?' She looked unsure. 'She's not great at talking about problems. In our house, a lot gets swept under the carpet.'

'Well, I don't think there's any chance of that now that it's out in the open, do you?'

'I suppose not.' She seemed encouraged just hearing me say it. 'What should I do next?'

'Give yourself some time to come to terms with it in your own head, then maybe ask her if you could go for lunch, or a coffee and just tell her how you feel, perhaps? That's always a good place to start.'

'You're right. Thank you.' She dried her eyes. 'I'd better get back and help her look for Rover. If anything happens to him my life won't be worth living.'

'Don't worry, cats have nine lives,' I teased.

'But what if he really was a dog originally?' She looked upset again.

'Not sure, to be honest.' I had forgotten our other dilemma for a second. 'Still, I'll bet he's at home right now, curled up in front of the fire.'

I made her promise to text me and let me know how she was getting on, then sent her home, hopefully to get this thing sorted. Another human problem avoided for the time being, but my own childhood trauma had come to the surface and was not going to go away easily, I knew.

I headed out for a coffee and went to sit in the park and chill while I thought about Ronan O'Meara and the baby he refused to acknowledge. It had absolutely nothing to do with me, thankfully, but I couldn't avoid the growing realization that Myrtle was somehow relying on me after I'd promised to chat to her further.

Thankfully, I had a couple of nice, ordinary doggie dilemmas for the rest of the day. A serial barker who was a Dandie Dinmont; new to me, I'd never heard of the breed. This one had quite a rare addiction – to TV – and became aggressive every time her owner tried to change channel. Next up was a mongrel called Scamp. He'd only go for a walk in the baby's stroller. I hadn't been able to find out yet how he'd been allowed in the pram in the first place, but I was in my element.

*   *   *

Next morning I was still deep in thought as I prepared to head for Ashford to meet Denis Cassidy. My phone rang, and it was Mary, wondering if I could see Louis and Pedro that afternoon.

'No, sorry,' I said quickly – a bit too quickly, seeing how I had nothing to back up my refusal.

'It's just that . . . he wants to see you without Mike and today is the only—'

'Oh, OK then, that's fine.'

'It is?' I wasn't surprised that she sounded confused.

'Yes, sorry, I just remembered that my new client never confirmed. Tell Louis I'll see him at five o'clock.' It was the first lie I could think of.

She rang off, and I resolved to bring her back a muffin for her tea break, convinced I was driving her nuts.

Denis and Bartholomew were waiting as soon as I veered off the main road to their farmhouse. I don't know who was more excited, but I suspect it was Dinny.

'Well, aren't you a sight for sore eyes on this grey morning,' he greeted me.

'Well thank you.' I gave the little dog one of the treats I always kept in my pocket. We'd become best friends once I'd recovered from the melted-bed incident.

'You should wear that colour more often.' He winked as I took off my warm coat. 'And what have you done to your hair?'

'Washed it.' I laughed. I was pleased about the dress, though. It was another one of Bronwyn's, and I'd never have bought it myself. It was a wrapover in shades of purple and pink and it hugged my figure and yet was stretchy and comfortable, though not ideal for a motorbike.

'Come in, come in, the kettle's on. I've news.' He pushed aside a pile of newspapers and sat me down at the kitchen table, which had been wiped and set with brown bread and butter and jam. 'Alice Dolan down the road baked that fresh for me this morning,' Denis told me as he scalded the teapot. 'I swapped her six eggs for it.' He laughed. 'I think I got the better deal, I've so many eggs I could set up a stall. Remind me to give you some to take away with you.'

'I will, definitely.' I cut the warm, crusty bread as he had instructed and within minutes we were enjoying a mid-morning treat.

'Ah, real tea, you can't beat it,' I told him.

'And much cheaper than those bags, sure you're paying for the paper.'

'So, what news have you?' I urged, sensing his enthusiasm.

'I've enrolled in a computer course.' He was bursting with pride.

'Have you now? That's amazing.' I was delighted. 'I read somewhere recently that retired people are now proportionately the biggest users of the internet in the States.'

'Is that a fact? Well, maybe I'll start the same trend here in Ireland.' We chatted on until eventually I enquired about Bartholomew's mood swings.

'Oh, gettin' worse by the day. Last night he growled at me when I tried to shift him out of the armchair. And he frightened poor Alice half to death this morning. He wouldn't let her into the house practically, I had to shoo him away with me stick.'

It was an easy enough problem to deal with – Denis was just a pushover and the little fecker knew it. I started by asking him to ring his neighbour to see if she would call around for a few minutes while I was there. The poor woman was reluctant, but she came anyway. As soon as he heard the knock Bart was up and growling at the door. I immediately claimed the space, pushed him back by standing in front of him and moving towards him, then made him 'drop' and 'stay' in the corner. It took a while, and the poor woman was frozen by the time she was eventually let in. Then we all had to ignore the dog until she was leaving, when I forced him to 'heel' as we walked her down the lane.

'Now, Denis, you're going to have to practise and be firm with him,' I warned. 'This is going to take a while. And ignore him each time you come into the room at first, make him wait for your attention. That way he'll realize that you're the boss.'

'That's powerful stuff altogether,' he marvelled. 'I wouldn't have believed it if I hadn't seen it with my own eyes.' But I'd no idea whether he was capable of putting it into practice. He was a big softie, which was the main difficulty here.

'I wonder, Lulu' – he chuckled every time he said my name – 'could I ask you for a bit of advice about another problem I have?'

'Sure.' I wondered what was coming. He wasn't a man who'd ask for help easily, I suspected. He was proud and independent.

'Would ye take another cup of tea with me before you go and I'll tell you what I'm after?' he said and I agreed. I was beginning to realize I'd have to build in an extra half-hour for home visits generally; there was always something cropping up. Maybe it was that people were more relaxed in familiar surroundings, but I don't think I'd gotten out of one yet in the time allotted.

'You see, I'm trying to locate someone in England, but I don't know where to start,' he said, when he'd poured me another cup of the strong brew.

'Do you have an address, even an old one?' I asked.

'All I have is the name of a priest who used to know them, but any time I tried to make a call the number just rings out.'

'Would you like me to try?'

'I would to be sure, if it's not too much trouble?'

'Not at all. Give it to me now, if you have it.'

'Ah no, I'd need to think about it a bit first.' He looked flustered.

'Well, let me have a look, and I'll see if I recognize the code or anything. I spent a good bit of time in England after I left school. Do you know the area even?'

'I haven't a clue, to tell you the truth.' He got up and produced a worn piece of paper. 'It was a . . . sort of a friend who went away and I've never forgotten them, and I thought it was about time I did something to try and see if they were OK, that's all. Does that sound stupid?'

'Of course not. I'll tell you what, why don't I take it with me and try it from the office – that way I can at least establish if the number still exists even?'

'Right so, here it is.' He handed it over. 'You'll mind it though, won't you? It's the only thing I have . . .' He sounded agitated, which was not like him at all.

'Why don't I just make a note of it, that way you can keep it safely here?' I sensed it was important.

'Great stuff, thank you, Lulu, that's very nice of you, very nice indeed.'

'So, tell me what you know?' I asked him as I jotted down the name of a Father Vincent and a number that looked as if it hadn't enough digits.

'Well, he's a priest and he knew my . . . friend, that's all I know really.'

'Do you know what order he belonged to?'

'An Italian order, as far as I remember. The Sons of Divine Providence, I think they were called.'

'Great, that should help. And tell me the name of your friends?' I asked as I copied the details into my Filofax.

'Eh, Joan Lehane and . . . er . . . her daughter Catherine.'

'OK, well I'll make a few enquiries.' I saw his face. 'But don't worry, I won't mention your name until you decide what you want to do,' I assured him.

'Grand so.' He was easily satisfied. 'That's mighty. It's been a long time, you see, and it's, eh, a bit complicated, I suppose.'

'OK, why don't I ring you if I have any news?'

'Sure won't you be back next week to see Bartholomew?' he asked, surprised.

'Oh, yes, if you want me?'

'Of course I do. Won't I be practising night and day on him? And I wouldn't know where to go next if you don't come back.'

'You could come to me?' I was always conscious of money

132

with older people, and my charges were higher if I had to travel. 'It would be less expensive,' I said gently, not wanting to embarrass him.

'Haven't I plenty of money and no one to spend it on,' he cackled. 'Money's not my problem, Lulu. It's time that's my concern.'

15

I WAS LOOKING FORWARD TO SEEING LOUIS AGAIN THAT AFTER-
noon, even though I couldn't get Denis Cassidy out of my
mind as I drove back to Dublin. He was a dying breed in
modern Ireland, and I was determined to encourage him.
Besides, I reckoned he needed friends, so I'd have to get on the
case of the missing priest as well as send him his first email.
Today I'd sensed a vulnerability about him, and I wondered
if it really was just loneliness. Christ, half the world seemed
to be looking for someone to love them. As soon as I had that
thought, I realized that, for the first time in my own life, I
wasn't looking for anything, really. I was content and enjoying
where I was at. It gave me a surge of wellbeing.

That surge went 'puff' in an instant when Mary showed
in my first client that afternoon.

'Louis.' I saved the document I was working on and
looked up as I heard the door open. 'How are you do—'

'It's me,' Mike said, totally unnecessarily.

'Oh, right, it's just, eh, Mary mentioned that Louis
wanted to come on his own, so I wasn't expecting you.
Hello, Pedro.' I turned my attention to the dog in an effort
to buy some time.

'Actually, I lied.' He grinned. 'I pretended to be Louis. For two reasons. One, I was afraid you wouldn't see me and, two, Louis is doing my head in so I needed your advice when he wasn't around.'

'Of course I'd see you – whatever gave you that idea? There's absolutely no—'

'Oh, I dunno, the fact that you haven't looked me in the eye since that night maybe.' He raised his eyebrows at me. 'We sort of got off to a rather eh . . . unusual start, didn't we?'

'I suppose so.' There was nothing for it but to face up to it, I knew. 'Actually' – I took a deep breath – 'I really want to apologize. I've sort of, changed my life, you see, and I'm always so cautious and in control – normally, that is – that I went a bit mad.' My face was prickly hot, as if I'd just come in from a winter walk.

'You were a hoot – did you manage to find the contents of your bag? I'd have looked for them for you, only it was pitch black and I'd no idea what I was searching for.'

'Yes.' I squirmed. 'And I am so sorry for what I . . . how I behaved. You didn't leave your em . . . bill, by the way.' I decided to get it all over with at once.

'I was just teasing you, it was fine. The taxi driver did open all the windows on the way home, but other than that . . .'

'Oh God, I'm mortified.' I couldn't look at him all over again. 'I have never done anything like that before, I swear.'

'Well, I won't be inviting you out for a drink any time soon, that's for sure.' He winked. 'So now, pay me back by helping me sort out this mutt before he – and Louis – drive *me* to drink.'

'Of course. Sure. Anything.' I was so relieved I could have kissed him – on second thoughts, maybe not a good idea after the last time. 'What's going on exactly? Tell me everything.' I opened my notebook and resolved to start again with him.

'Well, I'm really not sure who's at the root of the problem, the dog or Louis. But I suspect it's the latter. He treats Pedro like a human, and the mutt is becoming more and more demanding by the hour. All he's short of is making me sleep on the dog bed while he snores and farts on the goose-feather duvet that Louis bought me last week.' He laughed. 'I only got it 'cause Louis claimed my €30 polyester one was lowering the tone of the place. Anyway, the upshot is that he sulks, growls, scratches the doors, destroys the couch – you name it – to get what he wants. Pedro that is, not Louis.' He tried not to grin. 'Although Louis has his moments. And frankly, I've had it with both of them; I'm actually beginning to dread going home.'

'OK, let's start at the beginning. How has it changed recently – from what you told me when you first came?'

'It's a thousand times worse; do you honestly think I'm the kind of guy who'd be consulting a pet shrink otherwise?'

'Right.' My hand was sore from scribbling. 'This could be difficult. The thing is—'

'The only reason I haven't legged it myself is because it's a great place to live – huge – in a brilliant location, and Louis is the ideal flatmate most of the time. Sorry, I know I'm ranting.' He scratched his head. 'Anyway, I wouldn't give the bastard the satisfaction of going, because if I wasn't around I swear he'd be sharing Louis's Gucci cologne and eating venison sausages.'

We looked at each other for a second and then we both burst out laughing.

'Jesus, what am I like? You see how bad it's become? I'm even beginning to think of him as human, a rival in every sense of the word. In fact, if he could pay half the rent I'd say I wouldn't be there.'

'You need a coffee.' I picked up the phone.

'Make it an Irish. With a double shot of whiskey.'

'Sorry, only the animals get treats in here.' I smiled back at him. 'Nescafé Gold Blend is as good as it gets for the humans.'

We chatted about the problem until Mary arrived with a tray.

'So, if you had to sum it up in one, what's at the root of all this?' I asked as I nibbled on a chocolate digestive.

Mike thought for a moment. 'I guess, since Emerson – Louis's partner – died, he's been finding it really tough. They were together a long time. He went wild for a bit – headed for a different gay bar every night, came home pissed.' He lowered his eyes. 'So you see I've had plenty of practice with drunks before I met you.'

'Please, don't remind me. In fact, the only condition I'm attaching to all this is that you never bring up that night again. OK?'

'Deal.' He grinned. 'It's just you're such an easy target. I've never seen anyone blush so easily. Chill, would you? It happens to all of us, it's not a big deal.'

'Not to me it doesn't.' I was tempted to tell him just how uptight I usually was, but I'd been wasting my patients' time waffling on a bit recently so I cut it right there. 'So, never again?'

'Pity, you're an easy target,' he coughed as he saw my frown. 'OK, then, back to business. Louis's had a rotten time of it, I know that. I think Pedro is all that's keeping him going at the moment. It's as if the dog's attention convinces him that he's worthwhile.'

'Well, you know what they say: Don't accept your dog's adoration as conclusive proof that you're wonderful.' I tried to think this through logically. 'The thing is, we can sort it out, and I can help. But I don't see any way of doing it without getting Louis on board.'

Mike sighed. 'It's not going to happen. And I'm not going to be able to stand it much longer.'

'It might. Why don't I ring Louis and try and see him alone, just to tease it out a bit more. Can I tell him you were in?'

'No, he already thinks I'm a dog-hater, he doesn't need any more ammunition. I probably should just get the hell outta there, but he's been very good to me and I really like sharing with him. For all his madness he's funny and decent and we sort of work as mates. And he's a great cook, which helps. You've no idea how many silver trays I've consigned to landfill in my time.'

'Trust me, I do. It's one of the reasons I changed my life.' I started to tell him, then stopped. There was something about him, it made me want to confide everything. He had such an easy way with him. I shook my brain clear. 'Anyway,

I'm glad you're sticking around. I suspect he needs you right now.'

Mike nodded. 'Yeah, probably, although all he does is bitch at me.'

'Well, I'll speak with him. How about if I just say I rang you as well? Then I'll ask him to come in on his own – as the principal carer – or should I say the pack leader?' I grinned.

'Well, I know where I come in the hierarchy, that's for sure.' Mike shrugged. 'Bottom of the food chain, that's me.'

'Cheer up, we'll sort it.' I gave him a few websites to look at, which he took reluctantly. 'I'm not really into all this dog-psychology shite,' he told me as he got ready to leave. 'A walk, a feed and a kick up the arse if you got too big for your boots. That's how our dogs were raised – and the kids too, come to think of it.'

'Yes, well times have changed, mister. You'd be pros-ecuted today.' I promised to call him by the end of the week, and he seemed happier as he and Pedro ambled off, unlikely allies, but then dogs don't judge, thankfully.

I had a new client that afternoon. Well, a new old client. A year or two back, I'd treated Doug Stewart for a sexual-addiction problem. He was a quiet, shy man, early forties, no friends, English but had lived in Ireland for the guts of ten years.

'Hello, come in.' I shook hands and led him inside. He was a gentle giant of a man and I'd always liked him. Life had dealt him a rough hand. His mother died when he was three and his father went off for a long weekend with his girlfriend and left him home alone. A neighbour rang the gardai after she'd heard him crying all night and he was taken into care. That was the end of his father and the end of life as little Dougie knew it. He was in and out of care homes for most of his life and had always found people difficult to communicate with. Once again, I knew I'd felt drawn to him because of his difficult childhood, which brought my own into sharp focus.

As part of my final year training as a psychologist, I'd been asked to spend a few hours each week seeing patients as part of a public-health scheme. They were people who were receiving welfare payments and had medical cards and were therefore in the system, but some of them needed emotional support, and the waiting lists at the time were up to a year. So I'd met Doug and given him as much help as I could and he still sent me the odd card at Christmas or Easter, although not since I'd moved.

'Are you keeping well?' I greeted him warmly now, wondering what he was doing with himself. 'How did you find me?'

'That nice Mrs O'Hara at the Family Support Centre gave me your number.' He looked older; his black hair had streaks of grey through it, but his eyes were still warm and chocolatey and he looked well cared for. 'I hope you don't mind?'

'No, of course not.' He had a little dog with him, a mongrel type that was probably a Spaniel cross, I guessed, another one with a tail that would take your eye out. 'Who's this then?'

140

'He doesn't really have a name, just Growler I call him the odd time.'

'Sit down, please,' I offered. 'And tell me how you've been?'

He'd been doing well, it transpired. He had a part-time job working in a large motor dealership. He ran errands and helped out generally and, although it was only three mornings a week, it gave him something to look forward to. He was entitled to rent allowance and had a small bed-sit in the centre of Dublin so he seemed content.

'So have you a problem with your dog?' I asked him after a while.

'I just want to know how to get rid of him really.' Doug shrugged. 'I've been leaving him in the park, but he keeps on coming back. In fact, he's home before I am mostly.'

'But why do you want to get rid of him?' I tried not to sound as if I was judging him, something I was always careful of. 'He seems devoted to you.' I smiled, looking down at the dog stretched across his shoes and gazing up at him.

'He's costing me a bomb, and he's a lot of trouble, really. Always wants to come with me and follows me everywhere I go, even though my flat's only one room with a kitchenette and toilet.'

'So what have you done? Have you put an ad up in the local shops or anything?' I was trying to think of ways that wouldn't cost money.

'No, I just keep leaving him in the park, hoping he'll go off with someone.'

'But Doug, you can't just—' I'd been about to say 'abandon an animal' but then I realized that someone had done

141

far worse to him as a child and could have kicked myself. 'What I mean is, there are other ways to find a home for him.' I paused.

'Well, that's how I came across him. He was wandering around the streets, upending any bins he could, scavenging for food.'

'How long ago was that?' My heart went out to him.

'Three years ago, not long after I last saw you.' He smiled. 'You must have turned me into a softie.'

'I suspect you were always that,' I told him, wondering how I could help. 'Tell you what. Why don't I ask around, see if anyone wants a dog? And, meanwhile, if I type up a notice for you now, would you ask your local shop to put it in on their noticeboard?'

'Would they charge?'

'No, I don't think they would. It's usually a service they provide. Can't hurt to ask.' I tried to encourage him. 'Will I do up the notice anyway? We can word it together.'

'Yes please.' He seemed happier and, within a few minutes, I'd printed off a couple of copies.

'Just in case you find more than one shop willing to put it up.' I stuck the stuff in an envelope. 'Is it OK if I keep one here, as well? And I have your number now, so if I ask around and anyone sounds interested, I'll call you.'

'Great, thanks.' He stood up. 'How much do I owe you?'

'Nothing.' I smiled. 'You didn't really need my services at all.'

'But I took up your time.' He pulled a worn old wallet out of his pocket. 'I do have the money, I've been putting a bit away each week for emergencies . . .'

'Doug, you'll offend me, put it away.' I gave him one of my 'I'm the boss' looks, and he nodded.

'Thank you, you were always very kind to me when I was . . . in trouble.' He avoided my eyes. 'I'm OK now though, getting on fine.' I sensed he was still a bit ashamed.

'That's really good news.' I deliberately hadn't gone into his past, in an effort to avoid yet another human dumping on me. 'I promise I'll call you if there's any interest this end.'

I gave the dog one of my special bones but even then he still looked to his master before he took it.

'Go on then,' Doug told him, and he made a lunge for the smelly treat and went off with it firmly between his teeth, tail wagging furiously. I found myself wishing the dog could stay with Doug. I sensed they were good for each other.

16

PAPERWORK HAD NEVER BEEN MY STRONG POINT, BUT I KNEW I had a build-up of admin jobs, so I got stuck in next morning. Then I needed to make contact with Ronan. And Louis, as I'd promised Mike. And Emily, who hadn't kept in touch, despite her promise. Normally, I would wait for the client to contact me, but she'd been so vulnerable that I was a bit concerned. And finally, there was the priest for Denis, so I sighed, made coffee, surfed the net and sent texts until I couldn't avoid work any longer.

The priest sounded like the least hassle, so I started there. The number Dinny had given me didn't exist, so I rang the first number I could see for his order in the phone directory. They didn't know the man I was looking for, but after being passed around and explaining my problem several times, they gave me a number for a priest in London who'd been there for twenty-five years. He knew immediately who I wanted and gave me a contact. I rang just to check that he was, in fact, working there, and ended up speaking to the man himself. I had to be careful, because I'd promised Dinny I wouldn't say too much without his permission.

'Sorry to trouble you, Father.' Damn, I thought, I hadn't

anticipated having to explain. 'I'm really just making an enquiry on behalf of . . . a client of mine who's trying to get in touch with some old friends.' I knew I sounded vague, but he must have heard it all before, because he was sanguine enough about it.

'No bother at all, always a pleasure to hear from someone in Ireland. How's the old place anyway?' he asked, in an accent that was more Washington than Wicklow.

'Oh fine, I didn't know you had connections here.' I wondered what the story was.

'Ah, just friends. I'm American, but I meet a lot of you folks and I feel I'm half Irish as a result.'

'We do tend to get around a bit,' I told him.

'Hell, that's an understatement – you're everywhere,' he declared. 'Well, tell your client that I'm alive and well and, if I can help him in any way, he just has to ask.' He wasn't pushing for information at all.

'Thank you, that's very kind of you.' I hung up and rang Dinny.

To my surprise, he wasn't delighted.

'Right so, that's grand, great altogether.' He sounded almost fearful. 'I'll, eh, think about it so I will.'

'Denis, is everything OK?'

'Sure why wouldn't it be? Thank you very much, Lulu, I really appreciate all you've done.' He sounded like he couldn't wait to get off the phone. 'I'll see you on Friday, so?'

'You will. Do you want to take down the new number?'

'Ah no, I'll get it again.' He was gone.

Well, I'd done what was asked of me, but I hadn't heard the end of this one either, of that I was certain.

Next, I decided to text Emily, just in case she couldn't talk, and also to avoid putting any pressure on her. I sent off an innocuous message and left it at that.

Louis was next, and he greeted me warmly. 'Lulu, darling, so nice to hear from you. Are you well?'

'Great, thanks, just touching base as I promised. How are things?'

'Well . . .' I could almost see him checking to see if anyone was listening.

'Sorry, I should have asked. Can you talk?'

'Yes, just making sure. Actually, I was just about to call you. I need to see you. Things are getting on top of me a bit. It's not Pedro though. It's Mike.'

'OK, shall I come to see you, or do you want to come here? It's just that I might be able to do more if I saw you all in your normal surroundings.'

'Great, I'm off tomorrow, and I presume Mike is working, as usual. Let me call you back once I've confirmed that.'

'Sure.'

I texted Mike to report progress and moved on to my real problem – Ronan O'Meara. Actually, the truth was I hadn't a clue what to tell him. I'd given it a lot of thought but couldn't come up with a plausible explanation, so I rang him and simply said that I was seeing Myrtle that afternoon and suggested I meet him later to discuss the situation. He sounded happy with that, so I called Myrtle then headed out to see her.

'I've come up with a plan,' I told her over tea and apple strudel. 'Is there another dog nearby, preferably female?'

'Several. But there's one boxer – Charlie, very cute – and

146

Deputy likes her. She's just moved in with her family, quite close to Ronan, actually.'

'Great, so what we need to do now is follow the same principle with Deputy – lots of nibbles along the route – then the added bonus of a treat at the house *plus* another dog to play with.' I was quite pleased with myself. 'Shall we start now, because it may take a while? I'll do it initially, if you like, just to break the association between you and Ronan's house?'

'OK, that's fine,' she said, but she sounded disappointed. 'Actually, when you said you had a plan, I thought it was a plan for Ronan.'

'Oh. No, I'm afraid not.' I was sorry I hadn't made that clear. 'To be honest, I don't know what anyone can do except encourage him and then stand back and wait. Besides, as I'm not supposed to know anything, it's difficult . . .' I didn't know what else to say, and she was so nice I really wanted to help. 'On second thoughts, why don't we do our first new walk together and we can chat en route?'

'Thank you.' We both drained our cups and, while I washed up, Myrtle got the lead and the treats. Deputy was ecstatic, as usual. I asked Myrtle to go ahead of us, laying the treats while I played ball in the garden with the dog. The idea was that she'd meet us at the new house; the owners were out but Myrtle had a key, as she seemed to have for every other house in the neighbourhood. Then, while Deputy got to know his new girlfriend, Myrtle and I could chat some more.

I'd anticipated some problems to start, but in fact it worked beautifully. Deputy was in great form, excited

147

anyway from our game, and when he found the treats his tail never stopped whipping the air. Then, at our new destination, his beloved mistress was waiting, with a big, juicy bone and a bitch. Heaven, I suspected and, if Deputy's prancing and preening were anything to go by, he agreed. We gave Charlie a treat as well, and within seconds the two were cavorting around the garden. We encountered a slight hiccup a minute or two later, when Deputy tried to mount her, but once we'd established that she'd been neutered, we relaxed and left them to it.

'I've been thinking, my dear,' Myrtle said as we sat in the garden, well wrapped up and drinking the hot chocolate we'd bought along the way. 'I think you should let Ronan know that I told you his situation.' She must have seen my face, because she went on quickly, 'It's the only way. We've all been encouraging him, his sister, Ellen, has even been emailing him photos and sends him constant updates – in fact, I think that's one of the reasons he pretends he doesn't understand the computer – he's avoiding dealing with this.'

'That's what people do sometimes,' I said gently. 'It's a coping mechanism.'

'But it's been two years. It's not healthy any more. There's a little boy growing up who lost his mother *and* his father at birth and, really, he need never have lost one of them. I know that someday Ronan's going to regret this and I can't bear that.' She looked at me sadly. 'He's a good man, and he deserves to be helped, and my daughter and I are just too close to it. Besides, he's beginning to avoid us because we push him a bit and so I really need your input. And I'm happy to pay for your time – money's not a problem.'

'It's not that at all,' I told her quickly. 'It's just that I no longer do that sort of work. But I can recommend someone who's—'

'No.' She shook her head. 'Trust me, he'd never agree, not in a million years. My only hope is someone he trusts. He hasn't responded so easily to new people since all this happened, as you know, from the number of women I've tried to introduce him to.'

Oh God, this was harder than I thought. 'I really don't think I can help, to be honest, it's a very delicate—'

'Please, I'm begging you, just give it a try,' she pleaded. 'I'm desperate.'

I knew when I was beaten, and she saw my hesitation and pounced. 'It's affecting my health – and I'm not getting any younger.' She must have seen by my face that I knew she was laying it on a bit thick, because she burst out laughing. 'I've gone too far playing the little old lady card, haven't I?'

'You're a witch; I'd say you're healthier than I am,' I told her, before caving in. 'Let me think about it, OK? I'll see what I can do.'

'Thank you so much. Joking aside, I am concerned; he's become very introverted lately.'

'I'm meeting him after this, hopefully – but are you certain about me letting him know that you've told me about his past?' I was still unsure.

'Yes, I'll risk it, that's how worried I am about him.'

'Well, at least I'll have some good news about Deputy, and obviously I won't be telling him about your, eh, matchmaking.' We both grinned like bold children. We chatted further, and I promised to stay in touch and let her know how I got on, although I pointed out that I couldn't break any confidences.

An hour later, I phoned Ronan. 'I've made some progress – are you free for a quick chat? I'm walking towards your office.'

'What time is it?'

'Nearly half past five,' I told him.

'Could you give me ten minutes? In fact, why don't you go to the Queen's and order us both a drink? It's been one of those days.'

'Sure, but just the one for me, I'm driving, and that bike is a brute. What can I get you?'

'I'd murder a pint of Guinness,' he said. 'Be with you in a couple of minutes.'

He was there by the time the pint had settled and I'd paid and found us a quiet corner.

'Sorry, I meant to say I'd pay.' He was out of breath. 'You should have told them you were with me. My credit is good.' He smiled.

'No worries, you can get me again,' I assured him. 'Anyway, I know where you live, remember? So, why was your day so bad?'

'Ah, the usual. This credit crunch is putting my clients under a lot of pressure. Today everything just seemed to go against me, you know the feeling?'

'I sure do, although – what do they say? Life is 10 per cent what you're dealt and 90 per cent how you handle it.'

'God, I hate people like you.' He took a gulp thirstily.

'Actually, it's my new life, I'm much more laidback these days,' I told him.

'So, what news have you got to cheer me up?'

'Well, hopefully Deputy's on the way to being sorted.' I decided to go in gently. 'We've found him a new route that doesn't involve you. And one that has the added bonus of a cute bitch at the end of it.' I explained how we'd done it and cautioned that it might take a bit of time, but Myrtle and I had tried it again before we parted and Deputy seemed to have forgotten his attachment to Ronan's pad.

'I could do with a cute bitch waiting for me at my front door.' He was intrigued by how we'd managed it. It was the perfect cue, one I couldn't ignore.

'Actually, I think part of the problem was that Myrtle was hoping to convince you to get a dog yourself, so she wasn't worried about Deputy's visits. In fact, she's more worried about *your* social life, to be honest.'

He laughed. 'Listen, between my mother and herself, there's no fear of me becoming a hermit, that's for sure. They're always dragging me off somewhere.'

I took a deep breath. It was now or never. 'She told me about your wife. I'm so sorry, it must have been an awful time.'

His whole demeanour changed. He said nothing for ages, then slowly took a long sip of his drink. 'What else did she say?'

'That you had a child.' I saw him stiffen. 'Look, Ronan, you don't have to say a word about it if you don't want to, and I won't bring it up again. It's just that everyone is concerned that you won't be able to move on with your life if

151

you don't at least try to sort this out in your head. Myrtle begged me to try and talk to you and see if I could help.'

He looked so angry as he scraped back his chair that I thought for a second he might upend the table. 'What do you know about moving on with life? You know nothing about what I had, or what I lost. And as for sorting it out in my head, I've done that. I *am* getting on with my life, and just because I'm not dealing with things the way everyone else wants, that makes me wrong, does it? Well, tough.' He stood up. 'And for the record, I don't want to ever discuss this with you again, is that clear?'

I nodded.

'I lost everything that night. Every single thing, do you understand?'

'You didn't lose your baby,' I said quietly.

'I never had a baby in the first place. So don't you dare sit there and judge me.' He leaned in and spoke very softly. 'And I could never look at someone day in and day out who reminded me of what that loss meant.' He made to leave then turned back and spoke harshly, 'And that's never going to change, so don't waste your time trying.'

17

I SAT THERE FOR AGES AFTER RONAN LEFT, WONDERING ABOUT life. You'd think I'd have been used to it by now, with all the problems I'd encountered, but seeing his raw, ripped-apart life for that instant made me realize how fragile it all was. And in that realization came the knowledge that I had never really dealt with my own fragility. Seeing him so vulnerable about his child made me understand that my own mother had somehow disconnected a bit from me and that made me a mirror image of that little boy. I was the child who'd partly been abandoned. Oh, I knew my situation had been nothing near as bad as his was right now, for either me or my mother, but I was learning more and more how even the slightest emotional withdrawal can damage a person and leave behind scars that never really heal.

I finished my drink and was glad of the air and the breeze as I whizzed along the coast road, a fluorescent moon guiding my route. Later, muffled up and sitting under the starriest sky I'd ever seen, I wished it wasn't all so complicated.

And, as the week went on, it got even more complicated. Everyone seemed to want to involve me in their lives and, consequently, I couldn't shake off my old one. And all the problems my clients faced seemed to prod me towards the realization that I needed to sort out my own childhood insecurities in order to fully move on as a healthy adult.

On Friday I went back down to see Denis and Bartholomew. Initially it was a breeze; he made afternoon tea and salad sandwiches with hard-boiled egg, beetroot and Heinz salad cream, and the taste reminded me of summer days on the beach in Dollymount in north Dublin. He was making splendid progress with Bart too, and he insisted on showing me everything they'd achieved. I was in and out the front door until I was so cold I had to call a halt. All I could hear was 'Sit' and 'Stay' over and over again, until I had to remind him only to issue the command once and not to use the dog's name if he was misbehaving. When I finally got in, I suspected Denis might have been using food as a reward, the way the dog was looking at him, but I ignored it and Bart did everything he was told while I was watching.

'That's fantastic, well done.' I praised him over and over again. 'That is real progress, you must be pleased?'

'Sure 'tis not me at all, isn't he the smartest dog you've ever encountered?'

'He's certainly up there,' I assured him, and we practised a few new things, such as moving the dog out from prime position by the fire and moving Dinny's chair into the space. There was a slight growl to start with but, after I'd made it happen, he seemed quite content and, once he'd stayed there for a couple of minutes without moving, I gave him a command which meant he was free to wander about. To our surprise, he didn't try to muscle back into his space but found a corner where he could see us and stayed there happily.

'D'ya know, I think all he wants is a woman about the place.' Denis was delighted.

'Too much testosterone with just the two of you perhaps?' I joked, but I predicted that he wouldn't need me at all before long. 'Oh, by the way, I'd better give you that number for your friend, the priest.' I pulled out my Filofax.

'Ah, he's not really a friend of mine at all at all.' He immediately looked uncomfortable.

'Well, he seemed lovely and said to tell you if there's anything he can help you with, be sure to telephone.' I scribbled the number down and tore it out.

'Actually, I wonder would you be good enough to make the enquiry on my behalf?' Dinny asked. 'If I gave you the names like?'

'Sure.' I wondered if he was nervous talking to people in authority. Some older folks were, I knew. 'You gave me the names already, I think.' I opened the original page. 'Joan Lehane and her daughter Catherine, is that right?'

'Aye.' He sounded ashamed, and his head went down as I said their names.

'So what do you want to know?' I asked him.

'Anything, really. How they are, first and foremost. And an address if they have one, sure they must live somewhere.' He guffawed, but it was an attempt to lighten his own mood, I felt.

'Would Father Vincent have stayed in touch with them, do you think?' I asked him.

'Oh aye, for sure. I'd say at the very least he has a phone number.'

'OK. Will I say who it is looking to make contact?' I

wondered if it was a family member he'd fallen out with.

He stared into the turf for a long while, but silences had never bothered me.

'Aye,' he said quietly. 'Tell him it's Denis Cassidy from County Wicklow.'

'OK, and I won't offer any information, only if I have to, is that OK?' I knew without knowing that this was a big deal for him.

'Grand.' He got up and poked the fire. 'You're a powerful girl, d'ya know that? You've helped me something fierce.'

'It's a pleasure, sure aren't you paying me?' I teased him. 'I'm not doing it for nothing.'

'Aye, but this is bigger than that. And you don't fuss me, I like that. You've helped me a lot more than you realize, Lulu. I'm in your debt.'

'Well, why don't I see what I can find out on Monday and call you in the evening? Would that be OK?'

'Powerful altogether.' He seemed a bit more relaxed. Maybe it was knowing that he had the weekend to change his mind if he wished.

On our way up the lane a funny thing happened. A dog appeared out of nowhere and bounded up to us, tail wagging furiously.

'Hello, who are you?' I crouched down to get a good look at him. As I did so, a strange thing happened: my tummy did a little flip. He was the image of the dog I had as a child – Gnasher – the one who'd stolen my heart. Only his eyes, though. This one was skinnier, and he looked like a Collie mix rather than a purebred, and he'd been tied up, I reckoned, because he had a rope around his neck.

'That's Pete,' Dinny said. 'Bartholomew and himself ignore each other for some reason. He lives next door, but they don't really look after him. Oh, they feed him an' all, and he goes out to the cows with the farmhands. But they don't give him much attention.'

'Hello, Pete.' I rubbed the back of his ears the way I used to do with another red-haired dog long ago and, to my amazement, he tried to jump up on my lap. 'You're a lovely fella,' I told him, and he licked my nose as if to say, 'I know.'

'I'll ring them and let them know he's escaped,' Dinny told me. 'Although they never worry about him – he goes missing for days on end sometimes.'

'That's a shame, he's gorgeous.' I felt the oddest pull towards this mutt; maybe it was time to get another pet, after all.

I left them at the roadway where I always parked the bike, preferring to walk down the lane and savour the incredible colours that seemed to change every time I visited. As I waited for a tractor to pass, I could hear Dinny and Bart practising 'Heel' as they headed back down the lane. His life was yet another story that I was on the fringes of. I just hoped I could stay that way. When I looked back as I pulled off, Pete was dancing along beside me, and it was only when I came to the main road that he left me. My last image of him was tail down, clearly asking me why I wasn't taking him with me. I was going soft in the head, I decided, refusing to look back again. That dog's eyes were almost human.

Maddy rang just as I pulled in to the van and took off my helmet. It was the only thing I missed about the car, not being able to chat on my hands-free phone.

'What plans have you to take me out on the town and out of my misery this weekend?' she wanted to know immediately.

'Actually, I was looking forward to getting home, ordering Chinese, having a glass of wine and watching telly. Can you believe that?'

'Worrying,' she said. 'But just what I need. Can I come stay in your trailer?'

'Yes, please.' I was delighted. 'I have a nice bottle of red and even a few cold beers.'

'Done. I'll collect the food. Usual?'

'Absolutely.'

'Fantastic,' she sighed an hour and a half later as we tucked in to a selection of dishes, warm and cosy, candle lighting and a choice of decent TV at our fingertips. 'Shame we're not a couple – I could be snuggling up to you, at least.'

'Not with those smelly feet,' I teased her. Maddy's feet were legendary in our circle. We were always buying her odour-eaters and stuff as a joke at Christmas. 'God, what are we like all the same? We should be out having fun.'

'I know. I'm just too knackered all the time.' Maddy yawned.

'But you're not even working at the moment,' I reminded her.

'Well, I am really. I did a voiceover yesterday.' She sounded wounded.

'So what did you have to say then? Go on, tell me the huge effort you made?'

'I said . . .' She put on a high-pitched Cork accent: 'Betsy's

158

Boutique, where classy Corkonians catch the latest clobber.'

'Yep, I can see why you're exhausted. Here, let me pour your wine, I'm worried about your energy levels,' I told her. 'By the way, I met a dog today. He had eyes like Gnasher. I suspect the people who own him don't really want him.'

'Rescue him immediately,' Maddy said, flicking channels. She discovered *Jonathan Ross* just starting, so that was the end of that.

We fell into bed around midnight, and she told me jokes through the wall till I threatened to smother her with her own pillow. It was one of the great things about a mobile home: the walls were paper-thin, so conversation was easy. Maddy claimed she could even hear me fart. It was like being in the Girl Guides again.

Next morning, she had a plan. 'Enough is enough,' she declared. 'One of the guys in the show is opening in a new play in the Olympia tonight. There's a party afterwards. Should be a laugh. Will we head into town and have a look in?'

'You mean go to the play?' I hadn't been to the theatre in ages; it sounded fun.

'Don't be ridiculous, I've seen the script. It's a new production. Worst thing I've read in yonks. It'll close within a week, trust me. No, I was thinking about heading for the Old Stand, or Hogan's or even that gay bar, what d'ya call it?' She grinned. 'Or all three, maybe? Then nip across the road around eleven, air-kiss all the luvvies and grab a few free drinks.'

'I'm still off booze,' I told her, grimacing.

'Sure didn't you have wine last night?'

'Only one glass. My first since *that* night.'

'Well then, you're back in business. Right, I'll head home, do a few jobs and meet you at the Dart station at nine?'

'You're on, I haven't been in town on a Saturday night in weeks.' Suddenly, I feel young. And giddy. 'Let's go party.' I jumped up and started tidying.

'Steady on, it's only backstage at the Olympia, hardly a major attraction. Still, you're right, you never know what might happen.' She was gone.

We ended up doing a bit of a pub crawl, but I watched my intake, never wanting a repeat performance of what had become known as 'the Mickey night', because of Mike's name and me trying to have sex with him. It still ranked – even at this distance – as one of the worst nights of my life.

In the George – the gay bar that Maddy was determined to check out – we bumped into Bronwyn and Susie. Both looked remarkably happy, dancing like they were glued together and laughing aloud.

'Want to meet the luscious lezzers?' I asked Maddy.

'Oh my God, yes. Lead me to them.' She grabbed my hand and we headed across the floor.

'Lulu, darling, what a lovely surprise,' Bronwyn gave me a huge hug.

I made the introductions, and I could tell Maddy was impressed. The girls looked stunning, Bronwyn in a turquoise silk wrapover dress, and Susie, all blonde and bubbly in a baby-pink smock dress that made her boobs look huge.

'Are you two a couple?' Bronwyn asked immediately.

'I tried, but she wasn't having any,' Maddy told them.

'Well, darling, Susie wasn't sure either when I met her.' Bronwyn pulled her partner close. 'And look at us now.' She swung Susie in a twirl and laughed.

'How's the dog?' I felt obliged to ask.

'Long story, we'll be in to see you next week.' Bronwyn raised her eyes upwards as the music started again and the floor filled, mostly with gyrating guys in tight trousers. 'Are you here for the night?'

'No, we're on our way to a luvvie party,' I told her. 'Talk to you soon.' I grabbed Maddy before she started gyrating herself.

'Ouch, I was just getting into that.' She pulled her hand away as I dragged her outside.

'That's what I was afraid of. Come on, there's people to meet, drinks to be taken.'

We ran across the road, and Maddy blagged her way backstage, as usual, kissing the security guy and calling everyone 'darling' as she went. I loved being out with her.

In the green room there were quite a few celebrities from the telly.

'Must be a slow night in town,' Maddy whispered. 'Now, what are you having? And none of that sparkling-water shite . . .'

'Go on, I'll have a glass of white wine,' I told her and stood beside her while she managed to grab the barman's attention immediately, even though the queue was four deep.

'Madeleine, is that you?' a soft voice asked, and we both turned together to come face to face with Ronan O'Meara and a red-haired woman of about thirty.

'Ellen,' Maddy screamed. 'My God, girl, it's been yonks.

How are you?' She handed me my drink, hugged the young woman and smiled at Ronan. 'This is my friend Lou . . . lu.' She never remembered.

'Hello.' Ronan's look was cool.

'Hi, Ronan, nice to see you again.'

'You two know each other?' Maddy had decided she liked him, I knew that look.

'Yes, Lulu's been helping me with my dog. Well, he's not mine but he thinks he is.' He seemed to like the look of Maddy too.

'Sounds like a problem to me, but no better woman to sort it out. I'm Maddy – haven't been Madeleine since I became a luvvie.' She grinned.

'Hi.' I noticed he held her gaze. 'Sorry, Lulu, this is my sister Ellen.' I smiled and shook her hand. 'How do you two know each other?' I asked Maddy.

'Ellen and I were in an amateur theatre production years back. We were great pals but then we lost touch.' Maddy made a face. 'She found a man and moved to Donegal.'

Something clicked in my brain. Ellen. Donegal. Wasn't that who Myrtle said had taken over looking after Ronan's son? I was pretty sure I was right.

'So, how've you been?' Maddy wanted to know all. 'Still married? Any kids?'

'One little boy,' Ellen smiled. 'Lucas, he's two,' she said without hesitating. She didn't look uneasy as she said it.

'Any photos?'

'No, not on me.' Ellen smiled. 'How come you're here?' She was making an effort to include myself and Ronan.

'I work with Gary, who's playing the male lead,' Maddy

162

said, waving at a couple but bringing her eyes quickly back to Ronan. 'How about you?'

'My friend Patsy from college is also involved,' Ellen said. 'So I dragged my brother out to keep me company in the Big Smoke for the weekend. Have to make the most of it, what's seldom is wonderful.' She laughed. She was very pretty in a classic Irish-beauty kind of way – pale skin, copper hair and freckles.

'Can I get you another drink?' Ronan asked, and Maddy swallowed at least half of her almost full beer.

'I'd love a bottle of Miller,' she said immediately.

'Lulu?'

'No thanks, I'm fine.' I felt like we should move away and leave them to it. He looked uncomfortable, which is why he offered to get a drink, I suspected. Ellen also shook her head.

He was back almost immediately, the initial after-show surge having cleared to a trickle. Somehow Ellen and I ended up chatting, as Maddy had become even more interested in Ronan once she had discovered they were brother and sister.

Eventually, some of Maddy's friends claimed us. She tried to persuade Ronan and his sister to join us, but Ellen announced she'd promised to call in to another party later. 'It's the never-get-out syndrome, I'm afraid.' She waved as they headed off, but not before Ellen had taken Maddy's number and asked her to meet for coffee the following day.

We partied on and left much later than planned.

'I want to know all about him.' Maddy linked my arm in hers as we headed for a cab. She'd just decided she was staying with me again. 'And don't leave anything out.'

18

WHEN I ARRIVED AT THE OFFICE AT LUNCHTIME ON MONDAY, the nearest I was getting to not working that day, I rang Father Vincent and asked for his help. He remembered my voice and was as pleasant as he'd been last time.

'So, my dear, who is it you're trying to get in touch with?'

'It's not me, as I said. It's actually a client of mine.'

'And do you mind me asking what you do?'

'Well, I'm actually helping him with his dog, he's having some behavioural problems.' It was never easy to explain what I did.

'Fascinating. Sort of a psychiatrist for animals, eh? Do you know what, as far as I'm concerned, most animals are fine. It's their owners that need changing.'

He was a lot closer to the truth than he knew. 'Sometimes, that's true, but dogs are smart, too. They take advantage if you let them.'

'Don't we all.' He laughed. 'I've been getting away with it for years actually. Anyway, tell me the name of the person your client wants to get in touch with. And why doesn't he just ring me himself, if you don't mind me asking?'

'I think he's a bit nervous, to be honest. He seems to have lost contact with them over the years.'

'No problem at all. That often happens. Now, what are their names, and I'll look them up for you?'

I told him and was surprised at his immediate response.

'Well, I don't have to look them up at all. Joan is an old friend at this stage. And Catherine, her daughter, is a lovely girl, inside as well as out.'

'Oh, great, thank you.' I didn't know what else to add really.

'May I ask who your client is, or would you rather not disclose that information?'

'Would it be OK if I just let him know you are still in touch with them and see if he wants to take it from there?'

'Certainly. And tell him to call me any time. And please, feel free to come back to me again yourself if there's anything else.'

'Thank you so much. And I can tell him that they're both well?'

'Yes, tell him Joan is thriving. And Catherine finished second level this summer and got top marks in all her exams. She's decided she wants to study medicine and has just been accepted by Newcastle University.'

'That's great news, I'm sure he'll be very happy to hear it.'

'As I said, she's a smashing girl, nice to everyone, young and old, rich and poor. She'll make a fine doctor, I think. Please tell him.'

'I will, and thank you again, I really appreciate it.' He asked for my number, just as a contact for himself, and I was happy to give it. I hung up pleased that I'd have good news to report when I rang Dinny that evening.

I had a busy day and it was late when I made my way home, more tired than I'd been in ages. As always, the rush of clean sea air and the view worked its magic and I felt lighter as I settled into my little house. Before I put all work thoughts out of my head after the long day, I had one more job to do. I yawned as I got out my notes and rang Denis Cassidy to tell him my news. To my surprise, he'd no time to chat.

'You'll have to come down.' He always shouted when he talked on the phone. 'Bartholomew's gone mad altogether. Did you not get my message?'

No amount of talk on my part would calm him down this evening, it seemed, and within minutes he'd hung up after insisting I come down the following morning. I fell into bed feeling a headache coming on.

After a very disturbed sleep, I felt wiped out the next morning, and my day was looking extra heavy, because I now had to try and get to Ashford, which could take me up to an hour, depending on traffic.

First up was Emily, along with her mother, the famous Julia. And of course Rover came in his basket, was let out and proceeded to demolish one of my plants.

'He does that all the time at home.' Emily was amazed. 'Have you any idea why?'

'Plant- and grass-eating are actually far more common in cats than we realize,' I told them. 'One theory is that plants have some properties that might help the cat get rid of hair balls from his digestive tract.'

'Charming,' Julia said. She had an odd face; she was very pleasant but had a way of looking at you that seemed to say, 'I have the measure of you, so don't be trying to put one over on me.' It could be quite disconcerting, I imagined. 'So, how have you been getting on with him?' I asked, concentrating on Emily.

'To be honest, we've been a bit preoccupied with other matters, haven't we, Mum?' Emily coughed. 'As I mentioned, Mum just told me I was adopted, and that came as quite a surprise, and we were hoping you might be able to offer some advice, given your experience as a counsellor.'

'Well, I'm happy to try, but it wasn't really my area of expertise ever.' The whole issue of children's rights was complicated, I knew. 'And I have changed my career, so while I'll certainly listen and see if I can contribute, it would be just that, if that's OK?' Emily looked like she was about to burst into tears, fearing I might not help.

'What I'm saying is, this would be an informal chat.' I smiled. 'Officially, Rover is my client.'

'Look, I don't know what all this is about really,' Julia suddenly burst out. 'It was years ago, and best left alone, that's my opinion.'

'But Mum, you can't open up something like that and then just ask me to ignore it.' She looked pleadingly at me.

'I think what Emily is trying to say is that the fact that she's adopted raises issues for her and—'

'What issues?' Julia had that face on again. 'She's my daughter, and I've had her since she was ten weeks old and that's that. I should never have said what I said in the first place.'

'But it's out now, and you can't just try and put a lid on it.' It was the first time I'd seen Emily in any way assertive, and I suspected it was definitely a new experience for Julia.

'Don't go getting all stroppy with me, young lady.'

I knew this could quickly disintegrate. 'Emily,' I tried again. 'Perhaps if you told your mum what you need from her?'

'Just some information, how it all came about, that sort of thing.'

Julia said nothing, simply stared into space and, just when I thought she wasn't going to say a word, out it all came.

'You were born in London. Your . . . mother' – she struggled with the word – 'was single, from a good family. After you were born, she moved to Belfast, initially, and then to Dublin. Her family was horrified that she had had the child, apparently, and didn't want to know. She only stayed a week in Belfast, because of the Troubles, and then found Dublin very grey and depressing, so one of the nuns told me. She barely lasted a month here before deciding she wanted her old life back. I got the impression she was quite a spoilt young lady.' Julia sniffed contemptuously, but I could see it was all a front. This was affecting her more than she was letting on and, deep down, I knew she was even more scared than Emily.

'So, she gave you up, and we had applied to adopt, and we got you and from that day on you were ours . . .' I knew she wanted to say more, but she belonged to a generation of women who didn't show their feelings easily.

'Was I always called Emily?' No matter how long I worked

168

with people, sometimes the things that were important to them still surprised me.

'No, she called you, em . . . what was it again?' She feigned nonchalance, but she was only fooling herself, from where I sat. 'Oh yes, Sophie, that was it. Bit odd, don't you think?'

But her daughter's face lit up. 'Sophie, oh my God, it's so . . . so girly, I suppose. Sophie.' She kept repeating it. 'It feels strange but I like it.'

'Emily's nice too, though,' I told her. 'It suits you.'

'What? Oh, yes, of course.' She knew what I was getting at. 'I love my name.' She patted her mother's arm. 'Sophie is just so, not what I would have chosen for me. It's sort of . . . pink and fluffy, like candyfloss.'

'Well, that describes your . . . her, from what Sister Jarlath told me.' Julia glanced around.

'What was her name, my birth mother's?'

'She was known as . . . Kitten, I understand.' Julia's face was a picture. 'I couldn't believe it myself.' She looked to each of us for confirmation that we couldn't either. 'But apparently that's what was on her birth certificate.'

'Kitten?' Emily and I said in unison, then looked at each other and burst out laughing.

'Ridiculous, I totally agree.' Julia misinterpreted our laughter.

'I think it's fabulous,' I had to admit. 'I'd love to have been called Kitten instead of Louisa.'

'This was more than thirty years ago,' Julia said dryly. 'There were no Peacheses or Britneys around then.'

'My God, Kitten and Sophie.' Emily tried the two together. 'I bet that made people smile when they were introduced to us.' She was already turning them into a pair in her head.

'I don't think you were introduced to anyone except customs officials and the nuns.' Julia wasn't having any of it. 'And then us. From that day on it was Julia and Emily,' she said matter-of-factly, in an attempt to claim back her daughter.

'And we were a great team, weren't we, Mum? Still are.' I could have kissed her for her sensitivity. 'I was so lucky you chose me.'

'Well, we always tried to make you feel special.' Julia softened. 'So why can't we just leave it at that?'

'Did you meet her?'

'No, that only happened if the mother wanted it. We just collected you after she'd signed the papers.'

I saw Emily gulp. 'And did she stay in touch?'

'No. I sent photos, via Sister Jarlath, at Christmas and on your birthday. But after a couple of years I gave up.'

'I see.' Emily tried to put on a brave face.

'That wouldn't be unusual, from what I know,' I told her. 'If Kitten . . .' it made me smile again '. . . was under pressure from her family, then the photos might not even have reached her. People went to great lengths in those days to keep things like that hidden, even within families. They weren't talked about, not like now.'

'I know that,' Emily conceded. 'Just one last thing.' She looked at her mother. 'I don't necessarily want to do anything about it . . . but I'm just wondering . . . do you have the name of the home, or hospital, where I was born?'

Julia was silent for at least a minute. 'I have a file, with bits and pieces, but it's been years . . .' Emily and I both knew, I think, that Julia could have recited by heart every detail of what was in that file if she'd wanted.

'Grand so, it's just in case . . .' Emily let it hang.

'Well, I hope that'll be the end of it,' Julia sniffed. 'What good is there in raking up the past, upsetting people?' I suspect she meant herself more than anyone.

'Well, Julia, I think you've been amazing, telling Emily all this. It takes courage.' I smiled. 'Although I'm sure you feel secure in the love you and your daughter have shared all these years.'

'And so you should.' Emily's eyes were damp. 'You've been the best mother anyone could have wished for.'

'Well, I tried, that's for sure.' Julia dropped her facade for a split second and hugged her daughter, and that was the end of it . . . but only for now, I reckoned.

Next I headed for Ashford, to see what chaos Bartholomew was inflicting on poor Denis.

The dog tried very hard to tell me himself as I pulled up at the end of the lane. He tore down to meet me, barking his annoyance, but not at me, I think, because he screeched to a halt in a way that would have done me proud if I'd managed it on my bike, sending muck flying everywhere. Then he wagged his tail at a rate of knots, as if to say, 'Come on in and sort this out.'

'Hello, Barty boy.' I rubbed his stomach and tickled his ear and gave him a treat.

'Woof, woof. Woof woof woof,' was what I heard, but I suspect it roughly translated as, 'You're not going to believe what he's done. Be prepared for trouble.'

'OK, fella, what's up?' I asked, grabbing my bag from the box on the back. 'Come on, show me what the problem is, there's a good boy.'

He kept sprinting off, barking wildly, then tearing back and looking at me as if to say, 'What's keeping you? There's major aggro going on here.'

Denis was waiting in the yard. He looked a bit frailer, I noticed, or maybe it was just that the harsh winter light lent a grey tinge to his face.

'Dinny, how are you?'

'I'm grand, Lulu, which is more than can be said for himself.' He indicated the dog. 'He hasn't stopped barking since all this happened.'

'What exactly has happened?' I asked as we reached the kitchen. 'You were very vague on the phone yest—' Even if the hysterical barking beside me hadn't reached a crescendo I could see what the problem was. Tucked up on the armchair – Bartholomew's armchair – was Pete, the dog from next door that I'd met on my last visit.

'OK, I can see what's causing the rumpus all right.' I dumped my coat and dealt with Bart first, going towards him with a determined look, using a command to stop him in his tracks, then physically forcing him to back off, until his tail glued itself to his anus and he disappeared under the table, where he sat, with a face on him that would sour milk, eyes darting between me and Dinny.

'Thank God you could come. I'm too old for this.' Dinny sighed. 'Cup of tea to warm your bones, Lulu? It's a right cold one we have today.'

'Lovely, the chill does seem to have gotten to me.' I stood

close to the fire, but it had only recently been stacked with turf, so there was no warm glow just yet. 'So, what's the story?'

'The story is that Pete was being sent to the pound. The neighbours decided he was too expensive and too much trouble, even though they only ever fed him scraps, from what I could see, and he was tied up most of the time.' Dinny scratched his head. 'So I said to leave him with me for a day or two and let me think about it. Some of those shelter places have too many dogs, and a good few of them get put down, from what I hear.'

'Well, I know there are some dodgy operators out there, like in any other sector, but mostly the people who work in these places deserve a medal. It's just that funds are so tight and, unfortunately, people abandon and mistreat animals every day and they're left to pick up the pieces.'

'I understand that, but our neighbours are odd – they don't get on well with anyone around here except me, and that's only because I make a real effort. In fact, you could say I force myself on them, so I do.' He laughed. 'I was afraid they'd just take the dog and stray him, to be honest, drive to the middle of the forest and let him out of the car.'

'Surely not?' But I knew it happened all the time.

'Ah, you're probably right, but I couldn't take the chance, I've known Pete all his life.' He poured what looked like tar into a mug, milked and sugared it without asking and left it beside me. 'That dog has had a tough life, I've seen it.' Dinny shook his head. 'And I'd say he has the scars to prove it. Not that the neighbours'd be cruel, mind. It's just neglect. Dogs like him aren't really useful any more around a farm.

173

Sure you hardly ever see a sheepdog, even. Cats chase mice, hens give you eggs, all dogs do is alert you to trouble and, as they get older and their hearing goes, sure not even that.'

'But they're great companions, aren't they?'

'Aye, you and I know that.' He sat down heavily. I'd whooshed the dog off the chair without any bother; he was just chancing his arm. Having been kept outside and tied up for so long, he went straight for maximum comfort, I reckoned.

'So what are you going to do with him? Do you really need another dog?' He had enough on his plate with Bartholomew, and I couldn't shift the earlier feeling I'd had that he was slowing down a bit.

'I was hoping you'd take him,' he said, adopting the same pleading look his dog had given me minutes earlier.

19

'ARE YOU JOKING? I CAN BARELY LOOK AFTER MYSELF.' I laughed nervously. Pete was now looking at me adoringly – or at least that was how I saw it. That face, as well as Bart's pleading 'Take him away' look, and Dinny's 'You know you want to' penetrating stare were all combining to gang up on me. Who said animals didn't understand what was going on?

'You told me the first time I met you, that day when Bartholomew destroyed your couch, that you wanted to get a dog.' Dinny tried to look as if he was doing me a favour.

'Maybe. But a pup – not the dirtiest, scrawniest-looking mongrel I've ever seen.'

'Shush, he's sensitive about his weight.' Dinny laughed heartily. 'Like all us men.' He patted his belly. 'Sure look, have a think about it while you drink your tea, there's a good girl. And there's a glossy red mane under all the dirt, that I know for sure.'

'No pressure then, eh?' I gave him what I hoped was a filthy look. 'So that's what you brought me all the way down here for?'

'Not at all, sure if I'm to keep him I need your help with

yer man there, he's acting as if I'm about to put him in a concentration camp.' We both looked under the table, where Bart got full marks for the most dejected face I'd seen in a long time.

'Yes, well, he's good, I'll give him that. I should ask my friend Maddy if she could get him a part in her soap on TV. Anyway' – I changed the subject – 'Father Vincent said to tell you he knows your friends and is in touch on a regular basis. Joan is very well and Catherine is just about to start college studying medicine.'

I was surprised that he looked so thrown by the news. 'She's going to be a doctor?' he asked in disbelief.

'Apparently. That's good, isn't it? They've obviously done well for themselves.'

'Aye, they have surely.' He stared into the fire. 'And without any help from me.'

I saw his face was ashen. 'Dinny, do you want to tell me what this is really about?' Here we go again, I thought. 'It's just that I sense they're important to you, but you seem to be fighting it for some reason. Am I right?' I went to boil the kettle to top up the teapot so that I could actually drink the stuff, and while I was there I emptied out the impossibly strong, sweet brew he'd poured into my cup earlier. But really I was just trying to give him a bit of space.

Just as I thought he wasn't going to tell me, he said quietly, 'Catherine is my daughter.' As I looked at him, I saw tears trickle down his face, and suddenly I was plunged into another parent/child story that wasn't straightforward, just like my own.

'But Dinny, that's wonderful, you must be so proud?' I

decided to ignore the story for the moment and try to give him a reason to tell me. 'That's every father's dream surely – to have a son or daughter a doctor? Isn't it like having a priest or nun in the family was in the old days in Ireland?' I topped us both up, and sat opposite him and played with Pete in an effort to give him more time. The stupid mutt obviously knew he should try and make an impression, because he flattened himself to the floor, head down, ears cocked, with a little black fruit gum for a nose and the saddest conker-brown eyes I'd ever seen.

'His nose is a bit like a Westie's,' I told Dinny. 'But his shape is all wrong.'

'Aye, he's a cross all right, but there's more Collie in him than anything else.' He held out his hand, and the dog moved with such speed you knew he was desperate for affection. He only stayed with Dinny for a couple of seconds, in spite of the pleasure he so clearly craved. Instead he came back over to my feet and plonked himself down with a sigh, looking up at me as if to say, 'I'd be no trouble at all, honestly.'

Feck it, I knew where he was going to live from now on, and it wasn't going to be Ashford.

'Would you like me to leave you alone, Dinny, and call to see you later in the week?'

It was as if he hadn't heard me. 'I'm glad I know,' he said. 'And I'm delighted it was yourself who brought me the news.'

'Did it come as a shock?'

'Aye, it did, to be honest. I haven't seen them since Catherine was four or thereabouts.' He looked as if he'd aged ten years in the same number of minutes. 'Myself and

177

Joan were stepping out together for about two years when she discovered she was expecting. Needless to say we were floored. I was a bit of a lad, even though I'd turned forty – can you believe that? And it was still a bit of a scandal around these parts, especially where my parents were concerned. Joan was nearly twenty years younger than me, and my mother didn't like her one bit, that's the truth. So Joan went off to Cork and had the child, and then came back and stayed at home for about a year with her parents.' He got up and stoked the fire, and I suspected this was all very painful for him. So did Barty, it seemed, because he slithered out from under the table, hoping no one would notice, and planted himself down between Dinny's legs as the old man sat heavily back into his chair.

'I don't mind admitting this to you, Lulu; I was an awful coward at the time. I should have gone straight out and married the girl, and that's a fact. But I didn't, and eventually she couldn't take the gossiping and sniggering behind her back, and she upped and left and went to live in London.'

'So what did you do then?'

'I did what most Irishmen in rural Ireland did in those circumstances, I continued on as if nothing had happened. And for a while the drink helped me forget. Wasn't that terrible of me altogether?' he asked, without looking in my direction.

'I'm sure you did your best, Dinny. They were different times, don't be too hard on yourself.'

'Aye, but that's no excuse. Anyway, my mother took a heart attack a couple of years later and was dead within a week. That gave me a quare shock I can tell you. So when

178

the funeral was over I got in touch with Joan's family and found out where she was and told me father I was going to sort this out once and for all.'

'What did he say?'

'Nothing much, you know what men are like. "Do what you have to but don't bring any shame on your mother's memory," was all I think he said. But I was fierce determined.' He stamped his foot hard to illustrate his point and nearly had a brain-damaged dog on his hands. 'So off I went, tracked them down and, to cut a long story short, she sent me packing. Refused to have anything to do with me so she did, and can you blame her?'

'What did you do then?'

'I hung around for a few days, bought flowers, all the usual stuff, but she was having none of it. I doorstepped her one day and begged her to give me another chance. That's when I saw the child, a gorgeous little thing with a mass of curls and my mother's piercing blue eyes. D'ya know what, Lulu? I was fierce sorry that we'd been so stupid as a family, depriving ourselves of this lovely little girl for the sake of what people might think.' He smiled. 'I can still see her to this day; she was holding her mother's hand and skipping along, without a care in the world. Anyway, Joan told me in no uncertain terms that I'd let them both down and that she didn't need me any more. So, feeling desperately sorry for myself, I headed for a local pub, drank myself senseless and took off for home with my tail between my legs.' He sat back in his chair. 'So that's the story until now, and d'ya know something? It's the only thing in my life that I regret to this very day.'

'No contact whatsoever?'

'Oh, I sent the odd big cheque. I wasn't short of money, even in those days. But they were never cashed. She was a proud girl, that's for sure, and I hurt her badly when I refused to stand beside her in times of trouble.'

'So why now?' I wondered.

'Ah, lots of reasons, but mainly just selfishness, if I'm honest. I'm old, I've no one left really – and to think you've just told me I have a daughter who's going to be a doctor. Wouldn't I be the right proud father now at mass on a Sunday if I hadn't been so stupid way back then?'

'I'm sorry.' I meant it. He was a lovely man who'd made one mistake. 'But maybe now is the time to try again to fix it.'

'Sure look, Joan is still a young woman. And still good-lookin' too, I'd bet any money. She was a stunner, that's for sure.' He smiled, remembering. 'She probably married a millionaire. And now she's raised a lovely young girl, from what you told me. Sure why the hell would she want to have anything to do with me?'

'Well, you'll never know until you try, surely?'

'I'm frightened, Lulu, and that's the long and the short of it. What if she laughed in my face?'

'Is it not worth the risk?' I asked.

'Aye, I suppose it is. But I need to think about it.'

'Look, would it help if I phoned Father Vincent again?' I couldn't believe I was pushing my way into another complicated family. 'Could I ask his advice, in confidence?'

'Would you do that for me?'

'I would, if it helps. But, sooner or later, it's going to

180

come down to you, Dinny. You can't hide behind me for ever.'

'I know that. But maybe if you just found out a bit more. Tell him anything you like, just to give me a leg up, so to speak.'

'OK, will do. And I'll call you as soon as I've news. Now, I'd better head.' I drained my cold cup and stood up.

'So, are you going to give this poor wee fella a chance?' he asked quietly.

'That "poor wee fella", as you call him, would buy and sell both of us, I suspect.'

'Tell you what, give it a try for a week. And if you don't want him, I'll take him back. Deal?' he held out his hand.

'No way. I need time.'

'Sure what have you got to lose?'

'I'm on a bike, Denis Cassidy. I cannot have a mutt as a pillion passenger.'

'Tell you what, you only live in Bray, I'll drive up behind you.'

'No.'

'Go on, sure what have you got to lose?'

Ten minutes later, with an ecstatic Bartholomew herding us out the gate like sheep, I took off up the M11 with an old man in a battered Volvo estate trailing behind. When I checked my rear mirror, all I could see was a scrawny, filthy mutt with his head out the window of the passenger seat, enjoying the rush of wind much more than I was.

This was either going to be an instant success or a complete disaster, I knew, and my instinct was telling me not to bank on the former.

20

ALL DENIS WAS SHORT OF DOING WAS OPENING THE WINDOW fully and drop-kicking the dog on to my deck as he drove past, so keen was he to get away.

'Cup of tea, Dinny?' I asked. I'd never known him refuse, so I was anxious to see exactly how keen he was to be rid of the mutt.

'Sure if I drink one more drop my bladder will explode.' He was all nervous cheer. 'Will you ring me and let me know how you're getting on?' He revved up. 'He'll be no trouble, I promise.' *Vroom vroom* was all I heard as he kicked the dust of Bray off his wheels.

Suddenly I looked at myself, dressed in a very fetching helmet, canary-yellow windcheater and muddy boots, living in a trailer in amusement-park heaven, with a scruffy dog of questionable parentage as my closest companion.

Right on cue, he came towards me with the most trusting eyes and sat on my shoe as if to say, 'What now, partner?' Those bloody eyes were almost human. Just seeing us as an outsider might, made me drop down on the steps of my deck and burst out laughing at what I'd become. My life was not for the faint-hearted.

'OK, looks like we're stuck with each other for the moment, but I'm the boss, got that?' I flexed my foot, and he reluctantly moved but stayed glued to my side as I walked towards the door.

Inside, he tried to make himself as small as possible as he crouched in the corner between the couch and the fire, as if afraid I'd change my mind and kick him out or, worse still, tie him up on the deck.

I hadn't a clue how I was going to manage him during the day. That was the first problem. I knew I needed advice, so I warned him to be good and headed off into town to the pet shop, having phoned the office to tell them I'd be back before too long.

The guy in the pet shop laughed his head off when I told him I needed to take my dog to work on my motorbike. One look at my 'Don't mess with me today' face had him scrambling around in the storeroom.

'Have you got the bike outside, love?'

'No, I just wear this helmet and padded jacket as a fashion statement actually.'

'Very funny. OK, gimme a look.' He hemmed and hawed for a couple of minutes, asked a lot of questions about the size and weight of the dog then said, 'Yep, I reckon I have something that might work. Go off and have a coffee and come back in twenty minutes or so.'

I did as I was told, and when I returned he had a sort of crate secured to the front of the bike on a platform. It was detachable and had a lid that folded completely back.

'You'd only need the lid if the weather was atrocious say, or if you wanted to store food in there, maybe?' he told me, and I didn't tell him that, unless Pete got his mangled coat shaved, I'd have to sit on the lid to close it, I reckoned. The man had even fastened a sort of baby seatbelt inside and put a grey blanket in the bottom with dog paws all over it.

'And look, here's a little plastic wallet at the side that you can store treats in,' he said. 'Not bad, eh?'

'Not bad? You're a genius.' My admiration knew no bounds.

'And look, here's another little pocket with a combination lock.' He pointed to what looked like an old-fashioned pencil case. 'So if you had to bring money or credit cards and didn't want to bring a handbag, you'd have plenty of room in there, even for a lipstick.' He winked at me. I was so impressed that I bought a dog bed, two bowls, shampoo, a collar and lead and a supply of food from him. I happily handed over most of what I'd earned that week and promised to put a notice up in my office recommending him for special doggie jobs.

'And if it doesn't work, bring the dog down and we'll adapt something else, love.' He was still waving as I disappeared round the corner with a backpack full of goodies and a sinking feeling that me and the scruffball were a family.

Back at the van I dumped the stuff and tried out the carrier for size. The dog was deliriously happy to see me, and when I called him towards the bike and patted the box, he stood stock still for a second as if to make sure, then shot into reverse and made a leap that wouldn't have been out of place in a cartoon strip, landing with a plop on his bum in the box, tail sticking out and wagging for Ireland. I strapped him in, locked up and started off down the lane at a snail's pace. He kept looking back at me, wet, pink tongue hanging out, eyes laughing as if to say, 'Come on, don't be a wuss, put the pedal to the metal.'

In the town, people pointed and laughed, and I tried to ignore them but all Pete was short of doing was waving. He woof woofed at everyone who smiled at him, hair plastered to his face. I'm certain he was thinking, 'I've finally gotten lucky.' Within minutes, I too was waving and tooting my horn, and it had to be right up there as one of the nicest journeys I'd ever made into work. Even a couple of curmudgeonly truck drivers honked and laughed.

At the office he turned into a Crufts obedience champion again, never running ahead or stopping to sniff, as if he was afraid I'd leave him behind.

'Oh my God, he's so cute.' Our normally reserved receptionist came out from behind her desk, which was amazing. She hadn't interacted at all so far with my clients. 'He smells though. Yuk.' She stepped back immediately. 'Who does he belong to?'

'Me, for a week at least,' I told her. 'Don't ask, I was taken in by a con artist posing as a helpless old man.'

'The worst kind.' She smiled. 'Here are your messages. Shall I get him some water? What's his name, by the way?'

'Pete. And yes please,' I replied.

'Come on then, Pete, you are so gorgeous that we might even have a treat in the kitchen,' Mary said, but he refused to budge from my side, just sat looking at me until I gave permission.

'It's OK, good boy, go on.' I indicated that he should follow Mary and he toddled behind her but kept looking back to make sure I was still there.

'Oh, by the way, Mike called, wondering if you'd have time to see him this afternoon at about four thirty? I said yes after I'd checked your diary but told him I'd confirm it as soon as you got back to the office. I didn't want to disturb you with Mr Cassidy. Is that OK?'

'Actually, I'm due to see Louis, his flatmate. It's complicated, so if you wouldn't mind being aware of not saying anything to one about the other, just for the moment,' I asked. 'Meanwhile, I'll ring Mike now and explain.' Louis had cancelled my proposed visit to his home – twice – so I knew Mike was getting anxious. I dialled his mobile and he answered promptly.

'That dog should have been named Charles, because he thinks he's heir to the throne,' he told me, without wasting time on pleasantries. 'He was asleep on my bed last night when I got home, and even though I did everything you told me to he refused to budge, and when I eventually lifted him, duvet and all, on to the floor, he snored in my ear while I froze all night with only that old rasher of a duvet that Louis made me give up.'

'You love that duvet,' I laughed. 'You told me you hated Louis for insisting it wasn't up to scratch.'

'See, he's finally gotten to me. I now can only sleep with goose feathers next to my bum. Next thing you know I'll be label-spotting myself.'

'I doubt that,' I told him. 'By the way, I got a dog – on loan, mind you.' I filled him in, then I told him I was definitely going to see Louis and Pedro that afternoon, so that calmed him down a bit. 'So how quickly can we meet after and you can fill me in? Sorry, I know I'm piling on the pressure but I'm already on the Net looking for a new place to live.'

'OK, I get it. How about tomorrow?' I suggested. 'I have Pete in the office today, you see – in fact I'm going to have to take him with me to your house – so I really need to get home and walk him.'

'What time are you meeting Louis? It's just that I have my last appointment to see a band in the pub in Shankhill where we played that night, so I could swing by your place later? I'd love to see this famous dog anyway. After Pedro I'd say he'll be a treat.'

His request took me by surprise. He was a client, after all, and I didn't want to cross any lines, but I supposed that with him the boundaries were already well blurred. 'O . . . K,' I said hesitantly.

'Or we could meet in the town and I'll go for a walk with you along the seafront and you can fill me in?' He seemed to sense my concern. 'That way he gets his constitutional.'

'Great.' I was happy with that. 'I'm meeting Louis at six so, allowing for everything, I'd probably be walking him about eight thirty. Does that work for you?'

'That's spot on, my appointment is for half seven and the punters will start drifting in after eight so, allowing for a quick chat, I could meet you at, say, Goggins pub at about a quarter to nine?'

That suited me too, so I spent an hour at my desk, with Pete again trying to make himself invisible in a ball in the corner. He could have been a cushion he was so tightly curled up, and I swear he was afraid even to snore in case it annoyed me. As soon as I began to get ready to leave, two eyes watched me like a hawk until I said, 'OK, come on,' then he was like a mass of jelly and nearly strangled himself getting to my side in case I'd leave without him.

Louis's place was an ordinary, end-of-terrace two-up two-down from the front, but once inside you came face to face with a huge glass double-storey cube on the back that looked on to still water and rustling bamboo. It was an area that had always been known as the fashionable end of the canal, but in recent years – mainly thanks to a few super-cool architects winning awards for their designs – it had become really trendy and sought after.

'Wow,' I said as I walked in. 'You get no idea of what's in store for you from outside.'

'That was the idea,' Louis said, clearly delighted. 'Isn't it fantastic?' Suddenly Pedro spotted Pete and went berserk, even though Pete ignored him and cowered in a corner right beside the front door, thinking it was his fault. It took all of my experience to get Pedro to back down. Eventually, I physically blocked him by advancing towards him, and in doing so forced him backwards into the kitchen and on to his favourite seat, but he was not happy. Unfortunately, Louis kept saying 'Bold boy' while tickling his ears and smiling indulgently at him until I had to ask him to leave it to me.

'Louis, we need to talk about this kind of behaviour,' I told him.

'Come on, I'll give you the guided tour first.' He was not keen to tackle the problem, I knew. 'Wait until you see the deck that looks as if it's suspended over the water.'

It was to die for. I could see why Mike didn't want to

leave. Louis had broken all the rules and yet it worked superbly.

We chatted over china cups of delicious coffee that came from a machine hidden within the wall of a kitchen that I knew must have cost at least €50,000. It was a cook's dream, even I, queen of instant everything could see that.

'So, we'd better talk about Pedro, otherwise I might be tempted to kick out your flatmate and insist on sharing with you myself.' I wasn't lying; he had impeccable taste and the attention to detail was something else.

'Well, darling, don't tempt me, because it's Mike who's the real problem.' Louis gave a sigh that wouldn't have been out of place on the stage of the Abbey Theatre. 'Truly, he is. Pedro's far worse when he's around,' he said as he saw my raised eyebrows. 'In fact, that's one of the reasons I wanted to see you without him. I don't know what to do, frankly. He's a great guy and all that – and he does walk Pedro, which I hate doing – but he just cannot accept that the dog is my soulmate, in a way I can't explain.'

'Louis, I know how you feel, especially with losing Emerson, but unless you give your dog exercise, discipline and love, you're really not doing him any favours in the long run. And you're shoring up trouble for the future, in my opinion.'

'Mike's been complaining again, hasn't he?'

I decided to avoid the question. 'Louis, I can see it for myself. The dog is at least your equal, in some ways I'd say he even thinks he's superior. Everything you do, he seems to have the same rights, except maybe for using the toilet.' I tried to joke to take the sting out of my words. 'Someone has to be the pack leader, or else he *will* take over and, even if Mike does move out, anyone else you bring in will have the same problems. And what if you meet a new partner? Don't you want to be able to share your life with whoever you please without having to worry about Pedro?'

'Whoever shares my life will have to share Pedro's too,' Louis said in a petulant voice. I knew I had to be careful here.

'I understand that, but for everyone's quality of life it has to be you at the top of the pyramid, Mike – or whoever – number two and Pedro number three. Trust me, Louis, it doesn't mean less affection between you at all. It just means you have to set boundaries for him. I'm sorry, I know it's not what you want to hear, but you're paying me for a service and I owe it to you to tell it as I see it.'

'OK, I'm willing to give your way a chance,' Louis said after a bit. 'I guess I do see him becoming more demanding each time I give in to him.'

'Of course he is. I see a huge difference – even since the last time we met.' I decided to get to work. 'But remember, dogs live in the moment, so they don't hold on to things the way humans do, and that's good, because it means you can start from now and you'll very quickly see results, I promise. OK?'

'OK.' I sensed he wanted it; it was just easier to blame Mike.

'So, here are a few simple steps to start with. Firstly, I want you not to greet him when you come home until he's calm. Ignore him until he settles down and then give him loads of attention.' I could see he was scared of losing the dog's

190

devotion, but I ignored the look on his face and persisted. 'Next thing you can do is let Mike feed him each day—'

'He'll forget, or feed him junk.' Louis was agitated already.

'Give it a try. I can explain to Mike how important this is if you like. And I think I can get him on board.'

'Would you? That would be fab.' He relaxed again. After a few more tips, I left and arranged to meet them both in the house together over the following weeks.

Now, could I get Mike to behave?

21

I WAS SORRY I HADN'T YET HAD A CHANCE TO SCRUB PETE as we sat on a wall and waited for Mike. He looked utterly neglected; the phrase 'dragged through a hedge backwards' was made for him and the smell was definitely getting worse, for some reason, despite me wasting some of my precious Jo Malone spray on him. But if being a model pet was going to win the day for him, then he'd scored 100 per cent so far. I found it quite remarkable that a dog who'd been ignored for most of his life and chained up for long periods seemed to know exactly how to behave around people. My guess was he'd learned that being as little trouble as possible meant he got into none, so he now sat, perfectly still by my leg, watching but making no noise and not moving, even when someone passed. It was only his slight change of posture, ears cocked, body a touch straighter, that alerted me to an approach, so that I sensed Mike before I saw him walking down the prom, hands in pockets, collar up.

'Hi there.' He smiled. 'Is it me or is this brass-monkey weather?'

'I walked down from home so I'm warm.' I stood up. 'Meet Pete, and excuse the smell,' I warned.

Mike hunkered down so he was almost level with the dog, who looked very nervous. I'd noticed he was much more wary of men, and Dinny had told me that the neighbour who'd owned him was a widower, and I imagined most, if not all, the farm labourers would have been male.

'Hello, fella, gimme a look at you.' He tickled Pete under his chin so that the dog stretched his neck with pleasure and therefore looked into Mike's eyes. 'You are one gorgeous dog.' He whistled. 'Most girls would kill for those eyes, I reckon. Although you smell so bad, I think maybe your mother threw up on you like she did on me. Shame you can't talk, we could have a man-to-man about this in an effort to avoid it happening to some other poor bugger.'

'You promised, remember?' I slapped him on the head, while Pete seemed to have decided Mike was a pal and was now revelling in the affection. I don't think the animal had ever had as much attention as he'd received since coming to me. Everyone in our office building had petted him, and Mary was besotted.

'He's a special dog, you got lucky there,' Mike told me. 'Look how calm he is, happy to just be around us.'

'Well, I'm afraid he spent most of his life tied up in a yard,' I told Mike, and he grimaced. 'So I suppose anything has to be better than a chain around your neck.'

'Well, Pete, your day has come. If she doesn't keep you, I'll take you myself.' He gave the dog one last tickle and we headed off, Pete walking perfectly in step between us with a tail so high it almost pulled down a few stars.

I filled Mike in as we walked, and he seemed relieved that Louis was prepared to try. 'You were right in what you said – people are beginning to avoid us. Even my mates are nervous about calling to the door, and they're usually big rugby types. Also, I happen to know that the local residents' association has spoken to Louis because the neighbours on either side are up in arms. Apparently he barks for hours sometimes during the day.'

'It's a difficult one,' I told Mike. 'In a way Louis has transferred most of the affection he shared with Emerson on to the dog.'

'Who are you telling? I can see it clearly. Louis is lonely, and he's scared of putting himself out there again really – despite his initial madness – that's why the dog is now a substitute for all he's lost.'

'Well, I'm hopeful he's willing to change,' I said. 'But you have to encourage him. I've suggested that you be the one to feed Pedro for the next week, so no messing, OK?'

'What, you mean no sweet-and-sour chicken balls when I run out of dog food?' He dodged another blow. 'I know, I know. I forgot that Louis doesn't like him to have stodgy batter, the stuff with beer that he makes himself is much lighter.' Mike grabbed Pete's lead and ran on ahead laughing. 'Come on, boy, let's have a run, these dog shrinks will drive us to drink.' Pete kept looking back at me, a bit frightened in case I disapproved, I think, so I ran and caught up with them, and he bounded along, ears back, with the biggest grin I've ever seen on a dog's face, until both Mike and I ran out of steam.

'Christ, I'm so unfit it's lethal,' he panted. 'But at least I'm warm. Fancy a drink before we head home?'

'I'm wrecked.' I hesitated, still nervous of him for some

reason. 'I really should get off to bed . . .'

'Well, I'm driving, so I'm only having one. Go on, you know you want to.'

'What about the dog?'

'Say nothing, leave it to me.' He broke into a fast stride, so that Pete and I had no choice but to jog behind him to catch up.

'My friend here is short-sighted, so the dog is her guide, is that OK?' I nearly choked as Mike helped me into a seat.

'Certainly, sir. What can I get you?' The barman was over to us in a second.

'Eh, pint of Guinness for me. Lulu?'

'Glass of dry white wine please.' My face was beetroot as I tried to look just past his face, the way I'd seen it done on the movies. Mike noticed and nearly corpsed.

'What are you like, you eejit? Sure he doesn't give a toss, any mention of a disability and they fall over themselves to accommodate you these days, EU rules and all that.'

'You are the biggest chancer I've ever met in my life,' I whispered, completely mortified. Pete had once again wedged himself under the banquette seating, as if he knew that he too was chancing his arm. 'He doesn't even look like a guide dog, they're normally Labradors.' I grinned.

'Relax, you're with your uncle Mike.' He stood up and paid for the drinks as soon as they arrived.

'Sorry I couldn't treat you, but with my eyesight I wouldn't have been able to find the correct money.' I took a gulp just as the nice barman came back with a dish of water for Pete. 'There you go, boy.' He stroked the tiny bit of head that was visible. 'Any time you know you're coming in, give us a ring and we'll keep an eye on the door. My name is Alan, by the way.' He smiled and handed Mike a card as he left our table.

'Do you know, people down here are so nice.' I told Mike about the guy in the pet shop making up the carrier for Pete, and he laughed at the idea of me zipping along the dual carriageway with a dog on a bike. 'Is it because strictly speaking Bray is in County Wicklow and therefore in the country, even if we are less than an hour from the centre of Dublin?' I wondered.

'Yeah, I guess so.' He took a slug of his pint straightaway. 'You can't beat the old community spirit. It's fairly gone by the wayside in über-trendy Dublin, that's for sure.'

'Well, I'd say your business is fairly cut-throat.' I was interested to hear more about his life. All I really knew was that he was in the music industry.

'Sure is. But I love music, always have, so I go into work with a smile on my face most mornings.'

'How come you're so laidback about everything?'

'Not everything, but most things aren't worth worrying about.'

'God, I was so not like that in my last job – mostly the smile had been wiped away by the time I got out of the shower and my phone was already beeping with messages,' I told him.

'Big mistake. I leave my work mobile in the office, and only one person in the company – Marisa, my assistant – has my personal one, and she never rings me unless it's a dire emergency. And so far I've resisted a BlackBerry. Sure, like everywhere else, there is a lot of politics in my game, but

I usually manage to slip in the odd gig, like tonight, where I just head off and listen to some raw talent.'

'And were they good?'

'They were, yeah. One of our A&R guys, Ritchie, picked up on them from a demo and he asked me to have a listen. They've got a different sound, so hopefully we'll be working with them. Mind you, I wanted to be up on stage instead of the head honcho from the record company sitting in the front row in a jacket, I have to tell you.'

'You love it that much, huh?'

'Pretty much. And you? Do you love what you do now?'

'Yeah, actually, I do. I think I've been searching most of my life, chasing something, running round in circles because I didn't really know what I was looking for and everyone else seemed to have found. For the first time in my life I'm content.' I sipped my drink. 'Happy in the now, as all the experts tell you to be.'

'And tell me, Lulu, were you always . . . eh, how can I put this diplomatically . . . as barking mad as you are now?'

'Do you think I am, really?' I was delighted.

'I do.' He looked puzzled. 'Is that not a hanging-offence kind of thing to say to a woman, or am I losing my touch?'

'No, it's fine by me,' I told him. 'I love being called mad. I honestly believe "sensible" must have been the first word I learned.'

'Good for you, I think.' He grinned as he swallowed the last of his pint, but he seemed in no hurry to leave. 'And the dog? Is he for keeps?'

'I've no idea.' I told him the story, and he ended up down on his knees in what looked like a very good black jacket, lolling about on a dirty carpet talking to a scruffy dog and telling him what a great boy he was.

'He's got the oddest eyes,' he told me when he sat back down again. 'He sort of looks at you as if he understands what you're saying.'

'Tell me about it, those eyes are what got me in the first place.'

We left shortly after, and Mike insisted on dropping me off, even though I protested when I saw his shiny 09 black car with the cream-leather seats.

'Honestly, Pete is rotten, and I don't understand why but it seems to be getting worse,' I told him, but he insisted that it was too late and too dark for me to walk home. The only good thing was that we weren't in his car long enough to leave any permanent reminder – I hoped.

'You're a funny girl, I can't figure you out,' he told me as he deposited the pair of us at the gate. 'Living in a trailer in Bray, driving a bike and sharing your space with a mutt no one wants.'

'And happy with my lot, thank you very much.' I waved him off, and he promised to text me progress reports on Pedro and Louis.

I woke early next morning and decided I could no longer stand the smell of Pete, so I turned on the shower full blast and he trotted straight in, which surprised me. Normally you had to coax animals under water, but he seemed to know what was required of him. Once I started soaping his belly, I found the culprit. What looked like the remains of part of a dead bird were caught in the knots of hair in his belly. It was small, and I was completely guessing that it might have once been a bird because of what looked like a tiny mass of feathers. But the stink on my hands told me this was what was causing people to recoil in horror. It was so embedded I had to cut it out, which explains why I hadn't felt or seen it before. And as soon as I sniffed the thing I gagged.

'Oh my God, that is absolutely putrid, how on earth did you get it in there?' I asked Pete, whose tail immediately went down, as if sensing he'd done something wrong. 'It's OK; it's not as if you went walking in the woods every day, that's for sure.' I gave him a hug. 'Stay, good boy,' I commanded as I went to fetch a plastic bag and knotted it tightly so that it wouldn't stink out my bin. The clean, shiny dog that emerged from the shower bore no resemblance to the one that had gone in. I'd combed him first, but I knew he needed proper grooming by an expert one of these days. Still, it was a vast improvement and I was looking forward to the reaction in the office. Shame Mike hadn't seen him like this.

'You are so gorgeous,' I told him as I turned my hairdryer on low and dried his coat, and he positively glowed, licking my face at every opportunity as if to say, 'Thanks, I didn't like the smell either.' I knew that was just a fanciful notion on my part, though. As a rule, dogs love rolling in anything they can find, and the smellier the better had been my experience.

Still, he positively preened on the journey to the office, and it seemed as if every schoolchild laughed and pointed out their car windows as we whizzed past.

If ever he'd doubted his attractiveness, he knew he was on to a winner, I reckon, when Mary clocked him.

'Oh my God, what have they done to you? You are such a beautiful doggie.' She hugged him to bits, and he licked her back with just as much passion, all the time keeping one ear cocked in my direction to make sure I wasn't going anywhere. It made me smile to see how much she'd lightened up since Pete had arrived on the scene.

'Ah, Pete, I reckon you have it sussed now,' I told him, as Mary gave him a lamb bone she'd saved from her dinner the night before and he toddled into my office and placed it carefully on his bed, where he proceeded to sniff it and lick it for hours before he even tasted the meat. It was definitely our biggest success yet as far as he was concerned. I got a text from Mike that read:

can't understand it, u seem 2 leave ur mark everywhere. my car stil smells of rotten fish dis morn.
Had 2 leve roof down even though freezing!

Oops. I decided it would not endear either of us to him if I explained further.

Emily was back, this time on her own. 'How're things?' I asked as I went to meet her at the door.

'Fine.' She looked nervous, but not as deflated as she'd been looking recently.

'And Rover?'

'Actually, I think my mother might be finally coming to terms with him. Mind you, he sits – and stays – no idea how, but she's delighted, so I'm happy too,' she told me.

'Great.' I waited, but she said nothing. 'And are you and

your mother getting on OK?' I asked. 'Have you talked at all since the last time you were here?'

'Yes, we have. Only because I sort of pushed it, really, which is not like me at all, as you know.'

'In what way did you push?'

'Well, I asked her more about Kitten.' We broke into smiles all over again at the name.

'And?'

'Well, reluctantly, she showed me the file.' Emily got a bit animated all of a sudden. 'It was so strange, seeing her name, it made her seem much more real somehow. You know, an official document connecting me to a stranger.'

'And how is Julia about it?'

'She's OK, I suppose. For the first time in my life I've asked for what I want, without always worrying about what the other person will think. It's quite, I dunno, liberating, I suppose.'

'Good for you.' I meant it.

'The thing is, Lulu, I want to pursue this. I want to find my real mother, and I'd like you to help me. Will you?'

22

MADDY RANG, SUGGESTING A DRINK ON MY WAY HOME AFTER work. I'd told her about Pete, and she was dying to see him.

'It's just, I've nowhere to leave him,' I explained. It was going to be a bigger problem than I'd originally thought, I knew. I couldn't go out after work, and in some cases I couldn't see people on my way to or from the office, because leaving him in a box on a bike wasn't an option and, in the case of some of my newer clients, it would be counterproductive to introduce another dog at an early stage. Besides, even though most owners loved animals, they didn't always want someone else's dog messing up their carpet. I knew I'd have to think seriously about getting a car. I dreaded the idea, in spite of the wind and rain and the ruined shoes. At least in a car I could leave the dog happily for an hour on a blanket on the passenger seat while I went about my business. I told Maddy of my dilemma.

'Well, not a problem tonight, babe. We can meet in the Happy Hound, if you'll pardon the pun.' She laughed. 'And yours will be delirious, I promise.'

'Will they let him in? The other night Mike pretended I was blind in a pub in Bray. I was mortified,' I told her.

'Stop right there and rewind,' she demanded. 'On second thoughts, don't. Hold it for later. Jesus Christ, girl, what are you like? I have to beat everything out of you. You know by now that you have to ring Madeleine and tell all as soon as it happens.'

'Nothing happened, it was busi—'

'I want a blow-by-blow, no details spared. I have great hopes for this relationship. If he can survive your vomit, he's one to be chased,' she declared emphatically. 'And don't worry about the mutt being allowed into the pub, most of their female customers are dogs themselves. Besides, I know the manager, Paul. Had a snog with him once. Be warned, though, it's a rough joint, but it's on your way home and I have a casting session nearby – can you believe it? I'm so excited! It's at three thirty, so I'll be waiting with a large G&T in my hand, whatever the outcome.'

Smiling, I hung up. I loved Maddy to pieces, she was better than any vitamin intake. As soon as I finished with my next client – a Chihuahua called Fred who chased cars and hated tyres so he tried to bite them; not conducive to a long life on a number of levels, his owner had decided – I rang Clodagh to see if she'd join us.

'Sorry, I'm snowed under,' she told me. 'Things are really moving rapidly with the new venture and I have a meeting with a prospective client this evening.' She was well on the way to setting up on her own, having had it with big corporate companies who think they own their employees.

'No problem, I'm just so happy for you.'

'Well, you can take some of the credit, you know. You were the inspiration.'

'You know me, I'll take half the credit for anything pretty much. But this has been all up to you. You're a power-ball.'

'Thanks. I just wish I had a bit more energy. I could do with getting up a bit earlier in the mornings, say five instead of six,' she said, deadpan.

'Clodagh' – I choked on my coffee at the very notion of getting up voluntarily before eight – 'you have so much energy that when you die they'll probably blitz you and sell you as a super-duper multivitamin. How about meeting this weekend, instead? You could come and stay and meet my new dog?'

'I'd love that. By the way, don't go on about my new job to Maddy, I think she's feeling a bit cheesed off with her lot at the moment, and you and I changing our lives isn't helping, I suspect.'

'Thanks for the tip-off, I'll be careful. But she's going for an audition this afternoon, so she's very upbeat.'

'Brilliant. Oops, gotta go, there's my other phone, text you later.' She was gone so fast I could almost feel the rush of wind.

The rest of the day was unusually quiet. In recent weeks, thankfully, days like this had been rare, so I took immediate advantage and left Pete asleep under Mary's desk while I went and did a bit of shopping, picking up a few trinkets for my office, such as a really nice doggie calendar and a cushion that boldly proclaimed DOGS DON'T DO ANYTHING FOR POLITICAL REASONS. I loved it, so it got pride of place on my couch. On the way back I went for a coffee on the spur of the moment and thought once again how much I loved my new life. When my mobile stayed silent it was the icing on the cake.

I'd hoped to get a walk in before I met Maddy that evening, but she sent me a message at four thirty to say she was there already, not a good sign as far as the casting was concerned.

Can I bring P in or shud I ask 1st? I texted as soon as I pulled up at the pub, where a large group of weather-beaten men stood at the main door, huddled together under the canopy, smoking.

Immediately a message came back that simply read sorted so I manoeuvred my way through the crowd.

'How'ya love, nice bruiser ye got there,' a gravelly voice said.

'I'm ringin' Health and Safety, this place is bad enough without findin' dog hairs in the oul pint,' a wizened face added, the toothless grin taking away the implied threat.

'Don't mind them, love, they're only teasing. Come in quick outta the cold,' said another one straightaway.

'Thanks a million.' I smiled at them all and headed in the door, where Maddy waved to me from a quiet corner.

'This place is buzzing,' I told her, as Pete took up his usual position under my feet. 'The recession hasn't hit Sallynoggin then?'

'Cheapest pint in south-county Dublin here, as well as cheapest petrol down the road, so they're always busy.' She gestured to a barman and I ordered a white wine. 'What wines do you have by the glass?' I asked, expecting a couple of choices.

'Eh' – he scratched his head – 'I'll show you.' He

disappeared and emerged thirty seconds later with a half-open bottle of something I didn't recognize.

'Just Chardonnay, love. That OK?'

'Em, maybe—'

He came a bit closer. 'To be honest, it's been open for a while. Not much call for white wine around here. At least a fortnight, I'd say.'

'Thanks for telling me.' I grinned. 'I'd love a glass of Heineken so.'

'Good choice. Comin' up.' He was off again. 'How do you know this place?' I laughed as I settled myself in.

'Real Dublin pub, I used to come here years ago when I hadn't a bean. Not much different now.' She grinned as she wrestled with Pete, trying to get him to play with one of her gloves. He wasn't having any of it, not with all these men around. 'He's a great dog. Bit quiet though, isn't he?'

'I think he's wary around men, to be honest. Wait and see after he's been here for a bit.'

'Well, you've joined the right gang so, Pete,' she told him. 'None of us have had a man in ages.'

He licked her hand as if in agreement but stayed where he was, out of sight, out of harm's way.

My drink arrived, and Maddy drained her glass and ordered another bottle of cider. 'I got the Dart as far as Monkstown and walked up,' she told me. 'So I'm having a couple, but I changed my mind about the gin, it's too early.'

'How did it go?'

'Not bad.' She grinned. 'I've already got a callback for tomorrow to meet the heavy hitters. Today was just an associate producer, a researcher and one of the storyline writers.'

'Great. What's it for?'

'A new TV medical drama.' She beamed. 'You could be looking at the next Meredith Grey or – what's her name? – the gorgeous blonde one?'

'Issy Stephens? I can never remember their real names. Katherine something, I think. Is it really that big a part?' I was delighted for her.

'Well, it could be, but hey, it's prime-time TV, so that means thousands want it.' She shrugged. 'They're casting six main characters and three or four regulars. And they let me read the entire thing, which might just mean they're interested.'

'And what about your current contract?'

'Expires at the end of the year, and unlikely to be renewed, except on a week-to-week basis, if that bitch Charleston continues wielding her axe.' Maddy's worst fears had been realized when 'Porky Pauline' – as we all now referred to her after seeing her photo – had indeed been confirmed as the new series producer. 'Jesus, Christmas is nearly here.' Maddy made a face.

'I'm ignoring it,' I told her.

'Any plans?'

'No. You?' I asked.

'No, there'll be the usual forty-seven for dinner at Mum's house, but I don't think I can be arsed. Remember the drama last year when everyone seemed to have fallen out with at least one other member of the family? It was a nightmare. Add to that the fact that my brother-in-law drinks a bit too much whiskey – as you know; my sister constantly tells me I need to lose weight – as you also know; and you can see why I just might prefer to feed the homeless this year.'

'It's all coming back to me all right.' I laughed, remembering. 'Well, remember mine last year? I think I moaned at you till Easter. I barely had three days off and even then I spent Christmas morning talking down a client who was suicidal. When you work in that business, it's hard to get carried away by it all.' I shook my head remembering. 'It's hell for a lot of people. It just magnifies all their feelings of what's not right in their lives, especially when they're watching what seems like the whole world on a party blitz.'

'Well, how about this year I come to you and we spend it in a caravan?' She suddenly seemed delighted by the notion.

'And walk Pete along the seafront on Christmas morning?' It sounded like heaven to me. 'And eat candyfloss and ride the bumpers on the way back?'

'Will they be open, d'ya think?' She was like a child.

'Are you joking? That big yellow one right at the front – they opened the day of the owner's funeral. His sons said it was what he wanted, but the locals suspected it was more what they wanted because it was a holiday weekend and the town was jammed.'

'Well, I'm on. Will I text Clodagh for a laugh?' Maddy grabbed her phone. 'She'll be horrified. Imagine not having her Kir Royale with caviar nibbles in front of the log fire with Lord and Lady Boyden-Jones, or whatever they're called.' She sent off a quick message and we got into the chat.

'I've news,' said Maddy. 'But first I want all the gossip about being blind in Bray with Mike. Sounds like a movie title, don't you think? *Sleepless in Seattle* just seems so pedestrian now, compared with 'Blind in Bray' and I'd say sex when you can't see might be very erotic.' Her laugh was a dirty cackle.

I filled her in, insisting it was just business.

'Business, my arse,' she decided, almost before I'd finished. 'He meets you late at night for a walk and a drink. Way too cosy. If he was only interested in you professionally, he'd have made an appointment like everybody else. Did you charge him?'

'I did not. He wanted to see Pete as well, if you must know.'

'A likely story. Sure you've already told me Pete is in your office every day. So come on, tell Aunty Maddy. Do you fancy him?'

'No, I do not,' I insisted.

'Even a teensy-weensy bit?'

'I dunno, I don't know what to make of him really, to be honest.'

'Ah ha, I knew it.' She pounced.

'Don't go jumping to conclusions,' I begged her. 'It's just that I've never met anyone quite like him before. He seems so comfortable in his own skin. What I mean is, he's straight yet he lives with a gay guy – most men would run a mile. He loves animals, and he's not afraid to be silly around them. He's head of a major international company yet he dresses like the post boy, and he's so laidback he's almost horizontal.'

'And you threw up on him and he still talks to you,' Maddy added.

'Give over, even for you you've milked that one to death.' I poked her. 'He's always telling me I'm mad, by the way, which he thinks is an insult. I keep trying not to smile with delight.'

'You have changed, Lou, that's for sure. You're pretty horizontal yourself these days. I like it.'

'So do I. The greyness has disappeared from my life.' We spent a few minutes discussing my clients and how looking at their lives was making me realize I needed to confront my own issues with my mother. It was nothing she hadn't heard before, although she said that maybe now the time was right for me.

'Any mention of dinner, another drink, a Sunday stroll with the dog, even?' she asked then, referring to Mike.

'No, and it won't happen. We're too – I dunno what the word is really – pally, I suppose. He sends me funny texts, but I don't see him wanting to snog me. Sure didn't he resist me that famous night, despite all my efforts to get my leg over?' I was finally able to laugh at myself, maybe because now that I knew him better, I realized it was just another thing he'd taken in his stride. 'Actually, I envy him in a way. He has life sussed.'

'No more than yourself.' She signalled for another bottle, but I shook my head.

'Ah, but I'm not nearly as successful as he is, that's the big difference. It's easy to change your life from where I'm standing. But he manages to work in the corporate sector, play the games, earn big bucks and not give a shit, really.'

'Cool or what?' Maddy was impressed.

'So what's your news?'

'Well, it's not major or anything, but a bit of progress has been made on the Ronan O'Meara front.'

'Tell me.' I was intrigued.

'Nothing much, as I said. But his sister Ellen rang me the other day and suggested lunch. We went out to that nice little fish place, Cavistons in Glasthule. And who strolled in at the end of it but Ronan.' I could tell she was pleased.

'And?'

'And he said he'd been shopping next door, which, in fairness, he had. Claimed he spotted us in the window. Anyway, he joined us for coffee and he was very nice. Insisted on paying our bill too, which made him extra nice. Do you think he's good-looking?' I knew she was keen.

I thought for a moment. 'Yes, I do. At first I thought he was a bit anal, I suppose.' I remembered the first night he'd appeared at my class, wearing a pinstripe suit and that ridiculous tie. 'But once he loosens up he's nice.' It was an honest opinion.

'He seems a bit lost, I always think. Do you know any more about him?' she asked.

I felt uncomfortable, but given his outburst in the pub that night, I really couldn't risk even giving her a hint. Besides, I never discussed my clients anyway, it was just that I couldn't help feeling Maddy was exactly what he needed in his life right now, and knowing she liked him made it harder.

'It's OK – sorry, I shouldn't have asked,' she said quickly, which was unusually intuitive for her. Normally she'd pester you for info.

'I know he really has had a tough time these past few years. And I think you'd make a great couple, so I'll help in any way I can,' I told her. 'Maybe I should invite all my new clients for Christmas drinks in the office, and you and Clodagh could be my staff for the night?'

'Less of the work, more of the party talk, please.' She thought it was a great idea. 'Aren't we lucky though? Clodagh with her new job, you with your new everything and me with a bit of romance and a possible starring role on TV. It's going to be a good New Year, I can feel it.'

23

AFTER AN INITIAL BOUT OF PANIC, I DECIDED TO GO FOR THE party, so I sent out invitations to all my clients – the animals. There were a few rules to be adhered to upon acceptance. These included:

Pets must wear a Christmas collar

Owners must bring a doggie Chris Kindle (max. €20)

Everyone to bring a favourite Christmas song on CD (non-returnable)

Be prepared for mistletoe traps in unusual places

Spin the Bottle in operation – participation a must – no human tongues!

Most of the rules came from Maddy, who set about organizing the thing with the enthusiasm of Jamie Oliver in a school kitchen. This was because she was full of nervous energy. Despite three auditions, she still hadn't heard back from the producers of the new medical drama, and one of the researchers had told her off the record that she was being considered for one of the leads.

'Oh God, Lou, this could be it,' she told me and Clodagh over and over again. 'What will I do if I don't get it?'

Her not getting it didn't bear thinking about, and I pulled

out all my novenas to St Anthony and prayed like mad. I even enlisted the help of my mother, who apparently had a relic of him, which was more of a surprise to me than anyone else.

The day before the party was a nightmare. We set up a huge marquee downstairs in the courtyard for the pets. Maddy used all her TV contacts in the props department, and the result was fake grass, loads of plastic trees, kennels with no backs – nothing on TV has a back – and masses of toys. We even managed to cordon off a few areas in case of troublemakers, and Maddy persuaded four of the regular extras on her show to be dog handlers for the evening and another four to be waiters – by assuring them that there would be loads of 'media moguls' (she meant Mike) talent-spotting at the event. Clodagh got T-shirts printed with **IF YOUR DOG THINKS YOU'RE FABULOUS, DON'T SEEK A SECOND OPINION** printed on the front and **COCKING OF LEGS ALLOWED, ANYTHING ELSE TO DO WITH COCKS BY PERMISSION ONLY!** on the back. I nearly had to resuscitate Mary when she saw them.

'Is it not . . . like . . . totally unprofessional?' she whispered to me.

'Probably, but how many professional people do you know who would have a Christmas bash for dogs?' I wondered.

'I suppose,' she mumbled, but eventually she got caught up in the whole thing and almost rendered us speechless on the day, when she disappeared into the ladies' and emerged wearing a red velvet dress with silver snowflakes glittering all over it – very short – with white fur trim on the hem and sleeves. White patent, over-the-knee boots and a Santa hat completed the picture. Rumour had it (according to Maddy) that she had red crotchless knickers on underneath.

Pete, courtesy of Maddy, was wearing a red scarf with white pom-poms and looked delighted to be part of it all. He kept going up to everyone as if to say 'Look at me, aren't I gorgeous?' To which the only reply was a rub or a treat and, from where I was standing, he was getting loads of both. It was those eyes again.

Upstairs, I was surprised to discover that my very large office was in fact only half a room and could be doubled in size thanks to a clever partition which I hadn't even known existed. Thankfully, the other half was vacant, so within two hours we had transformed the place with trees, garlands, holly, berries and masses of mistletoe, all of which were fake but fabulously lush. Maddy went around spraying everything with something suspiciously labelled 'Christmas in a Bottle', which sounded dire but actually worked a treat and filled the room with the scent of cinnamon and cloves.

We had lots of party food, provided at cost by our next-door neighbours, a catering company who I'd never even noticed. Mary worked her magic on them and offered to give out their business cards to our 'dozens of celebrity clients' in return for their services.

We'd invited people from my first, disastrous class, others who'd made enquiries on our website or dropped in for a leaflet and of course all our regulars. And when I looked around shortly after the appointed time, it seemed as if everyone had come. It was complete chaos, as excited dogs said hello by sniffing bottoms, and Petra the parrot – a new client whose owner (a sweet old lady) had contacted me because he kept saying 'Fuck you, asshole' to everyone he met – sat on all the men's shoulders and kept kissing them. The only real problem was Rover the cat, who Emily insisted on leaving with the dogs and who very nearly ended up as dinner after meeting Selina – a Staffordshire Bull Terrier, and not tolerating any cats today, apparently. Unfortunately, Selina's owner, a young guy covered in tattoos and piercings, was tucking into the beer and checking out the talent and not really interested, Maddy reckoned, until she marched him downstairs with his pet and managed to secure them both in one of the cordoned-off areas with a beer and a babe for company. Rover, though, had to be consigned to his travelling crate after that, because one or two of the dogs, including Bartholomew, were eyeing him up – for savaging, Clodagh reckoned, as she made the suggestion discreetly to Emily.

Maddy's mum, Connie, had come and I was thrilled. I always felt she'd been more of a mother to me than Martha, so I hugged her and dragged her into a corner for a catch-up.

The only slight problem I had was finding enough time to mingle, as all of my regulars seemed to want to up-date me on their lives, which wasn't part of my plan for the evening.

Denis declared himself 'pleased as Punch' that Father Vincent had said he'd be visiting Joan Lehane before Christmas, and promised to convey the message that Dinny would very much like to make contact. He was further de-lighted that apparently Bart had been so traumatized by

Pete's arrival that he'd been 'good as gold' since he'd 'seen him off the premises'.

I headed off, still smiling, to talk to Ronan O'Meara and Myrtle.

'Top marks, Lulu, this is wonderful.' Myrtle hugged me.

'Yes, it's a fun idea,' Ronan added, then Maddy joined us and Myrtle winked at me and pointed to the two of them behind his back.

'Presents coming up,' she announced, and I saw her give Ronan a warm grin just as Mary announced she was about to begin pulling names from a hat. Each person called had to pick a present and kiss the person who'd bought it. I introduced Myrtle to Denis Cassidy, who looked a bit lost, then added Julia to the mix in order to free up Emily and, when I left, the three oldies were chatting happily.

'Lulu,' Ronan said quietly, staring at his gran. 'I was just wondering if we might have a chat about—'

'I've made a New Year's resolution,' Emily cut in, not having heard him.

'Not a bit early?' I smiled, and looked at Ronan apologetically.

'I've found an address for my real mother and I've decided to just turn up at her door and introduce myself,' she told us both. I decided I needed a drink before I tackled this one.

As it transpired, I didn't have to deal with it straightaway because, right at that moment, Louis came up behind me, pinched my bum and said, 'Guess who?', which sounded odd until I turned around and discovered it was actually Santa who'd groped me.

'Santa, you really are a dirty old man.' I laughed delightedly as he grabbed me in a bear-hug. It was a brilliant costume, complete with padded tummy, full wig and beard. 'But do I know you?'

'You do now.' He grinned as Mike and Pedro joined him.

'Jesus, it's like a zoo down there, I need a drink,' Mike announced. 'There's teeth and testosterone in equal measure, I reckon. And the smell of farting is something else. Great idea, Lulu. It's been a while since I've been humped by a bitch in a pink tutu on arrival at a party.'

'Shall I take him downstairs?' A volunteer came to the rescue. 'I've a very nice Pekinese called Tootsie who'd love to meet him.'

'I've already tried, and I think Tootsie might just be missing an ear, if she's the one in the red ballerina skirt?'

'Ah, but I bet you haven't brought him to visit the fresh-meat-treat press first though?'

'He's all yours.' Mike handed Pedro over so fast Louis didn't have a chance to object. 'Drink?' he asked Louis and me, just as Mary came and persuaded Santa to join her in distributing the goodies.

'I'll come with you, and don't dare abandon me,' I told Mike. 'I've been trying to get to the bar for at least an hour, but some client or other keeps nabbing me along the way.'

'There must be a lot of bad dogs out there so?' he enquired.

'Are you mad? The dogs are all having a great time, it's the owners who need counselling.' I laughed. 'It must be my face, what do you think? Do I look like a soft touch?'

'No, you have a "Don't mess with me" look on you most

days. Still enjoying your bohemian lifestyle?' he wanted to know.

'You bet, and that's only because, when it comes down to it, I don't have to get involved at all if I don't want to, so I just say what I think most of the time, not what I think they want to hear. Does that make sense?'

He handed me a glass of white wine without asking. 'About as much as the theory of relativity.' He made a face. 'Thankfully, I've had a lot of practice with complicated people, living with a gay Santa, and if you throw into the mix a mutt who thinks he's royalty, you won't be surprised to hear that most of it rolls off me.'

'How's that going?'

'Stop working, you're off duty.' He slapped my wrist. 'Actually, not too bad, we're making progress, mainly because I've buttoned my lip. That's all I'll say until I'm paying you to listen.'

'Hi.' Clodagh joined us with a good-looking guy in tow, and Mike greeted her warmly. 'This is Joe Quinn.' She smiled at him. 'His mother, Mabel, is a new client of yours, so he wanted to say hello,' she told us both.

'Ah, Clint the Cocker Spaniel.' I only remembered my new clients' names by their pets. I decided to ignore Mike, who almost choked.

'Hello, and thank you, you've made such a difference,' he said. 'I can now get in the door of my mother's house with-out losing blood.' The music started, and Clodagh dragged him off.

'Clint?' Mike looked constipated. 'Where do they get them? Owner a fan of Westerns, I presume?'

'No. Mabel is a big country-music fan. Clint Black?' I explained as he raised his eyebrows. 'She met her latest husband line-dancing to one of his hits.'

'Latest husband?'

'Third,' I told him.

'You gotta be kidding me – that guy is no spring chicken, his mother must be ancient.'

'No, swear.' I made the sign of the cross on my throat the way we all did as kids when we were lying through our teeth.

He shook his head. 'There's a word for you, I just can't think of it right now.' At that moment, Mary killed the music and the present-giving commenced. I got a year's subscription to DoggyScopes, a horoscope hotline for pets to tell what the future had in store for them. It had been bought by Louis. I should have guessed. I thanked him with a smacker on his hairy face, and he laughed delightedly. 'Wait till you hear it, it's insane – American, of course,' he told me. 'I just couldn't resist it, and I'm so glad you got it, you'll appreciate it.'

'There's actually no reply to that,' Mike informed us. 'You two should get together, you're made for each other.'

Just as people were beginning to talk, reluctantly, about leaving, Doug Stewart appeared, and I was absolutely thrilled because I'd doubted he'd turn up but I'd left him a message anyway, trying to encourage him. I was even more delighted to see he still had Growler in tow.

'He's going next week,' was the first thing he told me, dashing my hopes. 'That ad of yours was a great idea. I had eight replies. A young couple want him as a Christmas present for their nine-year-old son, so I've agreed to keep him until Christmas Eve.'

I introduced him to Mabel, whose son was still keeping Clodagh company. I also noticed Ronan and Maddy laughing in a corner, so I decided the night had been a definite success.

When I went down to check on the mutts and other assorted creatures, it was bedlam but everyone there was having a great time. Animals had that effect on people. There seemed to be no aggro whatsoever, although the smell made me wrinkle my nose.

'Dead mouse meets baby puke is what the minders have decided,' Mike said as I almost collided with him. 'Although that very attractive one over there assures me you don't notice it at all after a while.' He winked.

'I'd say, snuggled up to Melissa, you wouldn't all right.' I laughed. She was about eighteen, blonde and very sexy. 'Were you planning on getting up close and personal yourself?'

'Nah, too much trouble explaining to them what life was like before mobile phones and decimalization,' he told me. 'And if I have to trawl through another Bebo page with a girl and laugh hilariously at three hundred photos of her mates drinking stuff with umbrellas, I'll take one too many tablets.'

'Serves you right for being in the music industry. Sure no one in a record company is over twenty-five.'

'True. Sad but true, I'm afraid,' he agreed, just as Louis joined us. 'Which is why I'm such a novelty at thirty-five.'

Louis fanned himself. 'I've just been kissed under the

221

mistletoe by the most divine reindeer. If he's male, I want him.' Mike and I burst out laughing. The food helpers and waiters, once they'd finished serving, had all put on Christmas costumes, so we had two reindeers, a couple of snowmen and an angel.

'Which one?' I asked, and Louis pointed to his left.

'Yes, definitely male, I recognize him,' I told a delighted Louis, who threw the mistletoe at Mike and headed off.

'You've just sent my flatmate off to grope that animal, and you haven't a clue whether it's even a human being – never mind a male – have you?' Mike pretended to be shocked.

'Not an iota.' I grinned just as Dinny came upon us.

'What're you doing with that mistletoe in your hand and a gorgeous woman standing next to you?' He gave Mike – who was just about to take a slug from his beer – such a slap that I heard his teeth smash against the glass. 'Would ye give her a kiss, for God's sake, and then pass it to me so that I can have a go. I've kissed a dozen women so far tonight, and I don't intend to stop until I'm black and blue.'

'I'd better do as I'm told, that man is dangerous.' Mike held the mistletoe over my head and leaned in and, at that point, somebody pushed against me – there was a chain gang going around the place singing 'Jingle Bells', so I guessed it was one of them – so that instead of offering him my cheek, I ended up kissing him full on the lips. It was just the lightest brush really, but it made my lips tingle, so I jumped back as if I'd been given an electric shock.

'Nice.' He winked at me, but before I had a chance to process what had happened, Dinny was in front of my nose. 'For God's sake, what are you, man or mouse? That wasn't a gooser at all,' he told Mike, depositing a big wet smacker on my lips, then swinging me around. 'That's how to kiss a woman,' he announced, but by the time he'd put me down I had my back to Mike, who'd been nabbed by Melissa and dragged into the conga train. 'Now, where's that fit-looking pensioner I saw earlier? I'd say she'd be game for a laugh.' He disappeared into the crowd, and I was left, standing there licking my still-tingling lips, wondering what had happened with Mike and why I suddenly felt differently about him. I glanced over to where he was: kicking to the left then kicking to the right, and by now wearing a ridiculous set of antlers as he clutched Melissa's waist. He looked completely chilled, as usual.

24

SUDDENLY, IT WAS CHRISTMAS EVE, AND THE USUAL MADNESS ensued. I was in the office, trying to catch up on last-minute bits. I'd bought some brilliant pet cards online, as well as a selection of trinkets, and I'd sent them in the post to all my regulars, but I had three new clients, so these last ones were being couriered. Mary, who'd loosened up even more since the party, had volunteered her services too, which was extremely nice of her, given that most people would rather be anywhere else in the world except the office on this day. Still, I was eating my way through a casket of Milk Tray – courtesy of a boxer called Charlie – and feeling no pressure at all. There were no clients crying and telling me how much they dreaded this time of year, and no suicidal ones for me to be seriously concerned about. Sending out yoyos to Yorkies was the height of my stress, and I was loving it.

'I keep forgetting to ask where you're spending to-morrow?' Mary waltzed in with two steaming cups of hot chocolate, which came with a dash of rum and a truffle each, courtesy of our catering friends, who'd had three new clients since our party, one of whom was Louis.

'In the van,' I told her excitedly. 'Maddy's coming, and so is Clodagh, which is quite unbelievable given that her folks are entertaining every night for a week and normally insist on her presence. And what's more, I ordered the turkey and ham from our local butcher, who's promised to have everything ready to go in the oven, including homemade stuffing and giblets for gravy. He's even given me the loan of a large pot for the ham. Can you believe it?'

'No,' she said dryly. 'In our local supermarket they give you a number and you queue up, and when you get it it's wrapped, so you don't even get a look. To order all you do is write down the weight and your details at the customer-service desk.' I knew Mary was spending the day with her elderly parents and an aunt and uncle, so I guessed she wasn't really in the mood to hear me banging on about how our local fruit and veg shop offered to peel and bag the sprouts, sold homemade cranberry sauce and even had all the ingredients for a winter fruit trifle – including the cream and custard – in a cute parcel with the recipe attached. Maura, the owner, told me that, last year, she and her daughter had been up until 4 a.m. getting them ready, but that Bray was full of younger couples who couldn't cook and hadn't the time or the interest anyway, so they loved all her ideas and were happy to pay a bit extra – even in these tough times – to impress their families and friends. I overheard one elderly customer the previous Saturday saying that she'd rather not pay her gas bill than deny herself Maura's treats, a comment that made me realize how lucky I was not to have any worries in that department.

I decided that now was the right moment to make Mary

feel needed. 'Well, here's a little something to use when you get an hour to yourself. It's just to say thank you for being the best front-of-house person a dog could ever hope to bark at.' I handed her a homemade Christmas box filled with luxuries for the bath and complete with a snipe of champagne. She was so happy, she hugged me with tears in her eyes, then produced a doggie Christmas stocking full of edible treats for Pete, who came out from under my desk to receive it and thumped his tail enthusiastically.

There was a knock on the door just then, and it was the courier, come to collect my packages, so there was a bit of a mad scramble for a minute or two and I didn't notice a second delivery of flowers, a big red-and-white hand-tied bouquet with the most amazing red amaryllis and incredibly scented white hyacinths, which all turned out to be in little pots in a box so they'd last for ages – and even come back again next year, the delivery woman told me proudly. I replied that she was completely overestimating my skills as a gardener, but I was thrilled.

The card said, 'Thank you for ensuring that no one gets murdered in our house this Christmas, love Pedro.' There were paw marks all over it and it had all the style of a Louis gift, I decided, until I saw a further line in the bottom-left-hand corner. It said: 'PS You're a great kisser!'

I was still smiling a few minutes later when Doug Stewart appeared at the door clutching a bottle.

'I wasn't expecting to find you in; I just wanted to leave this for you to say thanks.'

'Doug, come in.' I was delighted to see him. Just then I noticed Growler and realized that today was their last day together. 'And there's no need to thank me at all. I'm just sorry you and Growler are parting ways.'

'We're not – the bottle's from him.' He grinned and patted the dog's head. 'After talking to you at the party and seeing all the dogs and their owners, I realized that he was all the family I've got, so I found the couple another rescue dog.'

I was so happy I hugged him for a full minute. 'You have just made my Christmas,' I told him, and insisted we open the wine to celebrate.

That night, Maddy teased me endlessly about the flowers, but she didn't have a leg to stand on really, because Ronan O'Meara had asked her out at last and they'd arranged to meet early in the New Year for a walk and tea in that lovely coffee shop I'd visited with Myrtle. 'So shut up unless you can take it right back,' I warned, as she launched into some crappy Christmas love song for the tenth time and made kissing noises to the flowers.

We had Chinese takeaway and mulled wine – not a combination I'd be recommending any day soon, but Maddy had insisted – in front of the fire, while we watched *The Sound of Music* and looked forward to the big day. We were meeting Clodagh – who'd been forced at gunpoint to spend the evening with her folks – for ten o'clock mass in the town, so we headed to bed early 'in case Santa is hovering overhead', Maddy told Pete.

The dog slept at my feet, as he always did, although tonight he had a brand-new, ultra-luxurious fake-fur bed with paw prints on it, courtesy of Emily, and a musical hot-water bottle that played Christmas tunes, bought by Imelda, another new client. He was unusually excited tonight, maybe because Maddy kept leaping out of her bed and winding the music up again every time it stopped so that she could hear 'Santa Claus Is Coming To Town' one more time through the wall. I was nearly asleep five times over, so I eventually locked her out and drifted off saying a prayer of thanks for the way my life had turned around and asking for a happy and healthy new year for all my loved ones.

The day dawned crisp and sunny. Maddy gave me tea and a Buck's Fizz in bed. I knocked over the glass as I threw back the duvet – one of the perils of a small bedroom – which meant that Pete had his first taste of champagne. He loved it, if his furious licks were anything to go by, and when I got to the kitchen the fire was on, the television was blaring and Maddy was peeling spuds and quaffing bubbles.

'Can we do presents now?' I'd been feeling up the parcels the night before and was dying to ransack the pile.

'No, we have to wait till Clodagh is here.' She slapped me. 'How old d'ya think you are, seven?'

'I know, I know.' I almost wanted to stamp my feet. 'It's just that everything seems magnified and much more exciting because we're waking up on Christmas morning in a caravan. It feels like we're on holiday.'

'We are! But you're right, it does feel like the best fun, like we're camping out or having a Famous Five-type adventure or something. Anyway' – she handed me a knife – 'help me with these, that'll cure you.' We sang and whistled and got everything ready, even down to laying the table and putting hats and crackers on plates, and I made a little doggie table for Pete, complete with his new Christmas bowl, courtesy of Dinny.

Maddy drove to mass so that we could leave Pete in the car then head straight for the prom. I'd dressed in a red coat – I was still living off Bronwyn – and I'd bought a matching hat, gloves, and a scarf with pom-poms, which Maddy declared 'ridiculous', but I noticed she was wearing a black felt coat with a giant reindeer embroidered on the back. Combined with stretchy jeans, a gorgeous T-shirt and high black patent boots, she looked young and happy and carefree, and I wondered if Ronan O'Meara had anything to do with it.

Clodagh was waiting for us outside the church. She'd been for a run and looked positively radiant, her hair in a ponytail and wearing a stunning purple jacket and blue jeans. 'I changed in the car.' She laughed. 'Thought you'd disown me if I turned up in trainers.'

We sang all the hymns loudly and I was surprised that I knew quite a few people outside. Maddy declared me a true Dulchie, a Dublin person who'd become a culchie – which is how country people were known in the capital.

We had a long walk, which Pete adored, principally because there was so little traffic. We let him off the lead most of the time, and he bounded about the place sniffing every hole in sight, hoping to come upon a Christmas bunny, I suspected. Maddy and I were knackered after forty minutes, whereas Clodagh hadn't even gotten into her stride, but eventually we won, after I screamed 'Enough,' and so we headed for one of the amusement places, which was definitely open and populated mainly by young adults – on their way home, Maddy decided, because they were all way too raucous for morning time and the smell of alcohol nearly knocked us out. Anyway, we had a great time eating candyfloss Barbie would have been proud of and crunching through toffee apples with concrete coats. Pete watched patiently from the sidelines and made no attempt to join in, ducking and cowering deeper in his corner as the chairoplanes swooped or the bumper cars crashed while the three of us waved madly and called out 'Good boy' a hundred times, just to make him feel part of it.

Clodagh thought the van looked amazing. Maddy had bought two hundred white icicle lights for the deck, and they twinkled madly as we approached, made even more magical because the earlier sunshine had faded and the light was dropping fast. She'd even draped a nearby conifer tree and, given that it was the only source of light around the neighbourhood, Clodagh decided it was 'the dog's bollocks', and Pete agreed, it seemed, as he meandered up and down the laneway and urged us on.

Once inside we uncorked the champagne and checked on the turkey, which we'd decided to cook really slowly while we were out.

Clodagh added her presents to the pile under the tree as Maddy shouted, 'OK, let's have a toast. What shall we drink to?'

'Romance,' Clodagh said immediately, and we all knew that had to do with Joe Quinn, whom she'd introduced us to at the party and who had asked her if she'd go out for dinner once he returned from a ski trip to Italy.

'I might have a bit of that myself, you never know.' Maddy gave a dirty laugh.

'I'd say you might whether you want to or not if Myrtle has her way.' We'd discussed it the previous evening.

'Anyway, the thing is, I might not have time for luuuuvvvv, darlings, because I have news.' She made a fanfare sound. 'You are looking at Sara Jane Heath, junior doctor at St Anthony's and about to take the TV world by storm.' She waited while we took it in.

'Sorry?' Both Clodagh and I said together, then I got there first. 'What? You got it? When? How? Jesus Christ, why didn't you tell me?'

'They only finally nailed it the day before yesterday as the team broke for the holidays.' She laughed at our faces. 'I was dying to tell you but I decided to wait. I mean, what could be more perfect? The three of us together, sharing Christmas, each one of us with a life heading in a new direction. I mean, look at us: new jobs, a new home for you, Lou, and maybe even for me – wait till you hear what they're offering to buy me out for the next three years – and new men in all our lives.' She nudged me. 'And don't bother denying it. I saw you looking at him in a funny way the night of the party.'

I blushed, because I knew they'd drag the kiss story out of me eventually. As it was, I couldn't believe neither of them had copped it on the card.

'My God, Maddy, this is big.' Clodagh danced her round the room and I did the same to a delighted Pete. 'You've finally got the break you deserve. I am so thrilled for you.' And with that she burst into happy tears.

'What did your family say?'

'What did Porky Pauline do?'

The questions came thick and fast.

'No one knows, although I can't wait to see that cow's face when she realizes she can't dangle a manky ten-week contract – *maximum* ten weeks, by the way, maybe even week to week if she really hates me – over me any longer. That's my first task after New Year, and I'm dying for it. Anyway, I wanted my two best friends to be the first to know.' She grinned. 'I'll let my gang in on it tomorrow.'

'God, it's huge. You'll be a proper celebrity.' I hugged her again.

'And that fucking grotty hairnet can finally be burned.' She whooped.

'We'll be invited everywhere,' Clodagh said. 'I might even get to meet Ryan Tubridy.' He was one of her TV idols, and she lived in hope.

The next half-hour was absolute bedlam, so much so that the turkey was done and we hadn't even put in the roasties, so we wrapped it in foil and each took a job while we drank and laughed and caught up.

'So, what's happening with Mike?' Maddy slipped in as she made the gravy. The champagne had loosened my tongue, so it all came tumbling out, and I showed them the card that had come with the flowers. There were whoops and whistles and shouts of 'I told you so,' and 'You owe me a tenner,' as they slapped hands in the air and teased me like mad.

'OK, calm down,' Clodagh said eventually, 'and let's recap. We know that Maddy and Ronan have a date lined up—'

'And Myrtle made me a Christmas pudding, so I'm in, I reckon,' said Maddy, and we all cheered at that.

'And Joe Quinn texted me last night after twelve to say he was thinking of me.' Another round of whoops greeted that. 'So what exactly is the state of play with you and Mike, Lulu?'

'Listen, telling her she's a great kisser is not a bad start,' Maddy said firmly. 'I haven't even gotten that far myself.'

'Really?' Neither of us could believe it. Maddy was not one to waste time.

'Well, there aren't many opportunities to snog in full public view, usually with his granny beside you.' She laughed.

'I've nothing else to add,' I told them. 'I sent a text to say thanks for the present to both of them, and Louis rang to say it had all been Mike's idea and that he had gone to New York that day to spend the holiday with his folks. Then he invited me – and you two, by the way – to his New Year bash on 2 January, so I guess I'll just have to wait and see what happens.'

'Will Mike be back?'

'He'd better be,' I laughed. 'I'd like him there.' I only realized it as I said it.

'Bound to be, I'd say he wouldn't miss it. And we'll be right there with you anyway, babe,' Maddy said. 'I can't wait.'

'Me neither, I have great hopes for you two.' Clodagh threw in her tuppence worth.

It was almost five when we finally sat down, but everything tasted delicious, or maybe we were just starving.

'I keep forgetting to ask you, Lou,' Clodagh said. 'What about Becky, where is she spending the day?'

'With Mum in San Diego. Seemingly, she was missing her girls and her husband offered to buy tickets for both of us. I said no, sure she barely knows I've moved house even.'

'Well, you're coming home with me tomorrow, that'll make you appreciate yours, I reckon.' Maddy grimaced. 'You're invited, too, Clodagh, you know that.'

'Yes, sorry, I should have let you know, I'm being dragged to the races by Mum and Dad, along with about a dozen of the world's most boring members of the Rich List. I only said yes because they still haven't forgiven me for not going home today.'

My phone rang just then, and to my amazement it was Mum. I didn't even know she knew my mobile number; normally, the odd email was all I got. Anyway, she told me how much she missed me, said she couldn't believe I hadn't come to see her and that I was spending Christmas in a caravan, then promptly burst into tears. I assured her that I was fine, and Maddy and Clodagh both blew kisses back at her all the way to the USA and agreed with her that Barack Obama was probably the messiah.

She'd been dipping into more than the cooking sherry, Maddy reckoned, and we turned off all phones then and toasted what was shaping up to be a great day and a New Year that looked rosy on all fronts.

25

THE NEXT DAY WAS HAPPY BEDLAM WITH MADDY'S GANG, and I spent most of the day helping her mum and trying to persuade her to chill. Compared to my family, Maddy's were a cross between the Waltons and the Brady Bunch, and they constantly got involved in each other's lives without being asked, said whatever they liked and yet you just knew they'd always be friends. Because they'd known me practically all my life, they embraced me as one of their own, and just spending time with them always cheered me up. This year they wanted to know everything about the changes I'd made, and I got hugged and kissed more than usual as they all congratulated me and wished me well. They'd even bought me a 'mobile-warming' present of a pair of old-fashioned deckchairs, because Maddy told them being at my new place was just like being at the seaside.

Connie hugged me loads and told me how much she loved me, which she did often, and because it was such a contrast to my own mum, it never failed to make me gulp. And this year it hit home even more than before, and I resolved once again to talk to my own mother as soon as I could.

When Maddy finally dropped us off the following

afternoon I knew I'd miss their warmth, but I was ready for the simple life once more. I spent the next few days catching up on paperwork, giving the van a good clean and indulging Pete with two-hour treks in remote parts of County Wicklow, where there were plenty of new smells and lots of nasty stuff to roll in.

Becky and I had planned to spend New Year's Eve together, but our small family reunion never happened, simply because she forgot and made other plans and, for once, I hadn't bothered to nail it down. I was disappointed although not surprised; it was just that, this year, I really wanted to show her my new life and talk openly for once. For the first time, I realized that I hated having a sister I didn't really know. However, not sharing our lives bothered me but not her, or so it seemed.

When Maddy heard she dragged me off to a 'luvvie' party, and we had a great time, and Ronan texted both of us around midnight so she was happy. Clodagh had an unexpected date with Joe, who'd come back early from his ski trip because there was no snow. She rang us at midnight, so all was well with the world.

Between us, we'd made a ton of resolutions. Maddy wanted to 'Become a star and get laid'; Clodagh was slightly more modest, declaring her number-one ambition was to start her own business, with 'Find a nice man' a close second; while I didn't want anything really, except maybe to see where my friendship with Mike took me, but I was trying to be philosophical about it and it seemed to be working. I felt no pressure, although I was hoping he'd be at the party.

I did absolutely nothing next day; it had been my first big

drinking session the night before since the 'puke party', as the girls called it, so I was a bit tender, even though I'd been reasonably careful. As I settled in that evening, Pete started barking for no reason and kept trying to get out. I didn't let him go just in case it was teenagers with fireworks, which had been happening a bit since Halloween two months earlier, and he eventually settled down, but I noticed he cocked his ears at the slightest sound.

'You're a great watchdog.' I felt a bit nervous as I got ready for bed, so I double-checked that all doors and windows were locked. Still, I fell asleep in an instant and didn't stir until the alarm beeped – so not that nervous, obviously.

Next day it was back to work but, for the first time ever, I wasn't dreading it, in fact I was in great form as I strapped Pete on the bike and headed off. There were lots of moans and groans in the corridors that morning, although everyone cheered up when they saw Pete, wearing his shades on his doggie sun visor – Maddy's Christmas present – an instant smile-maker which helped combat those first-day-back blues which everyone, except me and Mary, seemed weighed down with.

'If I take one more trip down Memory Lane with my uncle Dan or eat one more slice of Aunty Eileen's pudding, I'll scream,' she told me the minute I saw her. 'Am I the only one who's happy it's all over?'

'Not if my previous life is anything to go by,' I assured her. 'Why do you think the Samaritans are at their busiest this time of year? All that enforced closeness and good cheer makes a lot of people feel the way you do.'

'Thank God for that.' She laughed, and we chatted a bit more, until I got a call from Louis, who was simply checking that I hadn't forgotten his big night.

I assured him I was looking forward to it, then enquired if there was anything I could bring.

'No, nothing, darling. Those fabulous caterers of yours are delivering everything – plates, glasses, the lot. And Mike's just phoned. He's on the way from the airport, and his office arranged a car for him, so he's going to stop at the off licence and collect whatever we need, which is not much. I got masses of wine as presents this year, so it's really only water and mixers. The caterers are even supplying a few kegs of beer and a couple of barmen, so I'm sorted. Oh, I do adore parties.' He sighed happily and I agreed with him, delighted to hear about Mike.

I had only two of my newer clients that day, so I went out and treated myself to a blow dry then headed home early to get ready.

The girls and I met in O'Brien's pub in Leeson Street, an old haunt of mine, which had always been trendy. Most of Dublin, it appeared, was on holiday until the following Monday, so the place was buzzing with movers and shakers who were not dressed for work.

In the end, by the time we'd beaten our way to the bar, we'd only time for one drink so we headed out into the cold January air and strolled up the canal.

'I want you to see the house from the back first,' I told them.

'This had better be good, I'm wearing new shoes and

they're pinching already,' Maddy told me, reaching down and stuffing a tissue against her heel.

'Well, you tell me. There it is.' They both looked up and gasped.

'Oh my God, that is seriously gorgeous.' Clodagh was impressed.

'Does Mike own it as well?' Maddy cut to the chase.

'No, I told you, he only shares. He's been looking for one close by though. The area's become really trendy lately, and it's within walking distance of town too, which helps.' I'd been dying to see it from this side of the canal and, in the dark, with lights and candles and lots of people moving around, it looked surreal. For a moment you didn't see the glass, because there were no obvious glazing bars, and it looked as if someone had removed the walls and you were looking straight in.

'It's magical, isn't it?'

'Sure is,' they agreed, and because of the cold we didn't linger, simply walked quickly to the nearby bridge, crossed over and doubled back to approach the house from the front. A stranger opened the door and ushered us in, and it was clear the party was in full swing.

'Lulu, darling, you look divine.' Louis swooped. 'And Maddy and Clodagh, welcome. Let me take your coats.' Within seconds we were in the middle of it all, but the first thing I heard was Pedro growling at a man who'd come in behind us.

'Is it only men he reacts badly to?' I asked Louis.

'Now that you mention it, it does seem to be mainly men.'

'Any improvement since you started the new regime?' I wondered.

'There was, but then I left them alone and suddenly Pedro is back as king of the castle.' Mike appeared and smiled at us.

Without even thinking about it, I went into work mode. I made a signal at Pedro and kept walking towards him until he'd backed himself into a corner in the hall. Using a command, I made him drop, then stayed with my back to him, talking to the others. He made one more attempt to get by me but I used the same signal and he dropped again, and this time he stayed put.

'Impressive.' Mike winked at me, and I hated it that I went red. I'd forgotten him for a second when I saw Pedro's aggression, because I immediately knew Louis hadn't really made an effort.

'Louis, we need to talk,' I told him and was instantly sorry. I sounded like a schoolteacher, and I was a guest at his party, after all.

'Be afraid.' Mike nudged Louis. 'I told you she'd get you eventually.'

'Stop it.' I seemed to be forever slapping him, but he was used to me by now so he dodged my hand easily. 'Sorry, Louis,' I said. 'I forget when I'm off duty.'

'No, you're absolutely right,' Louis surprised me by saying. 'And so is Mike. We were making good progress, and then Mike went away and I started treating him like my partner again. Within hours he was the boss, and now he's even growling at me occasionally.' He looked like he thought I was going to give him a lecture. 'Sorry, I'll start again tomorrow, I promise. I really am getting a bit fed up humouring him, to be honest.'

'Wow, Lulu, you're good, I have to hand it to you. I mean, I've always been scared of you, but now you even have Louis grovelling. I reckon you've made it, bigtime,' Mike said, tongue so firmly in his cheek it was practically poking through his jaw.

'Watch it, or I'll be forced to subdue you as well.' I grinned.

'That's me told. Let me get you all a drink.' Mike led the way to the kitchen while Louis took our coats then followed us in.

'Pedro is still there, in the corner,' he marvelled as we walked through the hall.

'Yeah, but let's see what happens when the doorbell rings again,' I warned him. 'It'll take practice and a united approach.'

'Can we talk about something else? And chill, would you, he's a dog – you lot are very sad,' Maddy declared, and pulled a face.

'Sorry, sorry, I'm off duty from now,' I promised. 'Let's start again. Louis, great party.'

'Happy New Year, girls.' Louis plonked several kisses on each of our cheeks and Mike announced he wasn't even going to try and follow that routine, instead handing each of us a glass of champagne and toasting our health.

'I wish the three of you everything you wish for your-selves,' he told us.

'In that case, you might even have a role to play.' Maddy smiled innocently at him while I tried not to choke out loud.

'Sorry?'

'Well, I've just been offered a major TV role, so I reckon it's only a matter of time before I have a hit single.' She winked at me, knowing the effect her words would have had, and I could have strangled her for being so brazen.

'Oh my God, darling, that's amazing, there's a director here you simply must meet. Come with me and, meanwhile, tell me everything while we find him.' Louis was in his element.

'So, how did your Christmas go?' Mike asked as Clodagh was enveloped in a bear-hug by someone she'd described as 'a future client' as soon as she laid eyes on him.

'Great, stayed at home,' I told him.

'You had Christmas in a caravan?'

'A very posh Christmas, I'll have you know. And the girls joined me. And Pete was there too. It was fun.'

'What about your family? Didn't you tell me you'd a sister at least?'

'Becky – don't ask. My mother lives in San Diego, and normally she forgets to ring us even, but this year she decided she missed her babies and her very rich husband offered to fly the two of us over to visit.'

'You didn't go? I'd have been off like a shot.'

I shook my head. 'Wanted to spend it in my new home with my new dog. Becky went; lots of drama apparently. So how about you? Louis said you went away?'

'Yep, my folks moved to New York a few years ago so I try and get over to see them at least twice a year. My sister Eve and her husband had a baby six weeks ago, first grand-child and all that, so they came over from the west coast and it was a big family thing. My other sister Lyndsey flew in from Toronto so it was fun.'

'New York for Christmas can't be bad.'

'No, I love it.' He told me all about it until Louis arrived back and dragged us off to get food. Next time I saw Mike he was deep in conversation with two guys in the other room, and the three of us bopped the rest of the night away with Louis and his latest conquest.

It was after two o'clock when Maddy and I finally jumped into a cab and headed back to the van.

'So, did you make any progress with Mike?' she asked as soon as we were settled.

'No, can't say I did.' I realized I was a bit disappointed. 'He's always the same – teases me, seems to enjoy my company, but it doesn't go anywhere.'

'He kissed you the last night,' she reminded me. 'That went somewhere.'

'But that was only because Denis Cassidy handed him the mistletoe and more or less ordered him to,' I told her.

'And he sent you flowers. And they weren't just your average, order-from-Interflora bunch. They were chosen with care. Did you thank him, even?'

'Forgot,' I admitted. 'But I did text him the day they arrived. Anyway, they were probably chosen by his secretary.' I was on a bit of a downer for some reason. I think I'd been expecting him to flirt a bit with me or something. Instead, he had appeared friendly, but he hadn't made any real effort to corner me for a proper chat. Then he'd simply smiled and waved when the three of us shouted goodbye, and I was annoyed with myself because suddenly it mattered.

26

NEXT MORNING I WAS MY NORMAL SELF AGAIN. IT WAS Saturday, so Maddy and I took Pete for a long walk, then bought a load of goodies and headed back to make pancakes with maple syrup for brunch. As we approached the house the dog started barking, and this time he strained to get off the lead, which he never did.

'He's been acting a bit odd lately, mostly at night,' I told Maddy. 'I wonder if there are strangers around? You know the way sometimes mobile-home parks attract burglars during winter? Guys in Hiace vans trying to see what they can steal easily, because in general no one comes near their holiday home between October and Easter the following year.'

'Lou, this is not your average mobile-home park. There are how many – four – chalets? And each one is well hidden from the other, so you'd have to know about them.'

'I suppose. Yeah, you're right.' I took out my keys and put one in the lock, but it wasn't necessary. 'It's open,' I told Maddy, puzzled.

'Did you lock it?'

'Yes. Well, actually, I don't know, but I think so.'

'OK, just let's check inside.' She went in first, but everything was exactly as we'd left it, even down to her handbag on the kitchen table.

'Well, that decides that then,' Maddy said. 'My bag's got my credit cards, chequebook, the lot, which was pretty stupid of me, actually.'

'I always lock up,' I told her, a bit bemused. 'And check the handle afterwards.'

'But hang on, weren't you texting as you went out?'

'Yeah, that's right. I was messaging Clodagh.'

'And I followed you out. I don't remember you turning back to lock up.'

'No, me neither,' I agreed.

'And let's face it, no burglar worth his salt is going to leave a handbag behind, even if we disturbed him. I had two €50 notes in the zip pocket.' She opened it and pulled them out. 'Besides, he couldn't have escaped without us seeing him, could he?'

'No. There are two doors but only one entrance off the deck, although he could have jumped the handrail at the back,' I supposed. 'I think I'm just nervous because of Pete being edgy, that's all. God, I hope I'm not turning into a scaredy-cat.'

'Well, I can stay again tonight if you like?'

'No, I'm fine,' I told her. 'I'd just better double-check as I leave in future, though. I guess I am a bit isolated here, especially in winter.'

'OK, firstly, Pete would alert you if anyone even approached the van, wouldn't he?'

'Yes, definitely.'

245

'And I take it you have the number of the local gardai on speed dial in your mobile?'

'No.' I didn't even like talking about it.

'OK, well that I can sort straightaway.' She dialled Directory Enquiries and I watched while she saved the number for me seconds later. 'And have you got a number under ICE?'

'ICE?' I hadn't a clue what she was talking about.

'I – C – E. In Case of Emergency. The police and other agencies have told everyone they should have someone listed in the event of say, an accident. That way they can simply spool through your phone and your next of kin should be there. It's a worldwide initiative, as far as I know, or all over Europe at least.'

'Wow, that's clever. How come I never heard about it?'

'Because you're living on animal planet.' She grinned. 'You're mine, by the way.'

'Your what?'

'My ICE buddy, stupid. Will I be yours?'

'Oh, yes, of course.' I hugged her. 'Thanks, Maddy.'

'For what?' She'd saved her details in my phone in seconds.

'I dunno, just for being there. And for being you. And for always making me feel better.'

'You're welcome. Now, finally, who's your nearest neighbour?'

'That house over to the left, but I've never seen anyone, in spite of them living just across the hedge. I notice a light through the bushes at night, that's about it. They'd come and go through the front door, obviously, and that's the other end of the lane. I often see one or two cars out there as I leave for work.'

'OK, come on, let's check them out.' She was out the door before I could stop her.

'Honestly, it's not necessary, I'm just being stupid. I'm tired today, time of the month and all that.'

'Come with me, I'm not leaving until I'm satisfied you'll be OK.' She grabbed my arm and led me down the lane. 'Nothing to lose by just checking to see if they're home,' she reasoned.

The two cars were there and, before I could stop her, she'd rung the bell and introduced the pair of us to a young woman, who immediately invited us in for a New Year drink, even though it was barely lunchtime.

'Any excuse,' she laughed. 'Jack, my partner, is down-stairs in the kitchen.' She led the way, and I asked if it was OK to bring Pete in. I was so addled I'd forgotten to leave him on the deck and secure the gate, and he'd followed us up the lane, naturally.

'Sure, we love animals. I'm Jill, by the way, and don't say it: I've heard every Jack and Jill rhyme known to man, including a few that aren't repeatable. We're about to rescue a dog, by the way, so maybe he could have a play date with yours?' She giggled. 'Have you any kids?'

I shook my head.

'Me neither.' She seemed pleased. 'And that's by choice. Loads of nephews and nieces but never had the urge. Neither has Jack, so we're happy, although my mother, who lives down the road, still hasn't given up hope.' She was amazingly open and friendly, and I liked her. I could see Maddy did too.

'Jack, where are you? We have visitors,' she called. 'It's the girl who lives in the van down the lane.' A man had his back to us as we entered the nicest country kitchen I'd seen in a long time. He was putting turf on the fire.

'We wondered when we'd meet you.' Jill smiled. 'Jack, say hello to Lulu and her friend Maddy.'

'Hello.' He was a big bear of a man in his late thirties, I guessed, with a mop of dark hair and a beard. 'Glad you dropped in.'

Jill produced four beers without asking, and we all sat around the fire as Maddy explained why we'd called.

'Well, I'm delighted you did.' Jack had a hint of a Welsh accent. 'If you ever hear a noise and you're worried, just ring and I could be with you in ten seconds. There's a gate at the back that we never use, but I'll check it and make sure the area isn't overgrown.'

'We were just saying the other day how nobody knows their neighbours any more; we only discovered by accident that an old lady of eighty-seven lives two doors up from us,' Jill said. 'I could easily check in with her and do a bit of shopping if she needs help. But everyone's so busy – and I suppose reluctant to get involved – that we're missing out, I feel.'

Maddy and I agreed, and then Jack called out the house number and gave me both their mobiles and I gave mine in return. I couldn't believe how nice they were, so much so that Maddy and I giggled our way down the lane an hour later, having had two beers and no food. Even Pete had liked them, although he had been given a rib bone to chew right in front of the fire, so I reckoned he'd be leaving me for them if I wasn't careful. I made a mental note to drop them in a bottle of wine to say thanks and felt much more secure as Maddy and I made pancakes, just as the light faded. We settled down with a big pot of tea and a stack of warm, doughy rounds to watch yet another old movie and stuff our faces.

That night, Maddy was staying with her mother, and she insisted on taking me and Pete home with her, in spite of my protests. Connie was thrilled and fussed over me no end. She was a real Dublin mother; she wore an apron and always had a pot of something simmering on the stove. Nothing threw her, and she seemed to be constantly in the middle of one of her neighbours' traumas and had tea on the go day and night, no matter who called. She made brown bread for me and tried to 'fatten me up', forcing an apple tart on me as I prepared to leave, then insisted on driving me home herself next morning when she heard Maddy had an interview to do. She was delighted to finally see my new home and was as positive as she always was about every aspect of my life.

'You're like another of my brood, always have been,' she shouted as she shot into reverse down the lane.

After a very lazy weekend, life returned to normal the following day, and the heavy traffic and Arctic weather combined to create the annual January blues.

'Is it me, or is the whole world extra grumpy this year?' I asked Mary, after a very angry woman in a jeep hurled abuse at me because I was two seconds late taking off at a green light close by our office.

'It's the bills,' she told me. 'Angela in the caterers told me her Visa bill arrived this morning for over €3,000.'

'Ouch, that'd do it all right. Thankfully, I didn't go mad, for once.'

'Does your diet start today, like the rest of the world, or could you be tempted by a warm apple fritter, courtesy of our new best friends next door?'

'Absolutely. Life is too short to diet.' I grinned. 'The caterers did Louis's party, by the way, and he was very impressed.'

'I'm glad, things are tough out there.' Mary got up to put the kettle on. 'By the way, you never told me your friend Maddy was famous. She's on the front of one of the papers today. Some big TV series.'

'Oh my God, which one? I have to get it.' I rummaged for my purse.

'There it is on top of the filing cabinet; I bought it for you. I guessed you'd want a copy. She looks stunning,' Mary called over her shoulder as she disappeared off towards the kitchen.

I was so excited I could hardly speak. There was Maddy – my friend Maddy – on the front page of one of the tabloids with three other women under a headline that screamed BET YOUR LOCAL DOCTOR NEVER LOOKED LIKE THIS? Of the four women on display, Maddy looked the best by a mile, and yes, I *am* biased. Her long hair was windblown, her dress was sheer and colourful and she radiated energy.

I dialled her number. 'Bitch, why didn't you tell me?'

'Tell you what?'

'About the photo.'

'What photo? Lou, it's early, it's Monday, it's January. Any of those things would make me feel a bit groggy, but when all three come together – well, what can I say? All I need is to find a stack of bills on the mat and I'll have to take a tablet. Besides, why are you ringing when I haven't even had my coffee yet? Whatever you're waffling on about had better be good, OK?'

'Oh, sorry. Listen, I'll go and leave you in peace so, instead of going on about how fantastic you look on the front page of today's paper.'

'What? Are you serious? Jesus, read out everything while I put on the kettle. Word for word, don't leave anything out.'

'How come you never told me you'd done it?'

'Done what?'

'Posed for a photo with your three co-stars.'

'I didn't. Are you on something?'

I described it in detail and read every word, including the caption.

'Oh my God, I remember now. At the final auditions they set up several different groups, did our make-up and then mixed and matched us. We were asked to bring a few different outfits. I assumed it was just for their own reference. Bloody hell, I didn't take it seriously at all, sure I was messing around half the time.'

'Well, it shows. You look a hundred times more relaxed than the other three,' I told her. 'Now, get dressed, go and buy it and ring me back for more detailed analysis,' I instructed. 'Meanwhile, I'll phone Clodagh.'

'OK. I still can't believe they've used one of those photos. Are you sure it's me?'

'I think I'd know my best friend, even when she looks a million dollars. And how could you not have suspected they might use them? Was it not a professional photographer and all that?'

'Yeah, I suppose, but you know, we were in a TV studio, it was all very casual, but now you mention it there were lights and touch-ups and all that, but sure they hadn't even offered anyone the job.'

'Well, they were obviously making final decisions, and seeing how you looked together in various combinations must have been a part of it. So, from now on, get your roots touched up every three weeks, buy a pair of huge, expensive sunglasses immediately and ditch those awful pink-velvet sweatpants. Meanwhile, go get that paper so we can really gossip.'

'You're on, sure I'll nip down to the local in my pyjamas. Isn't that the latest trend anyway?'

'Maddy, you're a star – there might be photographers waiting outside your front door,' I joked.

'In that case, I'll go in my bra and pants,' she decided, and we laughed so much I ended up having to run to the loo.

By the time all three of us had dissected every inch of the photos and agreed unanimously that Maddy was the youngest, prettiest, sexiest – and a lot of other adjectives ending with 'est' – it was after ten thirty, so I got down to work, already an hour behind. Luckily, I'd no clients scheduled that day, but when I listened to my answering machine, I realized that not everyone was as relaxed as I was starting off the New Year.

27

FIRST MESSAGE WAS FROM FATHER VINCENT. I DECIDED TO CALL him straightaway, hoping for some good news for Dinny.

After we'd exchanged pleasantries, he got down to business. 'I spoke to Joan, as I said I would, but I'm sorry to tell you it's probably not the news you were hoping to hear,' he told me. 'I'm afraid she asked me to tell you that she has no interest in rekindling the . . . friendship. I did my best, tried to get her to think about it for a while, but she was insistent.'

I felt he knew more than he was letting on, but I wasn't in a position to discuss it so I was at a loss to know what to do next. 'I'm very grateful for your assistance, Father, and to be honest, I'm not sure if there's anything else I can do. Would it help if I rang and explained his situation?' I wondered aloud.

'I don't believe it would. I've never heard her so adamant, actually, in all the years I've known her.'

I took a deep breath, deciding I'd nothing to lose. 'Would you at least ask her if she'd accept a call from me? And please explain that I've no real connection with Denis. We only became friends recently.'

He was silent for a moment. 'I will, yes,' he said eventually.

'Thank you so much, I wouldn't normally push, but I know how much this means to Denis.'

'I'll try her now, might as well strike while the iron is hot.' He said goodbye, and I wondered what a rejection would do to Dinny. He was more vulnerable than he appeared.

Within minutes, my phone rang. I was surprised to hear Father Vincent back on again so quickly.

'I just spoke to Joan.' He didn't waste time. 'She's happy to speak with you, but only in person. She'll be in Dublin next weekend, as it happens, for a business meeting. She wonders if you'd like to meet for tea at 4 p.m. on Friday in the lobby of the Shelbourne Hotel? She asked me to tell you she's tall and dark and she'll be wearing a black-and-white check coat.'

'Wow, that seems like a done deal, so?' was all I could think of to say.

'I think you'll like her. She's a very private person, though, so I was surprised she agreed to your request at all to be truthful. I think you've made the right decision, my dear,' Father Vincent said quietly. 'If there's any progress at all to be made, then this can only help your friend Mr Cassidy.'

'I see. Right, well, thank you very much. Would you give Joan my mobile number just in case her plans change? Otherwise, I'll be there at four.'

'I will of course. And do stay in touch if I can be of further assistance. God bless.' With that, he was gone.

I rang Dinny immediately and filled him in.

'So she wants nothing to do with me?' he said in a small voice.

'Well, that's not exactly true,' I told him. 'So stop feeling sorry for yourself.'

'But she refused to even talk to me?'

'Yes, but obviously she wants to hear what you've got to say if she's agreed to meet with me.'

'Can I come with you?' he asked, sharp as a button. 'I could stay out of the way but you could tell her I was around the place and it might make her change her mind.'

'Absolutely not, Dinny. I'm not really comfortable being in the middle of this at all, to tell you the truth, so I am definitely not playing any games of that sort.'

'You will go, though, won't you? I really need your help, Lulu.'

'Yes.' I'd no idea how I'd gotten here.

'I'll pay for your time, and your expenses, of course,' he added quickly.

'Dinny, this is not about money. I'm doing this only because we've become friends and I know it's important to you.'

'Thank you. I appreciate that more than you'll ever know, that's the truth.' He paused. 'I've made a mess of this whole thing, and I've wasted so many years,' he said quietly. 'All I want is to try and make up for my mistake.'

'I know that, Dinny, but sometimes these things are not that easy to fix. And you might have no choice but to accept that.'

'Should I give you a cheque to give her, I wonder? Maybe that would convince her I'm serious?'

'I don't think so.' He was such a sweet, decent man, I didn't have the heart to tell him that money might only make it worse. 'I'll do my best to persuade her to at least talk to you. That's all I can do.'

'You're right. Sure that's all any of us can do in life – our best. And I'll start a novena to the Sacred Heart tonight,' he told me. 'He never lets me down.'

'Try Saint Anthony as well,' I advised. 'He works for me.'

We chatted a bit more about what information I'd give Joan, and he promised to ring me later in the week for a final chat before I met her.

At that stage, it was past lunchtime, and I was starving. My next message was from Emily, but Mary had already made an appointment for her to come in the following day, so I checked my emails then took the dog for a walk and grabbed a sandwich en route. I had to leave Pete behind in the office, because I had two new clients who wanted me to visit them at home, which meant a serious detour to get him on my way home. I feared I was going to have to buy an old banger for days like today. Mind you, I hadn't known what today was going to be like, I told myself, so I probably wouldn't have taken the car anyway, even if I had one. Still, at least with the bike it was easier to double-back in rush-hour traffic, so I left him snoring, and Mary promised to bring him out for a pee before she left if I wasn't back. And both appointments sounded like nice normal doggy problems, so I was in my element.

By the time I got back to the office it was after six. Even now, Pete always looked at me with delight when I returned, as if surprised I'd remembered him – or perhaps that was just my imagination: my old need to be needed resurfacing. Still he sat by the door, not moving, waiting, hoping he was to be included in the next adventure, so I picked up my messages and said, 'Let's go home, Pete,' then I locked up and we headed for the bike, just as my phone rang.

'I just got my first two scripts,' Maddy announced. 'They're great. I've loads of scenes. Can you believe it? And I've news, so will I swing by your place?'

'Maddy, no one "swings by" Bray,' I told her. I really wanted to see her, because I knew she'd cheer me up, but I was tired too; the home visits had taken their toll.

'I've got mini Aero bars, a tub of cookie-dough ice-cream and a bucket of popcorn.' She knew how to get to me. 'And a T-bone-steak bone for Pete.'

'Sold,' I told her. 'It was the bone that did it. I've neglected poor Pete all day.'

'Great, see you in about an hour?'

'Yep. Will you stay?'

'No, better not. I've a wardrobe call at seven thirty, followed by a hair and make-up appointment.'

'Oooh, get you,' I teased. 'You won't want to be seen with me next.'

'Why do you think I'm coming out to the sticks to meet you?' She was still laughing as I hung up and wound my way into the last of the rush-hour traffic.

I knew Maddy had arrived as soon as I heard her car at the end of the lane. So did Pete, but he simply wagged his tail and kept his eye on the door.

'Wait until I tell you what Porky Pauline had to say when I told her,' she announced when we were ensconced on the couch with a shopful of goodies. Of course, she had to act the whole thing out, which had me in stitches. 'Can you believe how bitchy she was in the end? Hinting that I must have known someone and all that. I wanted to leave the mark of my hand on her fat ass, I can tell you, but you'd have been proud of me, babe, I kept my dignity.'

'And not often you do,' I told her. 'You normally act first and think later.'

'Yes, well, I would've done, but now that I'm famous, darling' – she flicked her hair – 'it might end up on the front page of some awful tabloid.' She stopped. 'Are you OK? You look a bit frazzled.'

'Just a heavy day.' I rubbed my eyes. 'So, what other news have you?'

'Well, rehearsals start on Friday, then we shoot the first six episodes by the end of the month, so it'll be frantic. Keep the last Friday free, by the way, because that's my last day for a while, and I intend going out on the town and getting pissed, with you and Clodagh in tow,' she announced. 'I'm not used to being so sensible, but early mornings on camera mean I'm going to have to cut back on all the stodge.' She popped a huge spoon of ice-cream into her mouth. 'Last blow-out,' she said as I poked her in the ribs. 'And no booze between now and then. Oh, except maybe on Friday night, because Ronan asked me to go to a movie with him. Without his granny – can you believe it?'

We spent an hour deciding what she should wear (new print dress from H&M), whether she should keep her hair up or down (down, sexier) and if she should drive (definitely not, because then he'd have to drop her home and she might get to invite him in for coffee and then she could jump on him). We laughed our way through the nosh, and by the time she left at ten thirty, I was feeling much better.

Next morning, when I got to the office Emily was already waiting, looking excited and apprehensive in equal measure.

'So?' I asked as we sat down. 'How've you been?'

'Good, thanks.' She looked as if she was bursting to tell me something.

'And how's Rover?'

'What? Oh, he's good, yeah.' She seemed distracted. 'But I need your help with my other problem.'

That's what I'd been afraid of. I really felt like I couldn't take on another life at the moment, what with Dinny's future resting on my already weighed-down shoulders.

'I've been doing some research, you see.' Emily's eyes lit up.

'About your birth mother?' I already knew the answer.

'Yes, and I've found her address.'

'I see. Emily, I think you need to be careful—'

'Oh, I will be, don't worry. That's why I want you to come with me.'

'With you? Where?'

'To London. I've decided to surprise her.'

'I don't think that's necessarily the best approach,' I cautioned.

'Oh it is. I just know it. She's living alone during the

259

week; I've hired a private detective, you see.' For someone normally so shy and retiring, she was a powerhouse of energy. 'So I reckon she must be lonely—'

'Emily, that doesn't necessarily follow.'

'I've given this a great deal of thought, Lulu, and I want to meet her.' Her eyes were shining. 'I need to speak to her and ask questions and, for once in my life, I'm not going to take my usual softly-softly approach. I'm going to check that she's home, then knock on her door – that way, she can't avoid me. And the only way I can find the courage to go through with it is if you're beside me.'

I couldn't believe it. Emily, who had been told what to do all her life, was not for turning on this one. She offered to fly me first class, put me up in a five-star hotel and purchase an open-ended ticket so that I could stay on if I wanted. Consequently, she was very hard to say no to, even with all my experience.

My next clients were John the oncologist and Gilbert the Yorkie, whom I'd only seen once before. Gilbert had turned savage, apparently, and had bitten a little girl who lived nearby. Her parents were threatening to sue. God, I loved simple problems like this. I was in my element for the next two hours.

As soon as he left I wrote up my notes, then went to make myself a strong black coffee before I rang Emily, hoping to have one last try at persuading her to re-think her happy-families plan. Mary stopped me en route.

'Fax just in for you.' She handed me a ream of pages.

'Thanks, want a coffee?'

'I have the kettle on, actually, so I'll bring one in to you if you like?'

'That'd be great, you're a star. I have a difficult call to make.' As soon as I said it, I noticed the fax was from Emily. My heart sank when I saw the lists of flight availabilities for the next several weeks as well as print-outs of the facilities at several top hotels. Just when I thought it couldn't get any worse, I read her last paragraph, where she told me how much it meant to her that I had agreed to go with her, how this was the most important thing she'd ever done for herself and how she'd never had a real friend before. She wrote that, in agreeing to be there for her, I'd given her a new sense of self-worth, and if she finally put her past to rest and was able to be at peace with herself, it would be all thanks to me. It was game, set and match to Emily.

28

EVEN AN AMAZING DRIVE HOME ALONG THE COAST IN THE LAST of the brilliant winter sunlight that seemed to have glued itself to Ireland for the past few days didn't cheer me up, so I stopped at the local takeaway for food, then at the garage next door for dessert, then at the off licence, in the hope of attracting one of the girls out to Bray for a girly night. As it turned out, Maddy's phone was off, which was unusual, and Clodagh wasn't answering, so I ate as much as I could cram down my throat in three minutes, I was so hungry, and was just about to uncork the wine when Pete's ears went up and he suddenly barked like mad and shot towards the door. I decided to let him out, and he tore off into the trees, growling. I was immediately sorry I'd done it, because now I was completely alone. I waited a while to see if he'd stop, but he was sounding more agitated than earlier, so I decided to ring my neighbours.

'Jill, I'm really sorry, my dog's gone mad,' I told her as soon as I'd introduced myself. 'I just wanted to check that you were home?' I felt like a complete idiot.

'Yes, I'm here. Jack is out, but listen, I'll walk down to you now, just to check.'

'Oh, no, please,' I said, but she'd hung up, and within seconds I saw the light of a torch and she called out to me almost immediately.

'It's only me,' I heard, followed by 'Hello Pete, come to meet me, have you? There's a good boy.' Suddenly she was at my gate.

'Jill, I'm so sorry to have troubled you, I don't know what I was thinking. I just got a bit of a fright when the dog went mad.'

'Not a problem, that's what neighbours are for. Actually, I was just about to pour myself a cup of tea, so if you want to make it up to me, I'll have one with you.' She smiled. 'Although let's have a walk around first, just to check, OK? That way, if there is anyone hanging about looking for trouble, they'll know there's more than one of us here. Why don't you grab your coat, it's gone quite chilly tonight.'

'Are you sure?' I still felt bad about calling her out for no reason. 'It's just that Pete isn't one of those dogs who barks for no reason, which is why it freaks me out a bit when it happens.'

'No problem at all, the fresh air will do me good; I was melting by the fire anyway. You're a great dog.' She stroked Pete, and he lapped it up. We walked the perimeter of our little woodland, but the dog was relaxed, all he did was sniff and bound around the place, tail wagging at this unexpected romp, so we came indoors after a few minutes and I put the kettle on.

'Actually, I was just about to have a glass of wine – it's been one of those days.' I pointed to the empty ice-cream tub. 'Will you join me?'

'Love to,' she said, and I showed her around the van and we chatted for half an hour or so. When she left she made me promise to ring them any time I heard anything. 'We're nearly always there, and we stay up half the night as well, so you're not disturbing us in the slightest.' She waved, and I waited until I saw her close the little wooden gate at the end of her garden. I was delighted that Maddy had made me introduce myself; it was nice to have them close by. I gave up on the alcohol and decided that a good night's sleep was what I really needed.

By the end of the week my brain was fried, and there was still the small matter of my meeting with Joan Lehane. I could have done without it after all the angst of the previous days, but it was yet another thing I'd taken on board that I hadn't had to, and Dinny was ringing me practically on the hour to make sure I was still going. Last night I'd finally told him to back off and, God love him, he'd been mortified.

As it turned out, I was at the Shelbourne Hotel way too early, so I strolled around St Stephen's Green and was heartened to see snowdrops and crocuses already pushing their heads up through the claggy black soil. The park was full of muffled-up families feeding the ducks and students lying about on the grass, damp though it must have been.

Ten minutes before the hour, I settled myself near the door in the foyer of the hotel and waited. I recognized Joan Lehane immediately, and I have to say she was a good-looking woman, much younger and trendier than I'd imagined.

'Hello, you must be Joan. I'm Lulu.' I stood up, in no doubt that she was the person I was due to meet. She was tall, with shoulder-length chestnut hair and, although her coat and jeans were funky, they were beautifully cut, and her boots and handbag were not from the high street. I found it impossible to place her beside Dinny.

'Hello, I hope I'm not late.' She smiled. 'I got caught up in the magic of Grafton Street, I'm afraid. My God, Dublin has changed so much,' she marvelled.

'It certainly has,' I agreed. 'How long since you've been here?'

'A long time.' She smiled again. 'Should we go get some afternoon tea?'

'Yes, there are tables just through here.' I led the way, and we settled into a quiet corner. Most of Dublin was still grappling with the January sales, I reckoned.

Once we'd ordered, I wasn't sure where to begin, and since I – on Dinny's behalf at least – had asked for the meeting, I felt obliged to start the conversation.

'So, how do you know Denis?' Joan took the matter out of my hands.

I explained how we'd met, and she threw back her head and laughed. 'You're a pet shrink? My God, Ireland has moved on. When I lived here people wouldn't have come near you if you'd been seeing a shrink yourself, never mind having your dog's head examined.'

'The Celtic Tiger has a lot to answer for,' I told her.

'And how have you ended up meeting me on his behalf?'

I explained how we'd become friends and how, eventually, he'd confided in me about his past. Her words, when they came, surprised me by their lack of bitterness or condemnation.

'He abandoned me at a time when I was the most vulnerable I've ever been in my life, but he gave me the most amazing daughter and, once I survived the whole thing, I knew I could cope with anything. It was awful, initially. I'd no money, my parents were horrified – mainly because he was so much older than me – and assumed I'd give the child up. I'd no friends either, I discovered. There was no bigger crime in rural Ireland at the time really, except perhaps if he'd been a priest.'

'That bad?' It was hard to believe – even though I'd heard all the stories about the influence of the Church and the shame such things were considered to bring on families.

'I'm afraid so, as much because we were a well-respected, middle-class family as anything. Pillars of the community and all that. My father, in particular, was scandalized. I think it spoiled me for ever in his eyes.'

'So what happened?'

'Oh, I hung around, kept hoping it would all work out but, with Denis's mother ruling the roost, that was never going to happen. Eventually, I couldn't take the pressure at home or the whispering every time I stepped outside the door, so I took myself off to England, like so many others at the time. I was lucky, I had an old friend – Marion, a distant relation actually – and her parents let me stay until the baby was born. They also got me a job – not an easy thing to find, either – and I saved every penny, and when the baby was born I found work at night, and Marion was studying so she was happy to earn a little money by keeping an eye on her once I'd fed and changed her and put her to bed. I worked seven nights a week, every week, and it paid off. I was moved to front of house in a short time, and within a year I was managing the restaurant. It meant I got to spend all day with my baby, and by the time Catherine was starting school I had enough money – only barely, mind you – to buy a small flat and pay a proper childminder. Then my father died and my mother sent me a large amount of money. I think she felt guilty, to be honest. She tried to get me to come home, but by that stage nothing would have persuaded me to go back.' She sipped her tea. 'That's about it, really. I've had – have – a very good life, and I own my own restaurant now and it's been very successful, and I'm happy, and my daughter is the best thing that ever happened to me.'

'I'm so glad it all worked out, but just seeing you it's hard to imagine that it wouldn't.'

'Oh, I wasn't always so confident, believe me. I spent a good many years with my head down, working as hard as I could, never going out, not spending a penny on myself.' She looked down at herself. 'All this finery came much, much later.' It was an old-fashioned thing to say, and in a way it summed her up. She was very proper, although each time she smiled I sensed a hint of mischief about her.

'So how is the bold Mr Cassidy? Still the same, I imagine?'

'Well, that depends on what you imagine, I guess. He still lives in Wicklow – he bought some land – still has a twinkle in his eye, and we liked each other as soon as we met, I think.'

'Is he still as handsome and debonair as ever?'

I almost choked on my scone. Neither were words I'd ever associate with Dinny.

'He came to my Christmas drinks, and he still had an eye for the ladies.' It was as diplomatic as I could be.

'Did he ever marry?'

'No, and I think he very much regrets his actions now where you were concerned,' I told her. 'I believe he did go to see you at one stage?'

'It was about a year too late, I think now, looking back. I really struggled for the first year or two on my own. I was so lonely. But then it somehow turned around – I suppose things always do – and I'd just realized I was getting on fine when he appeared, thinking he could just apologize and pick up where we'd left off. But by that time I'd too much pride.'

'I can understand that, you'd been through a lot.'

'I loved him so much,' she said simply. 'And that continued for years. Eventually I started dating. Then I met someone and he asked me to marry him but, somehow, no man ever matched up to my first love.' She smiled at me. 'So what's he like now?'

I had no idea what to say. 'Well, he's older . . .' It was the most ridiculous answer. 'He's in his sixties . . .'

'It's stupid, but in my head he's still the same as he was. I probably wouldn't recognize him if he walked in now.' She glanced around.

Don't tempt fate, I wanted to shout – knowing Dinny, he could be lurking behind a plant. But all I said was, 'He's a lovely man, very kind, makes me laugh all the time. I think you'd enjoy what he's become.'

'Sure look at me. I'm forty, and every time I look in the mirror I don't recognize myself. I'm a mass of wrinkles.'

I wanted to tell her that, compared to her former lover, she was a Page-Three candidate but instead we indulged in a bit of girly nonsense for a while, and just as I was working up to my next question she beat me to it – again.

'So why now?' She arched her eyebrows. 'Why, after all these years, does he want us back in his life? Is it just because he's getting old?'

'That might have something to do with it, but I think he's genuinely sorry for the way he handled it back then,' I told her honestly. 'I suspect he just wants to make amends.'

'He doesn't have to, it's not necessary.' Again she spoke without a trace of bitterness. 'I always knew he'd get in touch someday, so when Father Vincent rang I knew what my answer was. He doesn't have to feel guilty about us, we're fine, and we don't want for anything financially.'

'He told me he sent you money but that you refused it.'

'Yes, and that was mostly pride. You see, I needed him, not his money. Money wasn't actually a huge issue once I found a job. But loneliness was always lurking. I'd no one to talk to a lot of the time. And even when I worked, there were so many nights when I was dog-tired, I'd have given anything for someone to just take over for a couple of hours. Someone to put their arms around me or run a bath for me, or just tell me not to rush home, insist that I stay back and have a drink with the girls. Silly, I suppose, but I was young and shy and Irish in a big, sophisticated city.'

'It must have been very tough.' I was transported back with her and suddenly wondered if my own mother had experienced the same loneliness. She probably had, I'd just never considered what it had been like back then. Although she'd dealt with me in a different way, the only way she knew probably. And that way meant that I had felt lonely too much of the time.

'It was tough.' She looked sad. 'So when he blustered his way in – waving a cheque – I just sent him away quickly and quietly. And do you know why? Because I was afraid. And, basically, what I was most afraid of was my anger. When I saw him again he looked older and sophisticated, and for the first time I wanted to scream at him, "You should have known better, you should have minded me," and I was scared of letting it all out because I knew that if I cried I'd never stop. Seeing him again just added to the loneliness. So as soon as he left I boxed it all up and superglued the lid.' She smiled. 'And it worked. It kept me going until I turned the corner, and one day I realized I was over it all and, even better, I was happy with myself. And that felt great. So please assure him that we're fine, and that Catherine knows exactly what happened, and neither of us bears him any ill will. In fact, I wish him only joy and good fortune.'

'You're a remarkable woman.' I meant it. 'And I really admire all you've achieved and the way in which you've managed the hand you were dealt. So many people would have taken his money, allowed bitterness to take over and still refused to have anything to do with him all these years later, yet you agreed to talk to me.' I wasn't quite sure what I wanted to say next, so I paused for a second and Joan didn't rush in to fill the space like most people would have. 'Look, I'm just going to throw this at you for consideration. What if he simply wanted to try and put it right, even though you don't need it and despite the fact that it's years too late?

270

Would you be prepared to allow him to do that? It would mean letting him into your life a little bit, I suspect, and it would really be all for his benefit, I think, although perhaps it would allow you to finally put the past to rest in that tiny little place in your head where there's a door that has never been fully closed. That's if you're anything like me, anyway.' I sighed.

She stared at me for ages, not really seeing me, I suspected. 'I never thought I'd say this, but now that I've spoken about my anger aloud, I actually think I would,' she said softly. 'Just give me a day or two to discuss it with my daughter. If we're doing this, she might as well be involved. Anyway, if I'm truly honest, it's probably been on my mind for a long time that the two of them should meet.'

29

I WAS BRAINDEAD THE NEXT DAY, SO WHEN A TEXT CAME IN AT about four thirty I nearly didn't open it, except I suspected it might be Maddy or Clodagh trying to drag me into town to hook up with them. They'd been shopping since the doors opened and I imagined they were about ready to indulge in a spot of relaxation. Their mission was to buy dresses for the launch of Maddy's new show in a couple of weeks' time, and as I still had a plentiful supply of Bronwyn's stuff and money was tight, I'd decided against joining them, much to their disgust.

So I expected a moany text calling me a party pooper but instead I read:

Help! De mutt has taken ovr hse n had 2 go 2
pub 4 lunch. Any chance ud call about 6 n if
u bcom ldr of de pack wil ply u wit bubbly n
cook u fab dinner? X Mike

I sent back a message immediately:

Do u tink I can b bought so easily?

272

To which he replied:

Double rate of pay 4 weekend n real bubbly, not
cheap stuff?

C u at 6.

I laughed and gave in, pressed Send and jumped off the
couch, dragged Pete out for a very quick walk then dived
into the shower.

Maddy rang while I was on the Dart. 'That woman makes
the Taliban look like a bunch of wusses.' She was referring
to Clodagh, I knew immediately. 'She wouldn't even let me
stop for lunch. Instead she had this cardboard muck with her
that she called a multi-something bar which she forced me
to eat. When I downed tools at 3 o'clock she ordered nettle
tea – can you believe it? And I promise you, I wouldn't have
been stripped naked as often if I were a hooker. She told
me my underwear had lost its elasticity, so I can't imagine
what she thought of my face. Come into town quick and save
me. Otherwise I'll end up drinking from a can in an alley
somewhere, because she's insisting we go to a juice bar for
"refreshments". I'm not kidding,' she spluttered. 'Remind
me again why we're friends with her?'

'Because she keeps us on the straight and narrow.' I
laughed. It was what made us work as a trio, I knew. Maddy
kept us laughing and made life fun, Clodagh never let us fail
and wanted only the best for us, and I suppose I was the one
who always worked out the solutions that got us through
life's ups and downs. 'Anyway, you're on your own,' I told

her. 'I'm having my dinner cooked by Mike, who's promised to pour champagne down my neck if I can get Pedro to stop guarding the door to the fridge.'

'You go, girl, you lucky thing. Sure how could beetroot and ginger juice compete with that?' She giggled. 'Call me later though, and if I get truly desperate, I'll be over to Mike's house myself.'

'OK, I'll make him put your name in the pot so.'

'Make him put my name in the bottle, darling. Fuck the pot. Oops, here she comes with another pair of Spanx. Gotta go, she's spotted me dossing. I found a Sweet Factory kiosk and I've been eating jelly babies on the sly.'

Poor Clodagh. Whatever chance she had of converting me, she'd absolutely none with Maddy.

Mike answered the door fielding an antique shield and spear, one of Louis's favourites. 'I swear he's gone bonkers; all that caviar has finally sent him over the edge. He now definitely thinks he owns the gaff.'

'Fool.' I grabbed the spear and took a swipe at him. 'You've probably driven him mad with your antics. And Louis will kill you if you damage that,' I warned as I dumped my bag on the floor.

'Me! Driven him mad? What are you, crazy? I'm terrified of him. I tried talking to him through the keyhole. I even promised him the fillet steak I was planning to feed you.'

'Well, he's not getting my dinner, that's for sure.' I laughed and followed Mike to the kitchen. When I opened the door, Pedro gave me a doggy version of a 'You won't believe this idiot' look. As soon as he saw Mike he gave a low growl, but it was a half-hearted attempt at dominance.

I gave him my usual command and walked towards him purposefully. His tail went down and he mooched off towards his bed.

'Jesus, I actually feel sorry for him now,' Mike said. 'He looks like he's been castrated. Sure what hope has any male against you?'

'That's the idea,' I told him. 'Now, tell me what's been happening?'

'It's like it always is. When Louis's here he spoils the dog rotten, has him sitting on chairs, sleeping on the bed, douses him in Gucci aftershave, the lot. Result – Louis happy, mutt ecstatic and I stay out of the way. Just sometimes it gets out of hand, like when I want to sit down and he won't let me, but mostly in those situations Louis whispers sweet nothings in his ear and Pedro reluctantly allows me to live. Then Louis goes away for a few days and the hound takes over. Now, normally, I just don't put up with it – my boot to his arse scenario – but he's getting worse all the time. Today he really snarled at me, showed teeth, the works. But to be honest I really only invited you over because I do, in fact, need your help with something else as well.'

'Go on.' I eyed him suspiciously.

'However, I will feed you very well. Louis left the fridge chock-a-block with goodies, although mostly for the mutt, I do admit.'

'You intend feeding me the dog's dinner?' I enquired. 'Anything else I should know? And was there some talk of something long and cold and fizzy?'

'Oops, coming right up.' He darted for the fridge, and Pedro got a fright and growled again but this time, as soon as I looked at him, he slunk away. 'OK, I've said it before, so this is my last attempt. You two are going to have to take a united approach to the Pedro problem.'

'We are.' He grabbed the bottle and a glass – in an effort to shut me up, I reckoned.

'Dogs need three things. Exercise, discipline and affection. It's not rocket science. Have you seen *The Dog Whisperer*?' I asked.

'Who the hell is he?'

'Doesn't matter, we've talked about this before.'

'I know, I know. To be honest, I've more or less given up, I never wanted all this hassle in the first place, you know that.' Mike poured a glass of champagne and handed it to me.

'You not joining me?'

'Yes, but not with that.' He snapped the ring on a can of beer. 'Cheers.'

'Slainte,' I toasted him in Irish. 'OK, let's try it once more. It's very simple if you just see it from Pedro's point of view. He sees Louis as Number One, himself as Number Two and you as Number Three. In order to change that, you both need to agree a pattern. Have you been feeding him?'

'Yep, and he's nice as pie to me. Ditto when I shout "Walkies". But Louis treats him like a child – in fact, better than a child – for the rest of the time, and that's the problem.'

'Tell me again when all this started?' I prompted, while Mike got things together for dinner. He had fillet steaks marinating in balsamic vinegar with lots of black pepper and he was baking potatoes and throwing a salad together.

'I suppose it . . . stop looking at me like that – I can cook,' he joked.

'No, I'm impressed actually. You do seem to know what you're doing.'

'My God, a compliment.' He laughed. 'Anyway, it started really when I tried to get Pedro off my armchair – one I bought for myself when I moved in – which he'd taken over.'

'Were you rough with him or anything? Could you have hurt him?'

'I dunno, I didn't politely suggest he might consider doing me the great honour of letting me sit down on my own chair, if that's what you mean. I just shifted him, as you do. To be honest, Lulu – and no disrespect, you're good at what you do – but I've no time for all these mind games. He's a dog, end of story.'

'I'm just wondering if there's something else wrong. Has he been to the vet lately?'

'Are you joking? He only has to sneeze and Louis takes out his credit card. Our vet averages three foreign holidays a year thanks to Pedro.'

I wandered over to where Pedro was. He wagged his tail as soon as he saw me and came towards me with a posture that was not in any way aggressive.

'Let's have a look at you, there's a good boy.' I pressed gently on his back, and as soon as my fingers moved down his spine a bit his whole manner changed and he started a low growl.

'What's wrong, fella?' I looked at him, but as soon as I moved my hands up to his back again, his tail went down and he tried to get away.

'I'd like to get him checked properly,' I told Mike. 'He just might have hurt himself, and somehow he connects it with you. Actually, give me a second, I might just be lucky.' I whipped out my mobile phone and dialled my friend Alan, who was a vet with a practice within walking distance. 'I'm ringing a friend who's a vet. I just remembered he's nearby, although at ten past six on a Sunday I'd say I'm pushing my luck,' I told Mike as I waited.

As it happened, I wasn't. Alan had had an emergency call and was just shutting up shop but offered to have a quick look at the dog if I got there in the next few minutes.

'Could you drive?' I asked Mike as I grabbed Pedro's lead.

'Is this not a bit dramatic?' Mike wanted to know. 'And what about dinner?' But I was already halfway out the door.

Fifteen minutes later we had what I hoped was an answer.

'He definitely has a problem with his spine,' Alan told me. 'Hard to tell exactly what without an X-ray, but he's in quite a bit of pain, I reckon. He tenses up as soon as I touch him in a particular spot.'

'Thanks a million. You may just have solved a problem that I was having no luck with.' I felt sorry for poor Pedro.

'Give him these tablets – I've written the details out – and if your friend wants to bring him back on Monday afternoon I'll do a few tests, but I'd say we've found the source of his aggression.'

He refused to charge me, so I made a mental note to drop him in a couple of bottles of wine and headed back to the car to tell Mike all about it.

'Wow.' He was as surprised as I was. 'The poor mutt. I feel guilty now, how's that for a turnaround? Can you believe I was actually thinking about moving out?'

'Well, I only did this for Pedro – you're big enough to look after yourself.' I grinned. 'Besides, you can talk, he can't.'

'True, but it's the only advantage I have over him,' said Mike. 'So all that money Louis's been throwing at his own vet and he didn't pick it up.' He whistled. 'That says a lot.'

'It's not easy. He may not have even been aware of the aggression, so he wouldn't have been thinking of it.' We were back at the house at this stage and I was feeling that at last we'd made some real progress.

'I'll talk to Louis and suggest he goes to see Alan on Monday. Sure he's your local vet anyway. It makes sense.'

'Just a warning: I think Louis may fancy his own vet.' Mike winked, handing me a fresh glass. 'Anyway, how do you like your steak? Potatoes are on and salad's made. I even defrosted a berry crumble for dessert.'

'You're a boy wonder.' I sipped my drink. 'Leave Louis to me, by the way – if that's OK? Don't mention today.'

'Are you kidding? You'd have to pay me to get involved any more than I am already.'

'This is delicious.' I indicated the glass. 'What is it about men and champagne?'

'The bubbles get up our noses, the glasses are too thin and the whole thing's just too . . . what's the word? . . . "polite", that'll do. Or maybe girly. Anyway, I always swallow the

279

entire contents in one gulp. All this sipping is bad for my macho image.'

'OK, I think I understand in a weird sort of way. So, what's the other story? You said you needed my help?'

'Ah yes. Well, it's simple. You know my friend Paddy Russell?'

'No, should I?'

'You met him the night of the party. Tall, great sense of humour, from Galway?'

'Oh yes, sorry. Nice guy, in a clean sort of way.'

'You make that sound like a disease.' Mike made a face.

'No, just not my type.'

'And what is your type, I wonder? No, never mind, I'm side-tracking. The thing is, he fancies your friend, and I was wondering if we could put our heads together and come up with a plan.'

'That sounds terribly girly.' I laughed.

'You're absolutely right; this was all Louis's idea. He made me promise to talk to you and, as you know, I obey. Paddy's had a bit of a rough time, you see. Long story, nothing sinister, don't worry.'

'Well, unfortunately, Maddy's just met—'

'No, not Maddy, Clodagh.'

'Clodagh? Oh, that's different. Sorry, me and her just get used to all the men fancying Maddy, so I just assumed . . .'

'Hang on, I have a list. Louis made me write it all down. Is she seeing anyone?'

'No, she was, sort of. But I heard last night that maybe he was just proving a tad too intense.'

'Right, well, that wouldn't be a problem with Paddy. Any

more laidback and he'd be in a coffin. So, what do you think? Worth a shot?'

'Maybe. Let me run it by Maddy first. She's way better than me at these things. I'm useless.'

'Great.'

'Oh, I nearly forgot, Maddy said to invite you to her launch party.' I gave him the date. 'She said you were very nice to her about it the night she was here.'

'I'm a very nice guy, actually.' He raised his eyebrows at me. 'And stop putting yourself down, by the way. You're always telling me how useless you are, and you're not. Bonkers: yes; useless: no.'

'Well, thank you, I think.'

'Pleasure. Now is it OK if we eat here in the kitchen? Louis would kill me, but I can't be arsed setting tables and all that.' He dished up the food without waiting for a reply.

'Here's perfect. I live in a van, remember?'

'Of course you do, I keep forgetting. I think Maddy getting that part is a major achievement, by the way. That's all I said to her that night. I know the production company – they've made a few videos for us – and they're huge. And very well regarded in the industry too.'

'I'm so glad you said that, it means a lot to me. I'm mad about her; she's been such a good friend to me, closer than my sister, to be honest.'

'Right, I want to hear about your family. You keep telling me bits and pieces.'

I wasn't sure I'd even sorted it myself yet, but I started by sharing that my father had died and that I had a stepfather,

Ron, who was very nice, but my mother had this idea that, unless she nailed me to the floor, I'd become wild, so she spent a lot of time telling me what I was doing wrong yet never went the other way and rewarded me for all the things I got right. And she didn't do affection. Also I hinted that I'd always felt a bit of an outsider, so I'd spent my childhood trying to be perfect. And sensible as well. All in all, a huge admission for me. Only Maddy knew as much.

'Sensible?' He nearly choked. 'I've never met anyone—'

'No, no, you only met me after I broke free. I was so dull, so careful, it was painful.' It hurt just to remember.

'So who minded you then all those years?' It was an odd question.

'Actually, the only one who ever minded me was Gnasher, my dog. He was my whole world.'

'What kind of dog was he?' he asked very quietly.

'He was a mongrel. All black with one white eye. I found him and hid him in the shed 'cause I knew Martha – my mum – would go mad. Then, I picked my moment – in other words, when she needed a monumental favour – and I agreed on condition she let me keep him. She was too hassled to argue; it was the easiest way to get around her. Becky was always so demanding, you see, so the odd time I asked for anything I invariably got my timing wrong and she said no.'

'I can't imagine you not standing up for yourself,' Mike said. 'You're full of confidence.'

'Well, thank you, but I'm not. At least I never was. Actually, I'm doing OK now, I think. I'm happy in my own skin, if that isn't too much of a cliché.'

'Phew, thank God you said that, 'cause it sounded like a giant self-help-book quote to me.'

We both laughed. 'So how long did you have your minder?'

'Gnasher? Two years. We went everywhere together. He slept under my bed. I swear the dog was half human. And then, one day, he disappeared.' But I couldn't tell him the story.

'How?'

'I can't talk about it, is that OK? It still hurts too much.' I bit my lip.

He stood up and pulled me to him and wrapped his arms around me, and for the first time in years I felt protected, as if someone was once again minding me. 'Of course it does, but . . .' He tipped up my face so that I was looking at him. 'I want you to listen to me, because I know what I'm talking about. At your party, everyone was saying how marvellous you were, to them as well as their dogs. And sure look at me, and that big lump over there.' He pointed to where Pedro lay, on his back, paws in the air. 'Last night he'd have chewed my leg off before he'd let me into the kitchen. Then you arrive in and he's snoring like an oulfella. So any time you feel sad about your old dog, think how much good you're doing for lots of dogs now. OK?'

'OK, thanks.' I smiled at him. 'Maybe that's why I feel like I've found my perfect niche in life.'

'And you've got Pete now.' Mike smiled. 'Don't forget him.'

I nodded. 'Thank God for Pete – I'd be lost without him.'

30

'SO WHAT HAPPENED NEXT?' MADDY WAS ALL EARS WHEN I told her about how nice Mike had been after I'd gotten upset about Gnasher.

'Nothing really, he was just so warm and friendly, and he sort of took over. He lit the fire and made me sit in his armchair and brought me warm berry crumble and ice-cream and lots of strong tea. Then he insisted on driving me back to Bray – he'd only had one beer – and when we got here he came in, said hello to Pete then fed him the remains of the fillet steak, kissed me on the head and was gone.'

'Wow, that's kind of . . . I dunno, old-fashioned.' Maddy sighed.

'It actually felt really cosy, like I could trust him or something. Does that sound odd?'

'Trust is good, trust Maddy on that.' She giggled. 'Warm and cosy is also a great start. Oh Lulu, I'm so excited,' she started, singing the song of the same title until I had to hang up in an effort to get her out of my ear.

'Just one thing – do you fancy him?' She was back in a second.

'Yes,' I mumbled.

'Sorry, what was that again? Speak up, Aunty Madeleine can't hear you.'

'Aunty Madeleine will get a slap if she's not careful.' I laughed.

'Thank God I'm on the phone. As Mike said, you can be vicious,' she chided me. 'Well, all I can say is what I said before. I've great hopes for this.'

'But sure he didn't even suggest another meeting,' I told her.

'Listen, if he fed you crumble and drove you home, he's interested, I reckon. Just give it time.'

'Meanwhile, I'm off to London tomorrow night anyway.'

'Oh my God, I'd forgotten, it's the "Hi Mummy, I'm home" scenario with Emily. Are you OK about it?'

'Yeah. I'm a bit nervous for her, but I'm only there for moral support, and I've actively advised against it, so what more can I do?'

'Nothing – and remember: next time, call me before you commit. You know the rules. Whether it involves men, women or dogs, Maddy knows best.'

'Get off the line, mad Maddy.' I laughed and hung up, took Pete for a long walk then set about getting ready for my trip.

The next morning was hectic as I tried to cram everything in. Dinny rang first thing, even though I'd phoned him as soon as I left Joan and brought him up to speed.

'Any news?' he asked as soon as he heard my voice.

'Dinny' – I hoped he took my tone as a warning – 'I told you she asked for a few days to think about it.'

'I know, but that was Saturday.'

'That was less than forty-eight hours ago.'

'And you think she will meet me?'

'I think she will.' I softened slightly, because I knew how much this meant to him. 'But, as I said, she wanted to discuss it with Catherine first.'

'My God, Lulu, wouldn't that be something else all the same? My own daughter. Sure I'd be made up so I would.'

'I know you would, Dinny, so just behave yourself for the next few days. Go and light a few candles, like most people your age would.' I laughed.

'I'll tell you somethin' for nothin', if I went into a church they'd all faint, even the saints.' He chuckled. 'Still, I'll ask Violet Moore; she has a direct line to Our Lady – so they say in the village anyway. And I am still doing that novena to Saint Anthony.'

'Do it all. I'm off to London today, but I'll be back tomorrow night and I'll probably hear from her by the end of the week. And try not to worry, d'ya hear me?'

'I do, I do. And Lulu, even if nothing else happens, haven't I done my best? And it's all thanks to you. I'll never forget you for it either. Just one last thing – you didn't happen to take a snap of her at all, did you?'

'Dinny, I was terrified you'd jump out from behind a pillar with a camera of your own, so I was hardly going to take a "snap", as you call it.' He always made me smile. 'Anyway, I was trying to be discreet, Mr Cassidy, not a word you're familiar with, I think. And as I already told you, she's a stunner so you certainly knew how to pick 'em.'

'Oh I did, that's for sure. She was a looker all right. But I wasn't half bad myself, you know.'

'Get away with you, you're a flirt anyway, that I definitely do know.' He was still chuckling away as I said cheerio and hung up.

Just as I was leaving the office, I got a text from Ronan O'Meara asking if he could see me. I wondered what that was about. He and Maddy hadn't seen much of each other these past couple of weeks, but that was because she was working flat out. She set her alarm for 5 a.m. each morning, and when she finally got home it was generally after seven. Then she had to try and learn her lines for the next day and get some decent sleep before doing it all over again. Between rehearsals and costume fittings and publicity, it was a six-day week, and she was living for her time off the following week, I knew. I arranged to see Ronan when I got back, and by then I was fast running out of time, so I packed up my bits and left the office. Saying goodbye to Pete was hard; I'd grown so used to having him with me. Mary had offered to look after him, so I knew he was in for a real spoiling. 'You be a good boy.' I rubbed his head, and he nuzzled in, the way he always did.

'Don't worry, I'll bring him for a big walk this evening.' Mary was staying in my van, which I found hilarious, but she asked if she could and I suspected she needed the break, so it had all worked out fine.

'Great, here are the keys, and here's the number of my neighbours Jack and Jill. They're always around and they're lovely.' I hadn't said anything about Pete's growling, just in case it freaked her.

'Go, we'll be fine, I'm looking forward to it.' She was all business. 'And don't worry, I'll take messages, and if anything urgent crops up I'll text. Otherwise, I won't disturb you.' I'd told her about Emily and I knew she was fascinated by all my clients, but she was very discreet. In fact, Mary had turned out to be one of the best things about the office, and I decided to bring her something back from duty free. I knew she liked perfume, but she rarely spent money on herself.

Emily was a bag of nerves, but in a good way. 'Can you believe I'm doing this?' She didn't wait for a reply. 'I'm so excited just to see what she looks like.'

'What did you tell your mum?' I knew she'd opted not to let Julia know what she was doing, another thing I had cautioned her about. I just couldn't shake the bad feeling I had about all this, but there was no swaying Emily.

'Just that I was going over to see my friend Amy. It's something I do a few times a year now that flights are so cheap, so she didn't suspect anything.' She must have seen something on my face. 'I will tell her, Lulu, I promise. But, for now, I want this to be about me and my real . . . I mean birth . . . mother. Mum would have tried to persuade me not to go, or else she'd have wanted to come with me, and in a way this is my journey, no one else's, and I want to keep it like that.' She smiled. 'Although I know it's a journey for you too, and I can't tell you how grateful I am that you agreed to come. I know you're unsure.'

'I've just had some – although not that much – experience of these situations, and they're rarely straightforward.

At best, they're complicated and emotional and draining. And you're my only concern, because I know how much you want this to work out.'

'Well, at least I'll have given it my best shot,' she said. It was more or less what Dinny had said to me the other day too. Funny that all my clients were searching for something that would complete them. And helping them was, in a funny way, helping me. I no longer felt the same anger towards my mother that I had shouldered for years, although I knew I still needed to ask her questions. Families were so complicated, I was finally really understanding that.

We had a good flight, and our hotel was just off Kensington High Street, so we went and did a bit of late-night window-shopping, popping in to those that were still open. Then we had dinner and a reasonably early night in preparation for the big day ahead.

When the time finally came, I was more nervous than Emily. We'd hired a car, and she'd opted to drive, having done all her research in advance. We even had sat nav, so it was an easy drive to Tring, a pretty market town in Hertfordshire. It took about ninety minutes to get there, so we were ready for coffee as soon as we spotted Costa Coffee on the high street. There we had a final chat before we reached our destination.

'Should I call her Kitten?' Emily was full of excitement, and I was trying hard.

'Well, I think "Mum" might be pushing it a bit.' I hadn't meant to sound so flippant. 'Sorry, that came out wrong,' I told her. 'I guess I'm nervous too.'

'I can't wait to see what she looks like and get to know her a bit bet—'

'Emily, we've talked about this. A lot. Don't get your hopes up. We don't even know if she'll be at home.'

'I know, but I can't help it. Anyway, the private detective said she takes the dogs for a walk in the mornings and then heads out in her car around lunchtime most days. So we might be lucky. If not, I guess we'll just hang out and hope she comes back.'

'OK, so let's just go through it one more time. What are you going to say to her initially?'

'Just tell her who I am, then ask her if we could have a chat, take it from there, I guess.'

'And suppose she doesn't want that? Remember: this will all be a big shock for her.' God, the more I talked about it, the less convinced I became.

'Well, I'll take whatever I get. At least the contact will be there, and I'll have seen her. In some ways, I won't feel she's real until I've stood in front of her and seen what she looks like for myself. I wonder will I notice a likeness, even in her mannerisms?'

'I don't know. I really hope you're not disappointed, that's all.'

'I won't be. Stop worrying, you're normally so laidback.' Emily smiled.

We found the house easily. It was a stunning Victorian farmhouse covered in ivy, with lots of windows and what looked like the original front door. It was set on a site of about half an acre, we reckoned, but the house was close enough to the road for us to see that the front door was partially ajar and a jeep in the driveway had the back door open. We'd been there less than a minute when we heard a female voice call, 'Come on, boys, time for a walk.' We watched as two golden Labradors bounded into the back, and then we saw her.

'That's her, it has to be,' hissed Emily. 'Come on.' Before I could stop her, she'd opened the gate, which was hidden by trees, and was heading purposefully up the short drive. I ran after her.

'Hello,' the woman said as soon as she saw us. 'Are you lost?'

'No, actually, we're, eh . . . I'm looking for Kitten.'

'That's me.' The woman smiled politely, and by this stage I was close enough to see that Emily looked remarkably like her. They had the same wide face and strong jaw, and their eyes were almost identical.

'I'm Emily.' Emily looked at me. 'And this is my friend Lulu.'

'Hi.' The woman smiled at both of us. 'What can I do for you?'

'We're from Ireland,' Emily added. It was clear the woman hadn't a clue who we were.

'Nice place,' was all she said. 'I've been there.'

We had already arranged that if it all went OK, I'd scarper and wait for Emily's call. Now I waited, and it seemed like for ever before Emily said, 'I'm your daughter,' and I dreaded to think what she must have felt like, because my own heart was threatening to explode.

31

'SORRY?' AS SOON AS SHE SAID IT, I KNEW WE WERE IN trouble.

Unfortunately, Emily didn't.

'I'm so happy to meet you at last.' She looked and sounded like a child with her open, trusting face; eyes shining in anticipation of a reunion. 'I only found out about you recently and—'

'Hang on.' Kitten held up a hand. 'How did you find me? I left specific instructions with the agency that I wanted no contact.'

Emily's face changed. 'I'm sorry, I didn't get in touch with them. My mother had a file, this address was on it.' She was shocked, I could tell. 'I just wanted to see what you looked like, to see if I was . . . like you in any way.' Her voice was barely audible, and it almost broke with emotion.

I felt I had no choice but to step forward. 'Emily made some discreet enquiries, and we learned that you'd moved back here to do some work on your original family home. We have no wish to intrude on your life, if it's not convenient—'

'We can come back later, or tomorrow.' Emily looked at

me gratefully, as if I'd just rescued the situation. I found myself wishing it was that easy. The woman's manner had changed utterly once she knew who we were.

'I'm so sorry, this must be quite a surprise . . .' Emily tried again.

'It's a shock. As far as I knew, I had to consent to any contact.' Her voice told me we were an intrusion she didn't want.

'I suppose that might have been the case in years gone by. But a lot of the agencies have closed, there aren't any – or at least very few – Irish children offered for adoption now. And most people seem to trace each other through the internet, as far as I know.' I was trying to give her time to come to terms with the situation. 'I'm just wondering if there's somewhere you two could talk for a little while, so that Emily can explain a bit more of her reasons for coming here?'

'No, I'm afraid not.'

'Please?' Emily's face was grey. 'All I'm asking for is a few minutes of your time,' she pleaded.

'We don't want to cause you any embarrassment.' I felt it was important to reassure the woman. 'And if anyone else appears, we will, of course, be discreet.'

'There's no one else here except workmen,' she told us. 'It's not that. It's simply that I put all this behind me a long time ago. I'm married now, and I have other children and—'

'I have brothers and sisters?' Emily's eyes were on fire.

The woman clearly did not want to get into details. 'They don't know,' she said quietly. 'And I have no wish for them to learn of your existence. I'm sorry you've come all this way, but you must have known that this was the likely outcome. Now I really do have to go.'

'I'm not here to make any trouble, and I'm not looking for anything, I swear.' Emily looked frightened. 'But please don't send me away. At least let me come back, or meet you somewhere. Just so that we can have a proper chat.'

'That's all Emily's asking for.' I wanted to throttle the woman for her insensitivity. 'Just an hour of your time, at your convenience, and wherever you choose.'

'That won't be possible.' Kitten looked away. 'I have no wish to rake up the past. I signed away my rights and I chose not to have any contact. That hasn't changed, so I've really nothing to add.'

'Please, I'm begging you, just give me a chance.' Emily was crying now. 'All these years I've known there was something different about me. When I learned about you, a lot of things fell into place. Could you just talk to me for a short while? Then I'll get out of your life, if that's what you want. I promise.' She looked utterly defeated. 'I don't even know who my real father is, for instance,' she said quietly.

'He's dead,' Kitten said baldly. 'So there's nothing else to learn there. And I don't want to continue this, it's too . . .' I thought she was going to say 'upsetting', but instead she said . . . 'unpleasant. It was a part of my life that I'd rather forget. There's nothing else I can tell you. Now I'm going to ask you again if you wouldn't mind leaving, and please don't make any further efforts to contact me because I'm afraid I won't be available to meet you.'

'Don't you have any curiosity about me at all?' Emily

hadn't taken her eyes off Kitten since we'd arrived. 'Suppose I do all the talking, fill you in on my life. How would that be?'

'I don't think you understand.' The woman had an odd way about her that I hadn't been able to put my finger on up until now. In fact, it had only just occurred to me that I'd never come across anyone quite like her before. She was utterly detached and totally unmoved by any emotion. 'I have no wish to know any details, and I'm sorry if that upsets you, but better to know where you stand, I feel. Therefore I won't be keeping in touch under any circumstances.' I wondered what had happened to her to make her so unmoved by a child she'd carried in her womb and given birth to. The one good thing for me was that she made my mother seem like an angel. I shuddered. 'Now I really do have to go, so I must ask you to leave.' With that she dismissed her baby girl once more.

'Come on.' I took Emily by the hand as if she was still that child and, to my surprise, she let me take over. 'I'm sorry,' she said just before we moved away. 'I only wanted to see what you looked like and to let you know that I was fine, that I'd had a good life and to tell you there was no need to worry about me.' She sounded like the child I'd once been, desperately trying to win approval. And from the look on Kitten's face, that approval was never coming – although, as she looked at us, I thought I sensed a crack in her facade.

I was almost in tears myself at that point. 'Let's go, love.' I led Emily away.

Once I'd settled her in the car, I made an instant decision. 'Wait here a moment,' I told her, and headed back to Kitten, who was just about to get into her jeep. 'I just wanted to say something,' I told her, but in reality I'd no idea what it was. All I was certain of was that it would come out. 'You can be very proud of your firstborn child. She's a lovely girl, inside as well as out. She's no more capable of causing you pain or trouble than one of those dogs, so have no worries on that score. But I hope, for your sake, that no one ever does to you what you've just done to her. Because no human being deserves to be treated with so little respect.' I fished in my bag. 'I'll leave my card in case you want to talk to me further.' I dropped a business card on the passenger seat. 'And I hope your daughter didn't inherit your total lack of compassion. Actually, scrap that, because I know for a fact that she didn't. I don't think I've ever met anyone with so little regard for another person's feelings. And to think that in this case it's your own child.' I was shaking with anger. 'Shame on you,' I said softly, and for a split second I saw that shame reflected in her eyes, despite all she'd said, but that and the myriad other emotions that flashed briefly across her face were masked by a veil of aloofness on top of an ice-cold exterior. I suspected it was how she'd learned to cope.

I knew there was nothing more I could say then, so I turned away and headed back to do what little I could for a girl who deserved so much more.

I'd never seen anyone quite as shocked as Emily appeared to be. She was curled up in a ball on the seat, rocking backwards and forwards. Her face was whiter than the most brilliant paint colour and she was sucking her thumb like a baby. I took off my coat and wrapped it around her and sat in and turned the heat up full blast. As I manoeuvred out into the traffic, I saw Kitten watching us and, selfishly, I hoped she was suffering. After what I'd seen on her face at the end I suspected that she was a deeply troubled woman, and I felt a tinge of sadness for her for the first time.

For the rest of the day, I minded Emily as best I could. We'd checked out of our hotel, so I took her to the first decent-looking one I came across and, once inside, I settled her in a corner and ordered hot soup and strong tea. She ate virtually nothing and said very little either, but I had enough experience to know that she'd talk when she was ready. So I simply sat with her and made small talk and treated her like the invalid she was. We stayed there for almost two hours, and then I put her back in the car. She looked slightly less shell shocked when we reached the check-in desk at the airport. I bought water and chocolate and all the current magazines and red tops for gossip, and once our flight had taken off I pulled down her table top, left her a selection of everything, and I was happy that she drank a little water and flicked through one of the tabloids.

'Can I stay with you tonight?' she asked blankly as soon as we were through Customs.

'Yes, of course,' I told her. 'And if you give me your car keys, I'll drive. We have to collect Pete from the office on the way, and I could pick up some food as well.' Emily didn't reply, so I went ahead with my plan. I rang Mary en route to tell her we'd landed and that it was OK to leave Pete and head home.

'How did it go? Can you talk?' she asked.

'No,' I told her, but she guessed from my voice.

'I'm sorry,' she said quietly, and I thanked her and told her Pete had bought her a present.

At the office, Emily didn't move, and my gorgeous dog greeted me as if he'd been afraid I'd never come back, and I gave him the biggest cuddle and whispered in his ear to be nice to Emily. He jumped in the back of her car and, when I stopped for fish and chips, he climbed on to the front seat and sat on her lap, almost smothering her.

Once home I settled Emily on the couch, turned on the heating as well as the kettle, and by the time I'd brought our bags in Pete was her hot-water bottle. I noticed she kept stroking him, and he looked at her as if he understood every bit of her pain.

Again, she hardly ate a thing, but by the time I'd made up her bed and brought her in a cup of hot chocolate, she seemed a bit brighter. Pete looked at me as if asking permission to stay with her, and I patted him on the head and told him he was a great boy and he settled down right beside her. When I left them, she was still stroking his head.

Next morning, she seemed a good bit better. She was up and dressed by the time I arrived in the kitchen. I'd heard her mooching about much earlier – impossible not to where I lived.

'I hope you don't mind, but I took a shower?' She was on the banquette with her feet tucked up under her and Pete on the floor beside her. As soon as he saw me, he came to reassure me, that he was still mine, I reckoned, but I gave him a treat for looking after Emily and he headed back to resume his duties.

'Of course not. I told you last night, it's your home for as long as you need it.'

'Thanks, but I'd better head off.'

'When are you back at work?' I asked her. She was a librarian, and I knew she loved her job.

'I left it open, because I wasn't sure what would happen.' She looked sad. 'But no sense in wasting any more of my holidays, eh? I told Mum I'd probably be home today, so I should make tracks. She worries about me.' I think she was as struck by the irony of that remark as I was, given what we'd just experienced.

'Well, you know where I am, and I want you to promise to ring, or text, me at any time. Day or night, OK? I'll do whatever I can to help you, you know that. And you will get through it, I promise.'

'Thank you, I don't know what I'd have done without you, actually. You made the whole thing bearable. At least now I know the score. And even though, right at this moment, I feel as if I'll never get over it, I know that some people are given much heavier crosses to carry and they manage.'

'You'll manage,' I assured her.

She looked at me with the eyes of a little girl who'd just been abandoned and didn't know what would happen next. In many ways she reminded me of myself as a child, always wondering what I'd done wrong.

'And do you know something?' Her lip was trembling. 'Even though it didn't work out, I'm still glad I did it.'

32

MY FIRST APPOINTMENT WAS WITH RONAN.

'How are you?' I shook his hand automatically, but it always seemed as if I knew him better than I actually did, so this greeting felt a bit too formal.

'I'm good, thanks.' He sat down.

'And Deputy?'

'Not visiting as often.' He grinned. 'I think Myrtle's finally relaxed.'

'I'm glad. How's she keeping?'

'Same as ever. More social engagements than the two of us put together. She'll be dating online next, I swear.'

'It wouldn't surprise me. And you and Maddy, how's that going?' As soon as I said it, I realized I shouldn't have.

His face told me he was a bit thrown. 'Eh, I haven't really seen her, to be honest. She's busy, and I've been pretty tied up as well.'

'Sorry, I wasn't implying anything.' I decided to be up-front about it. 'It's just that I know you two keep in touch, that's all.'

'Yeah, we do. She's fun.

'I need a bit of advice.' His whole demeanour changed. 'It's about . . . Lucas.' The way he said the name let me know that he was unused to saying it aloud.

'OK, I'll do anything I can.' I was so pleased to hear him finally talk about the child that I was more than happy to listen.

'I've decided I want to have him formally adopted.' He didn't look at me. 'My family is not happy. My mother and my gran are on my case, I reckon, because they stop talking any time I come within a mile of them. And my sister, Ellen, says she won't let me do it, even though I know she already loves the child as if he were her own.'

'You've talked to her about it, obviously?'

'Yes. You see, he's four now, and that means he starts school in September, so he'll be based up there in Donegal. I know they love him, and they're all he's ever known, so it makes sense. For some reason, though, Ellen is adamant. I don't understand it, I thought she'd have jumped at the chance.'

'Maybe she feels it's not the right thing to do? For Lucas, I mean?'

'How can it not be right for him? They're his parents.' He closed his eyes and sighed heavily.

'That's the thing, Ronan. They're not. You're Lucas's father.'

Just like that night in the pub, I'd said something he didn't want to hear.

'I'm his father in name only. It means nothing. I've never bonded with him and, most important of all, I have no interest in raising him.' He stood up. 'I'm sorry, I shouldn't have brought this up. I'd better get back.' He headed for the door.

I knew I had to try and rescue the situation this time. I stood up and got there before him. 'Don't go. It's not my intention to upset you; in fact, I'd very much like to help if I can. Please, sit down.' I sensed he needed a moment. 'Why don't I make us some coffee?' Without waiting for a reply, I left the room.

When I returned with a tray a couple of minutes later, he was staring out the window. Pete was beside him, head up as if to say, 'It'll be OK, don't worry.' I smiled at the picture they made.

'You think I'm wrong – everybody does – but it's the way I want it,' he said quietly. 'Why can't any of you accept it? Why do all the women in my life want to change me, I wonder?'

'Do they?'

'Yes. There's my gran, my mother, my sister and you.'

'Does Maddy know anything?' I asked simply because I wondered what her take on it would be. She sometimes had a way of looking at situations that was different to the norm.

'No, and I don't want her to. Is that OK with you?'

'Of course,' I assured him. 'Have you talked to anyone else, someone not so close? Even, dare I say it, a man?' I grinned. 'Less hormones flying and all that.'

'No, the only one I'd consider would be Ellen's husband. And he's decided to stay out of it. Sensible enough, I suppose.'

'Probably,' I agreed. 'Although it will affect him too, in a big way.'

'Yes, but Ellen's the driving force there, always has been. He'll go along with whatever she wants.'

'Ronan, would you at least meet Lucas?' I decided to cut to the chase. 'I just wonder about your ability to make such an important decision when you've never really had any-thing to do with your son.' I watched him carefully. He was such a complex man; I was learning a bit more about him as time went on.

'I saw a bit of him . . . initially.' He sounded defensive.

'I know that and, believe me, I think I understand how difficult this must be for you, and you have my word that I only want to help you make the right decision. For you and for Lucas. It's just that, he's a little boy now, with a personality, and—'

'Don't you see? That's exactly what I couldn't cope with. He'll be so like her, I just know he will, and every time I look at him I'll be reminded all over again of what I lost that day.' I realized he had tears in his eyes, so I busied myself with the coffee to give him a moment. 'I just don't think I could bear it. Believe me, this is not the way I want it to be.' It was the first indication he'd given of that.

'And tell me, what would be your ideal scenario now, given that there's nothing you can do to bring Audrey back?'

He looked at me as if he'd never thought about it. 'What do you mean?'

'Suppose you could have any relationship you want with Lucas, what would that be?'

He looked blank. 'I've no idea.'

'Well, thinking about that might not be a bad place to start,' I suggested.

'I suppose, in an ideal world, I'd want him,' he said after a long silence.

'And what would that entail?'

'I guess I'd need him with me. I'd want to make it up to him, be the best dad I could possibly be.' He put his head in his hands. 'Even the term "Dad" scares me to death. Little boys need so much.'

'When it comes down to it, all they need – like any of us – is love, really. Two parents would be the ideal, but one good one isn't half bad either.' For about the hundredth time in the past few weeks, my own childhood jumped up and hit me a smack in the eye.

'I can't do it,' he said simply.

'But do you know that?' I asked him, deciding to go for broke. 'At least if you met him and spent a bit of time with him, you'd be able to make a decision. And do you know something, Ronan? It's OK to be scared. And it would be OK to decide you'd be no good for him. I think maybe that's all your sister wants.'

'How do you mean?' He looked puzzled.

'Well, I've only met her once, and I could see that she loves Lucas. I think she's doing the most unselfish thing possible by refusing to adopt him. Having him legally hers is probably what she wants, deep down, more than anything. But maybe, like me, she's not sure that, ultimately, it's the right thing for you.'

'So what are you saying, exactly? That I have to give this thing a go? Then what happens if it doesn't work out? If I can't bear to look at him? What will that do to the child?' I knew he wasn't asking me really; he was asking himself.

304

'I wouldn't be suggesting for a second that you uproot him, tell him who you are, then dump him if it doesn't work out. That would be cruel. But what have you got to lose by meeting him, spending an hour with him, just seeing how you feel? He doesn't have to know anything except that you're his uncle.'

'I don't know if I can do it,' he said after an age.

'Well, at least you're thinking about it, that's a good start.' I smiled. 'We've come a long way from that night in the pub when you told me to mind my own business.'

He wasn't listening; his eyes looked far away.

'Why don't you just live with the idea for a while?'

'Would you talk to my gran, get her to speak to the others and persuade them to lay off?' he asked.

'I will if it helps you decide.'

'Thanks.'

'And just for the record, I think you're very brave.'

'Do you?' He looked like no one ever gave him any praise, or maybe that was my own personal angst.

'Yes I do, and I've no doubt that, whatever decision you make, it'll be made with care and consideration. And at the end of the day, that's all anyone can ask of you.'

He looked at me for a second, then went and stood at the window again. I made a few notes, just to give him the space and silence he needed as he struggled with emotions which I suspected were threatening to smother him. When he turned back, I don't know who was more surprised, me or him.

'I think you're right, I need to meet him,' was all he said.

33

HE LEFT SHORTLY AFTERWARDS TO MAKE ARRANGEMENTS, BUT not before he'd asked if he could use me as a sounding board. I told him I was happy to help in any way I could. Now that he was seeing Maddy, I felt we had a personal connection, even though I couldn't mention anything about it to her.

Two hours later, Myrtle rang. 'I had to tell you straight-away.' She sounded breathless. 'Ronan's just called in. He's decided he wants to meet Lucas.'

'That's wonderful,' I told her. I have to admit, I'd wondered if he'd have the courage to go through with it.

'It's all my prayers answered.' She was close to tears by the sound of her.

'Well, just let him take it at his own pace, that'll be very important.' I felt I had to urge caution. 'This is a huge step for Ronan, so please be careful as a family not to put him under any more pressure than he's under already.'

'Of course, I'll say that to my daughter as well. You're a very wise young woman, do you know that?'

'Not always.' I laughed. 'How will Ellen deal with all this, by the way?'

'That was one of my worries. But you know, deep down,

it's what she's always wanted. She adores the child, but she knows that, long term, it would be better for Lucas and for Ronan if they were together. But we'll be keeping a very close eye on her, believe me. We're very conscious of her role in the boy's life.'

'That's good.' We chatted for a while longer, then I had to go because Joan Lehane was holding for me. I promised Myrtle I'd keep in touch and wondered what the next conversation would bring.

After we'd exchanged pleasantries, she got down to business.

'I've spoken to Catherine, and she thinks it's time to meet Denis, as long as I'm happy about it, so I was wondering if you could set it up?'

'Sure. That's great to hear.' I knew Dinny would be over the moon. 'When were you thinking?'

'I'll email you details, if that's OK? Probably in a week or two. We'll come and spend a weekend, and I can see my family; I hardly had a chance last time. So I might suggest, say, lunch on the Saturday. Would you join us?'

'Yes, if you'd like me to, but wouldn't I just be in the way?'

'No, I think it would help. It might just be a bit awkward, especially in the beginning.'

'OK, well then, what if I join you initially and then I can slip away if things are going smoothly? That's supposing Denis is OK with all of this, of course.' But I knew he'd be delighted with my support as well.

'Great. Talk to you later in the week. I have your email address on the card you gave me.'

We said goodbye, and I dialled Dinny's number straight-away.

'Joan wants to meet you, and she's bringing Catherine,' I told him, and part of me wished I'd been there to see his face.

'What?' He sounded gobsmacked. There was a silence, which I didn't break, giving him a moment I knew he'd need. 'Are you serious?' he whispered finally. 'She said that?'

'She did. She rang just now.'

'Well, isn't that mighty altogether. When? Where? I'll have to get a new suit.' The old Dinny was back.

'Hold your horses.' I laughed. 'It hasn't been set up yet. She's suggesting lunch one Saturday over the next few weeks.' I filled him in, and he was like a child. 'She's asked me to join you. Would that be OK?'

'What, sure aren't you the one who organized this whole thing? I wouldn't have gone without you,' he bellowed, the way he always did when something was important. 'I want you to be the first to meet my daughter.' He didn't say anything for a second, and I thought I heard him swallow hard. 'Lulu, you've no idea what it's like to say those two words out loud.'

'Well, hopefully you'll be introducing her to half of Wicklow before long.' I smiled just hearing the emotion in his voice.

'My God, I think I need to lie down. I haven't had this much excitement in years.' I was happy for him. He deserved it.

I promised to ring him with all the details, and I left him planning a trip into Sean Connolly Menswear in Wicklow town to be 'kitted out from head to toe'.

Being knee-deep in happy families made me think about Emily, so I texted her to see how she was. She rang me immediately.

'Do you think there's anything else I can do?' she wanted to know. 'I just feel so sad all the time.'

'I don't think there's much more any of us can do,' I said gently. 'Except wait, and hope that when Kitten's had a chance to think about things, she just might change her mind. I'm sorry; I know this is not easy for you.'

'I guess I just never saw it ending like this. I know you warned me and all that, but somehow I was so sure that once she saw me she'd be delighted. How wrong was I?'

'She must have buried it all very deeply,' I told Emily. 'And maybe us turning up like that was just too big a shock initially. She might change her mind eventually and feel she owes it to you to meet you properly but, for the moment, all you can do is wait and see.' I didn't feel very hopeful though, she'd seemed so adamant.

'Would a letter help, d'ya think?'

'Hard to say, but somehow I doubt it. In some ways, maybe you not getting in touch again would make her feel you're less of a threat. I think that was her big worry.'

'If only she knew I wouldn't hurt a fly – it's just not in my nature to cause anyone any trouble.' Emily sighed. 'Surely she'd have known that just by looking at me?'

'I think she would have ordinarily, but the circumstances weren't really your normal everyday occurrence.' Hearing her dejected voice, after Dinny's excitement, brought me back down to earth with a bang.

'I should have listened to you in the first place and not gone tearing in,' she said quietly.

'Well, at least she's seen you, and she knows you want to meet her. Maybe once she thinks about it logically she'll realize she overreacted.'

'Yeah, I suppose,' she said – but neither of us would be betting on it, I knew.

I spent the next few hours writing up notes on all my clients. What with Ronan and his impending meeting with his son; Emily's mother and her unwillingness to form a bond with her firstborn; and Denis's possible new family, it seemed as if I was engrossed in parent-and-child relationships yet no nearer to sorting my own. Just as I was finishing up, my phone rang. It was Mike, I was delighted to see.

'Am I interrupting some revolution in dog therapy?' he asked when I answered.

'No, actually, I seem to be deeply embedded in the lives of my four-legged friends' families,' I told him. 'And they all seem to be connected with children, which is a bit surreal.' I sighed. 'No matter how hard I try, it's the owners who are keeping me busy; the dogs are much less complicated.'

'Well, I have a nice normal – by your standards anyway – referral for you,' he said. 'Our next-door neighbour has a parrot who's been depressed since his owner's husband died, almost a year ago. He's plucked off all his feathers and has a twitch. I'm not lying.'

'Oh, I've heard of that.' I was immediately keen. 'Parrots are among the most intelligent of pets. There is a medication used to treat depression in animals, you know.'

'What, you mean Prozac for parrots, lithium for lizards?'
He laughed. 'You're kidding me, right?'

'No, I'm deadly serious.'

'Jesus, I should have known. Only you, Lulu. Only you.'
I could almost hear him scratching his head.

'I'd be happy to advise your neighbour. Give her my number.'

'Are you sure you're not on something yourself?'

'Just high on life, can't you tell?' I joked.

'Well, Rita will be delighted. She cornered me last night on my way in the door. To be honest, I thought she'd been at the gin bottle. But believe me, the parrot is not a pretty sight, and Rita has had a bad year, so I promised to ask you about it,' he said. 'So, listen, are you going to Maddy's launch party on Thursday?'

'Are you crazy? Of course I'm going. It's the most exciting thing to happen to me and Clodagh in years. Everyone's going. Are you?'

'Louis gave me no choice. Apparently, there's some gorgeous actor he fancies who's just been cast in the show and he's convinced himself the guy is gay. So expect a lot of drama. Anyway, how about we meet you and Clodagh for a drink beforehand? I guess Maddy will be too busy.'

'Yep, but Clodagh and I were planning to grab an early pizza; otherwise we'll end up trollied. Fancy joining us? She knows this gorgeous little Italian in Temple Bar. I can ask her to change the booking to four.'

'Perfect. What time? I'll probably head into town straight from the office. I'll leave the car there and walk over to join you.'

311

'Cool, I'll text you the time. I have a hair appointment, so I'll be finishing early. This is a big night for me too, you know. My best friend is famous.'

'Yeah, the show is getting a lot of publicity all right, and Maddy is featuring a fair bit. Is it any good, d'ya know?'

'It really is, I've seen a few of the rushes, and Clodagh and I were on set one of the days.' I was so excited for my friend. 'Maddy deserves this more than anyone else I know.'

'By the way, Pedro is behaving much better since he saw your vet. Did Louis tell you he does have a back problem?'

'Yes, and I'm delighted we found out what the problem was. Good result.'

'Any news on the Clodagh/Paddy Russell thing? Could I bring him along on Thursday?'

'I haven't had a second to chat about it to Maddy. Sorry. And d'ya know, I think Thursday's not a good night. Clodagh will be too preoccupied.'

'OK, it's shaping up to be a good party anyway. As long as I stay away from trollied dollies I might even get home smelling only of aftershave. Bye.' He was laughing as he hung up.

I worked on, and it was an hour later than I expected when I was ready to leave the office. On impulse, I decided to indulge in a bit of late-night shopping so I left Pete snoozing away and headed for Dundrum town centre, where I bought a gorgeous purple dress in Harvey Nicks and shoes and a bag in House of Fraser, despite my earlier resolutions not to indulge. Passing through Bray later, I decided to treat myself to a pizza and have an early night. I was looking forward to Thursday and was in high spirits as I parked the bike and gathered up my purchases. Suddenly, Pete took off, barking madly, which gave me a real fright. I dumped my bags on the deck and, as I followed him, I heard a noise of someone scurrying off in the distance. It could have been an animal, but it sounded like footsteps. 'Pete,' I called, and he came immediately, tail wagging as if to say, 'That got rid of him.'

'Come on, there's a good boy.' I had no idea if the dog was simply reacting to some night creatures – Jack and Jill had warned me that there were rabbits about; most of their newly planted garden had suffered as a result.

I let myself in and turned on the deck lights. Something wasn't quite right. It took me a few seconds to figure it out, but then I realized that the place was not as I'd left it. A drawer was slightly open and there was a book on the floor. In my bedroom, the wardrobe where I kept most of my stuff looked different, as if someone had rifled through it, although I couldn't be sure I wasn't just paranoid by that stage. I rang Maddy, but her phone went straight to message. Clodagh answered immediately, however. 'Call the guards, I'll be there as quick as I can,' she told me.

'But I'm not—'

'Lou, please, just do it. Based on what you said, someone's been in. I'm on the way.' She hung up and I did as instructed.

Two young gardai, one male, one female, arrived almost straightaway. 'We were in the town.' Clare Grogan introduced herself and her colleague Tim Hynes. 'Tell us what happened. Anything missing?'

'That's the odd thing – nothing appears to have been taken but my things aren't where I left them,' I told them.

'Also, there's no sign of a window broken or anything, so I'm worried that someone may have a key.'

'These locks are used a lot, so a bunch of keys would undoubtedly have one that fits,' Tim Hynes said. 'You might consider getting a locksmith out.'

Jack and Jill arrived then, having spotted the garda car coming down the lane.

'Are you all right?' Jill was out of breath.

'Yes, come in.' I explained what had happened, but by this time I was beginning to feel a bit stupid about making a fuss. Clodagh appeared shortly afterwards. 'Don't get stressed out: break-ins to mobile homes are very common in winter.' Clare confirmed what I knew already. 'Even though these are really chalets, people still see them as holiday homes and therefore think they're empty in winter. Have you someone to stay with you tonight?'

'Me,' Clodagh offered.

'Are you sure?' I knew she was up to her tonsils in work.

'Certain.'

'OK so, that's grand. And I'll radio in all the details, and we'll keep an eye on the place for the next few weeks, OK? We generally have a car in the area all night anyway, because the slot machines in the amusement places are easy targets. So we'll include this place on our rounds; that way you can sleep easy,' Tim Hynes told me. 'Try not to worry. As Clare said, it was probably just an opportunist hoping to get some jewellery or small electrical items left behind. And ring this number if you discover anything missing, or even if you're just nervous. There's always someone on duty, and they'll radio whoever's out and about.'

'Thank you, I appreciate it.' I felt a bit stupid for taking up their time, but the others assured me I'd done the right thing.

The gardai left after having been assured that no money or valuables were missing, although I had nothing of value in the van really, and most of my jewellery was simply fashion stuff. But about €200 in my bedside locker was still where I'd left it, so everybody reckoned the intruder had heard me arrive home.

Jill put the kettle on, Jack went to get their bottle of whiskey to 'liven up the coffees' and Clodagh offered to stay as long as I needed her. Once again, I was delighted I had Pete, who seemed determined to protect me.

34

MADDY'S LAUNCH TURNED OUT TO BE JUST THE DISTRACTION I needed, because it gave me no time to think. Clodagh insisted on staying for a few days and went off next morning to collect her laptop and all her paraphernalia as well as her clothes and washbag.

'I'm here for a while – no arguing, thank you. Although maybe we should stay in my place on Thursday? Let's see what happens.' It was typical Clodagh, and I was more than happy to have her boss me around.

On Wednesday evening, we had a real girly night. Maddy came to stay, and we did face packs, eyebrows, the lot, all in our dressing gowns, then we opened 'just the one' bottle of bubbly to toast her big break. Clodagh headed off to bed shortly afterwards, because she was off for a run along the seafront at dawn, and Maddy refused to sleep in the 'doll's bed' that was my second guest room and insisted on bunking in with me instead.

'What are we like, the pair of us?' She wriggled her feet in fleecy socks and sipped the hot chocolate I'd made her. 'We've both had great success, yet here we are, sleeping in a caravan like the two urchins we are.'

'Listen, you're the star, not me, and once the series goes out you won't be able to walk around Dublin without having to pose for photos.' I marvelled at how little she'd really changed in all the years I'd known her.

'And what about you? Are you happy? What I mean is, are you really content with your lot?'

'Yep, I am.' I was so glad to be able to say that. 'I love my job and my life, and while I may not stay here for ever, what it's taught me is that the simple life suits me. I always thought I needed lots of "stuff" to survive, but in fact I don't.'

'And what about your mum and Becky? You OK there?'

'Yeah. Haven't heard from either of them in ages, actually. And dealing with all these dysfunctional parent-and-child relationships has made me see I need to talk to Mum, tell her how I've felt all these years.'

'Well, I won't ever let you take responsibility for any of that.' Maddy shook her head. 'It was your mother's failure – you know that, don't you?'

'Yeah, finally I do,' I told her. 'Whatever happens, the parent has to be the one to sort it out, but I suppose not all of them face up to it. Just because we're adults, it doesn't make it any easier, I guess.'

She sighed. 'It's as if the string that binds most families together got severed in your case.'

'Well, the father thing would account for some of it, I suppose. And I'm just happy not to be trying so hard any more. You've kept me going too, so many times, don't forget that.'

'I'm so glad we became friends.' She hugged me. 'It's going to be a great year for the three of us. Clodagh is flying, and you're completely chilled and enjoying life and I'm riding high at the moment too.'

'And has Ronan anything to do with it?'

'I'm not sure actually. Initially I felt a strong connection, but he's sort of, I dunno, pulled back a bit lately. But then so have I. Work's been all-consuming. I'd say it could go either way with him and, to be honest, I don't really know what I want. Besides, there's a cute new director on the show who's taking a lot of interest in my performance.' She giggled and stretched her furry toes. 'I'll introduce you to him tomorrow and you can tell me what you think.'

'Can't wait.' I finished my camomile tea and snuggled down under the duvet. 'Mike's going, by the way. We were supposed to meet him beforehand, but he texted me today to say he had a late meeting and would have to drop out, but he'd see us all there.'

'I sense great times ahead for you two.' Maddy winked. 'Can I be bridesmaid?'

'Idiot, you know we have that pact already.' I prodded her under the covers then switched off the bedside lamps. 'Although how you sense great times ahead when he just cancelled dinner with me is beyond my comprehension.' I laughed and we both settled down.

'I do like him more as time goes on, though,' I said into the pitch-black hole that was night-time in the country. 'He sort of gets me, I suppose. It's like I've known him for ever.'

'I think you're a match, all right.' She giggled. 'And Maddy knows these things.'

We yawned at the same time then were asleep within

seconds, although I did have to kick her once or twice during the night because she was snoring.

Next day was a bit manic; I had a new poodle called Bambi, white with a pink bow, as a client. It was another classic case: his owner, Joanna, had treated him like a king since she'd got him as a pup, imposed no discipline whatsoever, never exercised him and, as a result, was killing him with kindness – literally. He was so fat he could hardly walk. And now he wouldn't tolerate strangers anywhere near her and she was surprised!

I just about managed to get my hair done, but had to work a bit later as a result and so ended up changing in the office. Mary was taking Pete for the night, so they headed off together, after she'd told me I looked the best she'd ever seen me look, which I took as a compliment. The purple dress was very fitted, with a chiffon, see-through outer layer, so I felt sexy, and a bit funky thanks to some of Maddy's jewellery and my new shoes and bag.

I met Clodagh in town but we were both running late so, after a trillion texts, we had cancelled the pizza place and headed straight for Krystal, where the party was being held. The first person we met was Maddy, along with the other main stars, posing for a photo outside. Judging by the number of photographers, it was the place to be tonight. We waited and admired it all from afar, then Maddy broke free and dragged us inside, talking a mile a minute, telling us who was here so far and declaring Clodagh hot and me a ride.

There were loads of people from TV and radio, and a good number of soap stars over from London, along with a few we recognized but couldn't quite place.

'Failed *X Factor* finalists, one or two of them, then there's that irritating guy from *I'm a Celebrity*, and yer wan who looked like she never wore any underwear on *Strictly Come Dancing*. Oh, and that good-lookin' guy from *The Apprentice*, along with the bitch who never shut up moaning.' Maddy had filled us in on everyone within thirty seconds. 'Oh, and one or two *Big Brother* finalists.'

'How can you possibly tell all that?' Clodagh wanted to know.

'I can't, I'm making it up, but with reality-show contestants you can't go wrong.' She handed us each a glass of champagne and we nabbed a tray of gorgeous nibbles from a cute waiter, who kept feeding us once Maddy had winked at him.

Before long, Louis and Mike joined us, with Louis carrying a huge bunch of flowers for Maddy.

'Oh my God, I feel like a bride or something.' She was thrilled. Mike gave her a big hug then handed her what looked like champagne in a wooden casket.

'It's Dom P.' She sounded amazed as she peered into the carrier bag.

'Nothing but the best,' Mike said. 'I'm just looking for an invite to all the top parties now that you're really famous.'

'Done.' She kissed him full on the lips. 'As long as you mind Lulu at them all, she has a few bad habits that tend to get her into trouble.' She winked at me.

'And haven't I had first-hand experience of most of them?' Mike avoided my eyes.

'Wow, Lulu, you look amazing.' Louis grabbed me and swung me around. 'You too, Clodagh.' He gave her a hug.

320

It was madness but great fun. Maddy even insisted one of the Sunday papers take a photo of 'me and my two best friends', and she promised the photographer that if we made it on to the gossip page of what was arguably the paper most widely read over breakfast each weekend, she'd get him a walk-on part as an extra on the show. 'You're on,' he told her, and jotted down our names.

The time passed so quickly. There were speeches, then we got to watch the first episode, and everyone said Maddy was brilliant; even people who didn't know her were offering congrats. I was proud as Punch as I drifted around.

Clodagh had met a guy she used to deal with in her last job, and they were deep in 'potential-new-client' territory, Maddy and Mike were having what looked like a heart to heart in the corner, so I was pleased when Ronan O'Meara came up to say hello.

'I was wondering when I'd see you,' I greeted him warmly. 'How've you been?'

'Good, yeah.' He looked tired. 'I only just got here. Some party, eh?'

'Amazing,' I told him. 'I keep smiling at people I think I know and then I realize they're on TV. Have you seen Maddy?'

'Yes, only briefly though. She's in huge demand from what I can see.'

Shortly afterwards, the girl herself appeared and dragged him off to meet her co-stars.

'I think I've just been chatted up by a model.' Mike appeared at my side.

'At my Christmas party, you swore you were not getting

involved with young ones. Too much effort, was what you said, as I recall.'

'Ah, but this was different, this was a male model.' Mike grinned. 'Thankfully, Louis took him off my hands. Close, though.' He wiped his forehead.

'Well, I was doing quite well myself with an ageing DJ until you frightened him off.' I indicated a well-known radio jock with dyed blond hair wearing very tight jeans.

'Oops, sorry about that. I'd say he's just your type, too. You look great.' He smiled. 'Are you enjoying it?'

'Loving every minute,' I told him.

'By the way, Louis wants to cook the three of you dinner on Saturday night at our place. How you fixed?'

'I'm free.' I was delighted. 'And Maddy said she was planning to have a lazy weekend, because she hasn't stopped since Christmas and next week's her first break since she got the part, so I'd say you're on.'

'Great, will you check with Clodagh so?' Mike asked. 'My only job was to invite you all, and he'll swoop any minute to check up on me.' He looked around and was immediately nabbed by someone, so I excused myself and went in search of a drink.

Maddy introduced me to several more people, and before I knew it the night was coming to a close. For the first time ever, she swore she couldn't stay standing for one more minute, so we headed into a corner and caught up. 'God, if I have to make small talk with one more journalist I'll need an injection.' She grinned.

'Where's Ronan?' I asked. 'I haven't seen him in ages.'

'He had to leave. I was a bit disappointed, to be honest.

Apparently, Ellen's in town, and he had to meet her.'

'I think there's some stuff going on there,' I told her. 'I'm sure he'll fill you in.'

'Yeah, he mentioned that he'd a lot on his plate, which is fine. I'm just not sure himself and myself are going anywhere fast though.'

'Do you still like him?'

'Yeah, I do, but d'ya know, it wouldn't kill me if it ended tomorrow. I'm having a ball right now, with or without a man. What did you think of our director, by the way? Cute, eh, just like I said?'

'Yes, and you're right, he couldn't take his eyes off you. But this is your time to shine, I'm certain of it. I think you're right to just see where the Ronan thing takes you,' I told her.

'How about Mike?' she whispered. 'He seems to keep coming back to you.'

'Yes, we've had a few good chats. But he knows half the people here, from what I can see, so he's in demand.'

'He is, and from where I'm sitting, whatshername – the actress in *Fair City* – is determined to get her claws into him.' Maddy put on her evil face. 'Should I go rescue him?'

'No, he's a big boy, he can look after himself,' I told her. 'Did he invite you to dinner on Saturday, by the way?'

'He did, and I'm in. So's Clodagh. And if Mike doesn't suggest dinner with you soon – just the two of you – I owe you a tenner. He's interested, you mark my words.'

'Maybe, but it sort of suits me to get to know him a bit first. Does that sound strange? I'm kind of getting used to myself all over again and I like the fact that I'm not in a hurry

323

for anything. Even though a night of mad passionate sex with him might be just what I need.' I giggled, and Clodagh sat down and demanded to be let in on the joke. I took the opportunity to mention Paddy Russell, and to my surprise she remembered him and declared him 'quite fanciable', so Maddy decided we were doing all right for three spinsters.

'D'ya know, for once in my life I may not be the last to leave the party, I'm completely zonked,' Maddy said a short while later. 'What time is it?'

'It's after midnight – what say we hit the road?' Clodagh said.

'Only on condition that we can walk up to Burdocks, buy chips and sit on the wall near the park and eat them,' Maddy said.

'You're a star, you can't buy chips and sit on a wall eating them out of a bag,' I joked.

'Watch me, I'm starving again.'

'Me too,' I decided. 'Let's go.'

Maddy kissed half of Dublin on the way out. I snuck a glance at Mike and he was deep in conversation with the soap star, so I told Louis we'd see them both on Saturday and the three of us legged it.

Clodagh and the guy she'd been talking to earlier decided to go to a noodle place nearby, so I arranged to pick her up there in about forty minutes. We'd decided to stay in her apartment rather than pay for a cab to Bray, so we made faces at Clodagh through the window of her 'posh' joint and Maddy and I headed off for chips arm in arm, carrying our shoes and a bag each of presents she'd received.

We had tea and chips and fought over the last bite of spiceburger which we were sharing, then I walked with Maddy as far as Christchurch Cathedral, our parting spot. She hung out the window and waved her flowers and shouted that she loved me as she headed off in a cab. Then I caught up with Clodagh, as arranged, and we were home and in bed within half an hour.

Next morning, I woke early, showered and jumped in a taxi and headed for the office, where I'd left my bike. I was trying to decide whether to make a quick trip home, as it was still early and I'd left some of my stuff there, when my phone rang. It was Tim Hynes, the young garda who'd been at my house a while back.

'I just wondered if I might come and see you.' He sounded serious. 'I'm actually at your place now.'

'I'm in the office, but I could be there in fifteen minutes or so,' I told him. 'Is everything OK?'

'I just need to talk to you in person,' he said. 'I could come to you, if that's easier?'

'No, I need to collect some bits from home anyway.' I had a bad feeling suddenly. 'Has my place been broken into again?' I asked him. 'Or is something wrong with one of my family?' It was all I could think of.

'No, no.' He seemed anxious to say it, so that calmed me down. 'I'll wait here so, if that's OK?'

'Yes, I'm on my way.' I wondered if they'd found the intruder; maybe that was it. I thought of ringing the girls to fill them in, but Clodagh had been heading out the door for a run as I'd left and I was not going to wake Maddy, who was having her first lie-in of the year.

I put on a warm jacket and was on the road within a couple

of minutes. Because I was going against the morning rush-hour traffic, it was no time before I pulled up at the van.

Tim Hynes and Clare Grogan got out of their car immediately.

'Can we go inside?' she asked, before I'd even taken off my helmet. 'We need to talk to you.'

'Yes, of course, but please tell me what's wrong. Is it the intruder?' I opened the door, and all three of us stepped inside.

I looked from one to the other. I had an awful feeling about this; their faces looked way too serious. 'What is it?' I'd never wanted to hear an answer less in my life. I knew this even though I'd no idea what was coming.

'I'm afraid there's been an accident. It's your friend Madeleine.'

'The cab?' I was thinking aloud. 'Is she OK?'

Clare Grogan looked worn out. 'Would you like to sit down?'

'Just tell me, please,' I begged her.

'She was hit by a car as she was crossing the road near where she lives. From what we know, the vehicle didn't stop,' Tim Hynes said quietly.

'Where is she now?' I had a sudden, ridiculous urge to laugh and tell him that Maddy would get great mileage out of this. If she wasn't on the front page after the party last night, she certainly would be now.

'I'm very sorry to have to tell you this, but I'm afraid she didn't survive,' Clare said. 'She died at the scene.'

35

'I'M SORRY, WHAT DID YOU SAY?'

'You need to sit down.' They both grabbed me as I slumped. It wasn't that I fainted; my stomach sort of up-ended and my legs went from under me so I more or less folded up, and when they caught me I knew I was going to throw up, even though I hadn't eaten anything that morning.

'Are you telling me Maddy is dead?' I looked from one to the other, feeling sure I'd heard them correctly yet equally certain that I couldn't have.

'It happened about twenty minutes after she left you.' Tim Hynes looked like he'd never get used to delivering this kind of news.

'No, please God. Not Maddy.' I remember staring intently at them, just in case it wasn't true, and then, eventually, I ran to the sink. Afterwards, I stayed there, with my head resting on the cool surface, until I knew I had a chance of being able to deal with this.

'Please tell me, I need to know.' My heart was hammering so hard I had to do something to try to quieten it, so I sat back down quickly before my legs gave out again. I still think I felt that, once I knew everything, I could fix it somehow.

They filled in the details then and told me of the awful moments that had ended the life of my best friend. The taxi dropped her off and, as she was crossing the road, a car came around the corner at high speed, driven by two teenagers, according to the taxi man, who was stopped at traffic lights nearby. It hit her head on and didn't stop.

'The taxi driver rushed to her and called the emergency services. She was taken to the Mater Hospital, but she was dead on arrival,' Clare told me.

'What about her mum?' My stomach churned again when I thought of Connie.

'The guys who arrived on the scene found identification in her bag and sent a car to her family home. They were taken straight to the hospital at that stage. It seems like there was major confusion, because the taxi driver thought she was still alive. But it appears she died instantly.'

'I was her ICE buddy,' I told them, smiling at the memory. 'She made me put her in as mine. How come no one contacted me?'

'It all happened so fast, I'm afraid there just wasn't time.'

'So she didn't suffer?'

'No, she wouldn't have.' Clare hunkered down beside me.

'How did you know I was . . . the last person who was with her?' My stomach flipped again. 'And why did you call to see me?'

'The taxi driver told my colleagues she'd been with a friend, and Madeleine had told him you'd been to a launch party for her new show, so they went back to the venue and heard she'd left with you. Her mum begged us to call and tell you personally and, besides, we needed to check if anything unusual had happened. You didn't meet anyone or have a row or anything that might have meant someone followed her?'

'No.' I was stunned. 'You're not suggesting her death was anything more than an accident?'

'No.' Clare rubbed my arm. 'We're pretty sure it was just that, but the car seemed to head straight for her, so we wanted to check with you, just to be certain you had no further information.'

'Everyone loved her,' I whispered. 'Who could have done this awful thing and not even stopped to check how she was?' I felt myself swaying as I went hot and cold again.

'Are you OK? Is there anyone we can call?'

'Maddy would have been the one I'd have called.' I looked at the face of the young woman and wondered how many times she'd had to break news like this. 'She was my best friend. She shouted that she loved me as the cab pulled out of the rank; she slept in my bed the night before last. How could this have happened?'

'I'm so sorry, it's a terrible shock, I know. Can I get you some tea?'

I shook my head, wondering how, with all my experience of dealing with crises, nothing had prepared me for this. 'Clodagh,' I suddenly remembered. 'She's our other friend. I need to tell her before she hears it. Will it be on the news?'

'Yes, but no names have been released yet so don't worry.

Just give me Clodagh's address. We'll send a car and bring her here, shall we?'

'No, I'll tell her. Could you take me there please?' I asked Tim Hynes. 'I only have a bike and I'm not sure I could drive it right now.'

'Of course.' He nodded and stood up.

I'll never forget Clodagh's face. As soon as she saw me getting out of a police car she knew it wasn't good. She'd been sitting at her desk by the window working on her laptop when we pulled up.

'What's wrong?' she asked as soon as she opened the door. 'Lulu, what is it, what's happened?'

When I told her, she just walked ahead of us into the living room without saying a word. Then she sat down, put her head in her hands and rocked and cried. I sat beside her, and my tears finally came too. We sat like that, arms around each other for ages, while the two gardai made tea and discreet phone calls and tried to offer us what nobody could provide at that moment, the comfort of having our friend back.

Eventually, we both had to start making calls, simply because the press had gotten hold of the story and, because the TV show was about to start and the accident had happened while one of its stars was on her way home from the launch party, it was now a major news item.

First up, I phoned Becky. She was brilliant. I don't know why I was so surprised but I was.

'Lou, that is so awful, I can't tell you how sorry I am,' she said. 'Now, tell me what do you need? I'll phone Mum. She'll be upset, she was very fond of Maddy too.' She didn't

330

sound like my baby sister and it felt odd that she was looking after me for once.

I promised to call her as soon as I knew more, then I felt I simply had to go and see Connie, even though I was dreading it. Naturally, Clodagh wanted to come as well, so we headed off in her car.

Maddy's mum lived in an ordinary housing estate on the Northside of Dublin in a four-bed semi with a neat garden and snow-white net curtains. A couple of photographers kept a discreet distance, and across the road a TV crew was setting up. It made the whole thing seem absurdly real.

Once inside, I was struck by the silence. Maddy's family was like an unsophisticated version of the Waltons, she always said, and in the early days I kept asking – 'How can anyone call the Waltons sophisticated?' – to which she always replied, 'You haven't seen my lot around the dinner table.' As I got to know them over the years, I understood what she meant. Well, today, the big, noisy, unruly bunch was so quiet you'd think all of them had been silenced by a hit-and-run driver as well. When Connie saw me she just held out her arms, and I fell into them. 'Ah, Lulu, love, how am I ever going to get through this? What'll we all do without her, eh?' The rest of my tears came then, they gushed out of me as if someone had just severed a pipe, and eventually I had to pull back and allow Clodagh some time. What made it all the more surreal was that I hadn't seen Connie for a while but at the launch the previous night I'd sat with her for half an hour while she told me how proud they all were of Maddy. One by one the members of her family came to hug me, cry with me and tell me how much she'd loved me. 'It was the last thing she yelled at me last night,' I told Carla, her younger sister, through my tears. There were seven children in all, and Connie had been a widow for years. They were a typical working-class family made good. Connie's husband had scrimped and saved and bought this house shortly after their marriage. When he died he left her a decent pension and she'd gone out to work at night in order to educate the children. Even though she'd only two left at home, she still ruled the family like a mafia boss. Maddy and I had shared many a joke about her family over the years, and I'd attended nearly all of their celebrations – weddings, anniversaries and christenings. They were remarkably close, lived in each other's ears, welcomed every friend they met and, many times down through the years when I'd been lonely within my own family, they'd made me part of theirs. Hardly any meeting would occur where Connie wouldn't remind me, 'Don't be a stranger, treat this as your second home, darlin'.' I knew I might need that comfort now.

'Lulu, I was just wondering, is there anyone else we need to tell?' Sonia, Maddy's eldest sister, asked. 'The TV people are all in total shock, they've been on a couple of times. A few of the executives have asked if they can call over, but I've told them Mum's not up to it at the moment.'

'I think you're right to protect her,' I told Sonia. 'There's going to be a lot of interest in you as a family for the next while, so you need to be careful.'

'Actually, I wanted to ask you, would you handle the media? It's just that we've no idea, really, and you're used to dealing with all sorts of situations.'

'Yes, of course, I'll do anything to help, you know that. I

suggest you just stop answering the phone for the moment, unless you know who it is. And maybe I should put a message on the answering machine asking callers who are not family or personal friends to call my number? Would that be a good idea, do you think?'

'Oh yes, that would be brilliant. I think there are already several requests for one of us to make a statement.' She sighed. 'You're so good, thank you.' She hugged me, and I was just about to go to work on it when I remembered Ronan.

'Oh my God, you know Maddy was seeing someone?' I asked Sonia. 'Has anyone spoken to him? Does he know about this?'

'No, he never entered my head, to be honest. We all only met him for the first time last night. What'll we do?' She looked terrified.

'I need to speak to him.' All I could think of was that he'd already lost one woman he cared about. I'd no idea how he'd deal with this.

'Clodagh, I need to ring Ronan O'Meara.' I cornered her as she walked past with yet another tray of tea. 'I don't know if he knows.'

'Oh my God, I'd forgotten all about him, should one of us go to see him?' She was thinking aloud.

'Yes, you're right. But he may already know.' I took a deep breath and dialled his number.

'Hi there.' I knew as soon as he spoke that he didn't know. 'I'd say you three have a hangover.'

'Ronan, I need to talk to you. Are you in Dalkey?' I was trying not to give too much away, but hearing him sounding so normal made me want to bawl again.

'No, I'm driving back from a meeting in Howth. Is something wrong?'

'Are you still on the Northside or have you crossed the toll bridge?'

'Just at Clontarf, why?'

'I'm actually on the Northside myself – will you park in that car park beside the toilets and opposite that coffee shop near the church? I'll be there in less than five minutes.'

'OK, sure. I'm stopped at traffic lights about three or four minutes away, if it's the one I think it is.' He sounded wary. 'Lulu, is something up? You sound strange.'

'I'll tell you when I see you' was all I could think of. I had no idea how I was going to break the news. He'd had enough tragedy with women he cared about.

I jumped into Clodagh's car and headed off. She wanted to come with me, but she didn't really know him and I felt he'd need a bit of breathing space. My heart was hammering as I pulled up. I saw him immediately but he didn't recognize me in a strange car. He was on his mobile, chatting away, unconcerned. I said a quick prayer and walked towards him.

'Hi.' He leaned across and opened the car door for me. 'What's up?'

'Ronan, it's Maddy.' I'd no idea where to start.

'What's happened this time?' He was smiling. Everyone knew that Maddy always had some drama going on. 'I left her a message earlier but haven't heard back.'

'There's been an . . . accident. Last night, on the way home. Ronan, I'm so sorry, but it's not good news.'

'Is she OK? Where is she?' He still didn't look as if he

was prepared for what I had to say, but then is anyone, ever?

'No . . .' I couldn't say it.

'Jesus Christ, Lulu, what happened?'

'She left me and took a cab home. As she crossed the road to her house a car came speeding around the corner and hit her head on.'

'Is she OK? Is she alive?' He spoke so quietly I almost didn't hear it, but I knew I had to find the words.

'Ronan, I'm so sorry.' I hesitated but he needed to hear it. 'She didn't make it.'

'No.' He stared at me. 'No,' he repeated, then shook his head. 'Not Maddy, she had too much life in her.'

I started crying again then and we sat, our heads close together, and I knew he was crying too.

'Come back to her mum's house with me,' I suggested, hoping it would bring him some comfort, being with those who loved her most.

'I don't think I can,' he said. 'It's odd, because I didn't know her as well as any of her friends, really. But we'd talked a lot these last few days, and we even had a weekend away planned and now . . . all this is just such a shock. I can't quite believe what you're telling me.' He put his head in his hands.

'I know, it's hard to imagine. I don't think it's quite sunk in with me yet. Every so often it hits me and it's as if someone's just kicked me in the stomach I get such a jolt.' I knew I couldn't leave him like this. 'Please come back to the house for a little while. Connie, her mum, would love to see you,' I tried again.

'OK so.' He was in shock.

'Swap places, I'll drive.' I got out, and so did he. I locked Clodagh's car, and we made the short journey in silence. When I pulled up outside the house, he was taken aback by the media presence.

'Sorry, I should have warned you.' I could have kicked myself. 'It was always going to be a news story, but with the show and the launch last night it's taken on even more significance. Are you OK?'

He nodded, and we went inside. Photographers snapped, but I suspected they were simply taking shots of everyone.

Inside, Connie got upset again when she saw Ronan, and he looked a bit bemused to be surrounded by Maddy's entire family, some of whom he hadn't met before. A garda who'd arrived just as we'd pulled up followed us inside to let us know there was going to be a report on the lunchtime news on television, in case there was anyone else we needed to inform. I double-checked with Sonia, and she confirmed that all their relations had been told and the production company were taking care of her colleagues and friends, including those from *Southside Girls*, her last project. My phone rang. It was Mike.

'Is everything OK?' he asked as soon as I answered. 'There's a rumour doing the rounds that Maddy was in some sort of accident on her way home. I just heard it and I couldn't find out anything else so I decided to check in with you.'

'Oh Mike, it's awful, the worst possible thing to have happened.' I started crying again and I wanted him near me all of a sudden.

'Tell me,' he said very quietly. 'Is she OK?'

'She's dead' was all I could manage.

'Jesus Christ' was all I heard and for a second neither of us spoke. He must have sensed something of my need, because all he said was, 'Where are you? I'll come.'

I gave him Maddy's address, and he said simply, 'It'll be OK, I'm on the way. Call if you need me to do anything else.' Then he hung up, and the idea of him being there for me made me cry even more.

36

I HADN'T FULLY REALIZED HOW MUCH I NEEDED HIM UNTIL I saw him. Up until now, it had always been Maddy who'd been there for me, and the idea of him dropping everything and getting to me as fast as he could gave me the only minuscule bit of comfort I'd had since I'd heard the awful news. The other thing about him was that he had 'got' Maddy – as soon as I'd introduced them I could see that – and to me that meant he understood my loss.

'Come 'ere to me' was all Mike said as he came through the door. Then he held me so tight that for the first time I felt there was a possibility that somehow I'd survive.

'You'll be OK,' he just kept repeating as he rubbed my back and when eventually he saw Clodagh and went to her, I felt cold without him.

He sat with Maddy's mum for ages, and when I brought them tea he was holding her hand and listening intently.

'Thanks, love, what would I do without you?' She looked so old suddenly that it shocked me. I thought of all the times Maddy had laughingly told me that everyone in the family was terrified of Connie – well, today I was terrified for her. 'Are you OK?' she asked me. 'She's always looking after other people, never herself,' she told Mike. 'Maddy always said so.'

Mike stood up and put his arms around me again. 'I'll mind you,' he told me as he kissed my head, and I wanted to tell him that he made me feel safe but I hadn't the courage to say it.

I had to go outside then and make a statement on behalf of the family to the assembled media. It was one of the hardest jobs I'd ever had to do, so I kept picturing how Maddy would have laughed if she'd heard I was going to be on the six o'clock news. I kept it brief, simply said how shocked and devastated the family were and asked for privacy. The gardai had also asked me to appeal for any witnesses to come forward, which was the main purpose of doing it.

Later, Connie decided she wanted to watch the news to see what they said. They showed a clip of Maddy in the new series, which I wasn't prepared for, even though we'd been warned to expect it. I managed to bite my lip, but when they showed some footage of the press launch the previous night and a shot appeared of the two of us laughing with our arms around each other, it sent me over the top again. I was ashamed of myself, crying in front of her family, who were all trying to hold it together. Mike appeared behind me suddenly and rubbed my back again. 'Remember her like that,' he whispered into my hair. 'That's what she would have wanted.' I nodded, and when I looked at Connie the tears were streaming down her face too.

Ronan O'Meara left shortly afterwards. He wasn't quite sure how to handle all this, I suspected. He'd been close to Maddy, but they'd barely started out as a couple and now he had been thrust into the role of grieving boyfriend. I'd been keeping an eye on him, and I encouraged him to head off, sensing he needed the head space.

'I'm not sure what my role is in all of this,' he told me, confirming my earlier suspicion. 'I want to do whatever she would have wanted.'

'Well, how about you and I stay together during the funeral, that way we can be as close as the family need us to be without overshadowing them?' I suggested. 'I'm not sure what to do either.' And in a way that was true. Maddy had been closer to me than any member of my family, and right now I felt as if I'd lost a sister, mother and best friend all at once, yet we weren't related so I had no real idea what my role was either.

'That would be great, thanks. I'll stay in touch, if that's OK?' He looked far away. 'Just in case there's anything that needs doing, relatives collected, messages picked up, that sort of thing. I've been there, so I know how addled you can get, forgetting the most basic stuff.'

I hugged him, and he held on for a long time. I wondered again whether it would have worked between them. In many ways, he still wasn't ready, and the fact that he hadn't shared a lot with her spoke volumes.

About an hour later, Mike insisted on dropping Clodagh and I back to collect her car. We'd decided that I'd stay at her place so that we'd be nearer the family in case they needed us, and Mary had taken over Pete's care so I was free. She'd been another of my rocks; she'd phoned all my clients to explain what had happened then gone out to Bray to get clothes and all the bits I needed.

Mike dropped us off, then insisted on collecting food, so we lit the fire and curled up and when he got back the three of us ate pizza that no one really wanted while Clodagh and I reminisced about our friend.

He left shortly afterwards and told me to call him any time. He had to go to London the following morning on business but he'd cancelled as many of the meetings as he could and was planning to return the following evening.

The next day was even harder, mainly because neither Clodagh nor I had slept much and, also, reality had finally sunk in. That had happened for me as soon as I saw the newspapers. The story was front-page news everywhere, and most of the tabloids had shots of Maddy at the launch, looking alive and happy and carefree. My stomach heaved as I began to read, and eventually Clodagh suggested that maybe it was a bit too much for us at this time and so we agreed to put them away until we felt more able to cope.

Mike kept in touch, as did Ronan, and I got the nicest messages from my clients, delivered by Mary, who bought me a magnificent specimen plant with a card that said I should grow it near my kitchen window so that I'd always remember her. Emily left a hamper of home-baked goodies in the office for the family, Louis arrived with an armful of white, scented flowers and cried with me because he'd cared for Maddy too, and even Denis Cassidy had delivered a beautiful letter with a single rose to Connie's house for me. Each message reduced me to tears, and the ease with which they flowed told me that I was mourning for all that Maddy had represented in my life but which I hadn't realized until I'd lost her.

*　　*　　*

The gathering for the removal to the church was a bigger shock for Connie than the rest of us, I think, mainly because she'd been so isolated and protected over the few days. The short evening ceremony ended up taking almost two hours, as queues of people lined up to shake hands and offer support, including some well-known faces Maddy had worked with in television.

No one got much sleep after that, I suspected. When Clodagh arrived in the kitchen shortly after me the following morning, it was barely six o'clock and the sky was still sooty-black. I was sitting at her table going through the few words that Connie had asked me to say at the end of the mass, and I wondered aloud if I'd manage to hold it all together.

'You will,' Clodagh assured me. 'You're one of the strongest people I know.' She took away my mug and made a fresh pot of tea and a plate of toast, then we sat and reminisced again, which was all we seemed to do now.

When we arrived at the church, Mike was there, looking very different in a beautifully cut dark suit and white shirt, his tie lending the only splash of colour to an otherwise grey crowd.

'All I could see was black until I spotted you,' I told him. 'I'm glad you wore that tie – Maddy would have approved.'

'Like everything else that screams "Notice me" in my life, it was chosen by Louis.' He grinned. 'He's around here somewhere and, if you think I'm garish, wait until you see his jacket. It's not for the faint-hearted.'

I smiled, glad of the diversion his words brought to my

342

grief-soaked brain, which was his intention, I suspected. 'I think I spotted him as we drove in.' I smiled. 'It's loud all right.'

'Well, he claims he met Maddy in town on the day he bought it – just before your Christmas party – and she loved it. He was saving it for a special occasion, and he's been so out of sorts since he heard the news that when he announced this morning that she would have wanted him to wear it I didn't have the heart to tell him it sucked.'

'Is he OK?' I asked. 'I'd forgotten that all this will bring back a lot of memories of when Emerson died, and it hasn't really been that long.'

'Yeah,' Mike said softly. 'I think he's finding it tough. He really liked Maddy too. She had this ability to cut through all the bullshit so you sort of felt you knew her well, when in fact neither of us knew her at all, really.'

'Tell me about it.' I smiled sadly. 'It was just one of her talents. No matter how often I skirted around a point, she'd give me a couple of minutes – at most – before she'd tell me I was talking utter rubbish and then say what she thought the real issue was. It used to throw me when I got to know her first, but over the years I relied on it more and more, and when I had a problem I always found myself wanting to ring her, even to half tell her what was in my head, because she invariably made sense of it before I did.'

'So how're you holding up?' He reached out and pulled me towards him. He seemed to know exactly when I needed a strong arm around me these days.

'Thanks, I needed that,' I said into his chest, and as he loosened his grip slightly and tilted my face in order to look at me properly I saw someone I knew well heading towards me.

'Mum?' I said, confused. I felt myself stiffen slightly, which was at odds with my first thought which was 'Thank God you're here, I need you.'

Mike swivelled around just as my mother swooped. She grabbed me but didn't immediately hug me, simply held me at arm's length and said, 'It's OK, darling. It'll all be OK, I promise.' I must have looked stunned, because she too tilted my face up, but this time it felt like she was reminding me who she was. 'It's such appalling news, I am absolutely shattered.' She put her arms around me, and it was only then I realized that my sister Becky was with her. She grabbed me too, which felt odd, because my family were not huggers.

'How did you get here – I mean, when?' I asked Mum.

'This morning. I had trouble with connecting flights so I wasn't sure I'd make it in time, which is why I didn't tell you.' She smiled. 'I didn't want to upset you by not turning up after all.'

Either I'd got the wrong mother, or she'd had a brain transplant, I decided. Martha had never worried about up-setting me before.

'I'll see you later.' Mike made to move away, but I grabbed his arm – in a vice grip, I only realized a few seconds later, when he tried to prise my fingers away.

'No,' I said, and he practically fell over I pulled him towards me so fast. 'I'd like to introduce you to my family. This is Mike, he's a . . . client of mine but he's also a friend and he's been fantastic to me since . . . all this happened.' It was all I could think of.

Martha had him in a vice grip in an instant, but then she'd never been one to let a man away if she could help it. 'Thank you. Thank you so much.' She kept releasing him then grabbing him again. 'It means so much to me that someone's been looking after her for me.' It was so outrageous that it almost gave me the only laugh of the week, or it would have if it hadn't been so totally false-sounding. My mother barely knew my phone number, never remembered my birthday and would be hard pushed to recognize my face in a police line-up it was so long since she'd seen me.

'Hello.' Mike shook hands as soon as she put him down. Becky took over then, thankfully, and explained that when Mum had heard the awful news she felt she needed to see her two daughters.

'We should probably go in.' Mike indicated the thinning crowd. 'By the way, Ronan rang and said he might be a bit late so not to wait for him.'

'Thanks for telling me. Yes, we'd better.' I linked my arm in his and whispered, 'Could you stay with me, please? I'm not sure how much of my new, caring mother I can take this morning.'

'Sure.' He grinned. 'Families, eh? They're an acquired taste – at least mine is. Still, you must be delighted she came. Where did you tell me she lived again?'

'San Diego,' I murmured. 'And Martha is definitely an acquired taste, trust me.'

'She's a good-looking woman all the same.' He winked, and as I looked at her I realized why I nearly hadn't recognized her. She looked normal. Normal as in middle-class, well-heeled wife, that is. No cleavage – well, not much

37

YOU COULDN'T HAVE SAT THROUGH THE CEREMONY WITHOUT getting a real sense of Maddy, even if you hadn't known her. Her family had done an amazing job organizing it, in spite of their shock and sorrow. I'd always known they were a tightly knit bunch, but this smacked of a military operation. Everyone, it seemed, had a role. Her colleagues from TV walked on to the altar at the start with mementoes of her life as an actor. And each one told the congregation of the significance of it. There were lots of tearful laughs, especially when the awful hairnet she'd worn for so long on *Southside Girls* appeared. Everyone who'd ever met her knew how much she hated it. 'The minute they call "Cut", I yank it off. The make-up girls go mad,' she'd told me once. 'That's because as soon as I do it the bloody director calls for another take and they have to do my hair all over again, but I don't care.'

Her brothers and sisters all said the Prayers of the Faithful, each one special to Maddy, so that we prayed for all the things that were close to her heart. Her favourite nephew and her only godchild brought up the gifts, and all the while a gospel choir sang and people choked back tears. Maddy loved singing, she used to waft around the place clapping and singing 'Oh Happy Day' and always said she wished she'd been born black so she could sing gospel properly, and now this group sang their hearts out for her.

Just before the end of the mass I was asked to say a few words, and Martha was clearly delighted that I'd been chosen to speak. I was sandwiched between her and Mike, and she prodded me even before the priest had finished.

'When Maddy and I first found each other all those years ago, we knew, right away, that we'd always be friends,' I told the crowd. 'I just never thought I'd have to do without her. She slept in my bed the night before she died, she gave up Christmas dinner with her beloved family because I was on an adventure she wanted to be part of, and the last words she said to me as she leaned out of the taxi on the night she died were "Love you, babe."' I saw Connie get upset then, so I went on to talk about more general things, what a lousy cook she was, how she'd talk to anyone – homeless men under the arch at the Halfpenny Bridge or superstars she met in make-up – because Maddy treated everyone the same.

'I can't tell you how much I'll miss her in my life,' I finished up by saying. 'We had so many wonderful, crazy plans and, in a way, I'd built all my dreams around her.' I had more, but suddenly it was as if I'd only just realized that all my dreams had in fact died with her that night, or at least that's how it felt, so I simply shut up and bowed my head and let the tears flow. My legs refused to budge when I tried to get off the altar and I saw the priest rise, but Mike got there first. He put one arm around me and cupped my elbow with his other hand and led me gently back to my seat.

'I can't go to the grave,' I told him as soon as we sat down.

'That's fine,' he said. But as we filed out behind the coffin, so many people came to tell me they felt they knew me from overhearing Maddy cracking up on the phone sometimes when we talked, or simply to hug me and say, 'Don't give up on your dreams, she'll come back and haunt you if you do,' that by the time the cortege was ready to leave I knew I had to see this through and throw my white rose on her coffin and beg her to keep an eye out for me.

In the end it was Clodagh who finally cracked as the coffin was lowered, so I had to concentrate all my efforts to keep her going, which made it a bit easier for me. Mike and I linked her as we made our way back to the cars, and he rubbed her back and soothed her just as he had me.

'Thanks for rescuing me on the altar,' I told him when we were back at the hotel having lunch with her family and friends and anyone who'd travelled or had the time to spare.

'I'd love to take the credit but, to be honest, I probably wouldn't have done it except your mother practically drop-kicked me out of the pew.' He grinned. 'I would have expected her, or your sister, to go get you, but they seemed paralysed and suddenly I found myself in the aisle with a foot attached to my arse.'

I burst out laughing. It was so typical of my mother and sister, they were useless in a crisis, and anyway, if there was any crying in public to be done it was usually one of them so consequently neither of them knew how to react when they were forced into the role of carer with me.

'You really do overestimate my family if you think either of them would have come to get me,' I told Mike.

'Not that I wouldn't have done it or anything – I did, as it happens – but I just felt it should have been one of them.'

'Well, thank you for accepting the kick up the ass so graciously. For just a second or two I felt incapable of putting one foot in front of the other, which was strange, considering I couldn't wait for it to be over because I was so nervous.'

'You were perfect,' Mike said. 'If anyone is half as nice about me when I die, or cares as much, I'll be delighted.'

'Well, I think you'll be too dead to care one way or the other, no? But I'd bet Louis would be well into the dramatic speech at your funeral, and I'd also bet that it'd be one for the record books.' I giggled as Mike squashed his face like a bulldog.

'If (a) you're alive, (b) still talking to me and (c) you let Louis anywhere near my funeral arrangements, you'll have more to worry about than a suspected intruder,' he told me. 'And Pete will be useless because I'll be a ghost and, trust me, I will be lurking around you for years.'

Connie joined us then to thank me for speaking and I told her about my mother kicking Mike out to go and get me.

'Your mother's changed,' she said simply. 'I think she misses her two girls and wants more of them in her life.'

'Connie, there're not many people I could say this in front of, but it needs to be aired and Mike has some idea of my dysfunctional family after today, but you've been more of a mother to me for the last ten years than Martha has ever been.' Strangely, I didn't feel sad saying it, and in a way it was the final proof of how far I'd come.

'Come 'ere to me, darlin', and gimme a hug.' I did as she asked and she held me tight. 'You know without me saying it that I'm always here for you.' She sat back down. 'And now more than ever I'm going to need you to keep in touch, because I won't hear about you from Maddy.' This time, Mike and I both put our arms around her. 'But relationships with kids are complicated more often than not. We all make mistakes, and children when they grow up make them too. It's just that, as parents, we're always expected to get it right, and the fact is they don't give you a manual when you give birth.' She smiled. 'There should be a Reader's Digest, I think, or a Delia equivalent – a load of tried and tested methods that never fail.'

I thought again of all my clients and their various complications where kids were concerned and knew she was right. It was hard to be perfect, and the parent and child bond was so special that by its very nature it was also fragile. 'You're right, of course,' I told her. 'I suppose all relationships need to be nurtured.'

'Well, you're a great girl, always have been. I know your childhood wasn't what it should have been. Maddy told me that you'd lost out on a lot. But you've turned into a fine young woman and I notice you're much more content recently so I want you to come and talk to me any time if you need help, OK? In fact, come whether you need it or not.'

'OK.' I swallowed hard and hugged her again, and I noticed Mike watching the two us.

'And go easy on your mother, even if she is only doing now what she should have done years ago.'

'Yes, boss.' I smiled.

After a few hours of talking non-stop I was wiped out, so Mike offered to drop me home.

'I'm actually going back to Bray tonight, I've decided, so I'll grab a cab and pick up Pete on the way,' I told him. 'Clodagh's sister was always going to stay with her tonight anyway – she's up from Kilkenny for a course – so she'll be glad to see the back of me, I reckon. And you've been so good, I can't tell you how much your support has meant, but I'm sure you won't be sorry to get your life back either.'

'Well, you lot have sort of crept into my life, to be honest. You're quite a threesome.' He realized what he'd said straightaway. 'What I meant was—'

'It's OK, I know what you meant,' I told him softly. 'And you're right, we were quite a threesome, that's what's so hard about all this. When I think of my future without her in it, it just doesn't seem to work.'

'I know. Come on.' He put his arm around me. 'Let's go collect Pete.'

'Are you sure you have time?'

'Certain.' We said our goodbyes, and I promised to call Connie next day. By the time I sat in the car and the heat kicked in, I realized that I'd be asleep long before we reached Bray if I wasn't careful.

'I'll go get Pete.' I jumped out for air as soon as we arrived at Mary's. 'Will I borrow a towel so that he won't destroy your leather seats?'

Mike smiled. 'I love my car, but I'm not anal about it.' He

leaned out the window. 'And why are you worrying about my car seats? Where's the new Lulu you told me about when I first met you? Besides, have you not got enough on your plate just now?'

'Think I'm just trying to pretend that life is normal,' I told him. 'I really couldn't care less about your seats, if you must know.'

'That's my girl – normality doesn't suit you anyway.'

Pete was paralysed when he saw me first. After staring at me for a second he flung himself on me and danced about like a circus animal. He had a look of pure joy on his face and he licked me wet. In the car he sat on the back seat with his head as close to me as he could manage. I stroked him and talked to him and told him how much I'd missed him all the way home.

'OK, let's get you two inside.' Mike opened the door for me. 'You bring Pete; I'll carry in your luggage.'

The place was freezing, it was as cold inside as it was outdoors. 'Listen, I'm not sure you should stay here, it's like walking into a fridge. Why don't you stay at our place – we have a spare room?'

'No, honestly, it'll warm up really quickly once I turn the heat and the gas fire on,' I told him. 'Can I offer you a cup of coffee? Something stronger?'

'No, I'd better go check on a few emails. Sure you'll be OK?'

'Yeah, I'm fine. You go. And thanks again.' I reached out and gave him a hug and, just like before, he buried me against him and I felt safe.

'Goodnight. Call me if you need anything, won't you?'

'Will do.' I pulled away reluctantly, and he headed off, and I realized as soon as his engine noise died away that this was what I'd been dreading, finding myself alone with no best friend to have a giggle with if it all got too much. Pete jumped up on my lap, something he'd never done before. Even after all this time together he was usually so happy to be back with me that he made himself scarce until I'd settled in, just in case.

'Oh Pete, how will I ever get through this?' I asked him, and he looked at me with the saddest eyes as if to say, 'I know how much you loved her but you still have me.'

The tears came then, and I sat and cried a bucketful, and Pete never took his eyes off my face, just snuggled in tighter. Then I heard a noise and my heart jumped, but Pete wasn't worried so that calmed me down. I was still wondering if I'd imagined it when the door opened and Mike walked in. He took one look at me, blotchy and curled up in a ball with a dog, and said, 'As soon as I drove away I had a feeling you'd be like this, so I got us fish and chips so that you could at least eat while you bawled on my shoulder.'

If he'd given me a winning Lotto ticket it wouldn't have meant as much to me as what he'd done. 'I'm just so lonely without her,' I started again.

'I know you are.' Mike busied himself setting out the food, then he sat beside me, handed me a box of tissues and told me to tuck in. 'But you're strong, you'll get there and, knowing Maddy, she'll be up there watching over you and bossing God around, making sure everyone she loves is top of his list when it comes to happiness.'

38

THE FOLLOWING DAYS WERE SOME OF THE TOUGHEST I'D HAD to deal with. There was still a fair bit of publicity surrounding Maddy's death and it seemed everywhere I went her picture haunted me. Also, everyone wanted to talk about it, which I found the hardest part. Eventually – after I saw the photo of the three of us taken the night of the launch on the front of one newspaper – I stopped going into newsagents and asked Mary to warn people I wasn't up to discussing it just yet. Eventually I ran out of tears.

I was dropping in to see Connie every second day. Her neighbours were guarding her as if she was royalty and her children were cleaning, cooking and shopping for her, so I knew she was well looked after. In some ways, it was me seeking comfort from her instead of the other way round, and our meetings had a bitter-sweet tinge to them, because sometimes she'd look at me in a certain way, or smile Maddy's smile, and my heart would turn over. I knew she was suffering too, because most days she seemed to be looking for reminders of the daughter she'd lost. Whenever I visited she showed me a photo of the two of them, or pulled out a birthday card that boasted 'For the World's Greatest Mum', or wore a scarf or other item that Maddy had brought back from her travels. She looked so lost as she ran her hands over the precious items it made me realize that we needed each other equally now.

'I desperately want to feel her near me,' she told me more than once, and I knew exactly what she meant.

'Me too,' I agreed. 'Yesterday I went back through loads of emails she'd sent recently, and it was hard, but in a funny way it gave me comfort, as if reading her words brought her back into my life for a moment or two.'

'That's it, you've hit the nail on the head,' she told me. 'It all helps keep her memory alive.'

I was arranging some flowers I'd brought her as we chatted, because I knew how much she loved her garden and hated that in winter it was bare. Pete had taken to sitting right on her toes each time we called and he got permanently stroked as a result. I generally called on my way home from work, because early evening was a time most people were feeding families, or commuting, or still at work.

'Tell me about Mike,' she said out of the blue as I tidied up after the flowers. 'Are you two an item?'

'No,' I said. 'Although – and I haven't said this to anyone except Maddy – I'm beginning to wish we were. He's like the other half of me these days.'

'That sounds like a good start.' Connie took up her knitting. Pete didn't like it, he tried to steal her ball of wool all the time, but we both decided it was only because he was being done out of a rub when her hands were busy.

'Yes, but in a way, I'm not sure it'll go any further.' I sighed. 'He's made absolutely no effort in that direction since I jumped on him and told him I wanted a ride, then got sick all over him that first night.' As soon as I'd said it, I realized I might have offended her, but she threw back her head and guffawed so I relaxed and laughed with her. It was exactly what her daughter had done. Chats about everything had become part of our routine on these visits, and in a way she was so like Maddy – completely non-judgemental – that I found myself using her as a substitute for the sounding board I'd lost.

I told her the story then. She thought it was hilarious. 'Well, why don't you get all glammed up and invite him over for dinner some night to say thanks for the past few weeks? That'd be a good way of seeing if he's interested in you that way.'

'I'm not sure he is, that's my problem,' I told her. 'What do you think?'

'Well, I have watched you together and I do know what you mean. He's sort of the same with everyone, young and old. He's a lovely man though – and very easy on the eye – so you should take my advice and nab him. And he's very protective of you; I've seen him looking at you when you're not aware of it, so I guess there's only one way to find out. Get the mood right – the two of you nice and relaxed – and see if he pounces.' She giggled. 'It worked for me a few times in my youth, that's for sure. And if all else fails, I'll do a novena to St Rita for you. She's saint of the impossible.'

'I thought that was St Jude?'

'No, he's hopeless cases, and you're not that yet.' She laughed again and I was so glad we had each other. We were each exactly what the other needed these days, and I loved coming to see her.

'OK, I'll take some comfort in the fact that I'm an impossible but not a hopeless case,' I teased.

She laughed. 'My novenas always work, take comfort in that. How's your mum, by the way?'

'Good actually. She goes home tomorrow so I'm meeting her for a drink after I leave you. And this time I'm determined to air it all.' I smiled. 'Life is too short, as we both know.'

'Stick with her, it'll work out in the end,' Connie advised, and I stopped short of telling her yet again that I was closer to her than I'd ever been to Martha.

Maybe that remark was what prompted me to speak out an hour later, sitting opposite my mum over a late supper in a local bistro.

'Connie was asking after you earlier,' I began. 'In fact, I just realized that I'm probably closer to her than I am to you at this stage.' My heart started thumping as I spoke, but suddenly I needed to get it out there. It was the one area of my life I hadn't tackled, and Maddy had been pushing me more and more recently, urging me to tell my mother how I felt.

To my surprise, all she said was, 'I know that.'

It wasn't what I expected.

'Actually, I'm glad you brought it up.' She smiled but looked sad. 'I wanted to say that I was sorry for how we'd drifted apart.'

'Why were you always so tough on me? How come Becky had such an easy time growing up and I spent my entire childhood trying to please you yet never really succeeding?' It all came tumbling out, and I was glad.

'I suppose I was worried you'd turn out like your father.'

'Was he that bad?' I wanted to know.

'I thought so at the time. He was lazy and a waster, and it seemed like he cared only for himself.'

'Well, I sure didn't inherit those first two characteristics.' I smiled sarcastically. 'So you did well there, so well that I've spent my entire adult life working my ass off, being careful with everything and hating every minute of it.'

'I'm sorry. I know I made mistakes, I've been thinking a lot about it recently, even more so since Maddy died.'

'I thought you didn't want me.' I felt close to tears. 'So I kept trying harder, but nothing worked. All it got me was the very odd word of praise.'

'Can we start again?' she said simply.

'I guess we can try, but it feels a bit late, to be honest. You live away, and I'm more content than I've ever been – apart from Maddy's death, of course – and, for the first time in my life I don't need your approval. So' – I paused and took a deep breath – 'if we come together at all, it will need to be as equals and you'll have to be the one to make the effort. I finally gave up a while back.' I couldn't believe I was saying all this.

'OK, I'd like the opportunity,' she said, and held out her hand to stroke my arm across the table. 'And Lou, just for the record, I love you more than you'll ever know. So, friends, at least?' she asked.

'Friends,' I said quietly. 'And I want you to tell me more

about my father, in time.' I knew I still had questions but they weren't for tonight.

'I will,' she assured me. 'I promise.'

I nodded and then realized that I was content in her presence for the first time in years.

On the work front, it was business as usual. And a lot had happened to my clients while I'd been out of action, so there was a pile of stuff waiting. Luckily, I'd diverted my mobile to the office, and Mary spoke to everyone and kept them posted. Now, though, it was time to pick up the pieces, and I was glad to be busy doing something I loved.

My first foray back to work was to hook up with Denis Cassidy to meet his daughter, which, while it wasn't strictly a doggy dilemma, was a nice one to ease me in without too much hassle, or so I hoped, anyway.

It was all arranged. We were meeting for lunch in the Merrion Hotel, where the tables were well spaced and it was generally quiet enough anyway. When I met Denis he was very nervous. He'd come to Dublin the evening before 'to give myself plenty of time so that I wouldn't be confused about where I am', and he'd booked into the Westbury Hotel off Grafton Street, gone shopping for a present for each of them, then checked and rechecked the route to the hotel so he wouldn't get lost, even though it was less than a five-minute walk. He'd even timed it on each journey so as not to be late. His attention to detail told me how anxious he was. I met him for a cup of tea in his hotel, and he talked non-stop about the big event, insisting I check out his suit and tie and even inspect his nails.

'I want to look my very best for them,' he kept repeating, until I had to threaten him with a valium sandwich if he didn't calm down.

'What if they don't like the look of me?' he asked. 'I'm hardly what she'd want in a father. I'm an oulfella, for God's sake. A country one at that, which is even worse. She grew up in London, and you said yourself that her mother looks a million dollars. What if they're ashamed to be seen with me?' My heart went out to him. 'D'ya know something? I'm beginning to think I should never have started this. I'm a foolish eejit, Lulu, that's what I am.'

'Dinny, I don't—'

'Don't call me Dinny in front of them, please.' He was very agitated. 'Sorry, sorry, I don't mean to be rude. It's just that Denis at least has a bit of a respectable ring to it.' He brushed an imaginary speck of dust off his sleeve. 'I should have bought my suit in Brown Thomas or one of those other fancy stores, that was another mistake I made. This jacket is creased.'

'Din— eh, Denis, calm down, would you, you're stressing yourself for no reason.' I tried not to smile as I pictured him in BT's, Dublin's most expensive department store, in the middle of rows of Armani suits with trendy assistants fussing round him. 'It'll be fine, I promise, so stop worrying. Now, will you listen to me for a minute? They'll be as nervous as you, that's the first thing. And the second is that all three of you are going to have to accept each other as you are, that's the only way this is going to work. And finally, you look terrific, that suit is perfect. You couldn't have done any better. Now, relax, drink your tea and we'll

361

go for a stroll around St Stephen's Green and feed the ducks en route to meet them, OK?' I burst out laughing at the look on his face. 'OK, I'll feed them, just in case you get crumbs all over you.'

'Sure what would I do without you?' He laughed with me. 'I'd never survive this on my own, that's for sure.'

'You would, you're a tough old boot,' I told him as we gathered up our stuff and got ready to leave.

He calmed down a bit as we walked through the beautiful park. The spring bulbs had finally burst through and the wallflowers were already scenting the air, and with the soft early-spring sunlight it was impossible not to feel optimistic. He asked about Maddy's death and how I was managing and, for the first time, talking about it didn't upset me, mainly because he seemed to sense the enormity of my loss and understand how hard it had all been for me.

'You'll be grand, I guarantee it, Lulu. What you're feeling now is completely normal,' he told me, and I felt he understood more than most people. Perhaps it was his age, I decided, as I told him things about my mother that I hadn't been able to vocalize up to now. Maybe that final chat with Martha had done me good after all, and she had stayed in touch since she'd left, which I liked. I'd even gotten a funny doggy card in the post from her the other day, which meant she knew my new address at least. I swallowed hard, and Dinny squeezed my hand when he sensed that tears were threatening.

'I'm sorry, I'm not sure why it is, but some days are harder than others.' I blew my nose and made a huge effort to pull myself together. After all, I was here for him today, not the other way around.

'Of course they are, and they will be for a while yet, and all that stuff with your mother is coming out now because of your sadness,' was all he said, and we walked along in peaceful silence for ages, and I liked being with him.

Eventually, we made our way to the hotel. We were there a good twenty minutes before the appointed time, so I ordered some water and asked for the menu in an effort to keep him distracted.

'Tell me once more why you wouldn't take one look at me and turn on your heels,' he begged.

'They'd be very shallow if looks were all that mattered, they'll want to get to know you,' I assured him. 'Especially, Catherine, I'll bet she can't wait to meet her father.'

'My God, I'm a father, I still can't believe it myself,' he told me. 'Even though I've sat in my armchair night after night and thought about it and imagined her saying it, it still feels as if all this is happening to someone else.' He shook his head. 'I suppose that's because I always felt I didn't deserve to have them in my life, after the way I behaved.'

'Listen to me, Dinny – sorry, I mean Denis – if we all got only what we deserve then most of us would be a lot poorer as a result. Thankfully, life gives us some unexpected happy surprises, and this is one of them. And trust me, you do deserve it, you're a decent man.' I put my hand over his. 'And good things come to good people. That's what I believe anyway.'

'By the way, I keep forgetting to say, I'm paying you for today.' He shook his head as I tried to speak. 'I don't want any arguments now, so don't waste your time,' he warned. All of a sudden he stiffened, and when I followed his eyes I saw why.

Joan Lehane had just walked in. She looked as striking as I remembered. This time she was wearing a deep-plum, soft velvet coat with high boots and a matching big handbag. Her hair was loose and wavy, and more than one pair of eyes turned her way. She spotted me almost immediately, and then I watched her face break into a shy smile as she recognized Denis beside me.

She was at our table before I had time to get a good look at the young girl behind her, partly because a group of shoppers rose to leave just as she saw us, obscuring our view. Denis looked as if he was going to pass out with nerves, I noticed as I glanced sideways at him, having heard a slight gasp beside me. When I looked up again, I saw why. His daughter, Catherine, had just come into view. She was tall and blonde and smiling, but it was her eyes that made me gasp. It was like looking into Dinny's eyes, and in the brief moment I had to study her I realized that her mouth had the same lop-sided curve. Whatever else happened today, there was no denying that this exquisite young woman was related to him, and I found myself saying a quick prayer that neither of them was going to be disappointed with the other. If she was half as nice as she appeared, we were on to a winner, I reckoned.

39

'HELLO.' I RUSHED IN, AS THE OTHER THREE SEEMED LOST FOR words. 'It's so nice to see you again.' I shook hands with Joan and turned to her daughter.

'You must be Catherine. I'm Louisa.'

'Lulu, her name is Lulu, she's just trying to be posh,' Dinny 'call me Denis or I'll burst you' Cassidy announced, and we all laughed.

'Well, Denis Cassidy, you haven't changed, still embarrassing the women.' Joan smiled at him. 'It's nice to see you again after all this time.' She held out her hand, but Dinny, true to form, grabbed her in a bear-hug. He seemed so relieved that they hadn't run off as soon as they'd spotted him that he went in for the kill, was my theory. Joan looked at him for a long moment. 'You haven't changed a bit,' she told him, then paused before turning to her daughter. 'This is my . . . our daughter, Catherine,' she said proudly, and my heart skipped a beat just looking at the three of them together.

'Hello,' she said shyly. 'I'm happy to meet you at last. I've thought a lot about you over the years.'

As soon as she spoke, I knew it was going to be all right, and this meeting brought into sharp focus the horrible meeting Emily had had with Kitten recently. Looking at these three, I knew I could have left there and then and they'd have been fine.

Dinny, for once, was almost speechless. 'My God, but you're beautiful,' he said softly. This time there was no hug; he was afraid to push it, I'd say. Instead, he held out his hand and said quietly, 'And I've thought about how stupid I was to let you and your mother out of my sight every day since I last saw you as a little girl all those years ago.'

'I missed having a father,' Catherine said simply.

'Not half as much as I missed having a daughter.' He gulped. 'And in my case it was all my own fault.' He looked from daughter to mother and back to the young girl. 'I owe you both an apology and I offer it now from the bottom of my heart. I'm very sorry that I was such an idiot,' he told them. 'Seeing you both here makes me fully understand the extent of my stupidity.' It was an eloquent speech for a simple man, made all the more beautiful because it came straight from his heart.

'Thank you, Denis. That means a lot,' Joan said quietly. 'And I made a few mistakes myself along the way too. I was too proud that time you came to see us. I should have at least listened.'

'No, no, no.' All he was short of doing was stamping his foot. 'I won't let you take even a small portion of the blame. You were right to send me packing. It was no less than I deserved.'

We were all a bit tearful by then, so he quickly took

control. 'Now, I'd like to invite you all to have a glass of champagne to toast the future.' He signalled the waiter, who appeared immediately, with everything beautifully arranged on a tray.

'What a lovely surprise that you had organized all this,' Joan said as we raised our glasses.

'The only reason I didn't have it on the table was in case you legged it as soon as you saw me.' He grinned. 'Thank you, Joan, you've made me the happiest man in the world by agreeing to this meeting,' he toasted her. 'And Catherine, you've no idea how many nights I fell asleep wondering what you looked like and never imagining I'd have the great fortune to be sitting opposite you. I'm so proud to be able to call you my daughter at last. With your permission of course.' He touched her glass softly. 'And Lulu, in the midst of all your own troubles, you made all this happen and I thank you from the bottom of my heart.'

Joan wanted to know what had happened to me since we'd last spoken. I filled them in with one or two sentences then insisted I was coping well and turned the conversation around, because this was a happy day and I was determined to soak up some of their happiness for myself.

We had lunch while Joan and Catherine talked a lot about their lives. Dinny couldn't take his eyes off his daughter. He looked ready to burst with pride as he watched her go off to the ladies' a while later.

'Joan, once again, I'll never be able to thank you enough for what you did for me today,' he said as soon as Catherine was out of earshot. 'You've made my life complete.' It was another emotional moment. 'I mean it,' he told her. 'She's a

367

credit to you – a lovely, happy girl, and what a beauty she's turned out to be.'

'Thank you,' Joan said. 'And don't forget she's part of you too.'

'Aye, but she didn't get her looks from me, that's for sure,' he guffawed. 'I'll take any credit that's going, you know what I'm like, Lulu.' He nudged me. 'But Joan, you've done all the work raising her, and you've made a bloody great job of it.'

I left as soon as lunch was over, to give them some time alone. Joan and Catherine had agreed to call to Ashford on their next visit, and I suspected there'd be a red carpet the length of the M11 motorway out for them on the day, if Dinny had his way. Just seeing them together helped my own grief and made me believe that happy endings weren't just for the movies.

40

DRIVING HOME THAT EVENING, I FELT A BIT LOST, SO ON impulse I phoned Mike, hoping to tempt him out my direction for a drink once I'd deposited Pete. His mobile was diverted to his office, it turned out, and his assistant said he was in London for two days and had meetings more or less back to back both days. Disappointed because I hadn't talked to him for a while, I settled in to watch TV, but within a few minutes Pete started growling and I got nervous. It felt like it was happening more and more since I'd come back home, or maybe it was just that since Maddy's death I seemed to scare easily. I grabbed a torch, and Pete and I headed up to see if Jack and Jill were home and thankfully they were, so we drank tea and played Scrabble.

'Please, Lulu, don't walk up in the dark. I keep telling you to ring, and one of us will meet you at the gate,' Jack scolded.

'Sorry, it's just that I feel a bit stupid. I've been on my own almost since I could walk.' I laughed. 'So I should be well used to it and, normally, I don't scare easily. And when I opened the door just now Pete simply wagged his tail and headed for your house, so there was clearly nothing to worry about. And I'm sorry for barging in unannounced again, I think I might have to get an alarm fitted, just for the security of having it.'

'You're welcome here any time, in fact we enjoy hearing about your escapades, don't we, love?'

'We do, barge in any time.' Jill smiled, and I thanked them both for all their kindness. They'd become good friends and had taken to minding me like a child these past few weeks. Jack walked me home a couple of hours later, and I fell into bed and had one of the few uninterrupted nights' sleep I'd managed since my world had turned upside down.

I had a couple of new clients scheduled for the next day, and it was these that were keeping me going and helping to take my mind off things. It seemed that early spring brought lots of problem pets with it, either impulse Christmas purchases that weren't as easy to put away as the noisy, repetitive games, or New Year resolutions that involved getting to grips with the monster before the gardening season kicked off in earnest. Happily, for me, it meant lots of busy mornings trying to train people while making them feel we were, in fact, training their pets.

First thing after lunch I had another new client. This one appeared without a pet. All I knew was that she was called Katie Anderson, and Mary said she was English.

'Hello, I'm Lulu.' I smiled as I led her into my office, wondering what challenge this one would bring. Mary had enquired if she had a pet she wanted to bring along, but she'd been vague, so I'd no idea what to expect.

'So, how can I help you?' I opened a blank page in my notebook and waited.

'I'm not sure, actually.' She reminded me of someone, but I couldn't put my finger on it. I sensed she was nervous.

'Well, why don't you tell me how you heard about my services?' I thought that by encouraging her to chat I'd find out a bit more.

'Well, I found your card in my mother's car and I . . . eh . . . think that perhaps we might be . . . related.' The last word sort of fell out, and I knew that whatever her problem was she hadn't worked out what to say to me in advance.

'Related – how?' I smiled again, wondering what was coming.

'I think we have the same mother,' she said quietly, and my heart nearly stopped beating – just when I thought that nothing would surprise me where my mother was concerned.

'Martha?' I said quickly, prepared for anything.

'No, Kitten.' She looked puzzled. 'Who's Martha?'

'Martha's my mother – you're Kitten's daughter?'

'Yes.' She looked completely thrown. 'I've obviously got it wrong, but how do you know my mother, if you don't mind me asking?'

'I met her only once . . . with a friend.' I wasn't sure what was going on, but I wanted to encourage her. I also knew I had to be careful not to betray any confidences. 'Why don't you tell me what's on your mind, and if I can help in any way, I will?'

'I think my mother had a baby she gave up for adoption years ago. In fact, I'm almost certain of it. I found stuff, hidden away – and overheard one or two things as well. She's been very edgy these past few weeks, and then I found your card and I thought it must be you.' She looked dejected. 'Perhaps I should have checked a bit more before I came tearing over here, but I felt it was better to say what I had to say to your face. Besides, I was sure I was right and I guess I was curious to see what you looked like. But now that I see you' – she shrugged – 'you look nothing like me.'

'And have you spoken to your mother about this?' As I'd listened to her talking, I'd realized that it was Emily she'd reminded me of when she walked in. Their profiles were strikingly similar. This young woman had none of Emily's normal reserve, however, so in terms of character they were poles apart. Although it was interesting that her instinct had been exactly the same as Emily's when it came to finding a member of her family.

'Yes. Well, sort of. What I mean is, I've tried. Several times. She denies it, of course. In fact, she refuses to discuss it. But from what I've been able to find out, she had a daughter in Ireland about thirty years ago, and when I found your card I checked your website and you looked about the right age, so I put two and two together and decided to hop on a cheap flight and come see you.'

'I hope you don't mind me asking, but why would your mother not talk to you about it? I can understand why she might have wanted to keep it secret in the first place, these things were much trickier back then. But if she suspected you knew . . . ?' I let the rest of the sentence trail off, because even from one meeting I knew how big a deal it was for Kitten.

'There are a million reasons, none of which paint my mother in a good light, I'm afraid. She was a spoilt only child, used to getting everything her own way. When she got pregnant, the man was married, as far as I know, and very well known in political circles. Having a baby simply didn't fit in with her plans, I suspect. So she got rid of it and got on with her life, married a very rich man, had – has – pretty much a perfect life. My father dotes on her; everyone dotes on Kitten. She wants for nothing, moves in all the right circles, and now it's too late. It wouldn't fit her image at all, I'm sorry to say, if it got out that she'd had a baby by a married man and then abandoned it and never tried to find out what had happened to the child, even when she could well have afforded to at least look after her financially.' She looked upset suddenly. 'I should add that all of this is speculation on my part. My mother refuses to confirm anything. But I know enough to know that most, if not all, of it is accurate.' She paused for a moment. 'I was really hoping you could help me.'

'Why are you so keen to find answers?' I wondered. 'Surely if your mother chooses not to disclose these things, it's her right?'

'Because I feel she owes it to me to at least tell me if I have a sister. I've wanted one all my life. My mother has four sons, and she idolizes them. Don't get me wrong, she's not a bad mother or anything, quite the opposite. I never wanted for anything. It's just that she's a man's woman, always has been. Her father doted on her, still does, whereas her mother was ill a lot of the time when she was growing up and died when she was a teenager. So all her influences were male.'

'I would have thought, though, that a daughter would have made her very happy under those circumstances?'

'Not so, I'm afraid. And even though she's a very girly woman – if you know what I mean – she's drawn to men. It helps that she can wrap most of them around her little finger.' Katie smiled. 'Whereas me, I'm way too feisty for her. Also I can see through her: she can be quite manipulative. Men don't seem to notice it, though.'

In a funny way, her childhood reminded me of my own. Christ, I'm becoming paranoid, I decided, reading too much into every situation. However, one thing I was certain of was that I needed to think carefully about what I should do here. 'Katie, could I ask how long you're staying? It's just that I need a bit of time to think about all you've said.'

She looked at me for a moment. 'And you're definitely not my sister?'

'No, I'm not.' We both smiled together.

'Shame, we'd have gotten on well. Anyway, I'm here until tomorrow evening. Does that give you enough time?'

'Yes, more than enough. Would it be OK if I take your number and call you later?'

'Sure.' She called it out to me and I saved it in my mobile. We agreed to chat later and possibly meet the next morning.

On the way out, I grinned at the angelic-looking family waiting.

'When I see a group as perfect as you, I always think I'm just about to learn that there's a dotey dog making life hell.' I smiled at the kids. 'Would I be right?'

'Yes.' The kids nodded, and one of them yanked out an adorable-looking King Charles spaniel from under the couch. He had the most mischievous eyes I'd seen in a while.

'Her ate half my Lego pieces and chewed my sister's new ballet shoes and bit Granny and did a poo under the Christmas tree,' the younger one said without pausing for breath. 'And that was all on Christmas morning.'

'Well then, I think you'd better come inside. We may need to come up with a plan fast. What do you think?' I opened the door to my office.

The little girl looked as if she was about to burst. 'Otherwise Dad says Coco will get a kick up the bum and then he'll give her an injection himself to put her to sleep for ever and ever.'

'Janie, I don't think that's quite what Dad said.' A mortified mother tried to smile.

'Oh yes it is,' said the father. 'And a bit more besides.'

I led them in, delighted to have a nice normal problem for the next hour.

41

AN HOUR LATER, WE WERE ALL LAUGHING AS I SHOWED THEM
out. We'd made progress, and my next meeting with them
would be in their home. Mary was making the appointment
when my phone rang, so I left them to it.

'Well, what mischief have you been getting up to while
I've been away?' It was Mike. 'My secretary said you rang,
and you only ever call when you're in trouble.'

'No, actually, I've been a good girl, played Scrabble and
drank tea. That's about the height of my wild and crazy
life.' I laughed, then took a deep breath. 'Actually, I rang to
invite you over for dinner at the weekend. To say thanks for
everything. I don't know how I'd have survived the last few
weeks without you.'

'Hang on, could you repeat that please, so that I can
record it and play it back at every opportunity?'

'Very funny, I'd slap you if you weren't out of reach,' I told
him. 'So, can you come?' Suddenly, I desperately wanted to
get him alone.

'Actually, I've a better idea. Why don't you come to me?
Louis has a week off, and he's gone to Donegal to stay with
friends and he's taken Pedro with him and, believe it or not,

I miss the old bugger – the dog that is, not Louis. Since your vet got hold of him he's a different mutt altogether. How're you fixed for Saturday?'

'Sounds great.' I was delighted. 'Can I bring Pete?'

'I assumed you would; you two are surgically attached. I'll ring Clodagh, see if she's free too. You could stay over if you like? If you're very good, I'll buy you both breakfast on Sunday.'

'Eh, sounds good.' My heart sank. So much for Connie's instructions. 'Clodagh might not be free, though,' I told him. Not if I have anything to do with it anyway, I added silently.

'Well, why don't I ring her now and call you back?'

'OK.' I was already hitting speed dial on my mobile. Her number went straight to message. I sent a text asking her to call me before she spoke to Mike, but when she rang ten minutes later it was too late. He'd got her before my message came through, and she'd already accepted for Saturday.

'Oh Lou, I'm sorry, I feel like such an idiot,' she groaned. 'Let me ring back and come up with an excuse. I'll make it a good one.'

'No, it's OK,' I insisted. 'It was Connie's idea really, and I was never fully convinced. Anyway, I'd love to see you, you know that. I'm just in a funny mood today.'

'I know, I'm up and down like a yoyo myself. I saw Connie last night and she was a bit down. She misses Maddy so much.'

'Me too,' I told her.

'Me three.' She rattled off one of Maddy's phrases, and

I felt worse for having tried to exclude her from a nice weekend. 'Fancy coming to stay on Friday, and we could catch a movie in Bray?'

'I can't. I've got clients over from London. Listen, are you sure you want me tagging along on Saturday? I can easily say the clients changed days at the last minute.'

'No, you're coming, and that's that. He invited both of us. And do you know something? I'm not sure I'd be much good as a girlfriend at the moment anyway, even if he was interested, which he's clearly not. I'm a bit of a wreck, and it's been so long I've forgotten what it's like.'

'I could come over tonight?' Clodagh suggested. 'We could have a good oul moan?'

'OK, you're on.'

'Great, I'll be there about eight. I need to go to the gym first, I'm like a walrus at the moment. Will I pick up some food?'

'Ring me as soon as you're on the road, I'll have had time to see what's in the fridge by then,' I told her. After we'd hung up, I went for a walk to think about how I was going to handle the Emily scenario.

As soon as I had time to think logically about the situation I realized I was behaving like a counsellor, which I was not in this case. Emily had asked me to go with her to see Kitten simply as a friend. Then I argued with myself that she had paid me, but I reasoned that all she'd done really was cover my travel expenses. After an hour of going backwards and forwards and weighing it all up, I decided I had no responsibility to Kitten and that my loyalty was to Emily. I rang Katie and asked if she would like to meet someone at my office the following morning, provided I could set it up in time.

'Yes, I'll go anywhere, do anything you say if it helps me find out if I have a sister.' She sounded like she was about to burst into tears.

'OK, let me call you back.' I hung up and dialled Emily. As the number rang, I wondered about the wisdom of telling her all this over the phone, so I ended up asking if she had any free time that afternoon.

'Yes, I can come now, if that suits?' she said immediately.

'Fine, see you shortly.' I dialled Katie back. 'I need to talk to the other person face to face, I've decided,' I told her. 'I'm doing that this afternoon. I'll call you and let you know how it goes.'

'Fine, just one thing. Would it be OK if I came over and waited somewhere nearby? Just in case you need me?'

I had my doubts. 'I'd need your word that you would not . . . stake out my office, or approach anyone coming or going.'

'You have it,' she said simply, and for some reason I trusted her. 'Is there a coffee shop nearby where I could wait? And if you don't want me, I'll take a cab back to my hotel, I promise. I won't come anywhere near your office unless you tell me to.'

'Fine.' I gave her the name of a little place around the corner and told her to keep her phone on. I'd no idea how this was going to work.

Emily arrived shortly afterwards.

'So, what's up?' she asked as soon as she sat down. I filled her in as quickly as I could. At first, I thought she was upset, but then I realized it was as important for her as it appeared to be for Katie.

'But how did she find you?' was her first question.

'I left a business card on the seat of Kitten's car as we were leaving. Remember I spoke to her for a few minutes at the end? It seems Katie has known for years – or at least had a very strong suspicion – that Kitten had had a child in Ireland, so when she found the card and her mother refused to talk about it, she memorized the website address and made contact with me. She thought I might be her sister.'

'Wow,' was all Emily said initially. Then her face broke into a huge grin. 'I have a sister, it's what I always wanted.'

'That's what she said,' I told her.

'Do we look alike? When can I meet her?'

'Now, if you think you're ready.' I smiled. 'She asked if she could stay nearby, in case you wanted to see her.'

Emily burst into tears. 'Of course I want to see her, where is she?'

'I'll call her.' I dialled, and Katie answered on the first ring. 'There's a young lady here who's as keen as you are,' I told her. 'Come on over.'

I buzzed Mary and asked her to send Katie straight in as soon as she got here, and also to hold any calls. She would have done that anyway; it was simply a code we had for when I needed privacy with a client.

The door opened very softly a minute or two later, and Katie poked her head around the door, looking every bit as apprehensive as the girl standing beside me.

'Come in,' I said. 'Katie, meet Emily. Emily, this is Katie. I think you two have a lot to talk about.'

'Hello.' Katie made the first move, and I was immediately struck by how alike they were, even with different fathers. Seeing them together left me in no doubt that they were related. 'I think we might be sisters,' she said simply, before they grabbed each other and both of them burst into tears.

42

'MAYBE I SHOULD LEAVE YOU TWO TO TALK?' I SUGGESTED. 'I'll be outside if—'

'No,' they both said together.

'Please stay, you're part of this,' Katie said.

'We wouldn't be here without you, in fact,' Emily added. 'If you hadn't left that business card we might never have met.' She looked adoringly at her sister. 'I can't believe you've found me.'

'And I can't believe you seem as excited as I am.' Katie grinned. 'I expected you to feel – I dunno – jealous or bitter or angry. Or even all three. You have every right to be, you know that?'

'Maybe, but I don't feel that way at all. I was extremely lucky, you see. When Kitten gave me up for adoption, a very good family found me. I've been well loved and very well cared for.'

'Have you always known that you were adopted?' Katie wondered.

'No, that's the funny thing. Shortly after I met Lulu, which is a very long and complicated story in itself' – Emily smiled at me – 'I found out from my mum; she let it slip in the middle of a heated discussion. And I immediately decided I wanted to meet my birth mother. Mum was reluctant initially, I think she was worried on my behalf, but she relented and gave me all the information she had. I did some research then, but it was really Lulu who helped me, in fact I wouldn't have gone at all if she hadn't come with me. I wanted to see Kitten face to face, you see, not write or email or anything. And by pure chance she was at the same address, so it was easy.'

'Yes, the old house is her latest project.' I sensed it was one too many, as far as Katie was concerned. 'So you just turned up? How did she react?' Katie's eyes were like saucers.

'Not very well, I'm afraid,' Emily told her new sister. 'She was very cool, annoyed even, would you say, Lulu? She didn't give us much of her time. She sent us packing, basically.'

Katie said nothing, but her face told me she wasn't surprised.

'I was very upset, to be honest. Of all the scenarios I'd played out in my head, her refusing to talk to me was not one of them. Even after we came home, I spent weeks waiting for a call that never came. I kept thinking that once she'd had time to think about it she'd want to see me. I even sent a small card of my own to her at the address where we'd met. I don't think I ever told you that, Lulu?'

I shook my head.

'I did it just in case she wanted to see me, but she never wrote or called. I'm an only child, you see, and I desperately wanted to know if I had any brothers or sisters. I'd more or less given up, though, because I knew I couldn't force the issue. Lulu and I talked a lot about it in the aftermath of that disastrous meeting.' Her eyes looked sad as she remembered. 'She helped me through it. But now' – her face broke into a big grin – 'you've found me, which has made all my dreams come true.'

'Mine too,' Katie said, and there was an endless supply of tears, it seemed, but they were happy ones.

'I've so much to say to you,' Emily said.

'Me too. But Emily, I feel I have to tell you right at the start, I might be all you get.' Katie looked sad for a moment. I marvelled at the huge mix of emotions these two young women were dealing with, with dignity and mutual respect. 'I'd love to tell you Mum will come round eventually, but the truth is I feel she might never.'

She went on to explain all she'd told me, and I wondered what it would do to Emily but, to my surprise, when Katie had finished she said simply, 'Thank you for telling me that.' She paused for a moment or two. 'It's important for me to know that I haven't done anything wrong by trying to find her. And I have to accept that she probably won't want to see me again. But having you is . . . well, I can't explain it, it's incredible. I've wanted a sister all my life.' Emily wiped her eyes. 'I hope we can become friends as well as sisters. Having you is as important as anything I might have found with Kitten.'

'You've no idea how much it means to hear you say that. It's all I've ever wanted too.' Katie hugged her for the hundredth time. 'A sister who would be my soul mate.'

'Aren't we lucky?' Emily smiled at me. 'To have found each other at last.'

'You are, I think you'll each be very important for the other one,' I told them both.

'And some day – and I'm not even sure when – I'll tell her we found each other,' Katie said. 'Right now I'm too angry and hurt. And I'm so disappointed that, for all she's taught me about the importance of family, she failed miserably where you're concerned. But I love her, so I'll find a way through this. And eventually I want her to know that I have a sister now and, what's more, she's my friend.' As she spoke, I felt sorry for a mother who'd never really know how lucky she was to have given birth to two such beautiful girls. And who might go through life without ever really knowing either of them.

I sent them off to the kitchen for coffee then, to give them some time alone, and as they hugged me and left, I said a prayer of thanks that they'd found each other at last. Seeing them so happy made me ache for the best friend I'd lost. I desperately wanted to get Maddy's unique take on what I'd just been part of – she'd probably have frogmarched me on to a plane to tell Kitten what an idiot she was. Thinking of the situation as I sat at my desk made me think of my own sister so, on impulse, I picked up the phone.

'Lou?' She sounded surprised. 'Is everything OK?'

'Yes, I just wanted to say hi.' I'd no idea where to start really; we hadn't had a real relationship in years.

'This is one of those weird coincidences.' She laughed nervously. 'I was actually just thinking about asking you for some advice, but I wasn't sure . . .' Her voice tailed off, and I knew she felt as awkward as I did.

'Shoot, what's up?' I decided to go for it.

'It's a man, wouldn't you know?' She laughed. 'Listen, would you be up for a glass of wine some evening . . . and if not, no problem . . . it's just—'

'Sure, I'd like that actually. Let me have a look at my schedule and call you later, if that's OK?'

'Brilliant.' She sounded happy. 'I could do with your advice.'

Just hearing her say that gave me a nice feeling, and I hung up and decided to go for broke.

'Mum, it's me,' I said to her answering machine. I had decided I was not calling her *Martha* any more. I'd no idea what time it was in San Diego. 'Lou . . .' I added, in case she didn't know. 'I was thinking of you and just wanted to say hello so, eh, hello.' I felt ridiculous. 'Talk soon and, by the way, I miss you,' I added, and hung up feeling stupid.

I was glad to have Clodagh coming around that evening. I needed to share my happiness – and sadness – with someone who understood, and I knew she'd be a good sounding board too. On days like today, though, I wished I had someone special to go home to.

As it turned out, Clodagh got delayed and so did I, so we decided to stay in town and call to see Connie instead. We'd been alternating our visits to her, and both of us had noticed she'd been a bit low that week, so we decided a double helping of Maddy's friends might cheer her up.

Clodagh agreed to collect fish and chips for all three of us, a major indulgence for her.

'You must have had a bad day.' I laughed when she agreed

to my suggestion without even a little moan about the fat content.

'You said it. I've been trying to schmooze a client and I've spent a huge amount of time on the account, and today I heard they've decided to go with one of the bigger companies.'

'Ah, Clodagh, I'm sorry.' I knew she was working all hours trying to bring in new clients. 'You must be very disappointed.'

'I am, but hell, no one died.' It had become one of our shared ways of putting things into perspective these days. 'Now, will I ring Connie and check that she hasn't already eaten?'

'Done, she hasn't. She was just about to make herself scrambled egg. I said we'd be there in half an hour.'

I pulled up on the bike just ahead of Clodagh, and we trooped in with Pete wagging his tail, having already had a sniff of the food. Connie was in good form, which cheered us both up, and I regaled them with stories of my clients.

'You're perfect for that job,' Connie told me. 'You can sort out every aspect of their lives, practically. You're a marvel.'

'Thanks, but I'd really rather just deal with their pet problems.' I laughed. 'I think I was probably too encouraging when I met them all first, given that I was just starting off. Now if any of my new clients even mention their personal problems I hand out the number of a counsellor so fast they get whiplash. I've learned, believe me. Still, it's nice having you two to talk to, especially you, Connie. You have the same outlook on life as Maddy.'

'By the way, you just reminded me, Ronan O'Meara rang today to see how I was. He was asking about you.'

'Gosh, he's one person I've been meaning to ring.' I quickly stuck a reminder on my phone. 'How was he?'

'OK, I think. He wondered if I'd seen much of you, and I told him you'd both been very good to me.' She paused. 'What was the story with him and Maddy? He just doesn't seem her type somehow. He's very deep.'

'Well, I think they were just starting off, really,' Clodagh told her. 'And then things took off for her, which meant they didn't really have a chance to get to know each other properly. That's about all I know. Lou, you probably know more than I do, because you knew him first.'

'No, that's about the height of it. He's had a tough time these past few years, so I think it suited him to take things slowly, to be honest. I don't think even Maddy knew where they were headed, if anywhere.'

'It's just that I can't get a handle on him, that's all,' Connie said. 'It's probably just me after all that's happened. Anyway, tell me about Mike, he's someone I'd like to know more about too. Any developments there?'

I filled her in on the Saturday invite. 'So you see, I tried, but he didn't take the bait.' I shrugged.

'I didn't help either,' Clodagh groaned. 'Thanks to my stupidity, it's a threesome.'

'You know the first episode of Maddy's show goes out on Saturday night?' Connie asked.

'No,' we said together.

'So soon?' I was amazed. 'Couldn't they have delayed it? Is Maddy in it?' But I knew she was.

'They offered.' Connie sighed. 'The head producer or whatever they call him came around to see me. Very nice man. He wanted to see how I felt about it being shown. He assured me they wouldn't do anything to upset me, but I told him to go ahead as planned. It's what Maddy would have wanted. She would have insisted on it, in fact. And they have practically the whole of the first series recorded, he said. So I guessed it would throw out the entire schedule if it was delayed.'

My stomach was in a knot just thinking about watching it.

'Mike mustn't have known,' I said to Clodagh.

'Oh he did,' Connie told us. 'He phoned when the producer was here, actually. When I told him, he asked if I was sure I was up to it, then he offered to record it for me so that I could watch it later, but I told him I'd get the family around and we'd all see it together, that's what she would have wanted.'

'Maybe that's why Mike invited us both over to his place – what do you think?' I asked Clodagh.

'Yeah, I'd say it is,' she agreed.

We finished up shortly afterwards, having promised to be in touch with Connie before the weekend. Neither Clodagh nor I had much appetite for fish and chips really, although we were glad to see Connie tuck in with gusto. Saturday was another milestone looming for all of us.

Next morning, Emily rang, delighted she finally had the sister she'd always wanted. I urged caution because, as Katie had warned, I wouldn't be betting she'd ever have her birth mother in her life. It was such a wasted opportunity and, in my book, that made Kitten the loser by a mile.

So far, the only outright winner I'd encountered seemed to be Denis Cassidy. I was just thinking about checking in with him when my phone rang.

'Lulu, you'd better come quick. Bartholomew's gone mad.'

'That's amazing, I was just about to ring you.' I laughed. 'What's up?'

'Can you come down? It's like he's on drugs or something, I'm telling you, he's tearing around the garden, chasing his tail, wrestling with sticks. He's practically turning cartwheels. And Joan and Catherine are coming for the day on Sunday, so I'm up to ninety. The last thing I need is him ruining it.'

Ah, so that was the problem. 'Well, Dinny, I seem to recall that the reason you consulted me in the first place was because he was depressed, no?' I tried to keep the smile out of my voice. 'Remember the "male menopause in dogs" discussion we had?'

'True, you're not wrong, I have to give you that one.' I could almost hear him scratching his head. 'But sure now I'm thinking that was all in my head. I'd too much time to think, so I had. But now, well, there aren't enough hours in the day. I've had new lino put down on the kitchen floor, I've bought a new fridge and a modern cooker – one of those hobs, would you believe? With a separate oven, grill, the lot. And I'm on my way into town now to buy new cushions and covers for the chairs. Throws, Mrs O'Sullivan at mass said they were called. But Lulu, I need your help. With the kitchen as well as the dog. All I want is for him to calm down. Could you give him an injection or something?'

'Denis, I'm not a vet, of course I can't give him a shot. Although, mind you, I think it's you who needs to chill. Maybe a shot of something yourself. A drop of whiskey, perhaps?'

'You're a gas woman so you are.' He laughed with me. 'Look, will you help me one last time and pay me a visit before the weekend? I don't care how much you charge me. In fact, whatever it is, I'll double it. How's that?'

'OK, I'll come.' I flicked through the pages of my diary. 'And I'll only charge you the normal rate, otherwise I'll have no luck.' I laughed. 'How does Friday at eleven sound?'

'Fine, fine. Oh, by the way, could you pick up a load of flowers on the way? And a couple of vases to hold them? And if you could call into Marks and Spencer or one of those upmarket places and buy anything fancy they have to eat. Nibbles, I think they call them. I asked in the local shop could they order me some prawns in . . .' He seemed to be reading from a list. 'Prawns in filo pastry, whatever that is. And spring rolls.' He guffawed. 'As opposed to summer ones. Oh, and mini quiches, ham and cheese, that class of thing. But sure they're still laughing at me. Mary Grimes said that the fanciest thing they had in stock was a tin of steak and kidney pie. She'd never even heard of a spring roll.'

'Dinny, where on earth did you hear about them, never mind a country shopkeeper?' I wanted to know.

'On the telly, where else? That woman with the sexy voice who does the ads for Marks and Spencer. Sure you'd

391

buy anything from her. I've been jotting down the names for weeks. Will you do it? You'd be getting me out of a very big hole, I can tell you. I can't sleep worrying about what I'll give them to eat.'

'Why don't you just bring them out for lunch?' I enquired.

'Sure of course I'm bringing them out for lunch. Haven't I booked that very posh hotel in Newtownmountkennedy. No, this is for a snack after mass, I have to have a selection of stuff they'd be used to, fancy bits like they have in London.'

I gave up. 'OK, but my fee has just trebled,' I laughingly told him.

'Anything, Lulu, anything, just help me out here.'

'Would you like me to iron you a shirt while I'm there?' I joked.

'Don't be ridiculous. I've a brand-new outfit so I have. And sure the cleaners are coming on Saturday morning, they'll do that class of stuff. Goodbye now, Lulu, the gardener has just pulled up outside and Bart is giving him hell. I'll see you on Friday.'

Well, at least I've one success story on my hands, I thought, my mouth still open when I heard a click and realized he'd hung up. Once again, Denis Cassidy had rendered me speechless.

43

DURING THE COURSE OF THE WEEK I SET ABOUT CHECKING UP on the rest of my original clients. It was something I'd tried to do even before the accident, but since Maddy's death I'd been overwhelmed with paperwork and new clients and I'd neglected them. Thankfully, most of them had forced their way back in and dumped stuff on me, which had helped me as well as them, but I hadn't spoken to Ronan O'Meara very much since the funeral, although we had been talking to each other's voicemail several times. I decided to try him once more. I'd left a message when I got home the previous night but hadn't heard back.

'Lulu, I was just about to call you.' He answered immediately. 'I was in the North – in Derry – yesterday on business. I only got back late last night.'

'I don't suppose you came home via Donegal?' I asked, referring to where his son lived. It would have been a detour, but not a major one, if my geography was right.

'No,' he said quietly, and I knew he was still hesitating. 'Actually, I was hoping to talk to you about that. Would you have any time free today or tomorrow?'

'I don't. I'm sorry.' I knew without looking at my diary

that even squeezing in a trip to see Denis Cassidy had been pushing it. My accountant was due in on top of everything else and, as I'd already postponed it twice, cancelling wasn't an option. 'How about next week?'

'I was hoping to meet you before then.' He paused. 'I wanted to see if you knew about Maddy's show on Saturday?'

'I do – I only found out from Connie last night. She said you'd been in touch. It's nice of you to keep in contact, it means a lot,' I told him.

'Well, I know that watching the show will be hard for you, so I was wondering if perhaps you'd like to come and watch it with me and Myrtle?'

'Would you believe, Mike has invited me and Clodagh to his house for dinner.' I wondered if I should invite him too, but it wasn't up to me really.

'I see. Well, that's that then, I guess.' His voice sounded strained.

'I didn't know at the time, but that's obviously why he did it,' I explained.

'Will you be OK? Seeing it, I mean?'

I was worried about him and feeling guilty about neglecting him. 'Yeah, I'll be fine, although, just like you, I imagine, I'm dreading it a bit.'

We talked for a while, and I tried to bring the subject back to his son but he dodged my attempts and ended the conversation shortly afterwards, but not before I'd promised to call him after the show on Saturday evening.

As soon as I hung up, I dialled Mike and explained.

'Of course you should have invited him; in fact, I should

394

have thought of it myself,' he said immediately. 'Give me his number and I'll call him now.'

'Is that why you asked us for dinner?' I wanted to know.

'Sort of.' He seemed reluctant to take the credit. 'I wanted to see how you were doing anyway, and when Connie told me it was happening I decided it was going to be tough on everyone who knew her, especially you and Clodagh.'

'Well, you're a pet,' I told him, with a lump in my throat.

'Woof woof.' He added a howling noise to the barks and I laughed in spite of myself. 'You're seeing so many animals these days, you're mixing me up with one of them,' he said. 'A pet I ain't.'

He promised to call me back as soon as he'd spoken to Ronan, which he did a minute or two later.

'No good. He seems to want to watch it at home,' he told me, and I groaned. Ronan had sounded very down and I'd been hoping he'd come. 'I tried; even invited his gran to join us – and I haven't asked a granny on a date in ages.' He was trying to cheer me up.

'Well, thanks for that. You did all you can. I imagine this is hard on him. I just wish I had more of a handle on his feelings for Maddy. He seemed to be taking it very slowly, I don't think she was even sure if it was going anywhere.' I sighed. 'But, and I can't quite put my finger on it, he seems to be very affected by her death. And when I speak to him he appears distant, which doesn't make sense.'

'Maybe he had big plans for the relationship. We don't always share our feelings the way you girls do, you know.'

'Yeah, maybe. I guess we'll never know now. Anyway, is

there anything I can do to help with dinner? Make a starter, buy dessert or something?'

'Yes, yes and yes.' He laughed. 'All of the above. Will you come shopping with me and act as my gastronomic adviser?'

'I will, but you'd have much more success with Clodagh.' I wondered why I was talking myself out of his company when I was dying to see him. 'I have many talents, but none have to do with food.'

'Right, well, thanks for that. You're a great help. Tell you what, I'll email the menu to both of you, and you can indicate if anything I'm planning makes you want to throw up. Oops, sorry to mention the vomit word in your company. Talk later.' Once more, he left me listening to a dial tone with a smile on my face. I resolved to offer my services after all as soon as I got his email. It would be fun, going round a supermarket with him. I could even pretend we were a couple.

44

WHEN I FOUND MYSELF SHOPPING FOR DINNY THE NEXT morning, I knew I needed to get a life. I'd left Pete with Mary, so I filled his carrier and the box on the back of my bike and still had to wear a rucksack with flowers sticking out – and losing a few petals, I imagined – as I sped south on the M11 to Ashford.

'You're going to be paying me back for this for a very long time, Mr Cassidy,' I warned him as I unloaded the bike, with Bart dancing around my ankles.

'You're a real trouper, Lulu. Come in. I have money for you on the kitchen table – name your price,' he told me. 'And sure look at that dog, he's gone pure mad, just like I said.'

'Dinny, the place looks great and I haven't even seen inside.' I took in the garden. 'What on earth have you done?'

'Well, the two men I told you about – tree surgeons, I think they call themselves, can you believe it? – came with a skip and a van, and they cleaned up, threw out a load of concrete rubble and tyres and all class of rubbish that had been there for years. Then I got a painter in, and he gave the front of the house a lick of paint so he did. Next I got all the windows cleaned, then the two lads came back with a load

397

of pots and yokes for the windows and hanging bits and all that, and there you have it.'

'It's like a new house.' I couldn't get over it. 'I can't believe there are so many flowers in bloom this time of year. Grab some of these bags, will you, and show me the kitchen?'

Inside, the transformation was just as good. 'Dinny, the whole place looks bigger and brighter and more modern. I can't get over it.' I took in the new cushions and throws and rearranged furniture and painted presses. 'There's a TV programme in this.' I laughed.

'De-cluttering, they call it.' He was buzzing, I could tell. 'Sure I'd years of newspapers and magazines and books piled up, as you know. What do you think of the new oilcloth? Lino or Marmoleum or something they call it now.'

'Dinny, it's fab. The fact that you can even see it is a miracle, you were such a hoarder. Now if you help me unpack we'll put these flowers around and the place will be like a palace.'

'You're a great girl altogether.' He set about unpacking with a vengeance, and in no time at all the kitchen was filled with the scent of freesia and roses.

'I even managed to get a bit of lilac imported from God knows where,' I told him. 'The smell is divine, isn't it?'

'It is, Lulu, it is to be sure.' He looked years younger, more alive then I'd ever seen him.

'Are you excited about the visit?' It was a stupid question.

'Sure I haven't slept since I heard,' he told me. 'Imagine, my daughter here, in Ashford. And they're coming for mass too, can you believe that? I can't wait to introduce her to the priest and the doctor and everyone. I'll be proud as Punch, and that's as true as there's a God in Heaven.'

'Well, you deserve it.' I was delighted. 'Now, what's up with Bart? Tell me quick because I have to get back to the office before my accountant sends the sheriff after me.'

'Lulu, he's gone pure mad. I'm not telling you a word of a lie. Look at him now, leaping about like a frog. He's at it day and night.'

'Have you been ignoring him a lot of the time?' I asked.

'I probably have, I've had to keep him in the shed a few times while the workmen were here, and I suppose I haven't been bringing him out as much with me in the car because, to be honest, he'd have eaten half the stuff I bought. I'm not joking,' he said as he saw me smile. 'And I'm not talking about food, either. I couldn't leave cushions or parcels or anything on the back seat, sure he'd chew them to death while he was waiting on me, so he would.'

'Well, there's your answer, Dinny. He knows something is going on and he wants to be part of it. So, you're going to have to make a bit of time for a walk with him and give over half an hour or so for play each day.'

'Do you think?'

'I do, and you'd better start today if you want him calm by Sunday.' I laughed. 'Even if you only bring him as far as the Murrough in Wicklow town and let him run wild. Don't forget, Dinny, he was your whole life up until recently. All of a sudden you're off on an adventure without him and he's begging to be included. That's all that's wrong, in my opinion. Watch this.' I let the dog in, and he was so lively, it was as if he'd been wound up. Then I told Dinny to sit down, and I did the same, and suddenly Bart, happy to be part of it, lay down as well.

'Well, that's massive, it's the first time he's been relaxed in a week. You're a genius, Lulu, a pure genius.'

'Have you been keeping him out a lot?' I wondered.

Dinny shifted. 'I suppose I have been trying to avoid him dirtying up the place or sitting on the new cushions,' he admitted.

'That's OK, but how about buying him a nice new basket today, then? And making a place for him here? And buy a bag of dog treats while you're at it, and every time he's calm and well behaved give him one. That should do the trick.'

I left him soon after and made him promise to ring me on Sunday night and tell me all. He was my biggest success story so far and I was proud of him. And he'd given me Pete, who was so happy to have me back he did a Bart on it himself, tearing around the office, getting down on his front paws, begging for attention. It was such a change from the dog who used to crouch in the corner hoping not to be noticed that it made everything I'd done this past year worthwhile. I loved that dog to bits, and today I felt he'd finally achieved the total transformation I'd hoped for. I skipped lunch and brought him for a quick run around the only green space for miles instead, calling in to my catering friends on the way back and begging for a ham bone as a treat for Pete that evening.

I was so tired that even my accountant – whom I squeezed in for an hour at the end of the day – gave up after twenty minutes and agreed to come back on Monday, so I did a quick check on my emails before heading home. The menu from Mike was in, and I laughed when I read it and dialled his number. He was in a meeting, but rang me back just as I was about to go out the door.

'If you're cooking what's on that email then I'm Angelina Jolie,' I told him. 'And if that's the case then I've lost Brad somewhere along the way.'

'Well, you're a bitch straight out of Hollywood anyway, for even doubting me,' he said cheerfully. 'You refused to come shopping with me, and Clodagh's fecked off to London on business, so what's a guy to do? I'll admit it, I did have help – my own personal Nigella, if you must know, and what's more she's a babe – but I'm cooking everything that's on that email, and if you turn your nose up at anything I'll hold you down and force-feed you, that's a promise.'

'Cooking?' I teased him. 'Heating it up, you mean. I'd say your microwave will be turned up so high we'll all be at risk from the radiation, or whatever the hell it sends out.'

'On that note I'll leave you. I'm off for a pint with the guys from the office. You might as well type out your apology now and bring it with you tomorrow, save on the stamp.'

'Bye-bye.' I laughed. 'Can't wait.' I locked up and headed for home, determined to be in bed by ten and thanking God that tomorrow was Saturday. It had been quite a week.

I hadn't the energy to cook, so I made do with toasted ham and cheese sandwiches, even though I'd had very little all day. I let Pete out with his bone, and I laughed when he came back in with his mouth covered in muck. 'Did you bury that bone?' I played with him for ages and then we both curled up on the couch to watch a new drama series about a serial killer.

Just as I was about to get ready for bed, Pete started to growl. 'Not again, Pete.' I looked into his eyes. 'That TV show was a bit scary, don't make it worse.' I pulled him closer and listened. But his growl was lower and more sinister than at any other time. I turned his face to me and looked into his eyes. 'What is it?' I asked, as if he could tell me. 'What's wrong?' He jumped down and headed for the door then, and just as I was about to pick up the phone I heard a knock. Feeling relieved that that was all he'd heard I opened it quickly. Ronan O'Meara stood there.

'Ronan, you gave me a fright.' I laughed. 'Is everything OK?'

'Can I come in?' he said quietly.

'Yes, of course,' I told him. 'Pete, it's OK. Good boy.' I grabbed his collar, but he kept growling at Ronan, something he'd never done before.

'Sorry, he's not normally like this,' I apologized. Something about the look on Ronan's face bothered me slightly. 'How did you know where I live?' I wondered aloud. 'And why didn't you just ring me?'

He said nothing for a moment, just stared at me. 'I was afraid you wouldn't see me,' he said. 'You put me off the other day.'

'Only because I was fully booked. But we were to meet early next week, weren't we?'

'I needed to see you sooner,' he said.

'OK, but I wish you'd called first.' I realized I should have been more annoyed at him turning up like this, but something else was bothering me more and I wasn't quite sure what it was. 'So, sit down' – I indicated a chair at the small kitchen table – 'and tell me what's on your mind?'

He didn't make any move to sit. And Pete had glued himself to my leg and was staring at Ronan and looked ready to pounce, which was freaking me out a bit.

'I don't want you watching that programme tomorrow night with Mike,' he said. 'I want you with me.'

'Sorry? I don't understand,' I told him, but it was more to buy time than anything else. All I knew was that this wasn't his normal behaviour, and while one part of me felt there was no reason to be unduly concerned, another bit of me was noticing stupid things, like that he had one hand in the pocket of his overcoat the whole time, or that his eyes had a funny, glazed look in them.

'I want you to come to Donegal with me to visit my son,' he said in a normal voice, as if he was asking me for a cup of tea.

'Tomorrow?'

'No, tonight.'

'Ronan, it's after ten o'clock. Donegal is at least a four-hour drive. We couldn't call tonight even if we wanted to. It's too late.'

'I want you to help me get my life back together. To be a part of it. You can help me; you're the only one who can.'

'I'm willing to do anything I can to help you. We've become friends, I hope, and you were important to Maddy, but you're not behaving rationally, coming here like this, late at night. How did you know where I lived, anyway?' I asked again.

'Maddy told me,' he said. 'But this was never about

403

Maddy, it was always about you.' He stared straight ahead.

'Have you been here before? Have you been watching me?' It was out before I realized.

'Yes,' he said. 'I wanted to make sure he wasn't with you.'

'Who?'

'Mike. Maddy told me she thought you were right for each other, but you're the only one who can help me get my life back. I need you; he doesn't.'

'Ronan, I'd like you to leave. Now.' I went quickly but quietly to the door and opened it. 'Please go.' I held the door open.

'No.' He paused for a moment then slammed the door shut. 'I want you to pack a bag and come with me. Now, this minute.'

'I'm not going anywhere,' I told him. 'Ronan, this is not normal behaviour.' I realized my heart was thumping. 'I'll give you one more chance to leave, and we can forget this ever happened. Otherwise, I'm calling the police.' I picked up my mobile phone from the couch, but he was beside me in an instant. The space was tiny and he had his hand around my wrist in a split second.

'Ronan, stop it, you're hurting me.' He squeezed until I dropped the phone, then he took his other hand out of his pocket and I saw he was holding a knife.

'Please, this has gone far enough.' I was more scared than I'd ever been in my life. 'Let me go.' He saw me looking at the knife.

He loosened his grip and released my arm, then bent

down to pick up my phone. 'I wouldn't hurt you, you know that,' he told me. 'Come on, forget about a bag. We can buy what we need en route.'

'I'm not going anywhere with you tonight,' I said quietly.

He came very close to my face. 'Lulu, do as I say, please. I want you to walk with me to my car at the end of the lane. Here are the keys. You're driving.'

All of a sudden, I heard Pete barking. I was so confused I hadn't even noticed he was gone. It must have happened when I'd opened the door. 'Lulu, are you at home?' I saw the light of a torch coming and heard Jack's voice.

'Who's that?' Ronan asked. 'Is it Mike?'

'No, it's my neighbour, Jack. He checks on me every night about this time,' I lied.

'Get rid of him. That's why I brought this' – he held the knife to my back as he pushed me towards the door. 'Tell him you have a visitor. Go on,' he whispered. 'I'll be right behind you.'

'OK,' I agreed, not sure how I was going to alert Jack. 'But I'll have to open the door.'

'Just a fraction,' he ordered. I moved towards the door, and he had his foot out as I got there so that I could only open it less than halfway.

'There you are. Is everything OK? It's just that Pete—'

Ronan prodded me so I shouted, 'Jack, I have a visitor.' I couldn't see his face, so I prayed he'd see mine in the light of the deck and know how scared I was.

I could see his torch and knew he was coming closer.

'Get rid of him,' Ronan urged, but before I could do anything Pete had bounded on to the deck. Suddenly he flung himself at the door, almost knocking me backwards. He went for Ronan and, in the struggle, I saw blood and I screamed. Jack came bursting in then and I heard him shout over his shoulder. 'Jill, stay back. Call the police, Lulu's in trouble.'

45

'PETE,' I SCREAMED AS I TRIED TO GRAB THE KNIFE. 'NO, Ronan, please, I beg you, don't hurt him!' I saw Jack lunge at Ronan, who looked confused by the blood.

Sensing he'd caught Ronan off guard, Jack pushed him to the floor. In the scuffle, Ronan dropped the knife and, as it landed, I saw a foot come down on top of it. 'It's OK, I've got it.' Jill had fallen in her efforts to get to the weapon, and she held it above her head.

'Lulu, are you hurt?' Jack had Ronan held down and I rushed to where Pete lay.

'No, I'm fine, but Pete's been injured.' I could see a small amount of blood on his neck, but he was licking my hand so I knew he was alive. 'It's OK, Pete. You're a great boy. It's OK, good boy.' I kept repeating the words as I lay down beside him. 'Can someone get help?'

'The police are on their way,' Jill said. 'Jack, are you OK?'

'Yes, I've got him.' Jack was a big, burly man and he had no trouble pinning Ronan down. 'How did he get in?' he asked me, just as we heard the siren screaming up the lane.

'He's a client, I let him in. He's been watching me, that's

why Pete's been growling so much.' I threw my arms around my beloved pet and gradually eased him on to my lap. 'Pete's been stabbed.' It all hit me then. 'Please help me.'

Suddenly, it was chaos. Two policemen came storming in, handcuffed Ronan and dragged him away.

'I'm sorry, the knife slipped,' he told me as he left. 'I would never have hurt you, or Pete, or any animal. You know that.'

All I could do was nod. What had happened was totally out of character for him, I was pretty sure of that. And I knew how much he loved Deputy, so he wasn't a man to intentionally hurt any animal, as he'd said.

One policeman was on his phone, while the other checked we were all OK. 'Luckily, we were very close by. You'd been broken into before, hadn't you?' he asked, after introducing himself as Paul Keegan. 'There was a record of it at the station.'

'Yes, but please, I need help. My dog's been stabbed.' Each time I said the words, I could feel myself getting hysterical.

'We're on to it,' he told me. 'Jim, any word?'

The second policeman appeared. 'Yep, just got him. He says he'll meet us at the surgery. He reckons it'll be quicker and, besides, he has everything he needs there. It's only down the road.' He knelt down beside me. 'I'm Jim Doran. Are you OK? Will I carry him for you?'

'No, it's fine, he's not heavy,' I said, but as I stood up I seemed to lose the power in my legs, and all four of them grabbed me and Pete as I buckled.

'I've got him,' Paul Keegan said.

'We've got Lulu,' Jill said. 'Can you manage?' she asked, leading me to a chair.

'Yes, I'm fine. Sorry, I just stood up too quickly,' I explained. 'I need to go with him, though. I can't leave him.'

'I'll come too,' Jill said. 'Jack, will you be OK here?'

'Yes, of course. I'll lock up here and tell our neighbours what's happened, although I suspect they know something's up by now.' He grimaced. 'We were having dinner with our friends next door,' he told me. 'Pete sure knows how to attract attention when he wants help.' He scratched his head. 'We were upstairs in their front room instead of on the ground floor in the kitchen, yet he managed to get up on to a raised platform and tear at the door until we heard him. He had me by the leg in seconds. There was no doubting something was up – he wasn't taking no for an answer.'

We were walking out as we talked. 'I didn't even know he'd escaped until I heard his bark and your voice,' I told Jack as I handed him my keys. 'Thank God you came when you did.'

'It really was impossible not to.' Jill smiled. 'That dog will do anything to protect you.' She stroked Pete's head as the policeman gently carried him outside. 'He sure as hell loves you.'

We were in the car at that stage, and Paul placed Pete gently on my lap with a rug over him. 'I don't think it's too bad,' he said kindly. 'The bleeding's slowed to a trickle anyway.'

'Thank you.' I was trying not to cry. 'What happened to Ronan?'

'Another car took him to the station; we called for help as

soon as we realized the intruder was still here,' Jim Doran said. 'We'll need to talk to you at some stage, if that's OK?'

I nodded.

'Is there anyone I should call?' Jill wanted to know.

'Clodagh,' I told her. 'Her number is in my phone. No, wait she's in London tonight, I forgot. Will you ring my sister Becky?' I don't know why, but I wanted her. 'Her number is on speed dial five.'

'Her phone's off,' Jill said after a second. 'It won't allow me to leave a message.'

'Actually, could you try Mike? He's first under "m". I think I'd like him to know, at least.'

We had arrived at the vet's by then, so I left her in the car, gathering up my stuff as I carried Pete inside.

Joe Ryan, the vet, was waiting at the door. He introduced himself and quickly asked me what had happened.

I explained what little I knew as the vet carried him into the surgery and lay him on the stainless-steel table in the centre of the room.

'It doesn't look too bad, from what I can see.' He smiled at me. 'He's probably just a bit shook.'

'I think perhaps he climbed up a wall or pole or something to try and raise the alarm.' I was confused about what Jack had said. 'My neighbour is outside, she knows more.'

'Mike's on his way.' Jill appeared at the door. She told Joe all she knew then offered to ring Jack and check if he had seen anything else.

A veterinary nurse appeared. 'Hi, I'm Lisa.' She smiled. 'Are you OK?' I saw her looking at the blood on my blouse.

'Oh yes, I'm fine, I'm just worried about Pete,' I told her.

'Well, my dad's a great vet, even if I say so myself.' She grinned. 'So he's in good hands. Now, we'll probably need to run a few tests, so my mum, Maisie, is offering to make you some strong tea upstairs if you can face climbing the stairs?'

'Can I not stay with him?'

'I'll bring you back down in a few minutes. He'll be sedated anyway, so he'll be fine, I promise.'

'Thank you.' I let her lead the way.

'Mum, this is Lulu, her dog's been injured,' Lisa said a few moments later. Maisie shook my hand and I took the mug of tea she handed me and sat by the fire. She wrapped a rug around me, even though the room was toasty. As I sipped the warm brew I noticed my hands were shaking, so I concentrated on saying a prayer for Pete to keep my mind busy. I liked it that Maisie didn't talk much; instead, she pottered around, cleaning and humming under her breath. I found her presence very soothing.

'We've got the bleeding under control.' Lisa appeared at my side a few minutes later as I sat staring into the flames and trying to make sense of what had just happened. 'It was only a gash, really. Dad wonders if you're up to going downstairs just so he can run a few things by you?'

'Sure.' I stood up. 'Will you thank your mum for me? She's been very kind.'

'No thanks needed, she's been doing this every day, more or less, since I was born.' She smiled.

Mike was getting out of his car just as we came out the front door beside the surgery.

'Are you OK?' He sprinted towards me, and when I saw him I burst into tears.

'Oh Lulu, what am I going to do with you?' He enveloped me in a bear-hug.

'It wasn't . . . my . . . fa-ult,' I stuttered. 'It just happ . . . ened, he's been watch . . . ing me.' I blew my nose. 'That's why Pete's been growling.'

'Of course it wasn't your fault.' He tipped up my face. 'It'll be OK, I promise.' He smiled at Lisa. 'Mike.' He held out his hand.

'Lisa. We're just heading back to see Dad,' she told him. 'He's the vet. He wants to have a word about Pete.'

'How is he?'

'He was stabbed,' I told Mike. 'But it's not bad, apparently.' I saw his face change. 'Ronan didn't mean it, he wouldn't hurt an animal.'

'Ronan who?'

'Ronan O'Meara – that's who it was, he came to the van. He wanted me to go with him.' It was all so weird I thought I must have imagined the whole thing.

'He was the intruder?' Mike looked stunned.

'Yes, it's odd, isn't it?'

'It's unbelievable actually.' Mike helped me inside. 'Did the police get him?'

'Yes, will he be in trouble, do you think?'

'I dunno, I'd imagine he will. But let's not worry about that just now. Let's concentrate on you and Pete.'

'In here.' Lisa opened the door to a different room.

'I'm fine,' I told Mike as I came face to face with Pete. 'It's him I'm worried about.'

412

Pete struggled to get off the table as soon as he saw me.

'Well, looking at him, I'd say you don't have that much to worry about.' Mike smiled at the efforts Pete was making to get to me.

'It's OK, Pete, I'm here.' I went up to the table, and he gave up trying to stand, simply nuzzled against me. I bent down so that my face was level with his. 'You're the best dog in the whole world,' I whispered as I kissed his head and stroked him. Within seconds he'd settled.

Mike introduced himself to the vet and asked, 'How's he doing?'

'Well, the good news is that the gash was superficial,' Joe Ryan said. 'It didn't even need a stitch. But he appears to have had some sort of attack, or seizure, in his efforts to get help.' He smiled at me. 'That's some loyalty you instilled in him. How long have you had him?'

'Less than a year,' I told him. 'I sort of rescued him. He lived on a farm in Ashford and he'd been neglected a bit. He will be all right though, won't he?'

'How old is he?'

'I'm not sure, nine or ten, at a guess. I could check though – I have a client who lives next door to his original owners.'

The vet shook his head. 'I think your guess is fairly accurate. And what you tell me about him having been neglected is borne out by the X-rays. He has a few old injuries. The problem is, it's hard to be sure exactly what happened to him tonight – he may even have had a heart attack. Have you any medical history for him, the name of a previous vet, even?'

'No, I asked when I took him but, to be honest, I don't

think he'd ever been to a vet. He was a farm dog who wasn't really wanted after a while.'

'Well, I think we need to keep him here overnight, for a start. I've done all I can for now, and the painkillers and other medication should help. I have to warn you, though. He might never get back to the way he was.'

'What do you mean?'

'He might not be able to run about, or play like he used to. It's hard to tell. I could be wrong about this – dogs have confounded me many times in the past, I can tell you – so let's just wait and see how he is in the morning, eh?'

'He comes everywhere with me on the front of my bike,' I told Joe. 'In a special carrier. Will he still be able to do that?'

'Hard to tell.' He grinned; I imagined it was at the picture I painted. 'Let's see what the morning brings, eh?'

'I'll buy a car.' I was beginning to panic. 'I couldn't leave him at home, you see. He'd hate that, he comes everywhere with me.'

Mike put his arm around me. 'Let's not jump the gun, Lulu, just give him the rest of the night, OK? Can he come home with us?' he asked the vet.

'No, he needs to be here, but don't worry, he'll be well looked after.'

'I'll stay with him.' I wasn't going anywhere.

'You can't. You look exhausted, and the gardai think you should be checked by a doctor, just to be on the safe side.'

'I'm fine, honestly. Nothing happened, Ronan didn't hurt me.' I could feel my stomach heaving again. Please don't let me faint, I prayed silently.

'Jill said you almost fainted in the van.' Mike stared at me. 'That doesn't sound right.'

'I just stood up too quickly, that's all,' I told him. 'I promise you, I feel fine.'

'Lulu, I'll be here all night.' Lisa stepped forward. 'I won't leave him, I promise. And I'll phone you if his condition changes at all.'

The tiredness came over me like a wave then. I knew it was the scary events of the evening catching up with me, so I gave in.

'OK, I'll get some rest, but I'm staying in the van so I'll be close by if you need me – and provided I can come back first thing in the morning?'

'Come as early as you like,' Joe Ryan said. 'And what do you mean by "staying in the van"? Do you mean sleep in your car?' He looked concerned.

'She lives in a mobile home,' Mike said, and as he spoke the absurdity of my life hit me and I laughed.

'It's very comfortable, though.' Mike smiled at me, as if reading my thoughts. 'Don't ask,' he advised Joe and Lisa. 'It's a long story. Anyway, I'll stay there tonight as well and I'll give you my number so you can ring me if you need us. We can be here in a couple of minutes max. OK with you?' he asked me.

'Yes. Thank you.' It was all I seemed to say to him these days.

46

I DON'T REMEMBER MUCH ABOUT WHAT HAPPENED NEXT. MIKE spoke to the gardai and they agreed that my statement could wait until the morning, but I wanted to get it over with, so they came to the van shortly after we arrived home. Jill had phoned Jack and he had the place warm and cosy and well lit, although he and Jill tried to insist that I stay with them for one night, at least. I told them I was afraid that if I left I'd never go back, and they understood, and relaxed when they heard Mike was staying.

The interview didn't take long; there wasn't much to tell. I was as confused as anybody about why Ronan had been watching me. Jim Doran had spoken to his mother and his family – especially Myrtle – were confused and very upset by what had happened and wanted to speak to me. Mike immediately offered to ring Myrtle and reassure her, because I knew this would be a huge shock for her and I didn't want her worrying about me, on top of everything else.

It appeared that Ronan had been very depressed in recent weeks and was on medication. He had, in fact, made two attempts to visit his son but backed out at the last minute.

He had become convinced that I was the only one who could help him, he told the two gardai, and when he heard I was spending time with Mike he feared that he'd lose the relationship we shared, which seemed to have become much bigger in his head since Maddy's death. No one could understand why he'd had a knife; it was completely out of character.

'I can't really get my head around any more tonight, if that's OK?' I told the two men. 'But one thing I do know is that I don't want to press charges.'

'Maybe you shouldn't make that decision now,' Jim Doran suggested.

'I won't change my mind. Ronan needs help, and being in trouble with the law will only make things worse for him.' I smiled sadly, and Mike immediately took over and asked if they had enough information for the moment, so that I could get some rest. They assured us they were satisfied and left, promising to keep me informed.

Clodagh rang shortly afterwards for a chat about our dinner the following night. She had been confused when Mike answered my phone, he told me later, and she got an awful shock when he explained and she'd started to cry. I spoke to her briefly then, just to reassure her that I was fine. She was really upset that it had to happen the one night she was in London and promised to come straight from the airport the following day.

Despite my protests, Jack had asked one of the neighbours – a GP – to drop in. He checked me over and pronounced me fit as a fiddle but said I needed rest. I refused his offer of a sleeping tablet, but he left a couple with Mike in case I changed my mind. Before I knew it, I had been tucked up in bed by Jill with the electric blanket on, glass of warm milk beside me. I heard the three of them still talking as I drifted off wondering if Mike would be OK finding his way around the van.

I woke early, and it took me a few moments to work out what had happened and why my body felt so stiff. I eased myself out of bed, wondering about Pete, and staggered into the kitchen to find Mike making coffee with the door wide open.

'What's going on? Has something else happened?' I asked as I took in the scene. The main room looked topsy-turvy, with glasses lying about and coats on top of cushions and a duvet and pillow on the couch. It was an unwritten rule of mobile-home living, I'd been told, that you had to put everything away, otherwise the place looked as if it had been ransacked. It was something I'd always done, so I panicked a bit seeing it now.

'Nothing, just enjoying the peace and quiet,' he smiled, looking perfectly at home in my little kitchen. 'And it's a lovely morning – much milder. I guess this place has its advantages; you feel like you're on holiday the whole time, I bet.'

'You're right. Everyone says the same, that's why I like it so much.' I relaxed as soon as I saw he was OK. 'Where did you sleep, by the way? I should have made sure the spare room was ready.'

'It was, but you didn't tell me it was designed for skinny kids or midgets. I tried out the bed, but I wouldn't fit even with my legs curled around my neck. And when I turned

418

even slightly I hit the wall on one side or fell out the other. So I opted for the couch.'

'Maddy always said the same.' I giggled, remembering her expletives the first night she'd slept in the van. 'In fact, the night before she died she refused to go near it and climbed in beside me instead.'

'I did think of doing the same thing, but your snores through the wall put me off.' He grinned. 'Coffee?'

'Yes, please. I just want to ring and see how Pete is first.'

'I've just phoned. He had a good night. We can collect him this morning, although the vet agreed only because we were so close by. He's still a bit concerned about his breathing, so I propose we bring him home, keep him warm and transfer our dinner party here? Although that cooker gives me cause for concern – just as well I'm only nuking. Oops, I think I've just given the game away,' he ducked as I thumped him.

'I knew it. And you were all set to pass it off as your own, you cheat.'

'Yes, well, a man's gotta do and all that. So tell me, how are you feeling? Did you sleep?'

'I did actually, and I feel much better, although I'm really stiff; I think I went down with a bang in the struggle. Thank you for staying, and for coming out in the first place.' I rubbed my eyes. 'You seem to be constantly coming to my aid. I think it all just caught up with me in the end.' I told him the Dinny story as we drank coffee on the deck and explained that I'd been up early to shop for 'nibbles'.

'Well, I don't know why you think you've left your old life behind.' He raised his eyebrows. 'It seems that all your clients need your services for themselves, and in Dinny's case he needs a housekeeper as well.'

'Ah yes, but they're only paying me to sort out their doggie dilemmas, that's the difference. So I don't feel any pressure at all where they're concerned.'

'Well, why don't you get ready to collect Pete, and I'll clear up the kitchen,' he said after we'd finished. 'I'm afraid Jack and Jill – great names, by the way – stayed on after you went to bed. Jack had brought down a bottle of Scotch when he came to turn on the heat, so we chatted for ages. And, needless to say, none of us needed any encouragement to do serious damage to the whiskey. I think Jack was quite traumatized by the time it was all over. He thinks he's to blame for not keeping a better eye on you in the first place.'

'That's crazy. They've been amazing neighbours,' I said. 'I was just thinking I'll have to buy them a present to say thanks. I don't know what would have happened if he hadn't come to my aid. And them in the middle of a dinner party. Most people would have ignored Pete.'

'Don't worry, I made sure he knew how grateful we are.' He made it sound like we were a couple and I liked it.

'In fact, now that I think of it, I wouldn't have got to know them at all if Maddy hadn't marched me up to their door that first night we suspected an intruder.' I told him the story, and we agreed that it was likely Ronan had been in; he could easily have gotten access to Maddy's set of keys, which was what had confused us at the time. Maddy and I always had keys to each other's homes, in case of emergency.

'I wonder what will happen to him?' I was thinking aloud. 'Actually, I'd like to ring Myrtle myself later. I think his family need to think carefully about how they deal with this.'

'Well, why don't we wait and see what the police advise.' Mike stood up. 'Now, get dressed, and let's go see the real hero of the night. Besides, I've a lot of ingredients to prepare for my gourmet dinner this evening.' He grinned.

Just then there was a knock on the door. Mike answered, and my heart started thumping when I saw Ronan.

'I'm not sure this is a good time.' Mike looked at me for confirmation, but I knew I had to see him some time, and I was glad Mike was here.

'No, it's OK, come in,' I said.

Mike looked at me. 'Will I wait in the other room?' he asked.

'No, stay, please,' I said.

'I won't be long. I just came to say how sorry I am and to thank you for not taking this any further.' Suddenly he burst into tears. 'I don't know what came over me. I've been feeling so low about Lucas for a long time now, and Maddy's death heightened it all. I never meant to hurt you or Pete and I've no idea why I brought a knife.' He sounded distraught.

'It's OK,' I told him. 'I knew it was out of character.'

'I'll do anything to make it up to you,' he said.

'Then seek proper help. And deal with the issue of Lucas – you need to at least see him and find out how you feel,' I told him. 'That's how you can make this up to me.'

'I will, I promise. I'll make an appointment to talk to someone today.'

'Can I give you a recommendation?' I asked.

'You'd do that for me, after all I've done?' He sounded shocked.

'Yes,' I said, reaching for my diary and writing down a name and number on a piece of paper.

'I won't contact you again, I promise. But I'll never be able to thank you enough.' He held out his hand, and I accepted it.

'I'll check on your progress through Myrtle for the moment, if that's OK,' I told him. 'And for what it's worth, I think you'd make a great father, and I think Lucas might help you enormously.'

He nodded, than shook hands with Mike, who also offered to stay in touch. Ronan again seemed amazed as he left.

'You were amazing – I don't know if I'd have been able to be as generous.' Mike hugged me as soon as Ronan had left.

'He's a good man, I'm certain of it, and he was Maddy's friend too,' I said sadly. 'I owe it to her as well as him.'

Mike smiled and said no more.

Pete looked slightly brighter when we arrived, and he went a bit mad as soon as he saw me. But he struggled to get to his feet, although Joe said that was partly to do with the sedatives he'd been given. Still, he looked disoriented and shaky, but there was no doubting his desire to go with me wherever I was headed. He glued himself to my leg and wagged his tail as best he could, and all I was short of doing was smothering him with kisses and hugs.

'Keep a close eye on him, especially for the next twenty-four hours,' the vet told us. 'I've done all I can, but he needs careful watching.' He gave us his home and mobile number. 'Call me any time if anything changes, OK?'

'Are you sure? Even late at night? I don't want to disturb your wife.'

'Any time – I'll have my mobile by the bed. My family are well used to it. Normally, I'd keep him in, but there's nothing to be done except watch him closely, and I reckon he'll be much better if he's with you. Look at him, he's already rallied a bit just by seeing you.'

We thanked him and left, with me feeling I'd found a great vet and certainly someone I could refer clients to in the future. Pete managed to walk slowly to the car, but we had to help him on to my lap on the back seat, and I was glad to have a supply of painkillers to keep him comfortable. Even the short walk up the steps of the deck when we got back seemed too much for him, and he collapsed on to his bed by the fire as soon as he got inside. Still, he seemed delighted to be back home and wagged his tail and followed me with his eyes every time I moved.

Mike left shortly afterwards to get himself organized, and Jack and Jill arrived, closely followed by Clodagh, carrying an armful of flowers. I told her briefly what had happened, and she was as perplexed as I was and stunned that he'd called that morning. The only conclusion we could come to was that not being able to bond with his son had pushed Ronan over the edge in some way. I rang Myrtle, and she was distraught and blamed herself. I assured her I was fine, although I suggested she get the family together and assess their part in his breakdown. She wanted to come and see me, but I put her off for the moment, feeling I needed a bit of distance from the situation. She thanked me a million times for not pressing charges and for even speaking to Ronan afterwards.

I was well minded, and Pete got a load of presents and treats. Even a couple of local kids who didn't know us had heard what he'd done and called to see him with a stuffed toy cat, which Pete eyed with relish. We decided the cat's days were numbered just as soon as Pete got better.

We had a condensed version of the original dinner in the end. Mike decided to skip the starters and barbecue the fillet of beef instead of doing the whole beef Wellington thing. He made an enormous, colourful salad which gave me much-needed greens, baked the potatoes, filled three glasses with a delicious Merlot, and the three of us ate on our laps and had a good laugh. It felt like we were having a picnic, although Pete didn't really go for the little bits of meat we left beside him, which worried me slightly. He had the best spot on the couch, though, and he was stroked continuously by one or other of us throughout the evening. It was nearly time for Maddy's programme, so Mike made coffee and we settled down with some trepidation to watch the first episode, each of us conscious that we should have been watching while drinking champagne and toasting the celebrity sitting beside us. I had to bite my lip a few times in the minutes leading up to the programme.

No one said a word when she appeared on screen, looking alive and vibrant and very beautiful. In fact, none of us spoke at all until the first commercial break. I looked over at Clodagh and saw tears streaming down her face, and that made me hold on to mine, because I wanted to be strong for her. So I told her to shut up, because Maddy was probably up there looking down on us and calling us wusses and eejits and other unrepeatable names while she laughed her head off.

'You're right – I'm sorry.' Clodagh blew her nose and Mike sat in the middle with an arm around each of us and I felt safe and wondered what I'd do when he eventually left.

All too soon it was over, and before the credits rolled it faded to black and then faded up again on a smiling, glorious Maddy, arms outstretched as if embracing everyone. The picture was so full of life and so captured her essence that seeing the caption that accompanied it, simply giving her name and the years she'd lived, made me lean away from the screen as if I'd been given an electric shock. Then a line scrolled slowly underneath the picture that simply said:

Impossible to Forget

I think all three of us swallowed a huge lump in our throats at that. I picked up my phone straightaway and dialled Connie, and while they were as upset as we were, she told me they were so proud of Maddy and what she'd achieved. Just hearing that gave me strength, so when I hung up I was able to propose a toast to the girl who'd shared a huge chunk of my life and whom I had been delighted to be able to call my best friend.

47

THEY BOTH DECIDED TO STAY THE NIGHT, AND I WAS GLAD. I wasn't ready to be alone here just yet. My phone, which I'd left on silent, had masses of texts and voice messages; no one who'd seen the programme seemed to have escaped unaffected.

Clodagh took the spare room, and Mike slept on the couch again. When I woke up the next morning I was still stiff, so I padded out to the kitchen, stretching as I went. Mike was nowhere to be seen, then I found a note that said, 'Gone for a run. XX C.'

Underneath was written, 'Just in case you think we've all abandoned you, I'm incapable of running after two nights on your couch. Gone to get breakfast and papers. X M.'

Pete, who'd slept beside my bed, as usual, hadn't followed me into the kitchen. Just as I went to call his name, I heard him howl as if in pain. I dashed back into the bedroom and found him struggling to get up. He collapsed back down just as I got to him and looked at me as if to say, 'I'm sorry, I tried.' With my heart thumping even louder than it had during the incident with Ronan, I soothed him and told him it was OK and quickly dialled the vet's number. I was even more worried when he said, 'I was afraid something like this might happen. Can you come straight in?'

I was sitting on the floor ringing Mike when he walked in, carrying croissants and milk and all the papers.

'There's a lot of stuff about Maddy from what I can see,' he called out. 'I didn't know whether you wanted to read it or not, but I got them anyway.' I heard him dump stuff on the table and then he put his head around the door. 'Are you de—?' He looked at my face. 'What's wrong?' he asked quietly.

'It's Pete, he can't get up. I phoned Joe, and he said to come straight in.'

'Right.' He bent down and gathered Pete in his arms. 'I've got you, fella, you're a great boy. Lulu, are you OK to drive? My keys are on the table.'

I nodded. 'Give me thirty seconds to pull on some clothes.'

'On second thoughts, I'll put him on the back seat, he'll be more comfortable and that way you can stay with him. I'll ring Clodagh and let her know where we are.'

I was already stripping off, pulling on jeans, T-shirt and fleecy, grabbing socks and boots and pulling a comb through my hair as I moved like lightning around the van.

'Clodagh left her phone here, so I've written her a note and propped it up on the table,' Mike said as I climbed into the car.

'I've never seen Pete like this,' I told him as I cradled the dog's head in my lap. 'I'm scared, Mike.'

'We're almost there, try not to worry.' He zoomed around

a corner and pulled up outside the surgery. 'You ring the bell, I'll lift him in.'

But the door opened as soon as we got out of the car.

'Bring him straight in,' Joe said. 'Tell me what happened.'

I explained what little I knew, and then we stood around helplessly while he examined Pete, who seemed not to be in pain, at least.

'Can I stroke him?' I asked, torn apart by the way he was looking pleadingly at me.

'Yes, of course. That would help actually; it'll relax him knowing you're here.'

I crouched down so that I was at eye level and talked to him and kissed him and stroked him as much as I could without getting in the vet's way. After a few minutes I knew, from the way everything slowed down, that it wasn't good news.

'Lulu, I'm afraid Pete's had a heart attack,' he said quietly. 'He's deteriorated quite badly since yesterday.' He looked at Mike then back at me. 'Even if he pulls through, it'll only be for a short time, I feel.' He gave me a few seconds to digest the news.

I closed my eyes, and then I felt Mike beside me.

'I'm very sorry, I don't think it necessarily has anything to do with what happened the other night. He'd had some sort of attacks before, in my opinion. I think it's just his time.' He came over to me. 'Lulu, this is a hard decision but I think the right thing to do for Pete would be to put him to sleep.' He touched my arm. 'Would you like me to give you a few minutes alone?'

I shook my head. 'Are you sure there's nothing we can do?'

'He might rally slightly, but you'd be back here again before long, and in order to make him comfortable enough for you to take him home I'd have to keep him heavily sedated. He'd have no quality of life.'

'And if we . . . do it, what will happen? Will it hurt him?'

'No, I promise. He'll simply fall asleep. He won't know anything.'

I looked at Mike. 'What do you think?'

'Oh, Lulu, I'm so sorry.' He gathered me into his chest and stroked my hair.

'Do you think I should do it?' I couldn't even cry as I asked the awful question, hoping that someone would help me and knowing no one could.

'I think we should be guided by Joe,' Mike said. 'I don't think he'd be suggesting it if there was another option.'

'Is there no other way?' I begged the vet, but he shook his head.

'Lulu' – he took my hands in his – 'the most honest thing I can tell you is that, if he were my dog, I'd be doing it for him,' he said softly.

'OK.' I couldn't believe that with one word I had given permission to kill my constant companion, the one source of unconditional love in my life. 'This will be the second time a dog I love has died in my arms,' I told both men, and suddenly I was young again and the feelings of horror and helplessness came flooding back.

Mike kept me close to him. 'I know, but just try and hold

on to the fact that you're the best thing that ever happened to Pete,' he whispered. 'And I think you're doing what's right for him, instead of what you want.'

'Would you like to stroke him while I give him a sedative?' the vet asked.

'This won't . . . this isn't it?' I panicked.

'No, just to make him drowsy and ease his discomfort.' Mike led me over to where Pete lay, still gazing up at me adoringly.

'I love you, Pete, you've been the best friend in the world to me and I'm so sorry that there isn't another way.' I could feel the tears at the back of my throat.

'Hold on, if you can.' Mike had both arms around me. 'Be strong for him for just a bit longer,' he whispered. 'Don't let him see you upset, if you can manage it.'

'It'll take a few minutes to take effect.' Pete didn't even flinch as the needle was inserted. 'Good boy.' Joe patted his head. 'Now, can I get you two a coffee or tea?' I knew he was just trying to keep me occupied. I shook my head, afraid I'd throw up if I had to swallow anything.

'Will we share a cup of tea?' Mike asked. 'You're cold and shaking, and I think it would help.'

'OK.' I thanked Joe, and he nodded and went off quietly.

'Oh Pete, what am I going to do without you?' I looked into his eyes. 'How will I ever get on my bike again without you sitting in the front, laughing at me and ready for whatever adventure came your way, eh?

'I love him so much,' I told Mike as I stroked Pete's warm back.

'I know you do.' Mike rubbed my back and then let me

whisper sweet nothings into Pete's ears as I kissed and cuddled him and watched him getting sleepy.

Joe came back with a tray of tea, and Mike made me have a few sips. I was grateful for the warmth that spread down my throat.

'I think it's time, if you're ready,' Joe said with his back to me. All I could see was the needle he was holding.

'Are you certain this is the only way?' I was sure everyone could hear my heart cracking wide open.

'Believe me, I wouldn't be advising it except that I know it's the best thing we can do for Pete.' He looked sad.

'OK, let me hold him, though.' I climbed up on to the table and pulled Pete on to my lap, and Mike kept me steady while I held Pete and said, 'Good boy,' over and over, his favourite expression, because it generally meant a treat was coming. I said a quick thank you to God that he'd no idea that, this time, all that was coming was a lethal injection. The moment I saw the needle go in was the moment my heart broke. Pete knew none of this, thankfully, and he even gave a tiny little wag of his tail before he drifted off. All I know is that it was peaceful and he didn't suffer, and as I kissed him I prayed that I'd never have to endure this particular torture again.

'He's gone,' the vet said softly, and then he left and Mike let me cry, and I pounded his chest with my fists and wondered what I'd done to have been given so much pain to endure in such a short space of time.

Eventually we left, after Joe suggested we let him organize for Pete to be buried at a pet cemetery nearby. 'You can have a plaque erected in his memory,' he told us, and I agreed without really thinking. It didn't seem to matter much now that he was dead.

Outside, I was surprised to find that life was continuing as normal, the sun had come out and everyone was getting to grips with a new day.

Mike tucked me into the passenger seat and sat in himself.

'Remember the day I was worried that he'd damage your posh leather seats?' I smiled, remembering how much Pete had loved being allowed to come everywhere with me.

'I do. I can still see him looking at you as if to say, "Me, ruin a seat, don't be ridiculous".' Mike grinned.

'Maybe I should take him home and bury him myself.' I had another moment of panic.

'You've no real garden, have you? And besides, you don't know how long you'll stay in the van, so isn't it better to have somewhere you can always go?' he suggested. He and Clodagh had mentioned me moving the previous night – I think both of them were worried about security – but I wasn't ready to leave my little sanctuary yet. 'Anyway, I'm not sure if you're allowed to bury a pet in your garden any more.' He made a face. 'I bet there's some new regulation somewhere in Europe.'

'That wouldn't bother me,' I told him. 'Sure who'd know?'

'True.' He started the car. 'Is there an internet café anywhere around here?'

'Yeah, just around the corner there. Why do you ask?'

'I want to show you something.' He pulled out into the traffic. 'Which way?'

I gave him directions and, within thirty seconds, we were outside Surf 'n' Swallow, Bray's newest technological advancement.

'Now, before I show you, I want you to know that this was Maddy's idea.' Mike seemed a bit uneasy. 'I'd never intended to show you under these circumstances, obviously, but if I don't do it now you'll think I organized it after Pete died, but in fact I was working up to bringing you to meet someone new anyway.'

'Who?'

'I just want to show you something, then I'd like to go for a walk along the seafront and explain all, OK?'

'OK, but it's cold, and we don't even have our coats. Couldn't you explain over a hot coffee inside?'

'No, because you might get upset, and I want you to be able to get upset if you feel like it, so we need space. Anyway, I always keep a couple of jackets in the boot, so you won't freeze, and I'll buy us two takeaway hot chocolates before we start. Deal?'

'Deal, and I'd like to give you full marks for coming up with an intriguing idea for taking my mind off one of the worst mornings of my life,' I told him.

'Thanks, but just remember what I said earlier – today is not the day I would have chosen, OK?'

I nodded, and we headed inside. 'Order me a large hot chocolate with all the trimmings to take away and whatever you want for yourself then come and join me.' He handed me €10. 'And pay for fifteen minutes or so on the net.'

'Thanks – I've no money on me. I've just remembered I never even offered to pay the vet,' I told him.

'It's sorted, he'll send us the bill later,' Mike said. 'Now go, do what you're told while I get set up.' He headed for a computer.

When I joined him he looked even more nervous. 'Maddy said I needed to find you a dog,' he told me as I sat down.

'But I had a dog.' I was confused.

'I know, but she said you'd never gotten over losing Gnasher,' he said quietly.

'Gnasher? How do you know about him?' I asked.

'Maddy told me, but you told me too, remember? That night in the pub?'

'Did I?' This whole thing was puzzling. 'Yes, I do remember now. I never talk about him usually. But what's that got to do with anything?'

'Maddy said I had to find you a Gnasher. I'll explain why later. But I wanted to show you this' – he clicked on the screen – 'because if I didn't show you now, you'd think I'd done it because of Pete. But the truth is, I'd already done it. Just tell me what you think? Did I get it right?' He clicked again, and up came a picture of a dog exactly like the one I'd lost all those years ago.

'I don't understand – Gnasher died years ago.' My brain was addled.

'Yes, I know that, and this isn't him, obviously.' He was treating me like a child. 'See, his name is Pouncer.' He pointed to a description on the screen. 'Much more sophisticated.' He grinned. 'But he's a rescue dog, and I had planned, as per Maddy's instructions, to get him for you. So all I want to know now is, did I get it right? Is he the same sort of dog?'

'Yes, he's the image of Gnasher.' I bit my lip.

'OK, don't cry, please. That's all I wanted to know. Now' – he clicked out of the site and took up the cups – 'let's get out of here and walk and talk.'

48

WE WERE WRAPPED UP — ME IN A JACKET FOUR SIZES TOO BIG
for me – and on the seafront drinking hot chocolate in less
than five minutes.

'OK, now please explain,' I begged, as a big mongrel
dashed up to us and a young girl apologized and tried to put
him on a lead. 'I miss Pete so much already.' I looked after
the dog as he bounded along, determined not to be caught.

'OK, where to start is the thing. Maddy and I had a long
conversation on the night of the launch. It was late, after
she'd finished all the publicity and the press had gone and
you and Clodagh were off somewhere, chatting to her mum,
I think.'

'I remember that,' I told him. 'I wondered what you were
talking about, sitting in a quiet corner.'

'Well, Maddy asked me if I was interested in you and—'

'She didn't?' I was mortified. 'She'd never do that to me.'

'She did, but only after she caught me watching you.'
He put his arm around me. 'Now will you listen and stop
interrupting?'

'Go on.' I was beginning to like the sound of this.

'She said she needed to know, because you were very

important to her, and she told me a lot about you, some of which I knew already. She said you'd been a loner as a child, that your mum had been tough on you because of your dad and that you'd spent your life trying to be perfect. She said you'd never gotten over losing your first dog and that she thought you needed another one just like him because you still felt that it was partly your fault he died.'

'That's true.' I could barely speak, because he was telling me this on the day I'd lost another special dog.

'Also, she said that you felt, deep down, that your sister didn't care enough about you to mind your dog and that that had sent you even further into your shell. Is that true?'

'Yes, I suppose it is.'

'How did he die exactly?' I sensed he felt I needed to say it aloud.

'He was annoying Becky, kept running off with her dolls, so she put him outside the gate. He wandered off and was hit by a car.' I could feel my stomach contracting even thinking about that awful day. 'I came home from school and couldn't find him, and Becky said she hoped he was gone for good. I ran up and down the road looking for him, and then one of our neighbours came to tell us a dog had been knocked down in the next street. When I found him he was barely alive, and he died in my arms before we could even get him to the vet.'

Mike said nothing, simply held me while I cried all over again at the horrific memory.

'I never really felt the same about Becky after that,' I told him. 'Even though I knew it wasn't her fault. I think what upset me most was that neither she nor my mother understood my loss, so while I'd always felt a bit of an outsider because of my father, losing my dog reinforced my aloneness. Oh, don't get me wrong, we all got on with life and I put it behind me, but somewhere deep down I never felt like they really knew me.'

'Maddy told me that she thought it was one of the reasons you'd become a psychologist – that you found the family you felt you didn't have by helping others with their families. Is that true?'

'I guess it is,' I admitted. 'Although I tried to get away from it by specializing in sexual addiction. And it's not as if I blamed my sister, really. She was too young to understand, she just put Gnasher out of her way, she never wanted anything bad to happen, I knew that. But I think it was that they didn't realize what he meant to me and, in my book, that meant they didn't really care much about me. And for years I tried to be perfect, feeling it was all my fault. I think I lost my confidence and worried that I didn't belong anywhere, really.'

'Well, Maddy was delighted when you eventually changed your life. She had me rolling around telling me how uptight you used to be. I couldn't believe it, to be honest, because as far as I'm concerned you're absolutely bonkers, have been since the first day I met you.'

'But I wasn't always, I was very unhappy, actually, now that I look back.' I smiled. 'But it doesn't bother me any more, isn't that weird? And that's because I'm finally content with my life. And do you know what I've just realized as you've been talking – although I know it's been gradually dawning on me for a while? I'm always going to be OK as long as I'm true to myself. Even though losing Maddy was like losing a

438

part of myself, and this morning, having to do what I did was truly awful, I like what I've become. Working with animals is amazing, I've learned so much, and I couldn't go back to the old me, ever. And even though I know I have some sorting out to do with my family – especially Martha, Connie's helped me see that – I'm OK. And I know my mother has some regrets, and since the funeral we've talked, and we'll get there, I feel. And I'm meeting Becky tomorrow night too, for the first time in ages, so I guess that's progress.' I felt exhausted all of a sudden, as if the past few weeks were finally catching up with me. 'Anyway, go on, finish the story.' I knew I had to hear the end of this.

'Well, Maddy said that if I didn't take it very slowly with you you'd run a mile. In fact, she made me promise to become your friend first before I even asked you out. She offered to help me, in fact. She'd planned a number of fun things for me to do with the three of you.'

'Such as?'

'Bringing you ice-skating was one. The circus was another – that's all I can remember. They were the two most frightening, I think. She said I might have to offer to put my head in a lion's mouth.' He laughed. 'And then there was the dog; she said, in her opinion, a new Gnasher was vital. She didn't think you even knew it yourself.'

'I've just realized something.' I bit my lip. 'She said all this to you on the night she died, yes?'

'I know, it's weird, isn't it?' he said quietly, and we walked along for a moment or two in silence. 'Anyway, eventually I took it as a sign.' He smiled. 'And you know what I think of all that shite.'

'I do indeed.' I laughed.

'So I set about finding you a dog like the one you lost. Maddy gave me a photo you'd given her, one of you as a child with Gnasher.' He took his arm away and pulled out his wallet. 'This one.' As I looked at it the tears came again. But this time the tears were for me, for all I'd missed out on while I was growing up. I knew now it was no one's fault, but relationships with children need to be nurtured and mine wasn't.

'I've just figured out something else that's odd.' I pulled away from Mike and stared out to sea. 'All the dealings I've had with people, especially since Maddy died, have involved children or families in one way or another.' I thought about Denis Cassidy and his new daughter; Emily and her sister; and even about Ronan O'Meara and the son he just might be able to reach out to at last. 'I'll tell you more about it another time,' I told him. 'But my new life has brought me into contact with loads of people whose family lives are not straightforward. And in helping them, in a small way, I've sort of found myself, perhaps because I understand them more now and I know that, at the end of the day, it's how we feel about ourselves that determines our relationship with everyone else, including our children.'

'Come here, you poor baby.' He pulled me towards him and put his arm around me and we continued our walk. 'It sounds like you've learned more out of this changing-your-life thing than most people learn in a lifetime – if that's not way too deep for an idiot like me, especially so early in the morning.'

'Well, it's hardly an ordinary day,' I said. 'I've seen an

animal I adored die because of a decision I made. And now I find out that you've found me another.' I choked back the tears. 'And I'm not even sure how I'd have felt about another dog if Pete had been still with me.' I tried not to cry. 'Yet now that he's not, the idea seems – I dunno – to comfort me a bit.'

'Good.' Mike pulled me close again. 'That's enough for me.'

'But that other dog, he's not for today, in case I forget to tell you,' I said quietly. 'Today is all about Pete.'

'I know that – didn't I say it earlier? I knew immediately it was the wrong day, but if I hadn't shown him to you just now, you might not have believed I'd already found him. You'd think I was trying to cheer you up.'

'Probably, but then all you've just told me is so incredible that it makes finding a new Gnasher the easiest to believe.'

'Pouncer.' He grinned. 'More suited to your new bohemian lifestyle, I reckon. He'll be pouncing around Bray before long, I hope.'

'I feel like I'll never be so carefree again, Mike.'

'You've come on a long journey this past while, that's for sure.' He hugged me tight again.

'I miss Maddy so much,' I told him. 'More than I ever would have believed. She used to drive me mad sometimes.' I laughed. 'But in a way she was my family. She was a mother and a sister and even a child the odd time. And I really loved her.'

'I know you did. And I know – maybe more than anyone else, thanks to that last conversation – how much she loved you,' he said softly.

'I'm so glad you told me all this today. It's helped me more than you'll ever know.'

'In that case I'm happy . . .' Mike held my hand then and it felt right. It was the first real boyfriendy thing he'd ever done.

'Are we . . . you know . . . going out . . . an item . . . whatever?' I asked him then.

'I should bloody well hope so, considering all I've done for you. Finding that dog wasn't easy, you know. He's not even in this country; he lives with an elderly woman in Devon. He belonged to her only child, who emigrated to Australia, and he's so lively she can't manage him, so she's put him up for re-homing.'

'Another mother–and–child story.' I shook my head.

'I think this Pouncer might be a handful, by the way.'

'That's OK. Gnasher was bonkers too, that's why my sister threw him out that day. He was always in trouble.'

'Well, we could always kickstart this relationship by going to visit him some weekend, if you like?'

'I'd like,' I told him.

'Good' was all he said. We walked on. After a while, he grinned and said, 'By the way, I forgot to tell you one last thing. Maddy said I could kiss you, but only after I'd seen the first episode of her new series. That way she said I'd know exactly what I was missing by dating you instead of a proper celebrity.'

'You kissed me already. Under the mistletoe, remember?'

'Well, all I can say is, if that's what you call a kiss, you're in for a real surprise any moment now.' He laughed.

'Well, before you surprise me any further, and in honour

of Maddy, I'm now going to take the biggest risk of my entire existence,' I told him. 'One that makes changing my life seem like a game of Ludo.'

'What's that?'

I turned around and looked him straight in the eye. 'I'm going to tell you something I've never told any man before.'

'What's that?' he repeated.

'It's mad, ridiculous, stupid, given that I've never even kissed you . . .'

'Properly.' He winked.

'Stop or I'll chicken out, just let me say it . . .'

'What's that?' he wanted to know again.

'I think . . . I think I'm falling in love with you.' I held eye contact. For me, that was half the battle.

'Well, as we're clearly into major confession territory, I think I'll have to go one better . . .'

'What's that?' I borrowed his line.

'Lulu, maddest girl I've ever met, even though we didn't get off to the most eh . . . how shall I put this? . . . conventional start, I *know* I'm falling in love with you.' He tilted my face so that we were very close. 'And there's only one person to thank for making me see it. And now I think I'd better rectify the kissing thing, don't you? Otherwise we might have a big problem.'

'Thank you, Maddy,' I whispered, just before I found out we'd have no problem whatsoever. And somewhere up in Heaven I just knew that my best friend, along with my much-loved dog, were rolling around laughing as they looked down on us.

Acknowledgements

The first time I heard about an animal behaviourist was when my dog decided my new boyfriend was trying to take his place in the pecking order and bit him on the lip. Mind you, said boyfriend was trying to climb into his bed at the time! My vet John Hardy recommended I talk to Orla Doherty of the Animal Behaviour Centre and she gave me the most amazing insight into the mind of a dog. With her help the dog was sorted and, thankfully, the boyfriend in question stuck around and is now my husband, so it all worked out. And that one dog became two so woof woof to George and Jessie, our two Westies who taught me most of what I know about dogs.

I also need to thank John Ryan, who edited the *New York Dog* and *Hollywood Dog* magazines. He sent me some magazines and talked to me as well which gave me a whole other perspective and an insight into how Americans treat their dogs. Jim Stephens of the Pet Behaviour Centre also gave me valuable advice and some excellent reading material which furthered my understanding of how dogs see things. And Eoin Stephens of PCI College talked to me about counselling and particularly sexual addiction therapy, so special thanks to both of them.

I had two editors on this book and Francesca Liversidge and Linda Evans both played a vital role. Thanks to all the team at Transworld, especially Larry Finlay who gives all his authors great support. And Eoin McHugh in the Dublin office is always there at the end of the phone.

Gil and Simon Hess do a fantastic job with my books as do all the guys in the office, and Declan Heeney and Helen Gleed-O'Connor put up with me all the time.

I'm lucky enough to have Marianne Gunn-O'Connor as my agent and she is a friend as well. And Pat Lynch in her office is always there if I need a moan or a hot chocolate! Thanks as well to Vicki Satlow who does great work for my books in Europe.

My family and friends put up with me when I'm completely engrossed in a book so thanks to my sisters Madeleine, Lorraine and Jean and my brother-in-law Donal and sister-in-law Claire. I love all my nieces and nephews and especially my new goddaughter, Jane McGuinness. My father-in-law Arthur also gives me great advice and takes me out to dinner when I'm desperate.

I don't know how I'd survive without Dearbhla, Caroline, Ursula and Dee who've been my friends for years. I also have Anna Nolan to thank for all her help and advice, and it's great to have my friend Niamh Kelly home from Switzerland after a long time away. Patricia Scanlan and Claudia Carroll understand and buy me lemon or coffee cake and listen when I get to that mad stage in a book. And Dave Fanning lets me rant occasionally (only when he doesn't get in first, mind you). Also Frank Hession, you've been my friend forever and Diarmuid Gavin, you never fail to make me laugh.

And thanks to all my friends and colleagues in RTE and especially *Fair City* for all the support and encouragement.

Finally Gerry McGuinness, where would I be without you? You make life one big adventure and I'm lovin' the journey.

TAKE A LOOK AT ME NOW
by Anita Notaro

Most of us can remember a defining moment in our
lives. A split second when time stood still and our lives
changed forever. For Lily Ormond, that moment
came late one night when she answered a knock
on the door and discovered that while she'd been
smashing garlic and rosemary and watching
the soaps, her sister Alison had drowned.

Coming to terms with losing her only sibling and best
friend was devastating, becoming a mother overnight to
Ali's three-year-old son Charlie was mind-boggling, but
discovering that her identical twin had been leading a
secret life for years was almost Lily's undoing . . .

And so begins a journey linked with four men who'd been
part of a life she hadn't even known existed. A journey
that forces Lily to come to terms with a father who'd never
really cared for her, a child who needs her too much
and a sister who wasn't what she seemed.

'An emotional rollercoaster that keeps
you turning the pages'
Patricia Scanlan

9780553816853